A Life
Like Yours

Also by Annett Holliday

Happily Ever After

A Life Like Yours

ANNETT HOLLIDAY

POOLBEG

This novel is entirely a work of fiction. The names, characters and incidents portrayed in it are the work of the author's imagination. Any resemblance to actual persons, living or dead, events or localities is entirely coincidental.

Published 2005
by Poolbeg Press Ltd
123 Grange Hill, Baldoyle
Dublin 13, Ireland
E-mail: poolbeg@poolbeg.com

© Annett Holliday 2005

The moral right of the author has been asserted.

Typesetting, layout, design © Poolbeg Press Ltd.

1 3 5 7 9 10 8 6 4 2

A catalogue record for this book is available from the British Library.

ISBN 1-84223-198-7

Typeset by Patricia Hope in Palatino 10/14
Printed by Nørhaven Paperback, Denmark

www.poolbeg.com

About the Author

Annett Holliday is from Dublin and has always loved writing, often giving herself the starring role in her self-penned school plays.

She met her 'surfer dude' husband Pete in Australia in the 1980s and after a decade of sunny climes brought him home to Ireland – they now live in Co Meath with their two sons. Her first novel, *Happily Ever After*, was published by Poolbeg in 2004.

Chapter 1

The small red and white bus trundled up the hill, belching out black fumes as it struggled to climb the slope leading out of Kilmadden, the picturesque village in County Meath that Grace Kelly had fallen in love with a year earlier. Back then she hadn't envisaged the difficulties that living in such a beautiful but remote place could bring. Like the awful and erratic public transport, or the fact that her elderly little Starlet car complained during every journey along the potholed back roads between Dublin and the lavish green countryside. She had fallen head over heels with Kilmadden and had dismissed all doubts about the village's considerable distance from the big smoke, where she and her husband Paul worked. She also had rejected her son Jordan's protests about living in the bog with a load of backward culchies that hadn't a clue about skate-boarding and where there were no shopping centres. In fact, it must have looked like the end of the universe to a twelve-year-old but to Grace's thirty-two-year-old exhausted bones it seemed like Nirvana after the bustle and pollution of Dublin.

Besides, it had been all they could afford. Upon return from their life in London to Ireland and subsequent soul-destroying forays into the property market in the capital city, where a carpark space could cost you the equivalent of the price of a chateau in Northern France, Grace and Paul reluctantly realised that they would have to move to the country. They found a nice neat little townhouse in Kilmadden after months of traipsing through much of the midlands. Kilmadden was within driving distance of Dublin and had a small attractive village, complete with trendy coffee bars and a considerably well-heeled horsy set. "Location, location, location," were the three most important things that counted in property, said the real estate agent, and Grace agreed. After a few months in a tiny apartment in Dublin City, where the ambulance and police sirens competed with each other for exceeding the sound barrier throughout the night, Grace was ready to move to Reykjavik in exchange for a good night's sleep.

So now she sat on the bus pondering if it would ever make it up the damn hill and pitying her poor car which had simply refused to start the long journey this morning so she had to take this awful bus into town to work. The bus managed its marathon climb up the steep hill and came to a sudden jolt at the top. Grace prayed fervently that they hadn't broken down. Her boss would definitely sack her if she were late again.

But thankfully not. She heard an elderly woman's voice call hello to the driver and slowly climb aboard with her walking stick. Grace aimlessly looked out the window and there it was, in all its glory, the house of her dreams. She had glimpsed it once or twice before on the crest of the hill, a momentary flash of this wonderful house through the pale evergreens that screened it from the main road. Today on the bus, sitting at a height, she could see it clearly. It was the house she had always sketched as a little girl, probably gleaned from watching too many of the old Hollywood movies her mother had so loved.

The house was large and had a long black slate roof with a peak to one side over a dormer window. To the other side there was a large chimney made from the same dark sandstone that covered the entire house. The windows and door were white, with tiny glittering diamond-shaped panes. It even had a princess-style turret that made it interesting and magical, and a rose creeper winding its way up the wall. There was a separate garage tucked away to the back and a long curving gravel drive. It was perfect.

Gleaming brightly, a shiny silver jeep sat in the driveway. Grace imagined with an envious pang the person lucky enough to live there. Just then the door opened and a tall glamorous blonde woman emerged, followed by two blonde children, both girls. The woman, who was smiling, was clad in shiny riding-boots, beige jodhpurs and a crisp white shirt. Grace marvelled at how perfect she looked, all pencil-slim and elegant, as she settled the two blonde angels into the jeep. Grace felt a stab of jealousy. How could someone look so perfect and live in that perfect house with an obviously perfect life, while she sat on an antiquated bus, pale and generous of hip, her mousy hair in frizzy tendrils, going to a job she hated to pay an exorbitant mortgage on a tiny townhouse that you couldn't swing a cat in?

She wished she didn't have to leave her cute dimpled baby Orla every day in a stranger's care, just to survive, but that was how it was, and here was Ms Perfect living in Grace's dream home, living the life she had always imagined herself living. Life just wasn't fair.

Fair didn't enter into it. Grace had made her own choices, and her own mistakes. She had fled to London as soon as she was eighteen, away from the dark depression of Dublin in the late eighties, and the obvious disappointment of her parents. She had been the unlucky owner of a bright and shiny older sister, Olivia, who had been head prefect at Saint Julias's and went on to shine even brighter at university where she studied Applied Science. Olivia was clever and dutiful – she never got caught smoking behind the bicycle shed or got a D in her entire life. Grace, however, was the misnamed clod, the mischievous/plump/dopey one. Her parents never voiced it, but Grace could feel their disdain, and the never-uttered but much-thought phrase, 'Why couldn't you be more like your sister?' lay hanging in the air every time she saw them.

So rather than suffer any more unflattering comparisons, she decamped to London with her even dimmer friend Dymphna Coffey, and they got useless jobs in large anonymous corporate companies, got drunk every weekend in one of London's many Irish bars and felt chronically homesick.

At least there Grace could paint a prettier picture of her life and make herself sound madly successful and happy. Then she met Samir.

Samir was exotic and darkly dangerous. He was a handsome Jordanian pilot who worked for Gulf Air and was based in London. Grace wasn't sure if she fell for his dark looks or his fabulous pilot's uniform which made him look like Omar Sharif, but she decided it was a mixture of the two before letting herself be thrown onto his single bed in Battersea to be ravished in a drunken haze. He told her he loved her and for the first time Grace Casey as she was then known felt adored and wanted. Her mother had carelessly named her daughters after movie stars of Hollywood's glamorous past. Grace was named after the leanly elegant cool blonde that was Grace Kelly and Olivia after the beautiful and glamorous Olivia de Havilland. Of course Olivia fitted her name beautifully while Grace accepted the irony of hers, never thinking for one minute that she would fall madly in love with and marry a man called Paul Kelly and thereafter the comparisons would be forever made, unflatteringly. But right now, she had planned a more exotic name for her new title when she discovered six months of passionate interludes later that she was pregnant with Samir's child.

Love soon flew out the window and so did Samir.

He tearfully admitted to already having a wife and three children back in Jordan (not bad for someone of twenty-eight) and begged Grace to get rid of the baby. If the airline ever discovered his digressions, being Muslim based, they would sack him on the spot. He could not escape Grace's tiny Streatham flat quickly enough, so Dymphna was left to pick up the pieces and support her friend through the next five tear-filled months before eventually Grace picked up her courage and, with bulging stomach, went back to Dublin and the ensuing storm. This time her parents did voice the "Why could you not be more like your sister?" routine and made it plain in no uncertain terms that she had brought great shame on the family. And this was all before they learnt that Grace's amour "Sammy" was in fact "Samir" and to boot a bloody Arab, as her father had shouted. The row this time could be heard all over Raheny.

Grace had to shut up and take it as she had nowhere else to go and after her son Jordan was born, she endured six months of open stares and the resultant tut-tutting of the neighbours as they spied her brown baby. Eventually she could endure no more, and escaped back to London to the ever-welcoming Dymphna, who got her a junior job in one of the top banks and even researched all the day-care facilities in the area so Jordan could be close by.

Grace thanked God for her friends and swore she would never go back and live in that narrow insular little world that her parents lived in. It was all right to give money to help to save the black babies, but it was a different kettle of fish to have them living with you, it seemed. At least in London she wasn't being stared at every time she crossed the door by her mother's best friend, the awful Mrs Maxwell, who frequently mouthed "brazen hussy" at her from behind her net curtains.

There were lots of black and brown babies in London with white mothers and she fitted right in.

Within a year she and Jordan were doing very well and had got a place of their own when Grace was promoted, and then one day Paul Kelly had walked into Alliance and Southern Bank where Grace worked and took her breath away. He was part of a contingent of contracted painters who were assigned to paint all the branches in the Greater London area.

Grace spotted him as soon as he strolled in and despite his filthy overalls and Rastafarian hat, she couldn't miss the dark brown eyes and the white bright smile. He had three earrings in one ear and a number of tied hippie leather bracelets on his large brown wrist, but it still didn't put her off. He looked like an Italian gypsy and when he smiled directly at her, she typically tripped over the coffee trolley and sent tea and biscuits flying as she fell to the ground.

She emerged from behind the counter beet-red and covered in coffee and Mikado fluffy bits, wishing the ground would open and cover her up, but he was standing there still grinning widely and muttering the immortal words, "I see you've fallen for me, then?" in a strong Donegal accent. This was enough to send Grace into an embarrassed rage and it took another three months of Paul apologising for laughing at her before she would even consider talking to him again.

Paul Kelly was the best thing that had ever happened to Grace. He thought she was amazing. Somehow to him, her curvy hips and petite stature were utterly feminine, and he told her she was beautiful. Her pale clear skin and baby-soft curls appealed to him and he almost made her feel attractive. He didn't mind a bit that she had a son and he would often joke with his own dark complexion, saying it looked like Jordan was his own but had a better tan. She would watch in amazement as this huge six-footer played so tenderly with her toddler on the floor, letting Jordan rip into his black curls and pull his earrings, and never minding a jot.

"He's a real sweetheart," Dymphna had pronounced. Dymphna, who was a real Dub, couldn't hack most 'bog-warriors' as she termed them, but she had a real soft spot for Paul. "Don't ever let him go," she warned Grace, "because I'll be right here behind ye, ready to snap him up."

Dymphna had had her fill of East End wide boys and was considering going back to Dublin to find a decent fella. She was far prettier than Grace was. She was tall and big-breasted and had shiny sleek black hair and a lot of confidence. Grace couldn't understand how Paul had fallen for her plain mousy self when there were stunners like Dymphna around.

Then on their twelve-month anniversary when Paul proposed, Grace accepted, though she seriously informed him that she could not take the name Kelly and be ever more linked and unflatteringly compared to her famous namesake – the timelessly elegant ice queen of fifties Hollywood, Grace Kelly, who went on to become an even more perfect princess. Paul had laughed loud and long and had said that Grace was truly hilarious. He hadn't guessed for one instant that Grace had been deadly serious.

So she in turn hadn't the heart to admit any further her gross insecurities and flaws, lest he should pick up on them himself, and so Grace Kelly she became and forever more was subjected to sniggers and comments about the glamour queen that she so wasn't. She was sure Grace Kelly, film star, didn't have hems that fell down with dancing wayward threads, and bitten nails or cellulite-covered thighs, but there it was. On the other hand, if Olivia had met a handsome Mr de Havilland (however highly unlikely) and had married him, she would have elegantly fit her noble name with her classical features and her graceful neck. Grace tried not to think too much about Olivia and instead basked in Paul's obviously deluded devotion.

Grace decided to get married in London in a registry office, thereby negating the need for her parents' lecture on getting married in a Catholic church while already having a child, and it also prevented her mother from having the stain of Grace's sin paraded around Raheny in a white Rolls Royce. No, it was far better all round, her mum had agreed, that it sounded more exotic too, getting married in England. It also meant her mother could embroider to all her friends and family about her successful daughter in London who worked as a manager in a top-class bank.

Grace bought into the fiction too. She embellished her job and her flat and Paul over the intervening nine years, needing within her to measure up to her family's ambitions. Being further away meant she could bullshit all she liked and no one was ever the wiser.

So when Paul broached the subject of returning to Ireland two years ago, while they were planning another child, Grace first baulked at the idea. She had quite liked fitting her parents into a once-a-week fractious phone call and an even rarer email to the ever-busier Olivia, who was now engaged to a handsomely successful solicitor called Connell who was about to build them a dream home in the Wicklow mountains.

The thought of being back in Dublin made Grace blanch, but Paul reasoned that they could hardly ever let Jordan outside to play in London and they could never ever afford a house there. The flat had been awkward enough for Jordan but how would another child fit in? Over the months he had cajoled and prodded and eventually won her around. So here they were, a year and a half later, with the delicious Orla and a huge mortgage for a tiny townhouse back in Ireland, but it least it had a nice garden and large rolling hills nearby and it was too far away for Grace's parents to visit much, so she hadn't really regretted it.

Except for days like today when the dubious Irish transport system, which travelled on its knees, kept her late, and the gridlock that had stifled its citizens made her wish for the quickness of the tube and the prompt bus service of London. She had hated leaving her job too, but she had already decided to cut down on her working hours for Orla's sake. Even though now with their crippling mortgage it wasn't possible as yet, she still planned to scale down her career for a few years.

She hadn't however planned to scale it down to the level of Charlie Conroy. He was the office manager of the large international bank that she was working for in the IFSC and was the sleaziest, most sexist cretin she had ever had the misfortune to meet. If Charlie had interviewed her instead of the recruitment agency, she would never have let those lascivious beady eyes languish on her obvious charms longer than ten seconds. However, she had accepted the job without ever meeting him and now had the dubious pleasure of him salivating over her daily with his sweaty palms and greasy comb-over. His nickname around the office was "Pervy Comb-over" and boy, did that moniker suit! He had a special dislike for working mothers, which he never managed to keep to himself, and the snide comments about why Grace was late for work almost always included a reference to nappy-changing or the ironing having to be done. If Grace didn't need this job so badly, she'd have gladly told Pervy where to stick it.

Today, she prayed that this aging little heap of metal would speed its way into Dublin so she could begin her day without attracting Charlie's attention and inevitably being told off and eyed over yet again.

Only two more days of work to endure and she and Paul and the kids were off to Ibiza for a blissful week in the sun, a late summer deal that she had managed to get really cheap. It meant Jordan having a week off in school-term time, but they hadn't had a decent holiday since before Grace had become pregnant with Orla, and she felt they all really needed it. Especially Jordan.

Jordan hadn't really settled yet into Ireland, where a brown face still wasn't the norm and the more the influx of dark complexions that peppered the population, the more irritated and incensed the indigenous population seemed to get. Jordan had been quiet and a bit sullen and she hoped he wasn't being bullied at school about his strong London accent and dark skin. He said little, but was becoming increasingly withdrawn and moody. Grace knew his hormones were bound to be raging at this preteen stage, but she couldn't help feel it was a little bit more than that. He seemed to resent Paul ever since Orla had come along and even though Paul was the only father Jordan had ever known, perhaps he felt a little bit envious that Orla was Paul's biological child. Grace and Paul had never made Jordan feel any different from the baby – in fact Paul had gone overboard with attention to him when their baby daughter had arrived to prevent any ill feelings – but something was bothering her son and Grace hoped that this trip away would bring them closer and she would discover what was the matter.

Her mind was full of her little family as the red and

white bus wound its way through the country lanes towards the city and her other life.

Kate Heathcoat noticed the bus as it stopped on top of the hill outside her house. She envied its occupants, off to their busy lives in Dublin, their careers. She dearly missed the hustle and bustle of the city and a job, but Des her husband had knocked the idea on the head when she had expressed a wish to return to the workforce, pointing out that she already had a full-time job in looking after Jade and Chloe and himself. He had made it sound important, that he needed her there to keep the rest of them afloat, but he didn't know how utterly bored she was with her endless days while the children were at school. The mind-numbing routine of going to the gym, cooking and cleaning until the house shone and the frequent empty shopping trips to the Blanchardstown Centre or Liffey Valley, all left Kate feeling hollow. All the wardrobes in the house were crammed with her retail therapy purchases that only seemed to cheer her up for the shortest time.

She had recently taken up horse-riding twice a week for something different to do. There was a real horsy set in Kilmadden, but it seemed to be a clique and so far the snubs she had received intimated that she was a blow-in and not welcome.

So she still felt a deep loneliness. It didn't help that Des was so busy with his business that he had to work late almost every night. In fact sometimes she complained that she felt like a single parent, but Des had retorted that someone needed to slave away to pay for her lavish spending on the gold credit card. She felt ungrateful complaining, seeing as she lived in this fabulous house with two beautiful children and a Pierce Brosnan look-a-like husband.

She was the envy of her old friends so she felt like a fraud and kept quiet about her emptiness.

As she said goodbye to Chloe and Jade at the school, she realised she hadn't said a single word to either of them along the four-mile journey and felt instantly guilty. So she gave them both huge hugs and promised a visit to McDonald's that afternoon when she collected them. They were terrific kids and were good friends with each other despite the two-year age gap. Kate would dearly love another baby, a little boy perhaps, to fill her day, but Des wasn't keen on revisiting nappies and late-night feeds. Besides, he had said, she didn't want to go ruining her figure again – look at all the trouble it took for her to lose the weight the last time. Kate's cheeks burned at the memory. Des always managed to do that. He always managed to take her back to the awful days when she was plain fat spotty Kathleen Cassidy. That was who she was when they first met and that insecure fat girl still remained hidden away, deep inside her.

Kate had met Des fourteen years ago, when she had been his work-experience junior straight after secondary school that September in 1987. Kate was painfully shy and had got through her secondary schooling comforting herself with chocolate bars instead of friends, which resulted in her being considerably overweight and covered in acne. She couldn't believe how handsome Des Heathcoat was or how kind. He had taken her on after the first six-week trial, despite her awful typing and timid phone manner.

She in turn gazed adoringly at him as he strode purposefully about. He was barely ten years older than her, but with great confidence he was building his computer business up off the ground. He was dark-haired and tall, with piercing blue eyes, and reminded Kate, or Kathleen, as she was then known, of Pierce Brosnan who played the dashing Remington Steel on TV. Kate took an evening secretarial course in Dorset College and was determined to become indispensable to Des, to repay him for his faith in her. Des in return was impressed by Kathleen's ambition and encouraged her to take on further studies, so within eighteen months she was a fully-fledged secretary and bookkeeper. One night, after almost two years of never noticing her further than the cash books, he pressed a gym membership into her hand and told her that she was really pretty beneath the thick glasses and puppy fat and to give exercise a go. Des said that she might even gain some confidence. Kathleen blushed profusely, but took the offer in the spirit it was meant and went home directly to her dark little room in her noisy house in Kilbarrack and took a long hard look at her podgy self in the mirror. She had fallen desperately in love with Des, who remained blissfully unaware, judging by the army of vacuous blondes he had paraded into the office over the preceding two years.

Yet Des was the only person who called her Kate

and treated her like she was someone. Her parents were more interested in escaping to the pub every night like they had for the past six years, leaving Kate in charge of her three younger siblings. No wonder she ate for comfort. While she was still at school, she was never allowed out to any of the discos with her classmates because she was forever baby-sitting and eventually the invitations had stopped coming and she had earned the title of being a stuck-up cow. Eventually she sought solace in Dairy Milk and Tayto crisps. They had become her substitute friends. Even now, she still baby-sat at almost twenty years old, because she had no life of her own.

She would take up that gym membership and save up for contact lenses. She would get Des to notice her if it was the last thing she would do. That night Kathleen was shoved into a box deep within her mind and a fledgling Kate emerged. One that would lose forty-five pounds of excess weight, trade in her granny spectacles for some contact lenses and would purchase her first bottle of *Born Blonde* to spice up her mousy tresses. After the six months of hard gym work and self-improvement, Des smiled happily at Kate one evening and asked her to join him for dinner. The rest was history. She became not only his significant employee but now too his significant other and within another year he had proposed.

Kate was reborn from plain ugly Kathleen, but yet Des could have her back there in a heartbeat with an ill-placed comment or a look at her rear. She had never felt his equal all through her married life. Theirs was a type of parent/child relationship she supposed, from what she had gleaned from watching too much *Oprah*.

She knew that she was hopelessly dependent on his approval, but she also knew that approval was something she had never had from her parents so she was happy to endure the situation. He had given her so much after all, even her looks. People now only saw the slim, perfectly groomed, blonde size-ten Kate – they never knew what she had been, and that's the way it would stay. She knew every day she was only a box of chocolates away from Kathleen and her podgy unhappiness. So she trekked to the gym religiously to keep her at bay. And when Des made any kind of remark, however flippant, about her not being to the gym enough that week or ruining her figure with more babies, it hurt her deeply. But she would never let him see that.

Today she decided, after her unsatisfactory riding lesson, that she might try to persuade him to agree to her having a part-time job, something that would lift the endless boredom that was threatening to consume her.

Chapter 2

It had been a blissful six days in Es Cana, Ibiza. Jordan had smiled all week and played happily in the sand with his baby sister, fished with Paul and even shed some light on his troubled existence in school. He was being teased about his accent and occasionally his dark skin, but he was also really having trouble with the schoolwork.

Grace was relieved but still resolved to go down to see the principal as soon as they got back. But for now calm and serenity was the theme in the Kelly household and they had enjoyed their week away from grey damp Ireland.

Orla was gurgling happily on her rug under the sun umbrella and the boys were larking about in the surf. It was a clear blue sunny day and Grace lamented that they were going home tomorrow, but she was making the most of her last full day and had turned a nice toasty brown.

Just then she heard a commotion. A man from Liverpool, whose son played with Jordan on the beach, was running towards his wife shouting that two planes had just crashed into the Twin Towers in New York and another had ploughed into the Pentagon. Grace felt her blood run cold and simply could not believe what she was hearing. She called Paul urgently out of the surf and relayed the message. Then the Liverpudlian came over and breathlessly told them what had occurred. Grace noticed that his hands were shaking. Paul took Orla up into his arms and held her tightly while Grace ran to the beach bar where, in the café that normally showed all the football games on Sky, she watched a real-life movie unfold in front of her eyes. Everyone in the bar was transfixed, staring open-mouthed at the large screen which was showing the second plane smash into the twin tower. A couple of girls were crying and Grace found herself thinking how incongruous it all was – everyone in their gaily coloured swimwear and lovely tans watching this absolute nightmare that was really happening. Grace left when she saw people tumble from the building and then saw it collapse. She ran along the beach until she reached Paul and fell into his arms and burst into tears. She then cuddled Orla while Paul went to see for himself. It was such an awful event that you had to actually witness the horror before you could comprehend it. They then sat on the beach until the sun disappeared into the sea, lots of nationalities but mostly British, Irish or German, and talked like old friends about what it all meant. Everyone spoke quietly in whispered hushes for some reason and no one appeared to want to leave. Eventually they gathered all the beach paraphernalia and wearily trudged back to the hotel. Now, Grace couldn't wait to leave and to get home. Sky News had said that all the world's airports were grounded while security was being tightened and she was fretful that they might not be able to get off the island.

Back in their room, Jordan seemed transfixed by the endless repeats of the planes crashing and then the buildings collapsing. To him it seemed like a film, Grace thought, so she spent ages explaining that it was all too real, and Bruce Willis wasn't going to emerge victorious and save everyone at the end. She knew he was too young to grasp the real terror of it and in the end she switched off the TV and they went out to dinner. But they all ate little and Orla seemed fractious so they returned early to the room and spent the remainder of the night on the balcony sipping a nice red wine and drinking in the beautiful view of the sea with the glittering lights of the bay looking more beautiful than ever. Grace felt that she knew at last what a heavy heart meant, for her heart did indeed feel heavy and she knew the world would never be the same again.

As if on cue, a huge storm blew up out of nowhere and within a couple of hours lightning flashed and thunder roared and it seemed like the gods were angry.

Grace felt like a frightened child and lay awake most of the night wrapped tightly in Paul's arms, and tried not to close her eyes where she could only see people desperately choosing to fall to their deaths instead of facing the flames and where planes were now weapons crashing into buildings, but eventually she fitfully slept.

The next day the television was full of the awful events of September 11th. Stories now emerged of the Arab-looking hijackers that had taken over the four planes and Grace watched as Jordan visibly winced at that report.

"Are you OK, love?" she enquired mildly, though she guessed at what the problem would be.

"It's just all I need, that's all. Things are bad enough at school without them all thinking I'm a terrorist now." He sullenly chomped on his breakfast.

"Will ye go way out of that, son, talk to your old dad!" Paul joked. "Sure, every time I opened me mouth in London, I was considered a terrorist!" But Jordan just rolled his eyes.

Grace felt sorry for her son and briefly thought of Samir. She had never perceived his airline pilot's job to be dangerous until now. She wondered what he would make of it all. Then her thoughts drifted on to Jordan again. Perhaps she should have made more of an effort to keep in touch with Jordan's real father, but Samir had made his feelings plain at the time. Grace had never realised the issues Jordan would have as he grew up.

He was always just her brown little boy. He still was.

"You won't have any problems back home, Jordan, I'm going to make sure of that."

Grace said the words precisely and wished she felt as confident as she sounded.

The tour rep came by later and assured everyone

that they would leave Ibiza later on in the day. There were some delays but they were not to worry. Paul looked at his dwindling wallet of pesetas and Grace remembered that Orla had only enough baby formula and nappies for another twenty-four hours and they both prayed fervently that they wouldn't be stuck at a hot airport for a couple of days while things crawled back to normal. Then Grace felt guilty for feeling so selfish, when there were literally thousands of families enduring immeasurable grief.

So she cheerfully packed all their belongings and hugged and kissed them all too often as they left for the airport. The very last thing she wanted to do was get on another airplane. It was funny. Airplanes had always held such promise for Grace – escape to better places, exotic climes – she had never ever thought of them as sinister weapons before. She also, much to her own shame, found herself scanning the proposed passengers for flight EI619 for any Middle Eastern faces, and her with a son of Middle Eastern origin. She could not even admit this to Paul, who would have been disgusted with her and she feared for Jordan, if this was his own mother's reaction.

Eventually, the flight took off for Dublin, several hours late, but the journey passed uneventfully and the crowd gave a resounding and unanimous cheer when the plane landed on the Emerald Isle. Everyone was glad to be home and safe.

Kate saw the horrible events unfold in her own kitchen

where she was busily preparing lunch for Jade and Chloe while they changed out of their school uniforms.

Des called her soon after to ask if she had seen the news and to tell her that several of his college buddies worked in Morgan Stanley on the 72nd floor of Tower Two, which had taken a direct hit, and most were missing, presumed dead.

Kate just watched the screen in a daydream, not believing it to be real, and she also let Jade and Chloe watch it, even though she felt it would scare them. They needed to see this history unfold and to learn what people sometimes did to each other when great hatred was involved. She made them toasted cheese sandwiches while tears spilled from her eyes thinking about all the mothers who were in those buildings or on those planes and who would never get to be bored again in their kitchens, wiping up endless crumbs, and she suddenly felt deeply ashamed, like she was flying in the face of God and all that he had given her.

Des arrived home sometime after four, which was practically unheard-of for him, and gathered his children closely to him, then poured Kate and himself a large Scotch.

"Today, it just doesn't seem all that important," he said as he told her about the clients he had cancelled. "Only this does."

"Shame it took something like today to make us all realise it," Kate replied, watching Des cuddle Chloe on his lap while Jade sat draped around his neck. She loved him when he was like this, which was all too rare these days, but now didn't seem like the time to approach the issue. So they sat, all four of them, in their large comfortable living-room and ordered pizza for dinner and watched Sky News until late.

That night Kate and Des made love like they hadn't done in years, raw and passionate, seeming to reaffirm life in the face of all that death. It had been a very strange day indeed, Kate thought, as she drifted off to sleep, trying to dismiss the images of people vainly waving those handkerchiefs from the burning buildings.

Chapter 3

Grace went back to work the following Monday and promised herself that she would not accept Charlie Conroy's spiteful comments any longer. She had begun to reappraise her life in the wake of September 11th and had decided it was way too short to endure the like of her boss's toxic tongue for very much longer. As she sat at her keyboard, she suddenly visualised Orla's little dimpled smile this morning and she felt sudden tears prick her eyes. Orla, who was the most affectionate cheery little cherub you could meet, spent most of her days with strangers who would witness that first faltering step and that first word instead of her mother. It just wasn't right. With Jordan, Grace had been so young it didn't dawn on her how much she was missing out. She was so busy just trying to survive for them both until Paul came into her life, but even now she saw a certain distance in Jordan, a lack of warmth, which she put down to his having spent so much time in crèches. He told her once when he was five years old that he had hurt his knee badly while playing on the swings and Grace had idly asked if his minder had given him a hug. "No, we never get a hug, not ever." And Grace had been shocked, but that was how it was, and she wanted better for Orla.

"Grace, nice to see you've got time on your hands." It was Charlie Conroy, leering over her shoulder, his eyes lapping up whatever bit of cleavage escaped her sensible white shirt. He threw a bulging folder on her desk. "I need these exchange rates applied to these corporate accounts before twelve." His fake smile became a sneer. "That's if you think you're up to it."

"What makes you say that?" Grace snapped, turning to face him. She doubted if he could accept a challenge if it came down to it.

"Oh, nothing." His face turned bright red and he tried to laugh it off. "It's just you seem a bit distracted."

Grace wasn't about to tell him she was in tears over missing her baby, which would be something he could bleat to his cronies at the pub forever about. "I am perfectly fine, as it happens. Twelve o'clock it is, then." She grabbed the folder and slammed her open drawer shut just so old Pervy would get the message and he slunk away in silence back to his corner office, no doubt to read his *Times* for another hour before he scampered off to the staff restaurant to stuff his large face with sausage rolls.

Grace set about the exchange rates, banishing her

children from her mind. She didn't open her thirty emails either, and they could just wait. Just then the telephone trilled.

"Mrs Kelly, it's Avril from *Cute and Cuddly* crèche here, I'm sorry to tell you Orla is not well. We have her in isolation and you will have to come and get her."

Grace was alarmed but also wary. This was not the first time she'd had such a call from *Cute and Cuddly* and had rushed off in panic only to find it was a false alarm. Orla had been extra bright and happy this morning, barely two hours ago – how could she have become so ill so fast? "What seems to be the problem with her?"

"She has a high temperature and is very grizzly," said Avril snottily. "You are aware, I'm sure, of company policy, Mrs Kelly – one sick baby cannot be allowed to remain on the premises causing infection to other babies."

Grace remembered the verbose twenty-page document detailing the myriad of rules and regulations right down to the colour of mucus that was permitted to trail down a baby's nose (clear fluid was fine, green forbidden) and she swore under her breath. She had to think quickly. It would take at least another hour and a half to get home to Kilmadden. Even if there was a bus waiting, which she doubted, there was the small matter of Pervy Comb-over – he would hit the roof if she just announced that she had to leave. It was only half past ten.

"OK, I'll be there as soon as I can. I'm travelling on

the bus, so please give her some Calpol in the meantime, would you?"

"OK," replied the sharp-tongued Avril. "As long as you sign the medical register when you get here."

Is this what they call childcare? Grace absently thought, while she turned off her PC and fetched her coat.

Darren, who worked across from her, looked concerned. His small pixie face was furrowed, making all his red freckles join together on his forehead. "Hey, Princess, are you UK?"

He had nicknamed Grace "Princess" on her first day, but the affectionate way he had said it, she for once hadn't minded. She could have called him "Carrot Top" in retaliation, on account of his flame-red hair, but instead she termed him "Daz" (short for Darren and also alluding to his white shirts which were all a dull shade of grey and invariably needed a good wash).

"Orla is sick and I have been summoned once again to take my unclean infected child from the hallowed halls of *Cute and Cuddly* – a misnomer, if I ever heard one."

"Jeez, Pervy will go off his brain," Darren replied worriedly.

"Yes, he probably will, but you know what, Darren? My baby comes first, and if he tries to make me feel guilty today, I'll tell him where to stick his job."

"Don't be too hasty now – the last person we had in that job was a big gorilla with numeric dyslexia. Here, throw me over that exchange rate file, I'll do them for you. I was getting a bit bored with Solitaire anyway."

Grace smiled. Darren was a good mate. Now she just had to face Charlie Conroy.

'Count to ten first, Gracie,' she reminded herself as she buttoned up her blouse all the way to the top before entering into his poisonous chamber.

Charlie appeared flustered as she entered. Obviously he wasn't working, probably more like surfing a porn site on the web. He cleared his throat and shuffled a few papers self-importantly. "Grace, ah, what can I do for you?"

"I'm sorry, Mr Conroy, but my baby's crèche has just telephoned. Apparently Orla has developed a high temperature and they are concerned. I have to go home."

"What?" His eyes darkened and a fresh sneer formed on his wide ugly mouth.

"Don't worry about the exchange rates," said Grace. "Darren has kindly offered to do them." She was making a supreme effort to be nice despite her hackles rising.

"That's hardly the point." He suddenly smiled. He was obviously enjoying this. "I mean, I can hardly have you running off every time your children have a sniffle – and while Darren is doing *your* work, who will do *his*?" His bushy eyebrows knit in a perplexed fashion. Obviously his own three children had never shamed him with a cold, or perhaps Mrs Conroy could afford to stay at home on Pervy's exorbitant salary.

"Mr Conroy, I have a sick baby to look after, and the crèche has ordered me to collect her. Now, I'm sure if your ill child needed you, you would be there. Surely what happened in New York last week has made you realise it is only work, after all." Grace was reddening visibly now. The next words out of her mouth were going to be 'I quit!' if this gobshite insulted her any further.

"Right, I see your point," he said at last, his face relaxing. "OK so, but don't make a habit of it, mind. I need all my team on hand. We are under-staffed as it is."

"Thank you," Grace replied curtly, not meaning it.

She fled his office and winked quickly at Darren before racing away for the eleven o'clock bus. She sprinted all the way to Abbey Street and thankfully made it.

Within an hour she was hurrying up the path to *Cute and Cuddly* childcare centre where a haughty Avril was frowning behind reception.

"She's in the isolation room," Avril sniffed.

If Avril's attitude to the parents was anything to go by, Grace hated to think what she treated the children like. Grace had liked the professionalism of the centre when she first managed to get Orla in, but now she wondered at her choice.

Orla was busy playing with some toys and seemed perfectly normal to Grace.

"She was very tetchy earlier and her temperature seemed a bit high," said Jenny, one of the two women who took care of the children. "Perhaps you could take her to her GP just to be sure." She smiled sympathetically and Grace could tell she was spouting crèche-speak and not what she really believed.

Grace lifted an ebullient Orla and returned Jenny's smile, thinking of the thirty-five pounds she would have to shell out to the local GP, to be told there was nothing wrong. "We'll see," she replied and walked to the door.

"If baby needs antibiotics she won't be let back to the centre until she has been taking them for twenty-four hours," Avril called out to her shrilly, as she sneaked past reception.

Grace just shook her head in disbelief. Firstly they'd had to get on a waiting list for this bloody crèche, then they'd had to shell out another mortgage to actually send Orla, and then she'd spent the rest of the time taking her home or to the doctor with some imagined illness or other. Grace wondered if it was all worth it. Judging by Orla's reaction of delight when Grace had arrived to take her home early, she wasn't ecstatic about being there herself. Grace knew she and Paul had some financial re-thinking to do. She would have to do some figures and try to find another way. This was not working. As she kissed and cuddled Orla to her in the bright September sunshine, while walking home to her little townhouse she was thankful that she had this wonderful dimpled baby to love and the rest was academic. She would work something out, but Orla's days at *Cute and Cuddly* were numbered, that certainly was for sure.

Kate got back from her riding lesson and sat in her large kitchen sipping coffee and aimlessly flicked through a magazine. She decided she'd telephone Melody and ask her to baby-sit that evening. She wanted to talk to Des about her returning to part-time study. If she wasn't going to have another baby she really needed something to occupy her mind or she would go crazy. She had always wanted to do a course in interior design and felt that it would be something that would benefit Des also. It would save him money if she could do all the decorating in the house. Also, she would put it to him that if she were happier then they both would be happier. She had made up her mind that she was taking the course, whether he liked it or not. The events of the past week had taught her that time was precious and no one quite knew how much of it they had. She lifted her mobile and called *Ban Thai* and booked a table for two at eight, and she then called Melody's mum Barbara to ask her if Melody was free.

"Oh, she's free to baby-sit all right, but not much else," huffed Mrs Tormey in an exasperated tone. "That wan's a right little madam."

Kate laughed and asked no further.

She gathered that Melody wasn't too popular with her parents lately. She had turned from being a Barbie-doll fan to a Brittany clone overnight, it seemed. She was almost eighteen now but she had been baby-sitting for the Heathcoats for two years and the transformation had been incredible. Melody had started off as a bookish quiet girl who wore mostly jeans and sweatshirts, but in the past year these had been replaced with tiny belly-tops, make-up and miniskirts. Melody had developed a stunning figure and wasn't ashamed to show it off.

Kate often saw her lately make sheep-eyes at Des, who was old enough to be her father, so she guessed that Barbara Tormey was having a hard time reining young Melody in. Soon she'd be off to college and that's the last they would see of her, so she might as well get her as often as possible in the meantime.

Kate arranged with Barbara the proposed time of seven thirty that evening and then phoned Des to complete the arrangement.

"I want no excuses – you have to be home for seven," Kate insisted. She knew from plenty of miserable experiences that Des seldom kept his appointments with his wife, especially where business was involved.

"What's so important, Kate?" Des seemed distracted, irritated even.

Kate decided not to enter into any arguments that would defeat her campaign before it even got started. "I want a nice dinner with the man I love – that's what's so important to me, Des. Just think of me as a client that you want to do business with."

"I love it when you talk dirty. Count me in," Des laughed, tension broken.

Kate rang off and smiled. She had learned over the years that when it came to Des Heathcoat you caught more flies with honey than vinegar. She went upstairs to choose something ravishing from the wardrobe for her dinner date. This had to go well. She was determined. And Kate determined was a sight to see.

Over in Number 7 Highgate Place, Grace was putting

her own plan into place. She was going to cook Paul his favourite Mexican meal tonight and have a couple of bottles of wine, while she explained that it would make much more sense for her to find a part-time job right here in Kilmadden. One that wouldn't take her away from Orla in the hours that she needed her, thereby dispensing with the astronomical crèche fee. Also, staying local would prolong the life of her elderly Starlet and save them hundreds of pounds in bus fares. She could perhaps get someone to look after Orla in the mornings or work weekends. She wasn't sure yet, but there had to be a better way than this. She also felt that Jordan needed her now more than ever and at his pre-teen age he might fall into mischief having those three hours alone every day.

She thoroughly enjoyed her afternoon with Orla, and even tackled a huge pile of the avalanche that was her ironing while an exhausted Orla had a long nap. She happily chopped onions and peppers like a true domestic goddess before the novelty of being home in the middle of the day on a Monday wore off. Paul was in for a surprise tonight. She had just made the salsa when she heard Jordan's familiar slam of the front door.

She smiled as she hurried out to meet him but the smile froze on her face when she saw the torn shirt and the blood streaming from his nose through a bloodsodden hankie.

"Jordan!" she cried in shock.

"I'm OK," he said wearily as she led him to the kitchen.

She noticed there was mud on the back of his shirt and his jersey was covered in a mixture of grass and bloodstains.

"What happened?" Grace tried to keep the rising hysteria out of her voice as she applied a cold compress to the large bruise that was emerging under his left eye.

"A few hard guys started on me on the way home from school. A really brave crew of them, four guys beating on one. They started calling me Bin Laden and a terrorist and then they pushed me to the ground and gave me a good kicking. I hate it here, Mum. Can we go back to London? At least I'd have my friends to back me up there."

She could see he was fighting back the tears.

A million guilty thoughts raced through her mind. At the forefront was the fact that Jordan was alone coming home from school, obviously without friends. She felt so awful. Ultimately it had been her decision to return here, and now it seemed Jordan was paying for that. She felt an idiot for never thinking for a minute that Jordan would be some sort of target because of the colour of his skin.

As she soothed her son and took his bloody torn clothes from him and made his favourite snack, she felt surer than ever that the decision had already been made for her. She was going to quit her job and that was that.

Kate and Des were enjoying their meal in *Ban Thai*. She had worn her sexy black Valentino and got her hair blow-dried at *Zoot* so she felt as glamorous as she could be. It always lifted her confidence. Des ordered the Sambal Seafood and Kate had her usual Spicy Garlic Prawns and they were having a nice cosy time when Kate saw it was now time she approached Des with the real reason she had cornered him into this date.

"Des, remember you and I were discussing the possibility of another baby and –"

"Not that again, Kate," Des cut in. His face was suddenly contorted into a scowl. "I thought we had decided it was a non-runner."

"If you let me finish," Kate replied coolly. Her pale blue eyes were steel. "*You* decided that it was a non-runner. And I happen to agree for the moment. But I am feeling increasingly isolated and bored all day, while the children are at school. I feel I am wasting my days away. I have always wanted to do a course in interior design and I also feel it would benefit both of us if I was interested in something and had more to offer. I could redesign the house or even your offices, in time."

"OK, OK. Let's take it one step at a time now, Kate. Don't get too far ahead. You're always saying that there is so much to do at the Beeches. How would you fit it all in? And what if the children are off from school or even ill, what would you do then? And you know how often I have to entertain clients. How would you handle that with your college workload?"

"I have thought it all through," Kate calmly replied, as if reasoning with a small petulant child, which was in fact what Des appeared to resemble most of the time. "I thought I might hire a nanny or home help if you like. Someone local who could help out on the days I need her and maybe do a bit of light housework, help with the kids, that sort of thing."

Des looked a bit dubious. "I don't know, Kate. I mean, having some stranger in our home all the time. It might not work out."

Kate took his hand. "Well, at least let's give it a try, Des. It's either that or nappy patrol for the next two years. The lesser of two evils."

Des smiled at last. "Jeez, I'd forgotten what a persuasive person you can be, Kate Heathcoat. All right then, we'll give it a try. As long as she doesn't look like Mrs Doubtfire or do any of the evening entertainment when important clients are in town. I want you beside me at those times."

"Fine. No problem." Kate's spirits soared. She had never expected he'd cave in so easily. She would enrol in the next course she could find and put an ad in all the local shops tomorrow. At last she could feel she was going to be interesting and useful again. She just hoped Jade and Chloe would take to the idea as easily as Des had.

She poured them both another glass of white wine and was glad she had worn her sexiest underwear tonight. Des was going to get a reward for his good-natured acceptance of her new ambitions.

She smiled at her handsome husband and marvelled at how incredibly lucky she really was.

At the Heathcoats', Jade and Chloe were immersed in

The Little Mermaid video in the den while Melody slipped quietly upstairs and flicked through Kate's heavily stocked walk-in wardrobe.

A lot of the stuff was too old for Melody's taste, but it was classy and had all the right labels – Rocha, Costello, and even a few Dolce and Gabbanas. She picked her way through Kate's underwear drawers and found numerous flimsy pieces of lingerie that she quite fancied and settled for a pair of silk cream cami-knickers. They had never been worn as they still had the price tag on. She stuffed them quickly into her jeans and quietly shut the drawers and turned off the light. She would text Suzie with the words *"Bingo, Suze!"* and Suzie would know that Melody had filched another piece of expensive clothing from Kate's burgeoning wardrobes. That Kate had far too much, anyway – it wasn't though she would ever miss a lousy pair of knickers.

Melody skipped downstairs as she decided she'd better check on the kids before she had another sip of vodka and Red Bull. It wouldn't do if she lost this job. She would make sure she wouldn't lose it. It was the only thing she had to look forward to in her lousy boring life. If Kate Heathcoat had to spend one night in Melody's stinking damp cottage with her bratty siblings and her drunken father she would go crazy. Melody lived to come here and spend some time in its crisp clean surroundings and spend a few hours imagining that she belonged here herself. Then, like Cinderella, she was transported back into her grimy cellar and her depressing reality. Melody was determined that she would do well in her exams and get as far away from her measly existence as soon as possible. Or maybe she would just marry her boss like Kate did and get everything handed on a plate to her. Either way, Melody wasn't going to end up a wrecked depressed drudge like her mother had, that was for sure.

Paul and Grace sat in their tiny kitchen long after Jordan and Orla had gone to bed, drinking homemade sangria and pondering on their future.

Paul was concerned about Jordan's beating, but seemed to feel it would all die down in time, and that Grace was panicking and rushing headlong into a decision that might leave them a lot worse off financially.

Grace persisted. "Paul, if you work out what we're paying *Cute and bloody Cuddly*, then deduct from that the amount of times I will be docked pay for leaving my job to take Orla to another doctor for some perceived illness, plus the cost of running the car down on all those long journeys, I am sure we are making very little. Just let me work out the figures and have a scout around to see if there are any decent jobs going around here. I'm not saying we're going to do this tomorrow, but at least agree to me looking into other options, ones that don't have my kids in danger or enduring miserable days with strangers. I want to enjoy Orla while I still can, you know."

Paul gave Grace a hug. "I know. The kids are our priority. Right. Let's look into it."

Grace's face was wreathed in smiles.

"That's more like it, Mr Kelly. Now, give us some more of that sangria if you want me shouting *'Ole!'* later on."

That was settled, the worst part was over. Now she just had to find a decent job. Goodbye, long bus journeys and Charlie Conroy, and hello village life.

Chapter 4

Kate placed her advert in the local Spar on its cluttered notice-board among all the other adverts for ironing services and baby-sitters. She'd fashioned it on Des's PC and was rather proud of her handiwork. She printed it on Chloe's bright pink paper so that it would stand out. It read:

Help!!

I need an Angel…

Can you be my extra pair of hands?

I live in the Kilmadden area. I require a sane and willing person to collect two very cute school-going children several afternoons a week and endure some light housework and perhaps not so light homework. Timetables can be flexible to suit.

If you are an angel, please call Kate on . . ."

And she provided her mobile phone number below in a fan of cutaway tails.

The notice had an angel on the top with a grubby face. A nice touch, she thought.

Kate was getting excited at the prospect of returning to the outside world of study and adult conversation. Her brain felt like sawdust from lack of use. She dropped into the local library and gathered copious books on interior design. She needed some impetus to stimulate her stymied brain that lay idle from years of Barney and Barbie. She would prove to Des that their lives would only improve from this new venture.

Now she had to break the news to both Jade and Chloe. Jade, at just six years old, was a total pet and would happily approve of anything Kate did, but Chloe was a precocious nine and would probably hate the idea. She felt Kate should always be at her beck and call, a little like Des did. Chloe was definitely her daddy's girl, so Kate was aware she might encounter some opposition. She knew she would have to sell the whole thing to Chloe if harmony was to endure.

That afternoon she telephoned the National Institute of Higher Education and came up with a list of part-time courses that would suit her. Griffith College had a very good two-year RODEC course. Now all she needed was the right person to come along that would tie the whole plan together, and she was on her way. She felt quite exhilarated as she headed her jeep towards the Leisure Centre.

The gym would be no problem for her today. She would gladly take a spin class and twenty lengths of the pool. She had something to look forward to and it made her feel excited about life again, something that she hadn't felt in quite a while.

Grace stopped off at Spar that evening to get some much-needed chocolate (to soothe her frayed nerves – another month of Charlie Conroy's smart comments and she would need larger jeans) and some pasta for the dinner. The entire family was living on twenty-minute miracle meals, which invariably involved pasta. Grace was always too exhausted to cook anything more complicated.

Then she spotted a bright pink job advert with a cute angel on the top and tore off one of the little tails with the mobile number below. This might be just what she was looking for. It seemed a bit vague but she would call this Kate person that evening and find out more.

Kate's telephone rang at seven thirty. Obviously not a *Coronation Street* fan, she mused wryly as she put the TV on mute and grabbed the phone.

"Hello, I'm ringing in reply to your advert for an angel? My name is Grace and I live locally. I believe I might just have a battered pair of wings behind me somewhere, and I may be what you're looking for."

Grace had rehearsed that little speech, thinking whoever wrote the advert obviously had a great sense of humour, and hoped her approach would do the trick. Luckily enough the laughter that rang down the phone told her she had been right.

"I'm Kate Heathcoat," replied the laughing voice.

"I'm going back to college to take on further studies and I need someone to help out, another wife if you will. Would you like to call up to the house sometime this week? I can fill you in on all the details – then we can both decide if it's something we can agree to."

Grace liked the tone of the other woman's voice. It sounded young and friendly. Her accent was cultured, but not as toffee-nosed as some in Kilmadden. Grace didn't intend to become a maid. "That would be fine – whereabouts are you?"

Kate gave her the details and they arranged to meet up the following evening at eight.

Grace wasn't too aware of the place names around Kilmadden, but dutifully wrote down the address – she could drive out there early and get familiar with where she had to go. She decided not to tell Paul too much about it until she had met the woman and seen for herself if it was something she would be interested in. Certainly Jordan's black eye and quiet mood was a sobering influence in her decision to progress with the idea of a local job.

Grace had called the school to alert them to the fact that Jordan was getting a few racial insults and the Principal had assured her that such behaviour would not be tolerated at St Peter's. There were a number of different races and colours moving into the area and Mrs Cooper assured Grace that the school did its best to assimilate and blend all the different cultures. Respect was very important, she said. So Grace felt a little bit better and hoped that what had happened to Jordan was an isolated incident.

The following evening Grace told Paul that she was going to a sort of interview.

"That's great, love," he enthused, with half an eye on the football match. Jordan and himself were entwined on the sofa, munching on popcorn, immersed in their macho little Mecca of soccer, which was usually the living-room.

"Do you know where Killetstown Cross is?" Grace asked absently, while searching for her keys. She had put Orla to bed early so as to give herself enough time to find the place.

"Nope," Paul replied, not taking his eyes from the screen. "What's the full address?"

Grace fetched the scribbled note. *"The Beeches, Killetstown Cross, Fox Hill, Kilmadden."*

"Oh, Fox Hill is on the Dublin road on the way out of Kilmadden, where the bus goes into town," Jordan piped up. "A guy from my class lives up there. That's where all the really posh houses are. He's even got a tennis court."

Somehow that information made Grace nervous again. She didn't want to be a skivvy at some large mansion and have to wear a uniform. Then she remembered the woman's tinkling girly laugh over the phone and doubted she would be too pretentious. She combed her hair again just in case and slicked on some of her best Lancôme lipstick and put on her best wool jacket. At least if she was well dressed, she wouldn't feel like the poor relation when she got there.

"Right, I'll be off, so. Don't let him eat too much rubbish," Grace said, pointing at Jordan. They barely lifted their heads as she went out of the room. "Thanks for all the encouragement," she muttered crossly underneath her breath. Then she told herself to cop on. She had deliberately played the interview down with Paul and now was accusing him for his lack of interest. Grace couldn't even figure herself out sometimes. She headed her car towards the Dublin road. She had made sure she had a good half hour to get there in case she lost her bearings.

All the houses on Fox Hill were large and enclosed, most had security gates and large tracts of land about them, and each one was nicer than the next. Grace gasped at a few of them. Some had ornate horses carved into their large steel gates, and many had accompanying stables. She drove slowly, irritating other drivers, but she didn't care. Then as her car struggled up the steep hill, the large granite wall of her dream house came into view. There it was. The carved granite plaque said: *THE BEECHES.*

Grace was astounded. She was actually going to meet the owner of her dream home.

She sat in the car for what seemed like an age, pondering on whether or not she would actually go in. She wasn't sure she wanted to go beyond those gates and catch a glimpse of the perfect house and its owners. Could she go to this house every day and work there as a type of servant, without being incredibly jealous of the person who lived there? She wrestled with herself inwardly for a few minutes and then got out of the car to ring the brass bell over the steel intercom that sat neatly embedded in the wall.

Just then she saw the little blonde girl run arou
from the rear of the property into the front garden. She
was laughing happily, her blonde hair glittering in the
evening sun. Then the woman Grace had seen a few
weeks earlier appeared, pursuing the girl, carrying a
water hose and sprinkling her. She was also laughing
and obviously wet. She still seemed pristine despite wet
jeans and hair and Grace watched them for a second
before turning to go back to her car with a serious case
of cold feet. Just then she heard the woman cry out to
her. She was waving her hose around and coming
towards the gate. Grace smiled and turned around,
cursing herself for not being quicker. She would have to
go through this after all, it seemed.

"Hi! You're early. Grace, isn't it?" Kate Heathcoat
was smiling broadly, while still clutching the hose. Her
blonde hair was wet and stuck to her head but she still
appeared effortlessly beautiful to Grace.

Her neat size-ten figure was encased in plain dark
slim-fit Capri pants and a simple white vest top, which
showed off not only her ridiculously slim thighs but her
well-toned, golden arms. Grace had always had fat
thighs and chunky arms and spent ages wondering at
anyone who possessed neater legs than hers, but this
just wasn't fair.

She felt suddenly conscious of her generous thighs
and her mumsy jacket that covered a multitude. But
Kate Heatcoat was smiling so earnestly and seemed so
nice, she found herself smiling back warmly.

Kate pressed a remote control and the large black

gates opened slowly. "Sorry about this! Jade and I were trying to water the plants and we ended up in our customary water fight. Come inside and I'll just grab a towel and make us both a nice cup of coffee."

Grace followed Kate meekly down the crunchy gravel drive, noting with despair that Kate appeared to have a neat and irritatingly slim bum too.

She smoothed down her wayward hair as she stepped delicately into the hallway after her hostess.

"Come right in, I'll be back in a sec," Kate murmured as she disappeared behind a door.

Grace drank in the incredible hallway. Outside the house looked rustic and quaint, but inside it was totally modern and tastefully designed. The hallway was large and square and dominated by a huge polished wooden staircase. A long landing overlooked the hallway and had a large coffee-coloured sofa on it flanked by two fat cream lamps. There were various colourful prints dotted about and numerous bowls of fresh-cut lilies. A large warm rug covered the wooden floors of the hall which led into what looked like the kitchen. Grace thought she glimpsed an Aga and the smell of freshly ground coffee filled the air, mixing with the scent from the lilies. Grace thought she had landed in the middle of an advert for *House and Home* and dismissed from her mind the terrible images of her own soccer-boot-strewn hallway, covered with coats and prams and any debris her family could drop there en route to the rest of the house. In fact, she guessed, most of her house would probably fit into this hallway.

Kate emerged from the room with a fluffy white towel

over her head. "Come through, Grace," she smiled, while drying off her hair.

She led Grace into the most incredible kitchen she had ever imagined, never mind seen. The room was very large and square. One entire wall was floor-to-ceiling glass, with large French doors leading onto a carefully designed patio area, and gave a fabulous view of the large garden. But right now, Grace was trying to take in the enormous kitchen with its light ash wooden units, which were adorned with ornate silver fittings. A huge Aga dominated and the halogen lights danced off the shiny black granite worktop, which gleamed brightly. Several cabinets were glass-fronted, and showed off fine crystal and china, neatly piled. A huge worktop island stood in the middle of the room and above it stainless steel pots and pans hung from a silver rack. Grace noticed there was a percolating coffee pot bubbling away in the corner beside a small silver portable television, which was showing the now too familiar images of Ground Zero in New York. On the counter were numerous cookery books, mostly of the low-fat variety, and again copious amounts of fresh flowers.

Grace felt as if she had entered another world.

Kate invited her to sit on a tall silver stool, which was set against a long breakfast bar area that faced the glass wall and the garden.

"Coffee?" she asked casually.

Grace nodded mutely as she tried not to stare open-mouthed at the patio, which had a huge paved area covered in large clay pots full of ficus trees and bougainvillea. She noticed the huge dark Java-wood patio furniture and the barbecue that overlooked the long perfect lawn, which was dotted with landscaped flowerbeds and mature trees.

"Your house is amazing," she said at last to Kate, who was busily pouring the coffee with one hand while tousling her hair with the other.

"Thanks," Kate smiled. "I love it, I have to admit. But it's a lot of work, trying to keep it all maintained. That's hopefully where you come in."

Grace smiled back. She liked Kate instantly. There were no airs or graces. Kate seemed, at least, to be very down to earth.

"Do you take milk?" Kate enquired, while opening a large wooden door that revealed an enormous stainless-steel fridge.

"Yes, thanks – and two sugars."

Grace noticed that all the milk was of the low or no-fat variety. It made sense, she realised. You didn't get to be size ten without some sacrifices. She imagined the wails of indignation she would get from Paul and Jordan if she ever dreamed of bringing anything less than full-fat milk or real butter into her house.

Kate brought the coffees, which were of course in trendy handpainted mugs that Grace noticed matched the sugar bowl and the napkins which lay on the breakfast bar. Kate also placed a plate of rich chocolate-chip cookies before her. Grace thought quickly, 'If she eats one, then I will.'

"Now," said Kate, sitting down at last.

"Tell me, as they say, a little bit about yourself."

So Grace launched into a compacted version of her life story – leaving out the fact of her almost-teenage pregnancy and her disappointed parents. She must have amused Kate, however, as several times she laughed outright as Grace described her hated boss and predicament over leaving Orla in the clutches of *Cute and Cuddly* Childcare Centre.

"I have often wondered about those places," Kate said, after Grace told her about Orla's frequent fictitious illnesses. "That's why I placed the ad. I could have just enrolled the children in one of the local crèches, part-time, but I would prefer them to be in their own home environment with someone who genuinely cared about them."

"True," murmured Grace, wondering if Kate would mind Orla being part of the package, "though they can't all be so bad, I suppose." There was no point in Grace taking the job, if Orla wasn't included. She wasn't going to quit her well-paid job to look after Kate's children, while her own baby languished in *Cute and Cuddly*.

"You'll want to take her out of there, if this offer works out," Kate said, as if reading Grace's mind. She took a cookie and nibbled its edge.

Grace took one too.

Kate went on. "I have no problem with that. I think if women networked a bit more like the men and helped each other, then we'd be in a stronger position."

"Couldn't agree more," said Grace, stuffing the last of her delicious cookie into her mouth. She noticed Kate was still nibbling hers slowly. "That would be great," she went on. "As I wouldn't want to leave her in the crèche much longer and I couldn't inflict my mother on the little darling. It's a miracle I'm not in psychoanalysis myself after living with her for nearly twenty long years."

Kate grinned at Grace's statement. Here was a kindred spirit. Not everyone, it seemed, got on with his or her parents. She had noticed in Kilmadden, which was a hugely family-oriented place, that there were a lot of grandparents heavily involved in their grandchildren's lives. She shuddered at the mere concept of her parents drunkenly rifling through her drinks cupboards or worse still looking after Jade and Chloe. Both children had only been to Kate's childhood home once or twice. If Kate's parents asked to see them, thankfully a rare event, Kate made sure it was on neutral territory, where there was little or no booze in sight.

"So," began Grace, interrupting Kate's reverie, "You're going back to part-time study?"

"Sorry, yes," replied Kate, while glancing at the television screen. "I have been thinking and talking about doing something for myself for ages now, but I just kept putting it on the long finger. But September 11th made me realise that life is all too short, so it has kind of galvanised me into taking action."

"I know just how you feel," replied Grace, eyeing the large cranes on the TV digging through the mountainous rubble. "It has had the same affect on me. I've realised that I need to be with little Orla more, and life is too short for me to put up with the likes of Pervy Conroy while I miss out on my baby growing up."

"Well, if you decide to take the job, it would mean you could spend more time with Orla and earn some money too. The hours might be flexible, but they wouldn't be too onerous, while the salary would remain the same. I just need someone I can trust and whom I believe will take over from me, like another mother, as it were. You'd be picking them up from school and maybe doing a bit of homework, cooking a snack or the odd time cooking a casserole if I have a late lecture. But it would be no more than three days a week and I'm sure I can be pretty flexible."

"It sounds great." Grace smiled. It wouldn't be too much grief, spending time in a terrific house like this, and having Orla by her side. She had met Jade and glimpsed Chloe, and they seemed tame enough. She thoroughly liked Kate too. She began to really want this job.

"The course is two years long." Kate went on. "So do you think you could commit yourself for that period of time?"

"I think so," Grace agreed. "That would take me almost up to Orla starting school – it would be perfect. Now I just have to convince my husband."

"Me too," Kate laughed. "Aren't men just like little babies when any kind of change occurs? Mine is sulking in the study because I am actually going to go ahead and go back to college. Honestly, you'd swear I was running off with the milkman."

53

"Mine is at home, sulking through the soccer, at the thought of me quitting a well-paid but lifestyle-poor secure job just so I can have the odd lie-in."

"And when did you last have one?" Kate enquired knowingly with a twinkle in her eye.

"Exactly," Grace giggled. She knew right then and there that she and Kate Heathcoat would become great friends.

Chapter 5

Grace was having lunch with Dymphna Coffey at the Harbourmaster Bar in the IFSC.

Dymphna and Grace had remained firm friends in the intervening years, despite Dymphna's early return to Ireland, just before the boom. She had managed, despite herself, to become very successful in her career, getting into a specialised sector of banking by being more computer literate than most of her peers. She progressed nicely in the banking industry, which in turn had afforded her the opportunity to purchase a nice little apartment on the Clontarf seafront – before it became unaffordable. Everything in Dymphna's life was rosy but the one thing that seemed to have eluded her was finding the right man, a nice single guy who had all his teeth and wasn't afraid of the "C" word: Commitment.

Today Grace marvelled at Dymphna's shiny black

bob and long lean limbs, which escaped her neat knee-length skirt, and wondered how any man could resist. They were both devouring spicy chicken wings, while dissecting Dympha's latest beau.

"Oh, Grace, he was totally 'bed and fled' but of course I fell for it all over again."

Grace was perplexed. "Bed and fled?" she echoed dimly, feeling really old and square for having to ask.

"You know the type," Dymphna replied, her violet eyes flashing with annoyance.

"They charm the pants off you, take you passionately to bed and then you wake up in the morning to discover that they have fled as fast as their insincere little legs will carry them."

"Oh, Dimples," Grace laughed, calling her friend by her old childhood nickname, "when are you at least going to play a little bit hard to get?"

Dymphna attacked another chicken wing, snapping it briskly in two. She licked her fingers. "All very well for you to say, my dear, with a gorgeous guy on tap. A girl like me has got her needs, y'know, and come to think of it, how is the hunky man from the bog?"

"He's fine, but you're getting off the subject – now please continue with the story."

Dymphna blushed – so Grace knew what was coming next. "Well, anyway, I didn't hear from him for a few days so I questioned Jason from Accounts who knows the staff where Mark works – at the Ballsbridge HQ – and lo and behold, Mark has been married for the last eighteen months to some poor cow from Limerick, who he only goes home to at weekends. Hence the three dates that only occurred during the week. I felt like a right eejit the next time I had to telephone international banking, I can tell you."

Dymphna had a complicated and mostly unsuccessful love life. Grace had endured years of tea and sympathy over Dymphna's poor taste in men. They seemed to be initially smitten but before long all faded away. She had been unlucky in one sense, Grace thought, but she seemed to be all too easily swayed by a smart line in fancy talk and a nice car or a good bottle of wine.

There had been a long succession of ne'er-do-wells and all too often married men that had passed through and Grace guessed that Dymphna had become increasing desperate over the past few years to land the big one. She was nearly thirty-two and most of her peers had settled into some sort of domestic bliss or co-habitation.

Dymphna now flicked her black shiny hair out of her eyes and sniffed miserably. "Honestly Grace, I am so sick and tired of the same old social scene. My bloody biological clock is ticking as loudly as Big Ben these days. Yet all the blokes my age that haven't yet settled down are pairing off with babes that are barely out of their school gymslips. I'm beginning to feel like I'm getting past my use-by date. At least that's how it seems to me."

"Don't be ridiculous!" Grace countered. "You, my girl, are a fabulous catch for any bloke out there – you're in your prime. It can't be all that bad, can it? Maybe you just need to broaden your horizons a little bit. Get out of the pubs and into the supermarkets. There's many a hunk to be found in Tesco's, looking lost and bewildered in the frozen food section."

"Anything seems to be worth a try," Dymphna replied earnestly. "I've just about exhausted my supply of men from the world of banking, that's for sure."

Grace thought fleetingly of her workmate Darren and then, picturing his carrot-red hair and freckles, dismissed him as a candidate. Dymphna seemed to be more particular about appearances than character, so the lovely but plain Darren would have to remain unloved for the moment. Dymphna had seen him once at Grace's office but hadn't given him a second glance.

"I'm quitting my job at Interfex Bank," Grace announced suddenly.

"What?" Dymphna screeched, putting down her chicken wing. "But why?"

Grace shrugged and fiddled with her cappuccino. "Oh, September 11th made me look at my life a little differently. And I've decided life is definitely too short to put up with the likes of Charlie Conroy at the expense of my kids."

Dymphna frowned. "But Grace, what about the financial end of things? I thought you and Paul were barely making ends meet as it was."

"We *are*," Grace sighed. "But I have had an offer of a part-time job locally and between the jigs and the reels, I'll be making almost as much as I am now, when you take the childcare fees out of it. Plus, I get to spend a lot more time with Orla."

"Why the doubts then?" Dymphna knew her friend and Grace seemed too unsure.

"I don't really know, to be honest. It's a little bit different to anything I have ever done before. I mean, I'm used to the gossip and bitchiness of the office environment, and I'm comfortable with all the organised coffee breaks. This is a kind of nanny job of sorts. I'd be collecting two kids from school, doing homework, maybe some light housework, or making lunches, that sort of thing."

Dymphna giggled. "Can't say I ever pictured you as some sort of Mrs Doubtfire."

Grace laughed. "Me neither, but if I keep eating the way I am at the moment, I'll certainly have her figure. I don't know yet. It's a bit of a gamble, although the kids seem really sweet and Kate, my prospective employer, appears totally normal. She is so nice you couldn't help but like her, despite her perfect figure and her fabulous house. Honestly, Dimples, it's like something out of *Vogue*. It would be nice to work in the lap of luxury."

"Just make sure it's the right decision, that's all," warned Dymphna sagely. "It might not be that easy to get another job like that in finance again if you leave. I have a feeling that September 11th will change the economy a great deal. The markets are already in freefall."

"It's changed a lot more than the economy," Grace replied darkly, dismissing several horrible images from her mind. She wondered absentmindedly if she would ever look at an aeroplane in the same innocuous way again.

"Now, I'm sorry Dimples, I really have to get back to work. Pervy Conroy will be standing at my desk looking at his watch if I am not back by two on the button."

"Doesn't the old creep have lunch then?" Dymphna grinned.

Grace shuddered. "I dread to think of what he gets up to on the net. The only time he seems to leave the office is either to stuff his fat face or perv on the female staff. I can't wait for the moment I can finally tell him to stick his job. Though I will miss Darren. He's an oul pet."

"Ginger-top you can have," quipped Dymphna, smoothing down her narrow skirt. "He has a face only a mother could love."

"You only saw him once," Grace admonished her friend. She felt quite protective towards sweet skinny Darren, who indeed seemed only to have his mother to love him.

"Once was quite enough," retorted Dymphna unperturbed.

"You see, Miss Fussy Knickers," Grace replied, "it's that attitude that has you single. If you dropped your standards just a little bit below Brad Pitt, you might just score yourself a fella."

"Meow!" sniffed Dymphna, unconvinced. "Now, come on. It's almost five to two. Your shoes will probably turn into pumpkins if we don't get you back immediately."

Grace laughed. Dymphna was such a funny dear friend. She would miss these girly gossipy lunches if she left her job in Dublin.

Doubts and counter-doubts filled her mind while she ran through the increasingly heavy rain that fell as she made her way back to the office.

By the time she reached her building, the shower had become a deluge and Grace was soaked through. She took off her jacket hurriedly and noticed with dismay that the front of her black shirt was soaking wet and stuck to her like a second skin, highlighting her two most obvious assets.

She cursed herself for not fastening up her jacket properly as she tried to wring her sopping hair out.

Darren was smiling from his desk. "You look like you've just been in a wet T-shirt competition. Old Pervy will just love it. I have an old rugby top here, if you'd like to change."

Grace was irritated. "Don't laugh, Darren, it's not funny. Anyway, I'm sure your tiny top won't cover me in the places I need it to." She glanced at her generous boobs and sighed. They had never been a problem until recently. In fact she had delighted in the fact that men seemed to ignore her too-wide hips, because their eyes never got that far. Her chest had always got all the attention. But Charlie Conroy had made her skin crawl, with his lascivious beady eyes constantly undressing her. And she wasn't the only one. Her office, with ten women workers, had an unusually high number of females sporting a Victorian taste in blouses and skirts. Grace marvelled at how this insidious form of sexual harassment was easily tolerated in Ireland and considered harmless. It would never have been acceptable in London.

Suddenly, Charlie Conroy emerged from his office and made a beeline for Grace's desk. Grace sat down immediately and switched on her computer.

"Have you got the overnight rates?" Pervy Comb-over enquired, his greedy eyes drinking in Grace's plastered-on blouse.

"Yes, I'll just get them." She could feel his gaze on her as she leaned over and gathered the file.

"Here." She almost threw it at him and grabbed another file quickly to her chest. He seemed to be rooted to the spot.

"Might need you to come in at the weekend, Grace," he announced suddenly. "The end of year filing needs to be boxed up and archived, now that the auditors have finished with them. I'm sure you could do with the overtime."

"No can do, I'm afraid," Grace replied innocently. "It's my son's birthday on Saturday and I need to keep the weekend free for him."

Charlie's face formed a familiar sneer. "Yes, well, I suppose it's late notice, but we really do need this filing to be done and it is part of your job description, as you well know. As we are understaffed you are aware that we cannot complete the filing in normal hours so – you will have to work late at some stage this month, to get it done."

He was now dark with annoyance. He then raised his voice. "Does everyone *get* that? We need all staff to put aside a few evenings or a Saturday this month to get all the filing archived. Now, anyone who has a problem with that, I suggest that looking at the Situations Vacant column might be a good idea."

With that, he stormed off and slammed his office door shut. Grace got a few nasty looks from some of her co-workers for raising the boss's ire.

Darren gestured "Looper", before returning to the box of KFC that was lurking underneath his desk.

Grace sighed heavily. She really would have to get out of here. She decided she would take this nanny job – it couldn't be any worse than this. She would tell Paul of her decision tonight. There would be no going back now. The decision was made. She was about to be out of Interfex International Bank and thrust into the unknown world of domestic bliss.

Kate heard the phone trill and leapt up immediately. She didn't want Des to answer it in case it was Grace calling about the job.

So far Des's increasing opposition to Kate's plans had shocked her by the intensity of his arguments. He had ranted and raved like a little schoolboy when she informed him that she had gone ahead and held interviews for an assistant. Obviously he hadn't believed she had been deadly serious when he had reluctantly agreed to the plan that night over dinner. Kate boiled when she remembered how he had agreed that she needed more stimulation in her life. It had all been a patronising charade. He never believed she would actually go through with it. How selfish could a man get, Kate thought angrily, as she rushed towards the phone. Des, thankfully, was sulking in his study, and hopefully wouldn't hear the call.

Grace was on the other end. Little did Kate know that Grace was receiving just as much opposition in her own home to the idea of her working for Kate. She was watching Paul from the corner of her eye as he seethed in front of the television, appearing to watch the football.

Stuff him! Grace thought, her dander well and truly up. It's my life and no man is going to tell me what I can and can't do. I'll work for whom I damn well please.

"Kate," she announced cheerily when the phone was answered, "it's Grace here, Grace Kelly. I just called to tell you that I have thought over your offer, and I would love to take the job." Paul harrumphed noisily in the corner and Grace turned away from him in disgust.

"That's wonderful news," Kate replied quietly, almost in a whisper.

Grace thought that maybe Kate's children had gone to bed, hence the hushed tone, yet then she registered a television blaring in the background. "Maybe we could have a coffee on Saturday afternoon to go over the finer points?"

Grace felt a bit awkward saying this, but she needed to sell the idea a bit more to Paul and discuss the salary before she said a final goodbye to Pervy Comb-over and her lovely pay packet. Paul was taking Jordan go-cart racing for his birthday so it would give Grace the opportunity to talk to Kate and finalise their plans.

"Yes, that's fine, Grace," Kate replied. "I have your

number, how about I give you a call on Saturday morning so we can arrange it. I'll call you then. And, Grace, thank you very much, you won't regret this."

Grace put the receiver down.

Paul stared blankly at the TV and said, "I hope you know what you're doing."

"Not another word, Paul Kelly!" Grace warned as she stormed from the living-room. "Not another word!" She flounced off to the bedroom in a dark rage.

That was the trouble with living in a tiny house like this. There was nowhere to go when you had a row. There were only two small bedrooms and Jordan needed his own space, so Orla's cot was in Grace and Paul's bedroom. So invariably, they had to creep about in the dark at night and be extremely quiet. There could be no reading in bed or watching TV even if they had wanted to, so now she just had to lie on the bed and fume about her row with Paul.

He had said that he thought she was stupid. Quitting a good pensionable job for some glorified cleaner's job at a posh house that would probably pay peanuts. And what if it didn't work out? Then she would be out of a good job.

Grace had railed angrily at that comment. She had known Paul for over ten years and had not been out of work for even one of them. She realised she hadn't ironed out all of the details, but the basic plan of working locally and having Orla with her was a good one. It infuriated her that she felt Paul believed she was stupid enough to act on a whim and quit her job, before setting all the finances in place.

She had retorted that maybe after ten years she should be able to relax a bit more and have the chance to spend a bit more time with the children, as she hardly saw them as it was. She inferred that if Paul were a better breadwinner that life would be easier for all of them. She felt guilty after that, as she knew Paul worked extremely hard for them all, but right now she felt like throttling him. This little house didn't help. It was so tiny it got on her nerves. Being in Kate Heathcoat's sprawling glamorous pile had done little to enamour Grace to her house as she returned home that evening. She hated her tiny untidy hallway where the boots and shoes clamoured for space with Orla's buggy. And the way the living-room was stuffed with just its shabby sofa and tiny bay window. Paul and Jordan had been watching TV, and crisp packets and drinks bottles were strewn on the floor along with Orla's fluffy toys and baby-bouncer – she literally couldn't move for bumping into things. She said nothing, but it all looked so dreary and depressing. Grace had felt a deep dissatisfaction ever since being at the Beeches and she felt deeply guilty for it, but that's the way it was. She wondered what Kate Heathcoat was doing over at her luxurious house, as she simmered away in her little dark bedroom, with the sound of Paul's football match blaring in the distance.

Kate was also fretting and simmering over at The Beeches. Jade and Chloe were in the den watching a video and Des was still sequestered in his study, supposedly working but she knew better. Des was in the middle of a king-size sulk.

Kate wondered at why Des was so opposed to the idea of her taking on further studies. Was she so insecure that he felt if she bettered herself in some way that she might get ideas above her station? If she was a designer, she might not be so acquiescent and the ever-loyal stay-at-home wife that he seemed to want her to be.

It suited him to have her at home in a gilded cage, and he didn't seem too keen on letting the door open. Kate began to feel a familiar knot in her stomach. She hated this feeling of insecurity she got when Des distanced himself from her. Whenever she did anything supposedly wrong, he would become cold and distant for several days, often completely ignoring her. This brought her back to the awful days of her childhood when she was Kathleen and ignored and unloved. Kate hated to be reminded of that former self and how that fat little girl still remained inside her just waiting for an opportunity to get out. She rose swiftly and lit an aromatherapy candle, then put on a relaxing CD of wave sounds lapping gently on the shore. She lay back down on her huge bed and wearily closed her eyes, as her mind drifted on to her family and back to that last day she saw them, her parents, a few months ago.

She spoke mostly to her parents by telephone. Sometimes they were coherent, mostly they were not. She felt a deep guilt about her parents. She knew she didn't do her duty by them and she had to admit that she felt ashamed of them. It was purely duty that got her to the shabby little council house that day. It was her mother's sixtieth birthday, so she steeled herself to get into the jeep and drive there with knuckles white on the steering wheel all the way, the obligatory bunch of flowers beside her with a card and £100 inside. She knew that's what they would be waiting for – the money – so they could be off down to the off-licence as soon as she left, but that didn't bother her. What bothered her was the way she felt as soon as she entered that house – it was that feeling that she hated the most.

As she turned up the road to her childhood home she noticed that many of the houses sported extensions or fancy renovations, making them appear cheerful and more affluent. But of course her parent's house stood out in its shabbiness. The garden was overgrown with a few tall weeds taking precedence and the pebble-dashed walls, once white and clean, were now dark grey and dingy. She walked slowly up the path towards the door, flowers in hand. She had deliberately dressed plainly in order not to be noticed, though she knew the jeep would stick out a mile. Her hair was tied back and she wore a plain T-shirt and jeans – not wanting to draw any unwanted attention from the old neighbours.

Kate rang the bell and, noticing that it didn't work, rapped hard on the peeling paintwork of the front door.

Her father eventually answered, smelling strongly of beer. He looked old, she thought. He was shabbily dressed in a stained grey cardigan and a dirty white vest. He was unshaven and she saw that his beard was entirely grey and his eyes were bloodshot.

He didn't smile or say hello but simply said, "It's you." And turned on his heel.

Kate followed him down the dark dank hallway to the kitchen. It all looked shockingly the same. She was amazed that each time the dirt and debris still surprised her. The tiny rooms that she hated so much as a little girl and had always wanted to escape from.

Her mother was sitting at the Formica kitchen table, cigarette in one hand, mug of tea in the other, as she vaguely watched the Channel 4 racing on a small portable TV on the kitchen counter.

"Kathleen, love, howiya," her mother rasped in her heavy chain-smoking voice.

Kate thrust the flowers into her mother's arms and gave her an awkward half hug.

Her mother smelled of cigarettes and lavender and at once Kate was filled with both revulsion and love. She came close to tears. She still loved them both, despite everything. Despite the fact that they had almost ruined her life and had neglected her for years, despite also despising them and everything they stood for over the years, she still felt a love.

"Put them in water, Christy," her mother then said, tossing the bouquet in her father's direction.

Kate sat down on a sticky chair, eyeing a mangy dog that sat scratching himself in a corner. Her parents were forever taking in strays, giving them more affection, if not care, than they had ever given their four children. Since Kate was a child, the house had been sticky and dirty. She had tried over the years to fix it up herself and then later when she married Des she had decorators come in and paint the place, but within a few months it returned to its former dingy self. You just couldn't help them, so she gave up. It also seemed as if she somehow made things worse. By trying to fix it up, it made them aware of how ashamed of them she felt. It was as if they weren't good enough. Kate felt they weren't and hated herself for it.

"Happy Birthday, Mum," she offered now, weakly.

"Thanks, love," Josie replied absently, while patting Kate's arm lightly. She never took her eyes from the one o'clock race.

"Would ye like a cuppa tea, or maybe something stronger?" her father enquired.

"Tea is fine," Kate replied, a little tersely. Alcohol was never far from their minds.

Josie opened her birthday card, expressed fake surprise at its contents and summarily despatched Christy down to the off-licence as soon as the tea was made, for a fresh bottle of whiskey. Her mother explained that they had only a few cans left for that evening, but now they could celebrate.

Kate smiled tightly and wondered in despair if they would ever change. She knew in her heart that things would only get worse as their alcoholism deepened and she worried about the day when they could no longer shuffle about the dirty little house together or when one or the other of their livers packed up and the other was left alone. What would happen then? She dreaded to think. Once again she failed to go there and remain detached.

She sat for another hour with her mother, enduring her barely concealed snipes at Des and his snobbishness and how her daughter lived the high falutin' lifestyle that made her feel she was better than the rest of them. When her father arrived back eventually with the whiskey and no doubt a few pints under his belt, Kate finally extricated herself and left.

She sped home out of Dublin like a maniac, towards the clean green fields, putting as much distance as she could between her and her parents. When she finally reached The Beeches she stripped off and went straight into the shower, where she cried for half an hour as she scrubbed dirty miserable little Kathleen from her skin, and put herself back together in time to collect the children from school.

As she put her plain clothes into the linen basket and donned her best cashmere skirt and jumper she began to feel more like herself again. Her family and her background were a deep source of shame and so she had kept them mostly a secret. No one would ever know how much it actually cost her emotionally to go back there. The briefest of visits would have her right back there, as scared fat little Kathleen who was left alone at night to look after her three smaller siblings. She had never had a childhood and always had to be the grown-up foraging for food from the neighbours, even sometimes driven to stealing when there was nothing but alcohol in that house. She never knew when she would go hungry so would always stuff her face with whatever she got her hands on just in case.

Now, eight weeks later, she lay on her bed remembering, listening to the calming wave music while tears streamed down her face. The memories from that house all those years ago were still deep and raw and Kate never wanted to go there again. Now she was slim and successful Kate Heathcoat and nothing would ever take her back there, not now and not ever.

Meanwhile, Des Heathcoat was seething alone in his study, an open and still unread textbook about Internet sales in front of him in case Kate came in unexpectedly.

He hadn't actually believed for one minute that Kate was ever serious about this idea of becoming an interior designer. He had humoured her at the start, believing this to be a whimsical idea, much like the horse riding and the pottery classes before that, which had all petered out after a few enthusiastic weeks.

No, this time it was different. He detected a determination in Kate that he had not seen before. This was a two-year course (albeit part-time) and she had already enrolled, and interviewed a nanny to boot. This new side to Kate made him feel uncomfortable. A knot had formed in his stomach and would not recede. He felt like Kate was drifting away from him. Des had carefully crafted and moulded his perfect wife over the years and now it all looked as though it might slip away.

Kate had seemed bored and distracted lately. What if she was already tired of him and slowly drifting away? He imagined all the young hip student types

that she would invariably meet in college and a deep
fear gripped him. It could only be a matter of time
before she fell for someone younger or more interesting.
He was already on the wrong side of forty. He was
aware as the years passed that the ten-year age gap
between them both seemed to widen. He felt older now,
although he would never admit it to Kate. He had
always felt her superior, from the moment the shy
bespectacled girl blushed into his office all those years
ago. He had been young, successful and handsome and
she had been in awe. And for years that's how it had
remained. But lately, despite all his dedication at the
gym, he could detect the slight sagging in his muscles,
and the ever so tiny paunch that he tried so hard to
keep at bay. In eight years he would be fifty while Kate
would only be forty. Kate would eventually tire of him
and leave him. Des couldn't bear that to happen.
Perhaps he should have agreed to trying for another
baby after all? All he ever wanted was a son to carry on
his name, but he couldn't bear another disappointment.
Nor could he bear another person taking Kate's
attention away from him.

Everything now seemed to be changing including
Kate and he hadn't the faintest idea of how to stop it.

Chapter 6

It was Saturday, the day of Jordan's birthday. Paul had planned to take Jordan go-cart racing with a few friends. Grace knew that becoming a cool thirteen Jordan wouldn't want her tagging along on what was essentially a blokes' outing, so she got up early and cooked Jordan's favourite breakfast of waffles and maple syrup instead, and had his cards and gifts ready and waiting for him to get up.

He eventually surfaced at ten and in a black mood. Smiling briefly while he opened his birthday cards and new mobile phone, he soon lapsed back into his sullen demeanour, while devouring his waffles in silence.

Grace fought back the urge to give him a swift clip around the ear, and quickly went upstairs to see if Paul was any more enlightened on the subject.

"I think it could be the fact that he asked six guys in the class to the go-carting and only two have agreed to go. No wonder the poor wee bloke feels a bit insecure and unpopular. But what can we do? I'm pretending everything is fine and normal, and the four of us are going, but I think maybe you need to talk to him, Gracie – he seems to be taking it badly enough."

"Fine, I will," replied Grace dejectedly. She gave Paul a quick hug. He really loved Jordan and she knew he tried to be the best father he could to him, something that was proving increasing difficult lately.

She went back to the kitchen and pretended to busy herself making some breakfast while Jordan fiddled with his new phone. She eventually sat down with some tea and toast and tried to broach the subject.

"Looking forward to today?" she began innocently enough.

Jordan shrugged, his large brown eyes downcast.

"Who's going along?" she asked.

"Only Gavin and Paul – everyone else was suddenly busy."

Grace took a sip of tea – this wasn't going to be easy. "Well, maybe they *are*. You're still relatively new around here, Jordan. It takes time to make friends. In a few months' time they'll all be your buddies."

"That's crap, Mum. You have no idea. They call me Bin Laden and a Muslim murderer. They tell me to go back where I came from. And that's the trouble. I don't know anything about the place I'm from, do I? Except London. I don't know anything about my real father or my real background. I hate it here! I hate this horrible little house in this horrible little village, where they have horrible little minds. I want to go home to London and back to my real friends, and most of all I want to see my real father!"

With that, Jordan fled the room in tears, bumping into Paul as he left.

Grace was stunned. She sat looking after Jordan but unable to follow and help him.

What could she say? It had always been a worry right in the back of her mind, the worrisome idea that Jordan would want to know his father some day, but she never envisaged that he would have so many problems with his colour and his background. All the anti-Muslim feeling that was blared out on the TV every day after September 11th didn't help, but she felt the problems went much deeper.

"I suppose you heard some of that," Grace said at last. She hadn't even noticed Paul was sitting opposite her.

His face said it all. He looked like he had been slapped. "Indeed I did," he said sadly. "Looks like we're in for some interesting times."

The words were said lightly enough, but she felt that he had been hurt deeply. He had been there for Jordan for over ten years, and he was Jordan's father to all intents and purposes. He must feel awful, to be dismissed like that.

"I'll talk to him later," Grace offered, while touching his hand. "I want his birthday to be a nice day, if possible. Please don't take it too much to heart. Just carry on as normal. I'll sort him out."

"Right, so," Paul replied, but his look didn't match his words.

Grace hoped that Jordan wasn't going to resent Paul and vice versa. She didn't want to be piggy-in-the-middle. A nice stress headache began to form in the middle of her head. She really didn't need this today. She was supposed to be meeting Kate later to finalise the details of her new job.

She went upstairs to find Jordan and see if he had calmed down.

She knocked on his door and he slowly opened it.

He looked worried. As if he expected a lecture.

She noticed his usually tidy bedroom floor was strewn with clothes and CDs but she ignored it for the moment. She sat down on the bed, resisting the urge to straighten the covers.

"Is school really as bad as you say, Jordy?"

"Most of the time." Jordan shrugged. "It wasn't too bad before September 11th, but since then it has got a lot worse. I'm too different. I look different, I speak different, and I don't have a lot of friends here. It's just no fun, Mum. Everybody asks me where I'm really from, and I don't know. I only ever saw Jordan on a map. I've only seen one picture of my father. Can't you find him, Mum, and why can't I meet him? Why didn't you ever see him again? Didn't you love him?"

"I did love him, Jordy, but there was the small matter of him being already married. I didn't know that when I fell in love with him – he never told me. When I got pregnant with you he got scared and he left me. I don't know if he still works in London, or even if he is still a pilot, but I will try to find out, if that helps. As for school, you are new and different at the moment, but eventually all this Muslim-bashing will die down and you will become just the same as everyone else, and someone else will become the new kid. Now, I want you to enjoy today and to say sorry to Paul. After all, you hurt his feelings earlier. He might not be your biological father, but he's the only dad you have ever known and he loves you."

"Not as much as he loves Orla!" Jordan replied belligerently.

Grace felt her blood rise. "Now, that's pure rubbish, and you know it. He loves you both the same. It's not Orla that he's taking go-cart racing today, is it? Now if you still want to go, I suggest you explain yourself to Paul."

"Right," Jordan reluctantly replied, and sloped out of the room.

Grace looked around again at the jumble of clothes and books on the floor. She decided not to focus on that today and headed into her own bedroom to get Orla. At least her baby still adored her implicitly and couldn't yet talk back. She needed to sniff Orla's downy neck and hug her to her.

She felt that somehow Jordan's problems and strong desire to see his father would be a divisive issue in the near future. God! She had thought babyhood and toddlers were problematic. It looked like the teenage years were the most traumatic yet.

Two hours later, the earlier drama forgotten, the house

was emptied of males and Grace gratefully enjoyed the silence and peace before going to meet Kate for coffee. Orla was nicely snuggled up in her cot for her morning nap. Grace had a long hot shower and was trying to find something nice to wear for her meeting with Kate when the phone rang.

Grace ran, clad only in her towel, to get to it before the noise woke Orla.

"Grace?" There was only one person with that commanding voice and it wasn't Kate.

"Olivia?" Oh no! Grace thought, what does my bright and shiny older sister want? She wasn't exactly the type of sister who called regularly for cosy chats. Grace tried to remember the last time they had spoken – it had been months ago, maybe even five or six months ago, Grace thought guiltily.

"Hi, sorry it's been so long. How are you?" Olivia sounded strange. Quite friendly even, which for Olivia was quite weird.

"Fine, we're all fine. It's Jordan's birthday today, the Terrible Thirteen. Orla's still cute though and can't talk back yet, thank God. And yourself? How are you?" Grace rolled her eyes. It felt so stilted and uncomfortable talking to her only sister. It always had.

"Oh, I'm so-so. You know, busy as ever."

Grace thought she could detect a slight tremor in Olivia's voice.

"I was just wondering if you and I could get together for a bit of lunch, during the week," Olivia went on. "It's been too long."

Grace almost replied, yeah, try thirty years, but she demurred. "Yes, that would be nice – are you still in Fitzwilliam Square?" Olivia worked for a high-flying firm called Scientific Innovations that Grace hadn't a clue about.

Olivia sighed. "Yes," she replied in a tired voice. "Are you still in the IFSC?"

"For my sins," Grace laughed.

"Right. So, can we meet somewhere in the middle, say the Davenport on Wednesday at around one?"

"That would be fine. I'll see you there. Bye, Olivia."

Grace put down the phone, perturbed. Olivia never phoned for a social chat and Grace hadn't heard from her since that telephone call months ago bragging about her new house being built in the Wicklow Hills.

Olivia and Grace had never been close. Moira Casey had made sure of that. Her mother had made divisive comments to Grace from an early age about Olivia. Olivia was smarter, taller, blonder and infinitely more suitable than Grace as a daughter. So Grace had hated the haughty snobbish Olivia ever since she could remember. Grace wasn't sure how it all started. She was just sure that they had never been like real sisters, even though there had been only four years between them. Grace was still going over the strange phone call when the phone rang again.

"Grace?" This time it was Kate.

"Are you still on for today, for coffee?"

"You bet!" Grace replied smiling. "I'm bloke-free for a few hours, so bring on the espresso!"

"Great," Kate enthused. "See you at one. Which do you fancy, *Mario's* or *Ibiza*?"

"*Ibiza* has great big fat mugs of cappuccino, so let's go there please." Grace badly needed some caffeine after her strange phone call from the Wicked Sister from the West.

"OK, see ya then." Kate sounded happy.

Grace ran to find something to wear, anything that hadn't got baby-food on it or a trailing hem. Kate was so elegant and well put together, Grace didn't want to look like an unmade bed like she usually did. She found her red linen pants and a crisp white linen shirt. Today Grace wanted a nice girly lunch where she could nail down an agreement with Kate that would change her future. And she was determined she was going to dress for success.

Kate was waiting at *Ibiza* when Grace arrived. Grace's heart sank when she saw her. She had flounced out of her townhouse feeling glam and classy in her red linen trousers and a slick of crimson lipstick to match, her hair behaving for once. But there was Kate, a perfect vision in a pale blue chenille knit suit that had to be Lainey Keogh. Her hair was piled high in a classic chignon and her face was delicately made up. Grace suddenly felt like a heffalump as she manoeuvred Orla's buggy through the myriad tables and chairs. She swallowed her envy as she smiled at Kate, who waved her over.

"Is this Orla?" Kate beamed at Orla in her cute pink fluffy outfit and Orla smiled and gurgled back, in great good humour after her long nap.

Orla was great with the public. She smiled and cooed on cue every time. Grace hoped she would always retain her sunny demeanour.

"I'll get her a highchair," Kate said, rising.

Within minutes they had Orla ensconced in her baby seat with a selection of toys, and had two frothy cappuccinos before them.

Before long they were like old friends. Dissecting marriage, men and housework, laughing and agreeing on most things, before getting on to the real reason they were there.

"OK, first and foremost, let's get the awkward stuff out of the way, like money. I used to hate going to interviews where you could never mention the salary, when it was one of the main reasons you were there. So I thought maybe if we settled on a fixed amount for the three days and then if I need you to work extra days we could agree an hourly rate. "

Grace smiled.

Kate continued. "Well, I'm in college Monday, Thursday and Friday. I know it's a bit stretched out – is that OK?"

"That's actually really good for me, Kate. Jordan has Speech and Drama on Monday and soccer on Fridays after school, so it's perfect. He'll only have to be alone for an hour one afternoon. He's just turned thirteen and I feel he's going to need me a lot more now he has become a dreaded teenager."

"It's all ahead of me, I'm sure. Jade's a little pet but Chloe is nine going on nineteen, you're going to have to keep an eye on her, and she's a real little madam. OK, so the days are fine. Now to the salary. How about three hundred and fifty pounds a week?"

Grace almost choked on her coffee. Obviously Kate had plenty of money and hadn't checked the going rates for childminding – although she thought it would be a little more than that, Grace had never expected this much. She was unsure of what to say. She felt a bit mean taking such a lot of money from Kate.

"That is more than generous. Are you sure you want to offer so much?"

Kate grinned. "You are going to be taking care of my most precious possessions in the world. I think I can afford as much as some people spend in a week on their gardener or in the beauty salon. I feel they're worth it. You'll hopefully be like another mum to them."

"Kate, I will treat them as well as I do my own. After what I have witnessed in *Cute and Cuddly* I would never want to have any child of mine in an institution like a large crèche again. It's a shame it's the best most parents have on offer."

"Yeah," replied Kate. "Someone needs to come up with a better idea for occasional childcare. That's why I'm so happy I found you. You have childcare problems and so do I, and we can help each other."

Grace agreed. She could never ask her mother or sister to help out with looking after her children, even occasionally. And as for Dymphna, well, poor old Dimples would have a heart attack if she were asked to baby-sit. Modern mothers were very much self-reliant. It was a case of having to be.

"Well," she said, lifting her coffee cup. "I accept

your kind offer and here's to a successful working relationship"

"Cheers!" Kate smiled as she raised her cup and clinked it with Grace's mug. "Now we just have to convince the husbands."

They both laughed, and Grace left *Ibiza* an hour later on a high. She had never imagined that Kate would be offering so much money. It would make her move from Interfex very easy. She would actually be earning more money now when she deducted all the petrol and crèche fees that she would be saving on. She was becoming more excited about the prospect of working for Kate and being at home more. No more Pervy Comb-over and his sleazy looks and smart comments. No more traffic gridlock and ironing all day Sunday. She couldn't wait for Paul and Jordan to come home so she could tell them the good news.

Kate was happy too. She had put the final piece of her career plan together and got Grace on board. It was all coming together. She was going to become an interior designer. At last!

She hoped that Des would come around to the idea when he met Grace and saw how nice she was and how well adjusted the children would be. Surely he wouldn't continue in his strong opposition. It would make life difficult for all of them. But one thing was for sure. Kate wasn't going to back down. She was going to achieve her dream for herself, no matter what her husband said.

Chapter 7

Grace scoured through her squashed wardrobe in a vain attempt to find something classy and professional to wear that would suitably impress her older sister Olivia. All she could find was a navy silk suit that had some kind of unidentifiable baby emission all over one sleeve (How did that get back into the wardrobe unnoticed, she fumed) or a plain black wool trouser suit with a missing button. It would have to be the black, she decided. She would wear a white silk shirt and leave the jacket open. Hopefully, it wouldn't be too chilly.

Grace wished she hadn't agreed to meet Olivia for lunch. She always felt like she was attending an interview, instead of having lunch with the only person in the world that she could call sister. She always felt Olivia was examining her for failure, just like her parents always had. She knew that Olivia would arrive immaculately groomed, clad only in Paul Costello with a laptop or lackey in tow and spend an entire hour making Grace feel inadequate, bleating on about her wonderful job and her even more wonderful fiancé.

Grace always felt like a bold child afterwards. Well, she couldn't get out of it now; she grimaced as she tried to comb her wayward hair, while Orla rummaged through her make-up bag on the bed. Might as well make the best of it. 'Anyhow, she will only get to you if you let her,' she remonstrated with herself. 'Be confident and stuff her, if she's her usual pompous self.'

"If she starts bragging, just leave," Paul had advised her the night before. He never had any time for Olivia either. He noticed the slightly raised eyebrow and the almost imperceptible frown that glanced off Olivia's face when she occasionally met him. He too felt that Olivia looked down on him, so Grace knew she wasn't imagining it. It had always been this way, as long as Grace could remember.

Well, today Grace wouldn't rise to the bait. She was determined that she would show Olivia that she was as successful and as happy as she was. She pulled on the black suit over the white silk shirt, then slicked on some red lipstick and she was reasonably happy. Scooping up a petulant Orla who was highly annoyed at being interrupted while discovering lipstick art all over Grace's duvet cover, Grace fled to the car. She was endeavouring to get to work early, so Pervy would have no reason to prevent her from taking a full lunch. Jordan had already cycled to school, in a surprisingly good mood. He had been a lot brighter since his go-cart outing the previous Saturday, Grace noticed thankfully, and Paul said the day had gone very well. Jordan certainly seemed more settled since.

Grace hoped that the outburst was a one off. She certainly didn't need Jordan to start demanding to see his biological father. She had enough on her plate for the moment. Her successful meeting on Saturday with Kate, which had left her determined to quit her job, had still remained largely unspoken about. The time never seemed right. She had briefly mentioned it to Paul and he was seemingly agreeable enough, but she still felt he had a bit of resistance to her leaving Interfex. So she had left the subject alone for the moment.

Grace quickly put Orla into her baby seat and stowed her myriad baby essentials inside. She prayed that her car wouldn't cause trouble today. Luckily enough it fired up after a few reluctant grumbles. Grace thanked the Lord as she sped towards *Cute and Cuddly*. She couldn't wait for the moment that she could tell the awful Avril that Orla was leaving, almost as much as the moment when she'd tell Pervy where to stick it. Grace imagined various different scenarios, where she eviscerated Charlie Conroy verbally as she handed him her resignation. Each time the scene became more outlandish, and it made her giggle as she raced towards Dublin. It helped take her mind off this infernal lunch date with Olivia the Awful.

The traffic was crazy as usual, and Grace was a little late as she parked her car and made the usual mad dash to Interfex. She raced into the office and glanced surreptitiously at Darren as she put her bag underneath her desk and quickly switched on her PC. Suddenly Pervy was behind her, breathing his heavy wheeze at the back of her neck.

"Bring the *Evening Herald* with you?" he said glibly, while drinking in Grace's very visible pale-pink bra beneath her silk shirt.

Damn it! Grace thought, I forgot this blouse was semi-sheer.

"No, Mr Conroy, but I did bring the *Sun* – you know, the one with the Page Three girls?" Grace replied, as quick as lightning, but almost instantly regretted it. Darren guffawed briefly in the background, before stifling his laugh.

Pervy visibly reddened. Grace looked at him in defiance, but inside her heart was beating a mile a minute.

"Just make sure you make up the time today, please," he replied gruffly before moving off to the next victim.

Grace couldn't believe it. She had called his bluff and he had backed down because he knew he was guilty. She resisted the huge urge to smile and punch the air so she busied herself at her desk instead before several emails arrived from around the office, congratulating her on her stance.

"You've got balls, Princess!" said Darren's missive.

Grace smiled at that and even took off her wool jacket. She knew that Pervy wouldn't have the neck to openly ogle her now, after she had outed him. Not today, anyhow. The rest of the morning passed in a busy blur, and before long it was time for Grace to go and meet Olivia for lunch.

She raced across the bridge onto Tara Street and on up to the Davenport, where she was to meet her sister at the bar, in record time. She couldn't spot Olivia so she went up to the bar to order a soft drink and scan the menu for lunch specials.

"Grace . . ."

Someone touched her arm.

Grace turned and was shocked to find that Olivia had been sitting at the bar almost beside her.

Olivia looked unrecognisable. Her normally glossy blonde sharp bob was layered and was now a dull light brown. Huge black circles rimmed her eyes and most noticeably, she was at least two and a half stone heavier. Grace was amazed at her sister's appearance. Olivia had always been so elegant and well put together. She was normally reed-slim and perfect in her appearance. Grace had always envied her easy grace and beauty. It had only been five or six months since they last met and Olivia had then been coiffed and immaculate as usual. But now, Grace had to gather herself together in order not to seem too shocked by the change in her sister.

"Sorry, Olivia, I just didn't see you there. I was in my own little world."

Olivia smiled slowly. "It's OK, Grace, I know I'm a lot different. No wonder you didn't recognise me. I'm as fat as a fool and my hair is shorter. You expected the old me to turn up."

"The old you?" Grace echoed, perturbed.

"I'll tell you while we have lunch. Shall we order?"

Grace nodded mutely – she was still too amazed to react.

They scanned the menus and chose their meals. Grace chose a salad, which was Olivia's normal choice and Olivia uncharacteristically ordered Southern Fried Chicken and chips. Grace hid her surprise and made small talk until the meals arrived.

Then Olivia began to talk. "I suppose you're wondering why I dragged you out for lunch and of course you're dying to ask why I've gained so much weight in the past few months." She looked at Grace askance.

Grace nodded again. She wondered when she'd get her voice back.

"The thing is . . ." Olivia started, then her bottom lip quivered, "the thing is, I don't *know* why, Grace. All I know is I am so unhappy. I am gaining kilos by the minute and I can't stop myself from overeating. I thought maybe you could help me."

Grace was again surprised. Olivia had never asked for help from her little sister. Grace had never seen her so unhinged. "Me?"

"Yes," sighed Olivia, gazing into the distance. "You are always so together, so definite. You have always done your own thing. I have envied you for years, Grace. You always did what was best for yourself, regardless of what others thought. Mum and Dad had no effect on you. You went off to London, had Jordan, and have always done pretty much whatever you wanted."

"I did what I had to, to escape their clutches," Grace replied mirthlessly. "I never had a plan, just a burning desire to get away from them."

"And *me*, you wanted to get away from me too, your terrible older sister."

Grace reddened profusely. Olivia was big into honesty as well as food at the moment, it seemed. "Yes, I suppose I did. I just got sick of always being compared to you. I could never live up to Olivia with her A grades and her gorgeous figure."

"Long gone now," Olivia interjected.

"Anyway," Grace continued, while eyeing Olivia's tempting chips, "that's why I went off to London with Dymphna. I just couldn't stay another minute in that horrible depressing house with those disappointed people. I was always such a failure in their eyes. Their faces, every time I stuffed up, spoke volumes. I just couldn't deal with it, and then I stuffed up again by bringing shame home along with a brown baby. So I gave up trying for their approval. It was never going to come, was it?" She slurped her diet coke, wishing that she had put vodka into it. This honesty session was dragging up unhappy memories that she would rather let lie dormant.

"And what about me? I was the dutiful one, the one with all the pressure and expectation to do well and excel. They pinned all their own frustrated ambitions on me. No wonder you hated me – you were always being compared unfavourably to me. I knew you would resent me but there was very little I could do about it. I'm not as strong as you, I needed their approval, and by being the perfect daughter, I got it. You weren't the only casualty, Grace." Olivia shovelled another piece of glistening golden chicken into her mouth. "Do you remember Mum used to watch all those old Hollywood movies and loved all those glamorous stars so much?"

Grace grimaced. "Who are ye tellin', don't I get reminded of my moniker every day?"

Olivia laughed. "Yeah, well, she used to show me pictures of Olivia de Havilland when I was five and tell me that's what she wanted me to look like when I grew up. Talk about pressure to perform!"

"So, why now?" Grace enquired sharply. "Why are you interested in telling me all this now, after all these years?"

"Because I lost a very dear friend in the Twin Towers on September 11th. Someone who never had a sister and often said I was like one. And it made me think after I lost him, why am I letting time pass while ignoring the one sister I do have? I'm sorry, Grace. I have been so selfish and wrapped up in my own life and problems, I'm a total stranger to you and your children, my own niece and nephew. I want things to change."

Grace felt instantly guilty. She had been so changed by the events of September 11th, so moved by the suffering of humanity, yet she hadn't even thought about her only sister, or her parents for that matter. She felt deeply ashamed. "Me too," she replied contritely.

"Good," smiled Olivia, her face lighting up.

"So what's the problem?" Grace then asked. Maybe

she could help after all. Weight problems she was an expert on.

"I wish I knew. I just feel dissatisfied, bored rigid and I seem to feel really down most of the time, when I have no reason on earth to. Lately I've been eating for Ireland, and it's not like the old me, but there is nothing wrong as such. Nothing I can put a finger on."

"And Connor, how are things with him?"

"His name is *Connell*, Grace – oh, that's right, you haven't even met my fiancé, have you? That's what I am talking about – you don't know anything about my life, or me yours. It's a disgrace."

"Agreed, but you didn't answer my question, Olivia – how are things between you two?"

Olivia's face darkened considerably. "I don't know. He is very sweet, and he loves me so much. It's just that there doesn't seem to be that mad passion I see in other people's relationships. I mean, my heart doesn't flutter when he walks in the room."

Grace thought briefly of Paul. She still felt her blood race when he walked around in his boxer shorts – that sexy brown back and cute bum.

"Does yours? Flutter, I mean, when you see Paul?" Olivia was asking.

Grace nodded.

"You see? That's what I mean. I don't feel that passion. I used to feel it in my job, and then I felt it a little bit when we decided to build our dream house. But they are all temporary highs. I just feel unhappy and unfulfilled at the moment."

"So you're filling it up with food," said Grace, directly quoting her WeightWatchers lecturer. "I do that too."

"Not lately, obviously," remarked Olivia dryly. "You're looking rather svelte."

"I just have a handle on it at the moment, but I still have wide childbearing hips, as Mum would say."

Olivia laughed. "You wouldn't want to be sensitive, that's for sure!"

"Do you love Connell enough to marry him?" Grace regarded Olivia with her serious blue eyes.

Olivia looked down at the floor. "You know, I'm not sure. I feel he loves me and I am with the best possible person for me. He would do anything for me, but I feel like this is my only chance to get married and if I pass on this one there might not be another guy."

Grace frowned. "I'm not sure that's enough reason to spend the rest of your life with someone, Liv. It's not fair on you or Connell. Marriage is tough enough when you're crazy about your partner. Love makes it bearable most of the time, but sooner or later, if you marry this guy, he is going to find out your real feelings. You won't be able to conceal it for too long and then whatever children you have will suffer if you split up. Be really careful Olivia, that you're not just marrying this man because you're thirty-six and you feel it's the Last Chance Saloon. That's not fair on either of you."

Olivia's face crumpled. "I know. I know you're right, but I'm so scared. The house is almost finished. I'm supposed to be out looking at wedding dresses and booking hotels but I just can't seem to move either way. I'm stuck. I feel my life is just becoming so fake."

Grace couldn't believe her ears. Here was her big confident capable sister who seemed to be so in control of her life, confessing that she felt mixed up and confused. It was a revelation. For the first time ever she seemed human, even fallible, and Grace even liked her, perhaps for the first time ever. "What would you really like to do, then?"

"What do you mean?" Olivia replied, perplexed, as if questioning her life had never occurred to her.

Grace looked right into Olivia's clear blue eyes. "If I could wave a magic wand right now and you could do anything you wanted or be anything or anywhere you wanted, what would you choose?"

Olivia blushed, and smiled. "This is going to sound really weird."

"Go on, try me, I'm an expert in off the wall."

"Well, I'd really love to be in Connemara, living in a little remote cottage and indulging in my real passion, which is art. I'd love to cash it all in and become an artist, and live quietly and simply and to never have to wear another corporate suit again. But most of all I'd love never to switch on another PC or drive in another traffic jam. I just feel so burnt out by it all – my job, and the pressure to succeed. I'd really love to just take off and do that."

Grace grinned. "Olivia, my dear girl, that is so achievable. What is stopping you? I thought you'd say, travelling to Tibet to live with the Dalai Lama or something outrageous. That is a lovely peaceful dream and all it takes is a bit of money, a resignation letter, and a 'Dear John' letter if Connell isn't part of the plan. Is he?"

Olivia laughed hollowly. "I doubt if he would be interested. Connell feels the Wicklow Hills are the outer Himalayas and he has a panic attack if he doesn't talk on his mobile for more than an hour. No, I doubt if he'd last two minutes in the wilds of the west. I think it would have to be a solo project."

"Well, then you have to figure out what you want to do. One thing is for sure. You are definitely not ready to go down the aisle if you are so unhappy you have gained all this weight in less than six months. It's a symptom of deeper problems. Problems that need to be solved before you can be happy again."

Olivia frowned. "You're right; I do need to sort myself out. But what about the wedding plans, the house in Wicklow?"

"You can put the wedding on hold. Tell Connell you need a bit of time to sort yourself out, take off to Connemara for a few days and spend some time alone, it'll help focus your mind. You need to do what's best for Olivia, no-one else."

"Right, I will. Thanks, Grace, I knew if anyone could talk sense into me it would be you. You're a rock of sense, you always were."

Grace was once again amazed. She had always felt so inferior and simple compared to brainy perfect Olivia – it was so great to be considered a rock of sense, of all things.

"I don't know who you are," Grace said finally, in mock seriousness, "but you are much nicer than the old Olivia. I could really get to like you."

Olivia smiled her first genuine smile. "There's more of me to like."

They both laughed and for the first time ever, felt like sisters.

Chapter 8

Grace couldn't believe her lunch with Olivia, and was dying to see Paul to tell him about what had transpired. She wondered about her mother and how she would react to Olivia dropping the high-powered job and matching high-powered fiancé to go off to the wilds and become a hippy artist. She felt her mother would die from the shame of her perfect daughter ditching her mother's dream.

Grace also felt she should telephone her parents and arrange a visit. It was ages since the kids had been over to Raheny. Even though each time she visited her home it taxed her emotionally, it really wasn't sufficient reason to keep the children away from their grandparents. That was her own personal baggage. If she and Olivia could become friends perhaps there was hope for her parents after all. September 11th had taught everyone how short life could be. She resolved to telephone her mother and father that evening and arrange to take Orla and Jordan over to see them both that weekend.

I can suffer them both for a few hours, Grace thought. If I can suffer Pervy Comb-over for seven hours straight, every day. They'd be a doddle after this. Anything would.

She decided to phone Dymphna now and fill her in on all the gossip about Olivia. Dymphna had been there all those years ago when Grace had suffered through comparisons with her older sibling, even at school where the nuns had practically canonised Olivia as being their favourite star pupil and most outstanding prefect. Dymphna understood the teenage angst between the sisters that had transformed into glacial coolness in their twenties. She had a brother that had become a priest and she was forever being unfavourably compared to Pierce, a missionary who was indeed a saint in the Coffey clan.

"I can't believe Olivia is fat!" Dymphna screeched, after Grace had told her the news.

"Well, not hugely fat, Dimples, but definitely not her usual skinny self. She's having a bit of midlife crisis. Apparently she's not too sure about the whole marriage commitment thing, or her successful lawyer fiancé, for that matter."

"She can pass him over here, so," remarked Dymphna, never one to miss out on an opportunity to snare a suitable candidate for her own wedding.

"And she hates her job," Grace continued. "She wants to up sticks and head off to Connemara and become a struggling artist, no less."

"Jesus!" exclaimed Dymphna. "All I need now is for Pierce to telephone to say he's run off with a nun for my day to be really complete. Does your mother know?"

"I doubt it," replied Grace glibly. "I didn't hear any screams from Raheny in Kilmadden lately. I'd say she'd be the last to know. Anyway, I'm going to ring her tonight. It's time I faced Depression Drive again."

"Rather you than me," sniffed Dymphna. "I'd rather wrestle crocodiles."

"How is your mother, by the way?" Grace asked and they both guffawed. Agnes Coffey wasn't quite as bad as Moira Casey, just pious and interfering and impossible to talk to. She was still a walk in the park compared to Grace's mother. Still, rather than answer copious questions about her commitment to Confession and daily Mass, Dymphna kept her distance from her mother, and so her sanity.

"As bad as yours," Dymphna giggled. "Now, I must go to a meeting in a few minutes. Give us a call after the weekend – let me know any more goss."

"Will do, if I survive a foray into enemy territory."

"Just double the usual Valium that you take beforehand," Dymphna quipped, "and call me on Monday." With that she rang off.

Grace wouldn't know what to do if she didn't have Dymphna in her life; she was such a character and a really good friend.

"Mum, it's me."

"Hello, Olivia. Sean, Sean, it's Olivia!"

"Mum, it's not Olivia, it's Grace."

"Oh hello, stranger. Sean, it's all right, it's only Grace."

Grace tried not to wince.

"Well, how's life in the sticks?" Moira always made a deliberate reference to Grace's move to County Meath. She resented the distance from Dublin that reduced her control over her daughter.

"Quiet and peaceful," Grace replied pointedly. "Anyway, Mum, the kids and I would like to see you and Dad and I was wondering if we could come over on Saturday to visit."

"What's seldom is wonderful, I suppose," sniffed Moira Casey.

Grace tried to remain equable. "So I'll take that as a yes, then?"

"Well, I can't speak for your father, he seems to spend half his life in that shed these days, but I'll be here all afternoon anyway, although I'll be leaving early to go to bingo, mind."

"Great," said Grace too brightly. "We'll be over about two."

"And will the man from the mountain be gracing us with his presence?"

Moira could never resist a jibe at Paul, whom she had always found to be unsuitable for Grace, being a lowly painter and a Donegal Northerner to boot.

Grace didn't rise to the bait. "I doubt it. There's a big job on and he's doing a lot of overtime. He works very hard for us all, Mum – he's a good man."

"Maybe soon he'll earn enough for you to stay at

home with little Orla," her mother said, but her tone was at least softer.

"Yes, well, I have something to tell you about that, but I'll fill you in on Saturday."

Grace almost said that she had lunch with Olivia, but she knew her mother would suddenly be full of praise and interest in her sister, and Grace couldn't bear that. She wanted to keep her feelings for Olivia at their new level of closeness and not have it clouded by her mother's favouritism.

Grace rang off and resisted the urge to go to the fridge and grab half a block of ice cream or into the drinks cabinet for a stiff shot of whiskey. She wished her mother didn't get to her so much, but she knew which buttons to press and boy did she use them. Dymphna was right – she'd rather wrestle crocodiles too than face her mother on Saturday.

But face her Grace would.

Dymphna was having her own morality crisis. She had a strange phone call that had left her confused and unsure.

Mark had called. Married Mark. Mark McCabe, tall, good-looking, impossibly charming, the rising star at the bank. With whom she had enjoyed those few sinful dates midweek before she discovered he was already spoken for.

Now he called out of the blue, and full of apologies. "I just wanted you to know that Carla and I have decided to call it a day," his silky voice had purred.

"And I would be interested, why?" Dymphna had replied sharply. She had felt such a fool when everyone else in the office had known Mark was married while she was waffling on about her fabulous new boyfriend.

"Well, you might be interested because we broke up over you. I can't get you out of my system, and I am sorry I never told you about my wife. But Carla and I, we were having problems. When I met you it brought everything to a head. I keep thinking about you, Dimmy, all the time and I'd really like to see you. Even if it's just the once to say sorry properly."

Dymphna wavered. She had fancied the fantastic butt off of Mark McCabe, but she and Grace had always had one golden rule: no married men. She knew Grace would kill her if she gave in but she could always bend the rule for a separated man, couldn't she?

"Call me during the week," she said at last, her tone still sharp. "And we'll see."

Dymphna knew she would get untold grief from Grace if she dated Mark again. After all, he had lied copiously the first time they dated. What's to say he still wasn't trying to fool her into a quick roll in the hay, while his wife was tucked away in Limerick. She could check with Maria over at Ballsbridge HQ to see if the break-up was for real. Maria would know, if anyone would – being on Reception and a total nosey parker, she knew everybody's business. She could find out from her if the tales of a broken marriage were true.

Then she could tell Grace – then it wouldn't seem so bad. Anyway, it was OK for Grace – she had a gorgeous man to love her every day. Dymphna got so lonely going home alone most nights to her pristine apartment and a ready-made meal for one. She needed someone to cuddle her and Mark was downright gorgeous. A brief moment occurred when she thought of Carla, Mark's wife, who was the real loser, having being cheated on, but perhaps she had voluntarily turfed the errant Mark out when she discovered his extra-curricular activities.

All the delicious memories of Mark's undivided attention and smoochy kisses mingled in Dymphna's mind. Her conscience was warring with her lusty loins. And so far, her much-deprived loins were winning.

Chapter 9

Kate was getting herself ready for Des's return from his four-day business trip to New York. He was always travelling overseas in order to keep clients happy and keep up with the latest Internet trends.

When Des spouted computer-speak Kate listened intently but could never grasp it all to the extent Des did and it left her cold as a topic of conversation. She knew she should be studying IT if she were really interested in Des's business but the idea of spending four years doing an IT degree sounded like a nightmare. Kate really wanted to do design and she was sure that would bore Des rigid. Today she was going to dress up, look fantastic, cook him his favourite meal and make a concentrated effort to sound really interested in his latest acquisition. Des was already feeling neglected with the idea of Kate attending college in a matter of weeks, so she needed to make him feel important, otherwise things could be tricky when Grace arrived. Des in a mood was not a man that you would want to meet. Kate would die of embarrassment if Des made a scene or was rude to Grace, so he had to be on board. This would all mean delicate handling of Des over the coming weeks. Nothing must rile or upset him, Kate was going to make sure of that. Everything must go perfect or life would prove to be very difficult indeed. She wondered if Grace had handed in her notice yet or if she had discussed the job offer with her husband.

Kate hoped Grace's husband was a little more easygoing than Des was.

She dressed in Des's favourite outfit, a black Louise Kennedy dress – then she sprayed herself liberally with Issy Mayake and arranged a fresh vase of lilies in the dining-room. In the fridge, two fat steaks lay marinating and the house shone like a new pin. Jade and Chloe would be excited to see their Dad but Kate had decided they would be in bed by eight, so she and Des could have a nice romantic evening. Given a little TLC, Des would be putty in her hands.

She had decided to surprise Des at the airport. His trips were so frequent, Kate hardly ever bothered to go all the way down to Dublin Airport, but in an effort to kick off her charm offensive, she decided to thrill the kids and go and pick up Daddy.

She collected Jade and Chloe from school and did the usual homework and snack time before making them change out of their uniforms and dress in their best clothes. She then told them they were off to the airport to meet Dad, and this was greeted excitedly with whoops of delight, as much for the idea of seeing all the aeroplanes and the promise of a burger there, as for seeing their father.

They all bundled into the jeep for the fifty-minute journey, leaving plenty of time to meet the plane. Des was due in for five o clock from JFK. Kate decided to get there a bit early, treat the kids to their burgers so she wouldn't have to cook for them later and they could be cajoled into bed that little bit earlier. That was the plan anyhow.

The traffic was extremely heavy-going towards Dublin and Kate was glad she had left in plenty of time. By the time they got to the airport and parked they had a scant twenty minutes before Des's plane landed so Kate hurried the children up to McDonald's for their meal. She didn't want to miss him in Arrivals, after all the travelling.

She was queuing up for the burgers when she heard Chloe call out to someone. She looked around to see Melody Carmody talking to Chloe.

"Melody, fancy seeing you here," Kate said, as she approached her baby-sitter with the children's food on a tray.

"Hi, Mrs Heathcoat," Melody mumbled.

"You look fantastic, Melody. I hardly recognised you. Your suit is lovely. You look very grown up in it."

"Thanks," Melody smiled. "It's Quin & Donnelly, actually. Their clothes have a lovely cut."

Kate almost said 'Baby-sitting must be paying very well these days,' but she thought she might offend Melody so she just nodded and said instead, "Are you here to meet someone?"

Melody brushed a long tendril of toffee-coloured hair from her carefully made-up face.

"Yes, actually I am meeting a friend, but their flight has been delayed, so I think I'll go downstairs to check again what time they might arrive. See ya, Jade and Chloe! Bye, Mrs Heathcoat."

With that she was gone, tottering off in too-high heels and a cloud of CK One.

There was no doubt about it, Kate thought, she was turning into a real stunner. She looked groomed and well put together. She had caramel highlights in her hair, and in the cream suit together with the grown-up make-up she could have passed for twenty-two at least.

Jade and Chloe were dawdling over their burgers so Kate had to hurry them up, in order to surprise Des.

They barely made it to Arrivals in time. Des came through and seemed to anxiously look around, as if he half-expected them. When he saw Kate a look of surprise crossed his handsome face. He looked so good. Kate was always surprised when she saw him after a while apart. She seemed to rediscover how handsome her husband was, the riveting blue eyes in his tanned chiselled face, the thick black hair that was tinged with a smattering of grey, the tall lean frame that wore business suits so well. She waved at him and a smile emerged on his face.

The children shouted "Daddy!" in unison and flew to him.

"This is a surprise, Kate," Des murmured as he kissed her cheek. He seemed distracted.

"Are you all right?" Kate asked. If she didn't know better she would say he was less than thrilled to see her.

"Yeah, just exhausted, love. And I've just remembered my car is in the long-term carpark, so I'll have to go and collect it."

"Oh damn, I forgot I hadn't driven you here!" Kate felt like an idiot. He had driven himself to the airport days ago because she had been too busy as usual. She felt guilty as well as stupid.

Des smiled at her. "That's no problem, it's lovely to see you all. You can drive me over there and then I can take these two rascals off your hands. Would you like to come home in my car, kids?"

"Yeah!" Chloe said loudly while Jade punched the air.

They really loved Des, Kate thought. "It's nice to have you home," she said, while putting her arm about him. And I'll show you how nice it is, later, Kate said to herself. She had missed her husband and he would discover how much, later, if everything went to plan.

Melody watched the perfect family scene from the mezzanine floor above.

Kate, looking all glamorous in her black dress, her blonde hair shining. Her arm draped around Des, like she owned him. Well, she did, some would say. She had it all. Des, that fabulous house and that luxurious lifestyle. Everything Melody ever wanted, except the kids of course, but that could be sorted, as Suzy would say. Melody hadn't expected Kate to turn up at the airport – she was a right bitch and no mistake. Melody would have to be a lot cleverer if her plans were to come to fruition.

She took out her mobile and sent a text to Suzy. There was absolutely no point in going home now, as she was all glammed up. She'd get Suzy to meet her in Temple Bar later and they would go clubbing. She wasn't going to waste all this effort, and if it wasn't going to be Des Heathcoat's lucky night, well, it would have to be someone else's.

Des glanced about surreptitiously as he and his family walked towards the revolving doors of the Arrivals Hall. That had been a close one. Kate never came to the airport – why now all of a sudden?

He wondered if Melody was there, somewhere, watching them. She had sent him a sexy text while he was in New York and he was left in no doubt as to what she wanted to do to him. He knew for ages that she had fancied him and he had watched her emerge from plain bookish schoolgirl to gorgeous vamp with a Brittney Spears body. Melody had flirted outrageously with him for over six months now, every time he took her home from baby-sitting – that dark two-mile drive down the winding country lane to her tiny little cottage. He would usually be a bit drunk, so he took little notice of her at first, but gradually the flirty talk got more and more suggestive and eventually it became obvious that Melody wanted more than just a chat. Des had always been faithful to Kate – well, all except for one or two one-night stands early on in the marriage when he had been overseas, drunk and randy. They had been instantly forgettable and to Des they didn't count. But this was different. It felt dangerous and Des thought it might be. That might be what excited him so much. It felt wild and dangerous and very flattering that someone of eighteen could find him sexually attractive. He hoped he wasn't sad and old, facing a midlife crisis, taking up with a teenager. But he was feeling old and sad some of the time these days. Though today, with Kate arriving at the airport, looking beautiful with the children, and seeming so excited to see him, Des felt a bit of a heel, thinking of someone else. He would be an idiot to throw everything he had away, for what amounted to a fling with someone young enough to be his daughter.

Perhaps it was fortuitous that Kate surprised him today. She didn't realise it, but she had averted her husband from being tempted to do something that he had fantasised about for months. That's where it should stay, a fantasy in his mind and that's all, Des decided. Now the difficult part would be to let Melody down gently. Without her going off and blabbing it all to Kate. Now that would really be messy. How could he explain that away? As he left Dublin Airport, Des Heathcoat decided that he had enjoyed a lucky escape and he would do nothing to endanger his marriage to Kate, not at the moment, anyhow. As he walked with his wife and two lovely children towards the short-term carpark he gave Kate a warm kiss on the lips as he clasped her hand. He was very lucky, he thought.

Kate was enough for the moment. Melody could wait..

Chapter 10

Saturday arrived, and so did Grace's proposed trip to Raheny to see her parents. For most people this would be a normal event to be looked forward to and enjoyed. For Grace it was something she had to steel herself for, a time to be endured and got through with the goal of remaining sane and unscathed at the end.

Paul found it all hilarious from a distance, Grace noted, while keeping himself away from them as much as possible. Paul had really sweet mother, Nell, who arrived down from Letterkenny occasionally, festooned in home-baked cakes and treats for the children. Nell was the exact opposite of Moira Casey. She fussed and clucked over her large brood and never had a cross word to say about anyone. Grace loved her to bits. If only her own mother could be as nice and uncomplicated.

Paul made them all breakfast as they discussed the day.

"Wish I was off to Dartmoor Drive with ye all, instead of havin' to go to work," he announced.

"Yeah, right," Grace replied sullenly, noticing his sly grin.

Number 13 Dartmoor Drive was aptly named. Dartmoor was the dark lonely moor and the number 13 was unlucky for some, particularly Grace. Grace had all sorts of names for her family home, notably Depression Drive, or Calamity Close just to name two. The humorous names covered the deep feelings of resentment and unease that Grace felt when she spent any time there. She tried not to seem unhappy in front of the children, though Jordan was very perceptive and could pick up on Grace's mood most times.

"What time do you think you'll be getting home?" Paul asked. This was doublespeak for how long do you think you can stick them?

"Oh, we'll leave there about four, I suppose. We can grab a Chinese for dinner, celebrate me switching careers."

"Sounds good," smiled Paul, chomping on another piece of toast.

Paul had become a convert to Grace's new part-time job when Grace told him how much Kate was offering and how much better off they would be in the long run. The idea of housework-free Saturdays appealed to them all – maybe they could start having some fun as a family again.

Now all Grace had to do was find a suitably nasty way to quit her job at Interfex, hopefully in such a way as to create as much inconvenience and humiliation as possible to old Pervy Comb-over.

"Are you looking forward to seeing Granny and Pops, Jordan?" Paul asked.

"Not really," Jordan shrugged. "It's really boring over there – there's nothing to do. Anyway Pop's never interested and Granny just wants to see Orla."

Grace rolled her eyes, but she couldn't deny it. Her mother was already showing favourites with her own grandchildren. Orla seemed to be flavour of the month at the moment. Until of course, Olivia had offspring and then they would take top position.

"Pop has a new aviary, Jordan, with some nice birds," Grace offered weakly.

"I don't think they're the type of birds Jordan is interested in," Paul quipped.

Jordan blushed. "No way, get real! I'm not interested in girls."

"Give it six months," Paul reminded him, "and you'll wonder what took you so long to notice them."

"Do I really have to go today?" Jordan whined.

"Yes, you do," Grace insisted. "You're not staying here alone if Paul is in work. Anyhow it's time you saw your grandparents, it's been ages."

And it'll be ages more before you go back again, she thought to herself. My weekend is far too short to spend all this time fretting.

Grace arrived at 13 Dartmoor Drive at two o'clock exactly. She knew if she were late she would get a lecture on punctuality, so she always tried to be right on time.

Anything to make the visit go smoother. She took several deep breaths as she knocked on the door of the neat semi-detached house that was virtually unchanged from her girlhood days. Mrs Bruton still twitched her curtains across the road when anyone arrived or left, and the once trendy façades of the 1950's built houses were now dated and old-fashioned. A bit like Grace's parents.

Grace's father answered the door. He was a quiet and unassuming man. He was largely ruled by his wife, and seemed to have no opinion of his own apart from his distaste for anything foreign or exotic, which Grace discovered when she had arrived home pregnant with Jordan. Sean Casey had roared and shouted his disapproval at the time. Now he seemed to genuinely like Jordan but Grace never really knew for sure.

He still complained about all the refugees that he claimed had flooded the country and were taking up all the accommodation and jobs. Grace found it ironic that he didn't see the correlation between Grace and millions of other Irish migrating all over the world to better themselves and a few poor east Europeans or Africans doing the same to the now newly affluent Ireland.

Every time her father ranted on about another darkie invading his space in a queue or in the bookies, Grace felt like shouting, "Do you realise that you have a darkie grandchild?" But she never did.

Instead she tried to keep the peace, and educate him that people were much the same, despite the different colours of their skin, and Ireland could benefit greatly from a bit of multi-culturism, but she doubted he would ever change. He had never been further than Kerry, so his mind remained insular and as polarised as ever.

Moira Casey, or "she who must be obeyed" as Grace often quipped, was the centre of the Casey family,

Moira had always been thin-lipped and disapproving. She was old-fashioned to the point of being Victorian and Grace could never imagine her mother young and happy. She had always seemed dour and downhearted. Except where Olivia was concerned – then Moira Casey seemed to come to life. She was genuinely animated and full of pride when she spoke of Olivia. That was what the problem was. Grace was made aware of the difference from a very early age. She wondered if her father had felt it – the same reluctant love Moira appeared to feel for her husband and second daughter.

Now Moira Casey was fussing about in the kitchen, cleaning out her cupboards as Grace and the children entered. Grace tried to cover her annoyance. Her mother had a habit of doing this, knowing a visit was imminent but finding some useless inane chore that absolutely must be carried out immediately, while the visitors waited nearby, feeling unwanted.

"Go into the parlour, I'll be another ten minutes cleaning this. These cupboards are such a mess, honestly, I just don't know where the dirt comes from."

Grace rolled her eyes heavenwards and retreated into the front room with Orla and Jordan. "Parlour, how are you!" she fumed. "No one, but no one, calls any room the bloody 'parlour' any more!"

It looked like a parlour though. The flowery curtains

battled with the flowery carpet and there were enough doilies and knick-knacks to open a craft shop. An ugly glass cabinet sat in the corner stuffed with medals that Olivia had won and some awful brass ornaments. This place was a nightmare for Orla to be – there was absolutely nowhere for her to potter about.

Jordan looked at Grace in desperation.

"Go and see Pops, I'm sure he's in the shed," Grace offered weakly. Her father had retreated there. Out of the line of fire, Grace thought, and can't say I blame him.

Grace sat down on the uncomfortable chintz sofa with Orla as Jordan quickly disappeared. If she's not here in ten minutes, I'm off, raged Grace. It was just so disrespectful. She knew it was a method of control – her mother still had to show she was calling the shots.

Her mother emerged a few minutes later. "Right, I'm all done, cup of tea, Grace?"

Grace tried a smile and nodded. She was already in bad humour and it had only been ten minutes since she arrived, but she was determined not to blow her top, as that was exactly what her mother thrived on.

They sat drinking tea in the narrow kitchen with its aging pine cabinets and tangerine walls, looking out the window onto the garden with its long aviary and huge shed.

"Is Jordan in there with him?" her mother enquired idly.

Grace nodded. "What does he do in there all day, Mam?"

"Avoids me, mostly," her mother said with a tight smile that didn't reach her eyes.

Grace would have loved to ask her mother right then if she was happy in her marriage, but they just didn't have that sort of relationship. Instead she asked, "Have you seen Olivia lately?"

Her mother pursed her lips. "Indeed I have. I don't know what's the matter with that girl. She's going through something strange. She's got some idea that she's unfulfilled, and not sure she wants to marry poor Connell. She's acting just like . . ." Her voice trailed away.

"Like what, Mum?" Grace echoed.

Her mother had risen and put her cup in the sink. "Oh, no one. I was just about to say her father, but she's nothing like Sean." She seemed to stiffen.

Grace waited.

"All this stupid talk about wanting to be an artist and taking off to the bloody wilds. It's crazy if ye ask me. That Connell is the most wonderful man and so successful – Olivia could never do better."

Grace was astonished to see tears in her mother's eyes. This indeed was a first, except when Moira watched those old-fashioned black and white movies, which always moved her.

"Maybe he just isn't for her, Mam. She's gained so much weight in the past few months – that means she's either totally contented or deeply unhappy. I know which one I'd put my money on."

"And when did you see her?" her mother barked, back to her waspish self. It didn't do for Grace to focus on any weakness of Olivia's. Her mother took it as a personal affront.

"We had lunch during the week. She rang out of the blue. But, Mam, that's beside the point. I'm really worried about her. She seems to be unravelling. No marriage is worth that. Olivia should do whatever she wants to, to make herself happy. Even if it means leaving Connell and her job to do it."

"It's all turning out so wrong," her mother said in a misty voice.

"What is, Mam?" Grace had never seen her mother like this before.

"She was always such a good girl. I really believed she'd never be anything like him, but here she is, thirty-six years later and true to form, she's become *just* like him."

Grace was totally nonplussed. Her mother seemed to be entirely somewhere else. Moira poured herself another cup of tea and sat back down heavily. She looked old, Grace thought sadly.

"I have to tell you something I have never told another soul, not even your father. Olivia is not like Sean, because Sean is not her father."

Grace was gobsmacked. Suddenly it all fell into place, like the last piece of the jigsaw puzzle. The large disparity between Olivia and Grace's appearances. The excessive pride her mother had in Olivia and the special love she seemed to have for her firstborn.

Olivia was a lovechild.

Grace didn't know how to feel. She was numb at the moment.

"Your father doesn't know that Olivia isn't his and you're never to tell him. The shock would kill him. The truth of the matter is, I was seeing someone else too, all those years ago when I was going out with your father, another man. But Seamus Costigan was never interested in settling down or taking a wife. No, all he wanted was to sketch and paint and travel the world. Sean was sensible and quiet; I knew he'd be good to me. So I kept going out with him, stringing him along, because I knew when Seamus found out I was pregnant, he'd be off like a scalded cat and he was."

"So Dad thinks Olivia is his," Grace said, the awful truth sinking in. She didn't know which amazed her more – the fact that her staid and sensible frosted-curls mother had been sleeping with two men at the same time or the fact that Olivia was her half-sister.

"Does Olivia know?" Grace enquired, though she guessed what the answer was.

"No, she would never forgive me," Moira Casey said sadly.

"But now she's going to do this, I feel it's all been for nothing. All the years I tried to point her in the right direction, fearing that she'd want to be a drifter like her father. Worrying that your father would suddenly look at her some day and realise that she wasn't his. But she was so good, so well behaved and anxious to please. I was so happy when she did well at school and university that I almost forgot it had ever happened."

Grace made a face. "And me? I was such a disappointment to you, at school and then later, getting pregnant. It seems I wasn't so unlike you after all, was I, Mam? Why did you make it so hard for me? This makes it all the more horrible, the way you treated me. Why did you do it?"

"Because I didn't want you to end up like *me*! Settling for a man that I didn't really love, so that I would have a father for my child. That was all, Grace."

Her mother's eyes were shiny. Grace thought she glimpsed a bit of love in them. Is that why her mother had been so buttoned up and joyless all these years? Was it because she had been suffering a broken heart and carrying a deep shameful secret for most of her life?

Suddenly, Moira Casey seemed very human and very flawed. But not nearly as difficult to like as she had been a few minutes ago. Suddenly there seemed to be a reason why she was the way she was.

"You have got to tell Olivia, Mam. This kind of a secret, it always comes out and then if she finds out you have hidden it from her, she might not forgive you."

"You must promise me not to utter a word of this to another living soul, Grace Casey!" her mother spat furiously. "I mean it. I will never forgive you if you tell anyone what we've spoken about today. I have trusted you enough to tell you what I have never dared tell anyone. I will tell Olivia, eventually. But in my own good time."

Grace looked at her mother as if seeing her for the first time. She wondered if she really ever knew her at all.

The rest of the afternoon passed in a kind of blur, and as Grace bundled up the children and they said their goodbyes, her mother grabbed her and hugged her fiercely. Grace's father stared in surprise but said nothing.

Grace drove back to Kilmadden in a daze, burdened with her mother's secret and unable to even tell Paul and share it with someone.

Somehow it skewed all her memories of her childhood, and she knew she would have to come to terms with it all in her own mind before she could accept it. She wondered, if this were her own reaction, how would Olivia take this news? At this very moment, it didn't bear thinking about. For the first time in Grace's life, she felt sorry for her older sister, very sorry indeed.

Chapter 11

Dymphna rolled over. She bumped straight into a brown hairy chest and remembered the passionate night before that she had spent with Mark. She had finally relented after she had interrogated Maria from Reception in Ballsbridge, and Maria had assured her that Mark had indeed split from his wife Carla. Mark had called twice during the week and had even sent Dymphna a bunch of beautiful flowers, with the words *"Please, please, please!"* on the card. So Dymphna eventually emailed Mark to say she was willing to give him another chance, at least to explain himself. Mark had collected her from work and they had a pleasant meal at Lovebites restaurant in Chatham Lane.

Mark had explained, over his seared salmon, that Carla had enjoyed the more than professional attentions of her boss before Mark had eventually got fed up waiting alone at home and decided to play the field himself. Dymphna looked into his clear blue eyes and decided that she believed him.

After a nice meal and a few delicious glasses of Merlot, they ended up back at Dymphna's apartment in a boozy night of romance and passion.

Now, in the cold light of her hangover, Dymphna suffered an acute attack of embarrassment to see Mark snoring beside her. She jumped up and fled to the shower. She washed her hair and showered while wondering what to do next. She should have at least taken her time before letting Mark hop into her bed. Grace was so right; she should have played it even a little bit cool.

Damn!

She wished she was at Mark's place and then she could leave. It's amazing how up close and personal you could get with a few glasses of wine under your belt and then when the next morning arrived, sense returned with your sobriety, to smack you in the face.

"Hiya, sexy," Mark drawled and leaned over to grab Dymphna and drag her back into bed. She had put on a pair of tight jeans and T-shirt.

"Hi, yourself," Dymphna replied, while delicately avoiding his searching mouth.

She was way too annoyed with herself to repeat last night's episode in the cold light of day. "Em, I have to go to see my friend today in County Meath and I was planning on setting off early – so if you'd like some breakfast, there's a great little coffee shop just a few minutes from here. If you're ready in ten minutes, I'll even pay."

If Mark was disappointed he didn't show it. He smilingly hopped up out of bed and headed for the bathroom, completely at ease, totally butt-naked. Dymphna remarked to herself that there was little wonder he was so confident. He looked so good the morning after the night before, even after copious bottles of wine, it made Dymphna downright jealous.

She had already trowelled on the concealer in order to cover up the black circles underneath her bloodshot eyes, and here he was perfect and bright-eyed. It just wasn't fair.

She didn't know why, but Dymphna just wanted Mark to leave. She just felt it had all accelerated so fast that she needed a little bit of time to take it all in.

An hour and a half later, after several coffees and one too many croissants at the coffee shop where they had made mindless small talk, Dymphna finally got rid of Mark and headed her little Fiesta towards County Meath. She hadn't intended to disturb Grace on a Sunday morning but she needed to talk to her friend and spill all the beans about Mark. Somehow she knew Grace would deliver a lecture, but perhaps that was just what she needed. She would text Grace en route before she got too far up the Navan Road, just in case Grace had any family plans. Sundays for single people could be so lonely, she mused. All the more weird that you needed Mark to leave so quickly, she thought wryly. She needed Grace's sensible head all right. As she sent off her text at the traffic lights, she hoped fervently that her friend was free. Her hangover was hurting and so was her conscience. It was Sunday and she needed absolution. It's not every day you sleep with a married man that leaves his wife of less than two years for you.

Grace got the text when she and Paul had just finished a long and fattening breakfast with the children. The kitchen looked like a bomb-blast had hit and the front room wasn't much better.

"Shit!" muttered Grace, "OK everyone, all hands on deck. Dymphna is coming over and we need this place to resemble a home by the time she gets here."

"Right." Paul grabbed Orla from her highchair. She was covered in egg and butter smears. "I'll renovate the baby. Jordan, you tidy the living-room."

They had the place looking presentable by the time Dymphna arrived, laden with heavenly smelling croissants and sweets for the children.

Dymphna unloaded her whole sorry tale to Grace over more coffee and croissants while Paul kept the kids at bay in the sitting-room.

Grace didn't issue her usual banner-waving tirade about "Married Men and the Dangers and Pitfalls Of" for Dymphna this time, in fact she was quiet and subdued and a little bit world-weary.

"What do you want me to tell you, Dymphna, that you don't already know? I mean, if you like him and he makes you happy, who am I to judge?"

Dymphna stared. Was this really her best friend talking? "I don't know who you are, but could you please send my friend back? You know – the gobby, opinionated one that we all know and love?"

"Sorry, Dimples, I know I'm not being much help. I've had a bit of a shock, that's all."

"What was it?" Dymphna was all ears. She had never seen Grace as quiet as this, not since that little blue line appeared in her pregnancy test all those years ago in London.

"If I tell you, you have to promise that this goes nowhere else. I am forbidden to tell anyone including Paul, but I do need to tell someone."

"I promise," Dymphna said, eyeing her friend seriously. "Go ahead."

"You know I went to Depression Drive yesterday? Well, my mother pipes up with a confession that Olivia is not in fact my father's child but someone else's. My mother was having an affair with someone else all those years ago, the guy made her pregnant then pissed off and she only goes and tricks my poor bloody father into marrying her."

"What?" Dymphna's eyes were like saucers. "No way! Moira Casey, a wanton sex goddess, I don't believe it!"

"Neither did I, not after all those years she made me feel like a trollop for having Jordan and all the while she was hiding her own dark little secret. I just feel gobsmacked. I'm angry, confused and most of all, I'm sorry for Olivia. She's going through something herself right now. This will hardly help, finding out her whole life was a complete lie."

"Is she going to tell her?"

Grace sipped more of her coffee. "She says she will in her own time. I need to get my head around it myself, but soon my mother is going to have to answer a lot of questions, a lot of questions indeed."

"Somehow my problems don't seem so important now," Dymphna announced, feeling brighter. "I knew it was a good idea to see you today."

"You I'll sort out later, me dear, when I get back to normal. You're not off the hook yet, Miss Coffey."

Dymphna smiled. "That's the Grace we all know and love – welcome back, ducks."

"At least I've told you now," said Grace. "So perhaps I can get back to normal with poor Paul – he hasn't a clue what's up with me, and I hate keeping secrets, but she made me promise."

Dymphna's pretty face darkened. "Well, that wasn't fair of your mother to do that. Don't keep a secret from Paul to suit her – it's your marriage and you tell each other everything, so do what suits you, OK?"

"You are perfectly right, Dymphna. I feel such a fake, hiding this from Paul. I will tell him, tonight. I feel a lot better now, thanks."

"*God*," said Dymphna, reflectively, "I'll never look at a grey-haired granny in the same way again!"

Grace laughed for the first time in twenty-four hours. Dymphna could always see a funny side.

Chapter 12

Grace was due to start her new job with Kate in less than two weeks and she still hadn't handed in her notice at Interfex. There had never been a right time, between Grace fretting over her mother and Olivia and her boss Pervy being on holiday leave. Grace could have informed HR by letter, but it wouldn't have had the same reaction or given her the same satisfaction. Grace dearly wanted to see Pervy's fat face when she told him where to stick his job. He was due back today from his week away and Grace resolved that it was now or never – today would have to be the day. She got to work early and told Darren and a few other work mates about her decision.

Darren was sorely disappointed. "Oh for fuck's sake, Princess! You're leaving me here with a few old fossils and two twits from Ballygobackwards! Who will I bore with my highly original and totally unsuccessful love life? Plus, you promised me you'd fix me up with that gorgeous Dymphna friend of yours."

"Sorry, Daz, I'm afraid she's already been taken."

"Some bowsie no doubt, complete with wedding ring," Darren smiled but Grace detected a note of derision.

"Darren, you know and I know that you would be fifty times better for Dymphna than Mark McCabe, but what can I do? She's over twenty-one, and she has crap taste."

"Mark McCabe . . ." Darren echoed. "I know that name, it sounds familiar."

"He's probably on the ten most wanted errant husbands list on the Internet or something," Grace replied with a frown. She put her arm on Darren's shoulder. "Don't worry, Darren, I'll still meet up with you as often as I can for lunch, and I promise to introduce you to any eligible single women I know that are under fifty."

"Jeez, thanks," Darren said darkly. "Now here comes the old pervert himself – we'd better at least pretend to be busy."

"Just think," Grace smiled. "After today, I won't have to pretend any more."

Charlie Conroy blustered in with barely a good morning and slammed his office door behind him. Not in a great mood, obviously, Grace thought.

She and Darren exchanged rueful glances. Grace thought she'd wait until after morning coffee before she dropped her bombshell. She knew two weeks' notice was the minimum she could give and it would take at least that to train someone in, even if they dropped in from heaven this minute, so old Pervy would not be pleased. But if he had some doughnuts under his large belt he might be more approachable.

Just then the telephone rang. Grace answered it while scanning another of Darren's smutty email jokes. He really hardly ever did any work, she mused.

"Mrs Kelly?" the shrill voice demanded.

It could only be one person. "Yes, Avril." Grace rolled her eyes heavenward.

"*Cute and Cuddly* here," Avril bleated on. "I don't wish to alarm you, but there has been a suspected case of meningitis in the crèche and The Department of Health has advised that all children be inoculated and the centre be closed provisionally for a period of at least three days."

Grace's mind raced. The word every parent hated hearing. Meningitis. Grace suspected that as the centre was prone to exaggerating everything, it seemed unlikely that it was serious, but if the Department of Health were involved, it might be for real.

Suddenly she just wanted to scoop Orla up in her arms and never let her go. If she did get this dreadful disease Grace would never forgive herself.

"What do I need to do?" She was entirely focused.

"All parents are to collect their children immediately. The Health Officer will be here with inoculations by the time you get here, but we're not sure what kind yet." Avril seemed even shriller than ever. No doubt she was under extreme stress.

"I'll be there in an hour," Grace replied tersely and put the phone down. Tears pricked her eyes as the horrible news sank in.

Poor little Orla, she just had to get to her, right now. She hastily packed up her bag and Darren was immediately beside her – he could tell by the look on her face that it was serious.

"Do you want me to tell Charlie you had to go?" Darren offered kindly when Grace told him the news.

"No, but thanks, Darren. I should tell him myself, because I have to tender my resignation anyway. Looks like it'll have to be now."

"I don't envy you the task," said Darren. "He's in a foul mood. Good luck and let me know how the baby is, OK? I suppose you'll be missin' for a few days."

"Yes, I'll have to see what the medical person from the health department says. I'd better go."

Darren squeezed her arm affectionately and almost made her cry – he was such an old softie. She made her way towards Pervy's dark domain. Somehow, even after all the times she had imagined she would relish this moment, she now felt nervous.

"Mr Conroy?" She poked her head through the door. "Can I see you for a moment?"

"Make it quick," snapped Pervy. "I'm very busy, and I've a lot to get through today."

He motioned her inside.

This wasn't going to be easy. "I hate to tell you this, but I have had a call from the crèche and –"

"Let me guess," Pervy boomed, pushing his chair

back, his face contorted into a red scowl. "Your baby has broken a fingernail, no, dropped its favourite toy, and you have to run off to fix it. Honest to God, you'd think we were running a bored housewife's club here and not an international bank!" He spat the last words forcefully.

Grace wasn't sure if she was more shocked or angry at his vitriol.

He went on. "You *waltz* in here day in day out with your stupid family issues and problems. It seems to me that you're just not up to the job – all you married women are the same. How I am supposed to run a department with half the people missing on the flimsiest of excuses?"

"As a matter of fact," Grace shot back, "there has been a case of meningitis at the crèche and the entire place is going into quarantine. My baby has been exposed to a potentially fatal disease and all you can do is rave like a lunatic. In fact, your foul temper and your infantile ranting I have grown entirely sick of. You are the most unpleasant person I have ever met, and that takes some beating. You can take this as my verbal resignation. I quit right now, this minute. I couldn't stand another moment working for the likes of you."

Pervy stood up quickly. His face was now purple – he was apoplectic with rage. "How dare you speak to me like that! You can't quit now. You must give at least two weeks' notice."

"Here!" Grace retorted, pulling up her blouse and flashing her new black bra at her boss. "Here's what you've been trying to get your greedy eyes on for months, consider it a week's notice for each. And don't think that the women who work here don't realise that you spend most of your time leering at them. It's only a matter of time before you get hit with a sexual harassment suit. Now if you don't mind I have a potentially sick baby to get home to, so you know where you can stick your job, Charlie bloody Conroy!"

If Grace hadn't been so angry she'd have laughed. She stormed from Charlie's office, slamming his door loudly.

She emerged to thunderous applause. Every woman in the large open-plan office was on her feet and even Darren and a few other men were clapping. They had obviously heard the whole thing.

Grace broke into a surprised smile, grabbed her shoulder bag and walked out.

It wasn't until she was safely in her car and making her way out of town that she realised what she had done. She had actually flashed her boss. Something she had never imagined she would do in a million years, but she had been so enraged by his belligerence, that she had acted completely out of character. Now she drove like a madwoman out of the city, complete with an embarrassed red face, to get to her hopefully still healthy baby. She was now officially out of Interfex – and what a way to dump a job!

She'd think about all that later. Right now she had to get to Kilmadden fast, and get Orla out of *Cute and Cuddly*. They didn't know it yet, but it was Orla's last day there. The idea of that cheered up Grace no end as she drove in speed towards County Meath.

By the time Grace got back to Kilmadden, the carpark of *Cute & Cuddly* was stuffed full of cars, jeeps and vans, and the reception was crammed with worried parents clutching departmental forms and babies and toddlers of varying sizes. The health visitor was explaining the medicine and fielding anxious questions. Grace learnt that the chances of Orla catching the disease weren't high, but it was a risk for every baby that had been exposed to the sick tot. The parents were given a red antibiotic drink for the children to take and were informed that the crèche would be closed for three to five days.

Grace grabbed Orla and left as quickly as possible, while informing a fractious Avril that Orla would never return even if hell froze over. Avril retorted that Grace would never get her three hundred pound deposit back either, in that case. Grace stared Avril right in the face and hissed, "See you in court, then. I'm sure the papers would love an in-depth look at what goes on in this so-called childcare centre."

Avril blanched visibly. "You wouldn't dare."

"After today, I think I'd just about do anything, Avril. So just try me!"

"There's no need for all this," Avril replied in a more conciliatory tone.

"Then I'll collect my deposit next Friday and we'll say no more about it," Grace said archly.

She took Orla through the large doors and smiled

ruefully. This had been a big day for the little guy. She wondered what she might do next. Paul would be chuffed to see her act so strongly, but she doubted she'd own up to flashing her boobs at old Pervy. Paul would probably divorce her.

Grace put Orla in the car and drove another couple of miles to the safety of their little townhouse. As soon as she had settled her little girl she sat down and telephoned Paul with the news. It was then that the events of the day overwhelmed her and the tears came. It had been the strangest of days. A day of endings, but now she could move on and enjoy some new beginnings.

Chapter 13

Kate was brooding in her large airy kitchen. It was over something she thought she saw the previous evening.

Melody had baby-sat for her the previous night, as Des and Kate had to attend a large business function in Dublin at the prestigious Westbury Hotel.

Melody and Des had seemed in deep conversation in Des's large Lexus, as it sat in the driveway outside the house after Des had collected her. Kate watched from her bedroom window and there seemed to be a kind of argument going on. It unsettled her a bit and she sat watching them quietly for a moment before seeing Des open his door and get out. He walked to the house purposefully. Kate then felt perhaps she had imagined a kind of intimacy between them. After all Melody was just a kid.

She went downstairs to greet her baby-sitter.

Melody was in the hallway, answering a text that had beeped on her mobile phone.

She glanced at Kate and seemed to frown.

Kate was clad from head to toe in a long Ben de Lisi black cocktail dress. Her hair had been freshly highlighted and she had spent ages getting ready, completing her look with a fine silver wrap and silver sandals and jewellery. Kate felt glamorous and she needed to be at her best tonight. The function was a large information technology awards event, which sometimes attracted the Taioseach and several ministers. Des had a lot of contacts there and he had inferred the importance of making a good impression.

Kate went into the kitchen.

"Is Melody all right?" she asked Des, who was swilling some orange juice from the carton and trying not to spill it on his Armani suit.

"Dunno," he shrugged. "She slammed out of her house when I collected her, in a black mood. Maybe she had a fight with her mother, or something. I was trying to find out from her, but she wasn't in the mood to explain."

Kate relaxed a bit. So that's why they had been talking in the car. What an idiot she was to worry.

"You look fantastic," Des then said.

"Don't look too bad yourself." Kate smiled. Des looked particularly handsome in his black Armani and a crisp white shirt. "I'll just go and get the kids settled, before we leave."

She went into the Den where Jade, Chloe and Melody were immersed in an episode of *Buffy*.

"Now, kids, you know you're not allowed to watch this – you know it gives you nightmares."

"That's what I've been trying to tell them," said Melody.

Kate switched the channel on to Nickelodeon.

"Are you OK, Melody?" she enquired.

"Fine, Mrs Heathcoat." Melody flashed a smile.

Kate spotted a designer bag at Melody's feet. "Is that a Prada bag?"

"Yes, it is, as a matter of fact – do you like it?" Melody's eyes seemed to be challenging her.

"Yes, it's beautiful, but they're quite pricey."

"I don't know how much it cost," replied Melody silkily. "It was a present."

"Someone is a popular girl then," Kate smiled.

"You could say that," Melody smirked.

Kate felt a flash of annoyance, and couldn't quite put a finger on why.

"We won't be too late," she said, kissed the children goodbye and left.

But it unsettled her. Why had Des been talking so animatedly to Melody? Who did she know that could afford a Prada handbag? Why did Melody seem to have an attitude with her these days?

"You're very quiet," Des said, as the Lexus sped effortlessly towards Dublin.

"Am I?" Kate smiled. "Sorry, I was just thinking."

"Don't know if I like that sound of that – usually your thinking costs me money."

Des laughed at his snide little joke but Kate didn't find it one bit funny. However, she didn't want to start a full-scale row en route to a big corporate event, an event that meant a lot to Des's business.

"I was just thinking about Melody, as a matter of fact, and hoping she is OK. She seems very unhappy."

"She's a teenager. They're always moody. Don't be too concerned. You're such a softy, Kate Heathcoat."

"I suppose you're right." But Kate couldn't quite forget Melody and that expensive handbag. No spotty teenage boy could afford such an item. Melody obviously had an older admirer. And she seemed cocky and knowing recently. Certainly not like that breezy giggly schoolgirl that had once blushed at the slightest thing.

Des and Kate enjoyed a really nice night, the function was a huge success and Des paid her lots of attention. Kate knew that Des liked to show her off at these corporate events and she didn't mind. It was nice that he was proud of her.

They got home just after midnight and Des stayed in the car as he always drove Melody home, but as they drove off, for the first time Kate felt uncomfortable.

She still felt unsettled now thinking about it all in her kitchen. It was just the way that Melody appeared to be changing lately. She seemed too knowing and too familiar with Des. Kate doubted if Des would consider Melody seriously. But you never knew. Men often went through a midlife crisis in their forties and Des often seemed restless lately. Kate was also aware that Des liked to control everything in their marriage and he was unhappy about her going back to college. But it was hardly a reason to have a bloody affair. You must be going mad, Kate, she told herself. Des has never given you any reason to doubt him. Melody might have a king-sized crush on him, however, so she made up her mind to watch that.

She wasn't about to give up an important dream of hers now, just because her husband felt a little bit threatened.

She was going back to college and that was final.

Grace had a surprise phone call from Olivia.

"Hi Grace, guess what? I am calling you from Clifden!"

"Clifden?" Grace echoed. Oh no! Had Olivia found out her mother's terrible secret? She didn't sound very upset.

"You got it. I took your advice and I've taken a couple of weeks off from my job and I've landed up here. It is so beautiful. I am smiling for the first time in ages. I just called you to say thanks."

"And how about Connell?" Grace enquired. "How has he taken the news?"

Grace was glad Olivia couldn't see her big red face. She felt awful concealing something so important from Olivia as her parentage, but what could she do?

"Well, he's a bit concerned. He's understandably worried that I mightn't come back at all. I told him I was unhappy and he thinks it's all his fault. But I think he realises I just have to do this."

"Good for you," replied Grace, relieved that at least things seemed to be looking up for her sister.

"So where are you staying?"

"Oh, I'm holed up in a cosy little guesthouse, just

outside the town. The views are breathtaking. I might even get around to doing a bit of sketching, if I can stop sleeping and eating!"

Grace laughed. "That's the good country air in your lungs. It gets to me too, every time."

"And Gracie, how's things your end?"

Olivia had turned over a new leaf, it seemed. She had never seemed interested in Grace's life before.

"Well, I quit my job at Interfex, would you believe. I told them where to shove it and I've taken Orla out of that awful crèche. I'm taking up a new part-time nanny position, that lets me take Orla with me. So, you're not the only one changing your life."

"That's great news, Grace. Poor old Mum would be utterly shocked and disappointed if she knew what we were up to. Have you seen her lately?"

Grace blushed even further. "Em, yeah, I saw her last Saturday. It was the usual scenario, but I got through it."

"Well, I'm not going to ring her just yet," Olivia, replied. "Not until I sort myself out a bit more. I'm not sure yet of what I'm going to do in the long run. I'm just enjoying a little time to myself at the moment. And I could do without histrionics or lectures."

"Enough said," murmured Grace darkly. "She'd be on the next train dragging you back by the hair. Enjoy the peace while you can."

Olivia laughed. "Will do. I'll call you at the end of the week and let you know how I'm doing, OK?"

"You do that," Grace said, genuinely meaning it. It

had been the first sincere and open phone call they had ever enjoyed.

After Grace put the phone down she spent a lot of her time that afternoon thinking of her older sister and regretting all the time that had been lost for them over the years. Thankfully it wasn't too late to fix it.

Dymphna was staring out the window. She knew she had to have the long range forecast on the currency rates report finished by this evening and she wasn't even halfway through yet, but she couldn't seem to get her groggy brain to function properly today.

It was Mark, of course. Whenever did she lose sleep and fret over her workload or her bikini line? No, every problem began and ended with men, it seemed. Mark had been troubling her all last night and most of this morning.

It wasn't anything concrete, but it was just the way he announced that he wouldn't be seeing her next Saturday or Sunday, as he was off to Cardiff for a stag's weekend with the lads. Dymphna didn't mind the fact of the weekend away and the fact he would be missing. It was the way he told her, shuffling around and looking at his feet, being totally apologetic about it, rather than being excited. Dymphna regretted that at the beginning of their relationship he had been deceptive, so she found it hard to trust him now. He might have been telling the truth, but that element of doubt remained.

They had been in her apartment, enjoying a takeaway and a bottle of wine when Mark announced it. Dymphna, who up to this point had been feeling warm and cosy snuggling in with her boyfriend, had gone right off the idea of a long evening of passion after Mark's bombshell, because she suddenly felt like he was only there for one thing, and anyway why had he suggested staying in? Did he have something to hide? Was he trying to conceal her from anyone who might know his wife and would spot them out somewhere? It all got too much for Dymphna and within an hour she had pleaded a migraine and got rid of Mark. She ended up in bed after a long hot bath, with a huge wodge of chocolate and the latest Marian Keyes. She tried to forget about him, but she found she couldn't settle, wondering was Mark really going to Cardiff or was he hot-trotting it to Limerick to make things up with the lovely Carla? She fretted about it all night long and so slept fitfully. She had woken late and spent all morning trying to catch up.

Dymphna didn't want to go down this road again and become the idiot fool girlfriend that everyone laughed at because she didn't know she was been taken for a ride. Or have Grace tell her she had already warned her all about married men and their deception. Dymphna didn't want a married man, or even really a separated man but Mark was so cute and she had been so lonely not having a man's arms about her that she had taken a risk. Now she just hoped it wasn't going to be a bad one.

All her friends were busily cohabiting and getting hitched and she felt time was passing and she was getting no nearer the altar, or even 'the seriously attached relationship with a future' basket. Mark seemed keen on her and lately there weren't too many offers from good-looking men that she was attracted to. She really liked him and dearly hoped she wasn't backing another loser who would break her heart.

Time would tell, but right now she needed to get this report done or it wouldn't be just her love life she had to worry about.

Melody was in her tiny drab bedroom that she had covered in Britney Spears and Christina Aguilera posters in order to disguise the peeling wallpaper and mouldy dampness. She was scanning an article in *Cosmo* that Susie had given her called "How To Snag Your Man In Just Ten Easy Steps". It advocated all kinds of sexy ways to win the object of your desire over and Melody felt she needed all the help she could get right now as Des Heathcoat seemed to be going off her, or at least having second thoughts.

She looked around the little dank room in disgust. It had never bothered her before she met Kate and Des Heathcoat and discovered how the other half lived. She hadn't known any better. Spending time in a luxurious house with children who had never even known a hungry night in a cold house or a hole in their only pair of shoes, had made Melody realise her life was sadly lacking. Being with the Heathcoats had opened up a new world and fostered a burning ambition for her to escape her hopeless future.

At first she aimed to excel at school and planned to go to college and succeed that way, but then another idea overcame that, one in which Des featured heavily. She could obtain all she desired a lot quicker if she got Des to fall in love with her. But now she seemed even further away than ever from her destiny.

That she would have to change.

She looked at the Prada handbag that had pride of place on her little dressing-table, and felt a bit cheerier. Des wouldn't have given her that handbag if he didn't feel something for her. He had given it to her last night when she baby-sat for them.

He had sat in the car outside her house and given her the bag and told her that he had been really flattered by her texts and she was a very sexy girl, but that Kate was sure to find out and he felt they should just be mates for the moment. Melody had retorted hotly that she didn't want his poxy bag and he could shove their friendship, until Des calmed her down and said that he felt she deserved only the best of everything and told her how much the bag had cost. Melody had been shocked and pleased at the price tag and forgave him, but her resolve to snag him had only strengthened. This might not be as easy as she had first thought but she would succeed in her plans. If there was anything she was sure of, it was her own steely determination.

Seeing Kate all dressed up in her finery last night, going to a ball no less, made Melody burn with jealousy. She used to like Kate, but now it just seemed like Kate was in the way, all smug smiles and condescending comments, taking Des for granted.

And the way she couldn't imagine Melody ever

having a genuine Prada bag! Like Melody was some kind of Cinderella, only suitable for rags and cellars. Of course, Des had made her promise she wouldn't ever let Kate see the bag – but she just couldn't resist. Because the bag was just the beginning, she vowed. She would show Kate some day what she was capable of, and that would be marching off with Kate's prince. She would then enjoy the look on the other side of Kate's smug face, that was for sure.

Maybe it had been a bad idea to go out to the airport and meet Des from his trip, but how was she to know bloody Kate would turn up and spoil it all? She realised that she would have to box clever on this one. Des would be putty in her hands when she got him to herself. She had learnt more than a few things in her early teens around the hay-barns of Kilmadden. She could see that Des was being taken for granted by Kate and sooner or later if Melody showed her sexy body off to him often enough, he would fall into her trap. She picked up the magazine again with renewed interest and decided that if her plan was to succeed, she needed all the help she could get, but she knew deep down that eventually she would succeed. Failure wasn't even in Melody's vocabulary.

Chapter 14

Grace rose early and managed to prise Jordan from his bed in time to give him a substantial breakfast and issue new orders for his after-school activities, as today she was beginning her new job with Kate. Orla was still snuggled into her cot and seemed to be having a lie-in.

Grace was nervous enough without being late. Kate was taking her along on the school run and then would basically go over all the chores and tasks for the day. Grace was torn between waking Orla and having a grumpy toddler on her hands all morning or leaving her for another ten minutes and being late. She decided to give her some more time and had a quiet breakfast with Jordan alone.

"How are things at school?" she enquired mildly, while chomping on some toast.

"A bit better, but there's still a lot of idiots who think I'm a Muslim and that I hate the Americans. I don't even know what Muslims do or what their religion is like. Except that my dad was a Muslim, wasn't he?"

Grace was taken aback by the question. She thought Jordan had forgotten about wanting to see Samir again. Deep down she felt a panic grip her.

She took a deep breath. "Yes, he was, Jordan."

Jordan shuffled in his chair. "I just want to know, that's all. I want to get to know him. I want to meet him. Can we find him, Mum? Can we look on the Internet and check his name out with the airline? It would be so easy."

He looked at her earnestly, her brown sloe-eyed boy with his chocolate skin and his dark hair. He looked so much like Samir. Grace felt her heart fill with equal measures of love and dread. She knew that she could not put off Jordan's request forever, but she hadn't explored how she would feel about seeing Samir again, or indeed how it would affect Paul – he had been such a good father to Jordan and had such disdain for Samir for abandoning them. Grace knew he would be against the idea.

"We'll try. I can try to find out if he still works for Gulf Air. But, we have to tell Paul first."

Jordan flung his arms around Grace's neck. "Oh thanks, Mum, you're the best!"

Grace laughed despite herself – Jordan hadn't been this happy in months. This wasn't going to be easy but now there would be no going back. Suddenly her nervousness about her new job dissipated. There was never a dull moment! She wondered what else the day would bring. It was only a quarter past eight and already her world had shifted slightly. She hoped the day would only get better.

Forty minutes later she had arrived at Kate's huge black gates and was buzzed through.

She spotted Kate at the door waving and a very handsome man who had to be Kate's husband Des clambering into a smart light-green Lexus. Grace drove her scruffy little Starlet along the gravel drive and tried to park it as far as possible from the large jeep and the Lexus.

She felt rather self-conscious as she approached the house, clutching Orla. Des seemed to be sizing her up. He stared quite brazenly at Grace, who felt he was taking in every wobble of her stomach and jiggle of her thighs.

"Grace, welcome," Kate beamed. "This is my husband, Des."

Des smiled winningly at Grace. He was extremely handsome, Grace couldn't help thinking, and so pristine in his appearance. He literally gleamed.

"Hi, Grace," he said, "and who is this beautiful little person?"

"This is Orla," Grace replied, smiling back, "and don't let the dimples fool you."

Des laughed, smoothing his dark neat hair in his driver's mirror. "Well, good luck – hopefully the kids won't be too much of a handful for you. I'll telephone you later, Kate."

Kate leaned down and pecked him on the cheek and then he drove off.

"Very nice!" Grace grinned at Kate, after he had gone.

"Yeah, he's not bad. Sometimes I forget how nice-looking he is until we spend a few days apart. Then when I see him again I look at him and go weak at the knees – until I have to clear up his smelly socks and then we're back to taking each other for granted again. But anyway Des's untidy ways will all become clear. First, we'll get these two angels off to school then you and I can have a nice cup of coffee and discuss the day-to-day routines. I dug out Jade's old baby seat for the jeep for Orla, if that's OK."

"That's very thoughtful of you, Kate, thanks."

Grace was again surprised by Kate's niceness and thoughtful ideas. She herself hadn't even thought of where she would put Orla. She hadn't even expected the jeep to be available for her, though she doubted Kate would wish to endanger her little cherubs in Grace's antiquated Starlet.

They set off for the school and both Jade and Chloe were very taken with little Orla, which pleased both of the mothers. It might make the children accept the change more easily. After lengthy goodbyes and waves to a delighted Orla, they went back to The Beeches and, over coffee and croissants, Kate went through Grace's daily tasks.

Grace found most duties to be what she had expected, except for all the clubs and activities that the children had to attend. It seemed exhausting, with ballet, piano, riding and drama lessons. The children had so many activities it seemed there was little time for them to just play, but Grace kept silent about it, for the moment.

"How are you going to get to college yourself?" Grace enquired of Kate. She must be aware of how inconsistent the bus service was.

"Oh, for the moment Des will take me there – it won't be a problem as he has to go into town every day anyway, and when he's overseas, well, I get to drive the Lexus, but he's not overly keen on that!" She made a face.

"Is he still not too keen on the college idea?" Grace enquired mildly – she got the impression Kate was dying to tell her.

"No, you could say that he still hates the idea. Honestly, Grace, it has nothing to do with you personally, but he doesn't want a stranger in the house raising his kids as he tells me, or me to be missing when he's got an important client coming to stay."

Grace bristled, half in indignation for Kate and half for herself. "And what about you, don't you have a say in your own life? If this is important to you surely Des will back you eventually?" She looked at Kate for confirmation.

Kate blushed profusely and looked out into the lush garden. "I hoped so, but Grace, I think he may not, you know. He seems to be punishing me already. He is quiet and withdrawn, as if I am doing something wrong, but I am not a bad mother because I want to fulfil my ambitions, am I?"

"No, you are not." Grace replied emphatically. "And Des will see that sooner or later. You have to persevere. Paul didn't want me to change jobs but already he's delighted with my better mood and a cleaner house. Just give it some time."

She smiled warmly at Kate who looked like a vulnerable child. For the first time since they met, Grace had found something that wasn't perfect in Kate's life. Even perfect people like Kate had their own problems and issues, it seemed.

"You're right, I will. If he sees I am determined and happy to do this, he will accept it more quickly. Thanks, Grace."

"No problem," Grace said breezily. She fervently hoped it wouldn't be a problem. She had definitely burned her bridges with both Interfex and *Cute and Cuddly*, and there was no going back. She needed this job and didn't want a tyrannical husband ruining it for her. They both sipped their coffees in an uncomfortable silence, worried for different reasons that this project might not succeed.

Grace got a call that evening from her father. This was about as rare as an audience with His Holiness, so she knew it must be serious.

"Grace!" her father barked down the phone. "I need your help. It's your mother. I just don't know what to do for her at the minute. She's been on a crying jag for the past three days and it's something to do with Olivia, but she won't talk to me about it, she just keeps sniffling into her hankie and lying about, and I'm getting desperate. Can you speak to her? I'm getting really worried."

153

Grace swore inwardly. This could get really complicated really quickly. "Has something happened?" she asked, trying to sound as vague as possible.

"Well, she got a phone call from Olivia's fiancé Connell to tell her that Olivia had just taken off to Connemara alone last week and he was really worried about her. Your mother seems to have taken it badly and she is talking about going up there and bringing Olivia back. Honestly, I can't see what all the fuss is about. Olivia is a grown woman and knows her own mind. I could do with a couple of days up there meself on me todd to tell ye the truth. But anyway, no point in me complaining, no one ever listens to me. Please talk some sense into her, will you?'

Grace sighed. "And since when has she ever listened to me, Dad? But I'll try anyhow.

Is Mam there?"

"Heavens, no – she'd kill me if she knew I was telling you – you know how she gets. She's off at bingo with Mrs Maxwell."

That old witch, Grace thought. Mrs Maxwell always looked like she just got off her broomstick. But how upset was her mam if she was off at bingo?

Her father read her mind. "She's only gone to bingo because I insisted. I thought it might take her mind off Olivia. Maybe you could call her tomorrow instead, and don't tell her I phoned."

"OK, Dad, leave it with me," Grace replied resignedly.

One thing was certain, she would have to calm her mother down. She had horrific visions of driving Moira

Casey to the wilds of the west coast to command poor old Olivia to come home to her sensible life. She hoped she could stop her mother from traipsing up to Clifden but she doubted it.

The next morning Grace duly called Moira to see how she was. Perhaps a win at bingo might have calmed her nerves.

"Mam, how are you?" she enquired while rolling her eyes heavenward – she had never been good at subterfuge.

Her mother's voice came back in a whisper. "Oh, I'm terrible, Grace, I really am. I got a call from that poor chap Connell about bloody Olivia. Honestly, the poor fellow is beside himself with worry. She's only gone and high-tailed it off to the country and not a word about her coming back. He called me to see if I knew anything. *Me*? Sure, she tells me, her own mother, nothing. Did you know she'd gone away on her own?"

Grace gulped. Her mother was the proverbial loose canon and could take Grace knowing any information and keeping it from her either extremely badly or very well. She decided to err on the side of caution. "She might have said something about taking some time out . . ."

"Well, she never told me anything or her future husband, for that matter. You didn't tell her anything, did you, about what we discussed?"

"Of course I didn't, Mam, that's between you and Olivia, but I do think you should tell her, and soon. But anyway, what did Connell say exactly?"

"Well, he said that she told him she was mixed up

and feeling unhappy and so she took off for a week or so. Then she called him from Connemara of all places, and said she was staying a while longer. Imagine! The poor fellow is worried sick that she'll cancel the wedding. I mean, what is she thinking of? Maybe we should go up there and sort it out. It's probably pre-wedding jitters or something. She'll listen to her mother and father, surely?"

Grace swore inwardly. "No, Mam, I don't think that's a good idea. If she needs some time to herself we'd better give it to her. Did Connell give you a telephone number or an address or anything?"

"Yes, he did."

"Well, maybe if I gave her a call and had a chat, she might tell me what it's all about. But, Mam, have you thought any more about telling her the truth about her father?"

The phone went silent for what seemed like a lifetime.

"I've thought of little else, but how would she take that news? She's already going off the rails as it is. I just don't know what to do!" Her mother erupted into fresh tears.

Grace took charge. "Look, Mam, calm down or you'll make Dad suspicious and you don't want that, do you? Just go and make yourself a nice cup of tea and I'll give Olivia a ring and I'll get back to you when I find out what's the matter."

"Would you, Grace, that would be great. I'd hate to see Olivia throw it all away at this stage. That lovely

Connell, sure she couldn't do better than him, and their beautiful house nearly ready – it would just break my heart."

Grace thought it would break her mother's heart if she couldn't brag to her friends and neighbours about Olivia marrying well and having a huge pile in the Wicklow hills, more than anything else. No wonder Olivia was confused.

"OK, Mam, leave it to me," she reassured her mother and carried on the charade just to protect Olivia. Her joke about Moira Casey dragging Olivia back by the hair from Clifden had almost backfired.

She telephoned Olivia straight away.

A Mrs O'Sullivan answered the phone and informed Grace that Olivia had gone off on a day out with a James McCarthy and wasn't expected until late.

Grace smiled wryly as she replaced the receiver. Olivia seemed to be having a whale of a time in Clifden, blissfully unaware of the whirlwind she was creating back in Dublin. And who was this James McCarthy? Grace couldn't wait till she talked to Olivia now. One thing seemed sure. It didn't look much like Olivia was going to be coming back any time soon.

Olivia was at that moment traipsing through Kylemore Abbey with one James McCarthy. He was the most wonderfully down-to-earth individual she had ever met. She had shyly gone to the local bar one night, where she was assured that the Irish traditional music was second to none and the *craic* was good. She had ordered a half of Guinness and sat quietly and self-consciously in the corner enjoying the music, when this man walked into the bar carrying a bodhran and Olivia just forgot to breathe because he was so gorgeous. He was extremely tall, at least six foot four and had a shock of blonde curly hair. His skin was as brown as a nut and he had the clearest bluest eyes Olivia had ever seen and a lovely wide smile that showed perfect white teeth. His clothes, however, were another story. Olivia, whose idea of casual was normally a cashmere sweater and linen pants, was amazed by the enormous grey shaggy mohair jumper the man wore that swathed his angular frame. It had so many holes it was almost threadbare and the dark grey cords he wore with it looked at least as old and half as decrepit. Olivia wondered if he was a New Age hippy or something. After he caught Olivia looking at him, he smiled winningly back at her and she blushed a dark crimson and tried to sink deeper into her velour chair, but eventually he approached her after a good session accompanying the group of musicians. Several Guinnesses later, Olivia found her nerve and discovered that James McCarthy was a dairy farmer and a local and apart from a year in Boston where he worked on building sites and hated every day of it, he lived outside Letterfrack, farmed a herd of dairy cows and never wanted to leave or be anywhere else.

Olivia loved his simple outlook on life and his calm sensible demeanour. She felt in turn calmed by him and had readily agreed when he had offered to show her his Connemara, weather and cows permitting. That had been four days ago and since then Olivia had spent a lot of time with James rediscovering her inner self and realising that she hadn't remembered a time when she had felt so serene or complete. She almost forgotten she had a life and a fiancé back in Dublin. Almost.

Today they walked through the stunning grounds of the imposing abbey, which overlooked a spectacular lake and she felt entirely at peace. It was raining softly and James was clad in a massive Aran sweater that looked as old as the hills and an equally elderly pair of faded jeans, but Olivia found she could not stop looking at him or admiring his handsome face which always seemed to be smiling or grinning. Now he was calmly telling her the history of the abbey while she was vainly trying to listen, all the while daring those full lips to kiss her. So far, James hadn't made a move on her, so Olivia wasn't sure if he just wanted her as a friend and anyway, what right did she have fancying another man when her engagement ring lay languishing in its box in her attic room back at the guesthouse? She knew she ought to feel ashamed and be on the phone to poor old Connell and begging him to come and fetch her but she didn't feel that way and she did come here to find herself. If that meant finding something she daren't ever have dreamed of, well, she just had to find out for herself.

She looked intently as James pointed out the statue of Our Lady high upon the hill overlooking the Abbey and she moved closer to him, smelling a mix of sandalwood and musk and his own scent. She longed for those long brown hands that played the bodhran so well to take hers and lead her off to make love in the long grass. She had never felt so unashamedly like the brazen wanton lustful hussy that she obviously was.

Olivia was feeling alive again, for the first time in a very long time, and she was relishing the feeling.

But deep in the recesses of her mind she knew she had a life and a fiancé and even a wedding looming back in Dublin and she could not stay here forever without facing the music. Eventually she would have to return and decide what her life was going to be. But for now she was enjoying the fairytale that was Connemara, and all the debris and hassle of her life in Dublin seemed very distant and far away indeed.

Dymphna was enjoying her own romance. Mark had come back from his stag's weekend bearing gifts, namely a bottle of *Allure* within a proper duty-free bag, so Dymphna had forgiven him and they had spent the entire evening in bed catching up. Since then things had been close to perfect, although he was making sounds again that he was off on a golfing weekend on Friday.

They had spent last Saturday together but not Sunday. Dymphna tried very hard to ignore that little distrusting voice in her head that every now and then made her doubt him. Yet when they were together Mark made her feel so special, like she was the only girl in the world. It was just a bit difficult to trust him completely. She knew guys went away on golf weekends all the time and she had to let go of this possessive streak, but just a little part of her worried that Mark was still visiting his wife in Limerick. She was afraid to even voice her fears to Grace who deep down had never really got over the disaster with the married Samir. That had really hurt Grace, to be taken in so comprehensively by Sammy and then to only find out he was married when she became pregnant and he hightailed it out of her life. Even now, fourteen years later, Dymphna doubted she could cope with the same set of circumstances as Grace had. Dymphna hoped if she became pregnant that Mark would support her but deep down she wasn't so sure. Still, having Mark in her life was infinitely better than not and she was going to enjoy him while it lasted.

Chapter 15

Grace finally got to speak to a happy Olivia the following morning.

"Hi," breezed Olivia, sounding chirpy and carefree. This was the exact opposite of how Grace felt at the moment. Between her mother's seven phone calls over the past twenty-four hours, each one becoming more histrionic than the last, and Paul's sulking over Jordan's determination to find his father, Grace felt a lot like heading for Clifden herself.

"Hi, yourself," Grace replied, trying her best to match Olivia's upbeat mood. "You sound a lot happier."

"Oh, I am. I'm having the time of my life. But I guess by your earlier call that all is not well back there, am I right?"

"You're right on the money," Grace grimaced. "The old dear had a worried phone call from Connell and he told her you had upped sticks and fled to the west. It took me all my time to convince her not to go there and talk some sense into you. Those, by the way, are her words not mine."

"Oh shit, I'll kill bloody Connell for involving Mam in this! He bloody knows what she is like. What will I do? She can't come here, not now . . ."

"Anything to do with a James McCarthy, by any chance?"

Olivia laughed happily. She sounded like a giddy schoolgirl. "Well, yes! We're just friends at the moment but, Grace, he gives me those butterflies in my stomach, the ones I've never felt before – he is just so wonderful. You have got to help me put Mam off, at least for a while."

Grace smiled. Olivia sounded like she was at last having a bit of fun in her life and who was Grace to try and stop her? "OK then, listen up. First you have to ring Mental Moira and tell her you are just having a well-earned rest for a while and you have sorted things out with Connell. Make sure you reinforce that everything is as normal. Then you have to ring Connell and placate him too, at least for another while, until you sort yourself out. Otherwise one of them, or worse still, both, will arrive on your doorstep sooner or later, probably with a shotgun and a priest."

Olivia sighed with relief. "Thanks, Grace, you're a star. I'll call Mam right now and then Connell straight after. I know it probably sounds like I'm running away from everything, but at the moment, being here, meeting James, well, it feels like I'm running towards my future. Does that make any sense?"

"It makes perfect sense," Grace agreed. "Now don't forget to ring me later and fill me in on all the juicy gossip regarding your new man friend, OK?"

"I promise!" Olivia laughed as she rung off.

Wow, Grace thought, this is going to come as a major shock to the parents, if Olivia decides to ditch the perfect partner and career and take up with this James person.

Grace didn't know how many more surprises she could take. Paul had surprised her with his very vehement opposition of Jordan's plan to find Samir. Even though Grace had already given her word to Jordan that they would both look on the net and try the airlines, Paul was dead set against it. They had had a huge row, which ended up in Paul saying, "Thank you very much for making me feel for the first time in ten bloody years that I'm not good enough to be Jordan's father!" And he had stormed out of the townhouse, which had shook as he slammed the front door, leaving Grace more frustrated than ever.

She felt she just couldn't win. She had fretted and worried that Paul would oppose the plan, but she'd never believed he would be so angry and against it. Jordan deserved to know his birth father, even if he was a deadbeat. Grace had known this day would eventually come. Surely Paul did too. He would have to like it or lump it, because she had made a promise to her son and she wasn't about to break it. Paul would just have to grow up!

Feeling like the whole world was on her shoulders Grace headed for The Beeches. At least spending some time in luxury would help brighten her day.

When she got there Kate was in an exuberant mood. She was so energised by her course that Grace found her enthusiasm infectious.

"It is so fantastic, Grace, I feel better than I have in years. It's just a totally creative environment and it has such a buzz. Most of these kids are teenagers and they have such talent and drive, it's amazing! First of all, I felt like an old trout among all these youngsters. There are a few mature students, but only a handful. But they all muck in and I'm just one of the gang – it's really good. They all seem so completely confident in themselves. I didn't realise I would feel so happy and it just feels so right, you know?" She then looked at Grace and giggled. "I'm sorry, Grace, I must sound like one of those poor deluded hippies who has just joined a cult. Anyway, enough about me, how are you getting on? The children really seem happy with you, and they absolutely love Orla, but are you doing OK? You seem a bit frazzled this morning."

Grace tried a small smile. "It has absolutely nothing to do with my job here – in fact I was delighted to escape the debacle that is my family life to come over here to this beautiful place and do something productive."

Kate looked concerned. "Tell you what, I haven't got a lecture until eleven o'clock, how about I tell Des to go on ahead and we can have a coffee and a chat first, and you can drive me into town in the jeep afterwards? Does that sound OK?"

Grace nodded. "That would be great, thanks, Kate."

Kate went off to tell Des and gather the children for school, while Grace tidied away the breakfast dishes. She heard raised voices in the distance and busied herself trying not to overhear.

Des rushed into the kitchen to grab his keys and briefcase and gave Grace a quick grin. He was extremely handsome, Grace thought. He was dressed in a smart white shirt, and an impeccably cut navy suit, which highlighted his dark hair and deep tan. He looked slightly irritated as he quickly hurried from the house.

Kate reappeared with a fully dressed but sullen Chloe and a lively Jade.

"Everything OK?" Grace asked.

Kate looked visibly flushed in the face. "We'll just get these two off to school and I'll tell you," she murmured, over Chloe's head.

They gathered all the children together and completed the school run in record time in order to get back for their much-needed coffee.

Kate put the coffees before them along with a huge plate of croissants. Grace didn't give a stuff about diets today – she was having at least two of them.

"I'm sure you couldn't help but hear the row earlier. Sorry about that. Des got a bit annoyed because I changed my plans. I was keeping him waiting and then I told him he wasn't needed after all and he got a bit huffy. He's such an overgrown child sometimes. "

"Tell me about it, I've got a sulking thirty-five-year-old at home that could pass for an immature two-year-old."

166

With that she told Kate about Jordan's quest for his father and Paul's overreaction, Olivia's flight of fancy to the west and her mother's hysterical tirades. After she had unloaded it all in great catty detail and got a few laughs from Kate en route, she felt a lot better.

Even Orla giggled beneath their feet with her dolly.

"You're a tonic, Grace," Kate laughed. "I know it's not really funny, but you tell it all with such wit. You have to admire Olivia all the same. She is brave to walk away from all the safety her life with Connell gives her to an uncertain future, albeit an exciting one. I don't know if I could have done that. Des makes me feel safe."

"I don't know if Paul makes me feel safe, but he does make me happy, most of the time, apart from now of course, when I could gleefully throttle him."

Kate suddenly looked wistful and Grace suspected, a little teary. "I don't think I could ever survive without Des. He has been my absolute life for the past ten years. But lately, since I've begun this course, I feel he's becoming increasingly distant with me, like I have disappointed him or something. Perhaps I have made him too much the centre of my world and he's feeling a bit left out now that I have something else to focus on. Plus the fact I haven't given him a son – it's something he always wanted, but after two girls he feels we have enough children. That's why I need a career – I don't see any more babies at the moment."

Grace grimaced. She didn't like the sound of that. From what she had already gathered old Des was a bit of a control freak, although mostly Kate seemed not to notice. "Surely, if Des sees you are becoming happier and more fulfilled it will benefit him and the children also. Wouldn't it make him happy to see you happy?"

"You would think so," replied Kate dejectedly, "but why does he make me feel like every minute I spend away from him, I am doing something wrong?"

Grace didn't reply, though she had an increasingly uneasy feeling about the length of time her job would last before Des tried to reassert his earlier control over his wife.

Although he was handsome and charming, instinctively Grace didn't like Des Heathcoat. She felt that if Kate drifted too far from his grasp there could be problems ahead.

As Grace drove Kate into town to Griffith College they talked some more about their dreams and aspirations and Grace realised that Kate was becoming more than a terrific boss, she was becoming a real friend.

Grace found herself tumbling out all her dark secrets about her dysfunctional family and how Olivia and she never got on and how she recently found out that Olivia was a secret love child and how her mother appeared to be coming unhinged.

Kate listened intently and then opened up to Grace about her own alcoholic parents.

"I have never told another soul, you know, Grace, about how ashamed I am of them and my background. I try to forget I ever came from them at all – most of the time it works!"

They both laughed. Even though it wasn't funny,

they found the common ground of being outsiders in their families strangely comforting.

"We're a couple of basket cases," Grace remarked.

"Looney tunes," Kate agreed, as the jeep pulled up outside the college. She hopped out. "Thanks, Grace," she said and Grace knew she wasn't just thanking her for the lift.

"For what?" she asked, puzzled.

"For being a good listener. I haven't been so open with anyone since . . . well, ever really, and it felt good not to be judged."

"You're perfectly welcome," Grace replied with a glint in her eye. "I'm an expert on dysfunction and basket cases, come from a long line of them and if you met my mother you'd know what I meant. So don't worry your head, as Paul would say. I enjoyed talking to you too. Saved me fifty quid in psychiatrist's fees. So off you go to your exciting world, Kate Heathcoat, and I'll see you later."

Kate laughed as she strolled away, portfolio in hand. Grace was an extraordinary person and, it seemed, was becoming a very good friend. Kate had never had a real friend before.

Des seethed all the way into town. He sped too fast along the country lanes in his Lexus and nearly collided with a car overtaking a tractor on a hairpin bend.

Bloody women, he cursed. Blast Kate and her bloody university course! She had become so uppity in the past few weeks, busy with this, studying that, she hardly had any time for him any more, and every evening she had her head stuck in a design book. And then this morning, she had shut him out in favour of the bloody home help! What kind of a fool did she think he was? In a temper he pulled out his mobile and keyed in Melody's number. It was time he taught Kate a lesson. No one took Des Heathcoat for granted, that was for sure.

Moira Casey put the phone down in a temper. Bloody Olivia, what a complete madam she was acting!

Moira felt incensed. Her older daughter had telephoned her and insisted that under no circumstances was she to even consider driving to Connemara or encourage poor Connell to do so. She had blathered on about privacy and needing some space, and whatever chance she and Connell ever had of actually getting to the altar, it wasn't helped by meddling mothers or well-meaning relatives and Olivia would be in touch again when she was good and ready. What kind of a daughter had she reared that treated her own mother with such derision and walked away from a perfectly good man and a mansion to boot? She would be very lucky if Connell ever took her back and she deserved to lose him with all the carry-on. Swanning off to the west like a real drama queen and expecting her fiancé and family just to put up with it!

Moira shook her head in amazement and then blanched at all the bragging she had done about Olivia to her friends and neighbours over the years. She had emphasised Olivia's achievements after Grace's scandal of an illegitimate child.

She also wondered how long more she could live with her secret and keep it from Olivia and Sean. The way her daughter was now going off the rails it seemed, whether Olivia liked it or not, Moira would indeed have to travel to Clifden and break the awful news. At least she would be far away when the fallout happened and perhaps Sean wouldn't need to know for another while. She decided to go against Olivia and dialled Connell's number. She would find out what the jilted fiancé felt about all this carry-on, because pretty soon it had to stop and Moira Casey was the very one to stop it.

Paul Kelly tried very hard to concentrate on the job in hand in front of him. He had to get his team of contractors to finish the hotel painting, as agreed, by the end of the week, despite the howling rain and strong winds, and two of his men being off sick. It was all he needed at the moment, a huge contract running seriously behind with all his problems at home. Paul found it impossible to focus for thinking about the row he had caused over Jordan's burning wish to find his biological father and play happy families. Paul couldn't admit it, but he felt truly hurt that Jordan did not consider him to be the father he had always felt he was. All those years of loving Jordan like he was his own. Paul had provided for him, had endured endless football matches and cut knees, but being there and being a hands-on father seemed to now count for nothing. He felt totally rejected and Grace couldn't seem to see how it was affecting him. He was supposed to just step aside and let some strange guy who couldn't be bothered all those years ago to take any responsibility, step in and be Jordan's dad. Well, if that was the plan, Paul wanted no part of it and he couldn't see a time when he could ever accept it, and as he tried to forget this morning and concentrate on his immediate work, he wondered if things between him and Grace would ever be quite the same again.

That evening Grace sank into her chair gratefully after what had been a tough day.

It was bad enough that a coldness to rival the North Pole had emerged between her and Paul after their quarrel that morning, but Kate's children had played up all day and Kate was late home (there was no sign of the sulking Des either). So Grace arrived home exhausted to a cold house with a fractious toddler in tow, to cook dinner. Luckily it was Jordan's turn to stay late for art class so she had got home just after he had arrived.

After dinner, she had just put Orla to bed, checked Jordan's homework and switched on *EastEnders* when a knock came to the door. Paul answered and she could hear a male voice outside. Dreading a visit from some evangelical bible-bashers or an insurance salesman, Grace tried to focus on the television and hoped Paul would get rid of whoever it was quickly.

Suddenly Paul was calling her name in his most polite voice and in he walked followed by a plump, balding well-dressed man whom he introduced as Connell, Olivia's fiancé.

Grace was embarrassed by the assorted toys strewn

172

across the tiny front room and the shabby but comfortable T-shirt and tracksuit bottoms that she had just changed into.

Paul looked no better in his paint-speckled jeans, heavy stubble and holey socks. Grace fleetingly thought they must look a lot like the *Royle* family to the affluent Connell, but one look at his face told her that Connell was too pained to notice what dishevelled state the Kelly household was in.

"Hi, Connell," Grace smiled, rising to shake his hand, which appeared to be shaking slightly already.

"Grace, nice to meet you," Connell replied, blushing. "I'm sorry to barge in like this, but I've had a disturbing call from your mother about Olivia and I really need your advice."

"I'll go put the wee kettle on, so," Paul announced and slipped quietly from the room.

Grace offered Connell a seat and he sat down heavily. He was very tall and somewhat overweight, but he had a pleasant childish face with nice kind eyes, Grace decided. He wasn't conventionally good-looking and seemed a bit like a large cuddly bear.

"So, my crazy mother has been on the phone then," Grace said lightly. She wasn't sure what stories her mother had been telling Connell, but she felt instinctively she had to diffuse the situation.

"Yes and, Grace, I *am so* concerned. Your mother seems to think Olivia is having some kind of mental breakdown in Connemara and she's insisting I take her there to sort it out. I talked to Olivia this morning and she seems a little distracted, but she won't give me any concrete answers about when she is coming back. I mean, we're supposed to be planning a wedding and moving into our new home soon. I'm just worried that I'm losing her. I can't just sit back and do nothing about it, can I?"

Grace swallowed hard. What could she tell this apparently sweet man that could possibly reassure him but yet not tell a blatant lie.

She stalled for time. "What did Mam say exactly?" she enquired at last. Hopefully she could decide what to tell him after she knew what he had been told.

Connell rubbed a hand over his thinning hair. "Well, she told me that Olivia has said that she must be left alone to sort herself out and an interfering mother or anyone else for that matter won't get her up the aisle, or words to that affect. I know she was having some doubts but surely that was just cold feet? If Olivia doesn't want to marry me, surely I should be the first to know."

Grace had to agree. Keeping Connell in the dark was a bad idea. Throw her mother's vivid imagination and control-freak tendencies into the mix and you had a recipe for a disastrous break-up.

She regarded Connell seriously. "My mother has a tendency to take the truth and run a mile with it, stretching it all the way. She means well but she does try to control all and sundry. I think you should give Olivia a bit of time. Surely you've noticed she's been a bit unhappy lately?"

Connell shrugged. "I suppose she has. I know she

has gained weight and got a bit down, but I didn't think it was anything too serious . . ." His voice trailed away.

Grace marvelled at the naiveté of men. Olivia was miserable for months, had changed beyond recognition and yet Connell had failed to notice it was serious. She wondered how well this man actually knew her sister.

"You're right, Connell," she said gently. "If she is having second thoughts, it's far better that they are dealt with now, rather than after the honeymoon. You can call Olivia tomorrow and have a nice chat. I'll talk to my mother and try to calm the waters. I really think storming up there will be counter-productive."

Connell nodded gratefully.

With that, Paul re-emerged with a tray of tea and biscuits, and the conversation about Olivia ceased. They then all made small talk about Kilmadden and Wicklow and the relative merits of each. Connell rose to go after another twenty minutes and thanked Grace profusely for her help.

She and Paul walked him to the door and saw him dejectedly climb into his large black Mercedes and drive away.

"He seems nice," Paul said, the cold war forgotten for a minute.

"Yes, but I've a sneaky feeling he's not going to be very happy in the near future,"

Grace replied, closing the front door.

"That makes two of us then," Paul said glumly and walked away.

Grace sighed heavily. Looked like the artic freeze was still in the air.

What a rotten day it had been. Grace wondered when it would get better. If she were a betting person she wouldn't wager it would be any time soon.

Chapter 16

The following day Connell phoned Grace and informed her that he and Moira Casey had decided, after another phone call, that they were indeed travelling to Clifden to see Olivia and that Grace could come along if she wished.

Grace made the air blue with her silent curses. This was a disaster and she could no longer see any way of preventing it.

Thankfully, it happened to be a Saturday and after a bit of persuasion Paul was entrusted with the children while Grace went on a wild-goose chase to Connemara to be a reluctant witness to the unravelling of her older sister's life.

The trip was interminably long, with her mother fawning over Connell like he was her long-lost son and heir. If she calls him 'poor Connell' one more time, Grace fumed, I'll string her up by her awful pearl necklace! Her mother came across as some awful caricature of Hyacinth Bucket, feigning a genteel middle-class background and pronouncing her words in a baffling Royal-Family-like accent.

Grace cringed at every mile that passed. If her mother had been upset, she certainly wasn't showing it at the moment, with her girlish laugh and her lengthy discussions about Olivia and Connell's proposed and increasingly unlikely wedding.

Grace felt like asking if her mother intended to tell Olivia about her real father or if that was going to be a wedding present?

It all seemed surreal as they sat now in the cosy front room in the guesthouse that Olivia was staying at, awaiting her return.

Grace had tried vainly to contact Olivia that morning, but she had already left on a trip. Now Grace sat with a weak cup of tea perched on her lap, examining the patterned carpet and dreading Olivia's return.

Connell was pacing, red-faced, peering out the large bay window constantly, before Moira entreated him to sit down and taste the wonderful homemade biscuits.

Just then Grace spotted Olivia approach. She looked carefree and happy, her blonde hair blowing in the wind, a pink healthy blush on her cheeks. She was wearing, of all things, a huge Aran sweater and jeans, clothes Grace had never imagined her in, never mind actually seen on her. Then Grace's attention was drawn to the tall Adonis-like man that was laughing alongside Olivia. He was just as Olivia had described, quite wonderful.

Grace glanced at balding, red-faced Connell in his

grey raincoat and sensible suit and decided he didn't stand a chance.

A moment later, Olivia burst into the room. Her face transformed from the carefree laughing one Grace had glimpsed a moment ago to one contorted in anger and irritation. Closely behind her stood the tall Adonis that Grace knew to be James McCarthy.

"What the hell are you all doing here?" Olivia exploded.

James seemed taken aback and retreated slowly until he was almost back in the hallway.

Moira Casey rose to the occasion. "We're here to bring you to your senses, young lady!" she retorted, while vainly trying to escape her comfortable armchair.

"Mam, I am thirty-six years old and quite compos mentis, thank you very much. And Connell, we spoke yesterday. I told you I wasn't prepared to come back to Dublin yet. You have no business barging in here like some caveman to take me back by force. And Grace, I thought you were on my side –"

"I *am*," Grace insisted. "I am only here to support you. I have been trying to get them to change their minds and turn back ever since the Naas Road."

James tugged at Olivia's sleeve and quietly told her he would see her later.

"Yes, thanks, James. I will see you later," Olivia said emphatically as her fine friend disappeared.

"Who the hell is he?" Connell thundered, showing more bottle than Grace ever imagined he could.

"He is a friend. I suppose I'm not allowed friends of

the opposite sex now? Really, Connell, you're such an old fogey!"

"Olivia!" her mother exclaimed. "That is outrageous! In fact, your whole behaviour to poor Connell here, has been totally disgraceful. I want you to come back home this minute and get back to normal. You have a wedding to plan, and a new house to get ready. This really has been totally out of character."

"Character?" Olivia echoed. "I haven't had any character to speak of for years, Mother. I have only been myself for the past few days, here where no one expects me to be the dutiful daughter, the perfect employee and the wonderful blushing bride, all rolled into one. Here, I'm just Olivia. There's no pressure on me to be perfect, and I like it. I'm not going back to that life – the truth is I just can't. So, if you don't mind, I think Connell and I have some things to discuss alone, so please excuse us. Grace, can you take Mam out for a walk?"

Grace motioned to her mother, who was not moving.

"I don't believe I'm hearing this!" Moira Casey raged. "You're an ungrateful little bitch, Olivia! You're just like your father, running away from your responsibilities as soon as the going gets tough, haring it off out of town the minute things got sticky!"

"My father hasn't got an irresponsible bone in his body," Olivia hissed back, moving closer to her mother, hands on hips. "He's put up with you all of these years, after all. The man deserves a sainthood."

Her mother's face curled up into a cruel sneer. "Sean Casey might very well qualify for sainthood, but your real father certainly won't!"

Olivia looked as if she had been slapped, and Connell seemed to be just as shocked.

Grace wished the ground would just open up and she would gleefully jump in – anything to escape this cringing debacle that was unfolding, breaking wide open her already dysfunctional family.

Moira Casey's hand flew to her mouth, as if trying to retrieve those fateful words.

Grace could tell she instantly regretted her outburst, but it was too late.

"What the hell do you mean by that?" Olivia demanded. She was now just inches from her mother's face.

"Your father is not who you think he is, that's all. Your *real* father ran off on me years ago just like you're doing now. He ran away for a useless dream and left me high and dry and pregnant with you. Your dad, I mean Sean, stood by me."

Olivia just stood there, open-mouthed, as if trying to process the information that had just turned her world upside down. Grace went to her and put her arm around her.

The air also seemed to go out of her mother who backed away and sat down heavily on the armchair.

"What do you mean?" Olivia asked at last, still in shock. She looked at Grace beseechingly. "She's lying, tell me that she's lying to me, Grace. She just wants me to come home and she's willing to try anything!"

"She's not lying, Olivia, I just found out. Dad doesn't even know yet."

"It's true!" their mother wailed. "I wish it wasn't true

181

but it is. Don't you think I would give anything for Sean to be your father? But the plain fact is that he is not, Olivia. I tried for years to pretend Seamus Costigan wasn't your blood and raise you to be different, but now you have turned out *just* like him, running away and breaking everyone's heart!"

She broke into fresh sobs and Grace didn't know whether to hug her or slap her for what she had just done. Olivia was plainly devastated. Connell just stood there, rubbing his balding head. He should be at least trying to *comfort* her, Grace thought absently.

"Look," she said finally, anxious to break the deadlock. "It's been a real shock to you, Olivia, and Mam is clearly upset. You said that you needed to speak to Connell – how about I take Mam over the road for a coffee and it'll give you two a chance to talk."

"All right," Olivia replied, eyes blazing. "But this isn't over yet, Mam, not by a long shot."

Grace took her mother tightly by the arm and frogmarched her across the road to a trendy coffee house that wouldn't have been out of place in Manhattan, never mind Dublin. She ordered two cappuccinos, while eyeing her mother who looked grossly out of place, crying into her lace hankie in her best tweeds that were more suited to an episode of *Glenroe* than this glossy chrome and beech-wooded palace.

"What are you playing at, Mam?" Grace stormed as she sat down. "Talk about choosing the wrong moment. Did you really mean to do that back there?"

"Of course I didn't!" sniffed her mother, all irritation

182

again. "I just got so annoyed with Olivia – honestly I could just smack the girl sometimes, to get a bit of sense into that head of hers."

"Mam, Olivia is a grown woman of thirty-six years. She is far beyond smacking. You should be more concerned that you have just turned her whole world upside-down with the news you have just sprung on her. She will need to know all the details, and this also means Dad will have to know and it'll have to be sooner rather than later."

Her mother's hand flew to her mouth. "Oh, poor Sean! How will I ever get the courage to tell him, after all these years? He will never forgive me – what am I going to do, Grace?" More tears began to flow.

Grace tried an awkward hug. "I don't honestly know, Mam. But after thirty-six years, I think you'll have to make it something honest and good. And please try to remember, it is you who has to make it up to Olivia and Dad. *You* have to be the one who is sorry."

Her mother brightened up a bit. "You're right of course, Grace. I'm just so ashamed of the past. It makes me a bit cross when I think about it. I just want to forget the whole thing ever happened. Tell you what, I'll try to be a bit nicer to Olivia, even though I still think she should come back right now to Connell and her proper life in Dublin, but I'll say no more about it for the moment. Sure, she might be patching things up with him right now. We'll give them another while – maybe you could get me one of those nice pastries they have over there in that cabinet – thanks, love."

Grace was once again amazed by her mother's ignorance of her situation. She truly never realised how much impact her actions had.

She rose resignedly and fetched a couple of cakes from the counter. She wondered herself how things were faring across the road in Sullivan's Guest House. Somehow she felt Olivia would not be patching things up, by any manner or means.

Across the street, Olivia was sitting meekly in an armchair, still letting the shocking news her mother had imparted sink in. Connell seemed at a loss for words. He still paced around like a caged bear rubbing his head. It quite irritated Olivia, who knew he was obviously worried about their relationship, but surely he could at least give her a hug, seeing as she was so upset?

"Sit down, Connell," she said at last, in a quiet sad voice.

He flopped down across from her, knitting his large hands together, looking as if he was attending an interview.

She took a deep breath. If she was going to break his heart, she wasn't going to be as cruel or as random as her mother had just been. "You know for quite a while I have been a bit low, and unhappy."

She paused, Connell nodded.

"Well, I have been feeling . . . like I was in a kind of surreal dream or something, like it wasn't really happening to me. The wedding, the house, even my job, none of it seemed like it fit me any more, and the closer

I got to the big day or even the big house, the more miserable I became."

"We don't have to get married yet," Connell said hopefully. "There's no rush at all. I don't mind putting it off for a while –"

"No!" Olivia said, a bit more fiercely than she had intended. "No, that's not the answer, Connell. I think if we are totally honest with each other you'll agree that we are just settling for each other. I am thirty-six and you are forty. It's like this relationship was the Last Chance Saloon for both of us, and even though I love you, there's no passion, no butterflies. And I want that, I need that, and I've decided it would be a great disservice to you and me if I go ahead with something that in the end won't work. You deserve someone who will adore you, and will give you everything you need. That person is just not going to be me. I'm sorry, Connell, but it's over. I'm not coming back to Dublin. In fact, after today, I doubt I ever will."

Connell couldn't believe what he was hearing.

He had never imagined it had been this serious. Even when Olivia disappeared, he still felt she would return to him. Now it all seemed such a stupid pipedream, the lavish house in Wicklow, the fancy hotel they had tentatively booked for the following summer. It was all turning into ashes. He couldn't say anything, not even that he loved her completely, in as much as he could ever love anyone. He knew he wasn't demonstrative or even romantic, but it didn't mean that he couldn't feel things deeply. He searched Olivia's left hand for the glittering diamond that usually nestled there. It was absent. Olivia noticed him looking and suddenly stood up.

"Wait," she said, and left the room.

A minute later she returned and handed him the ring.

"You'll be wanting this back," she said quietly, placing it in his large hand.

Connell looked at it for a brief moment and then flung it into the open fire where it was swallowed quickly by the tall flames.

Olivia was shocked for the second time that day.

"It means nothing to me, not without you," Connell replied bitterly and rose abruptly to go. "Please tell your mother and Grace I am sorry, but I cannot wait. I must go."

And with that he turned on his heel and walked out.

It was over. Olivia was free. And she had never felt so miserable in all her life.

Chapter 17

3 months later . . .

Dymphna stared out the window to the dark dreary December day. It was a scant two weeks to Christmas and Dymphna was low on that fuzzy Christmassy feeling that usually enveloped her as soon as the fairy lights were switched on in mid-November.

She had been feeling tired and overworked and a bit neglected by Mark lately.

He seemed distracted and removed. She tried all the lacy lingerie that Brown Thomas sported in an effort to revive his earlier ardour, but Mark still seemed to prefer boozy nights with his mates, football on the television or weekends away with the former, to being snuggled up in passionate clinches with Dymphna. He hadn't even mentioned Christmas yet.

Dymphna had envisioned months ago that by Christmas they would be inseparable, even moving in together, or at least planning a few days away over the holidays in a country hotel. Instead she now feared it would be dried-up turkey and arguments at her mother's in Raheny. It was enough to drive her to tears.

Just then the phone rang. It was Mark.

"Hiya, what's the story?" That was as close as he got with the charm these days.

"Busy as always. Why are you calling me? Aren't we meeting Sue and Dave tonight?"

Mark and his best mate Dave were like Siamese twins. Dymphna only got to go out to a nice restaurant if Dave and the awful social-climbing Sue came along. Dymphna had to suffer Sue's endless bragging about her girly weekends at Powerscourt or Dave's promotion that was almost in the bag and their forthcoming engagement. Sue's engagement ring sounded as big as the rock of Gibraltar and just as expensive.

"Well, that's just it. Sue's not well and Dave insists on staying in to look after her, twit that he is. Still, he's in 'lurve' and all that. I thought you and I could just stay in and get a video. Maybe you could cook me one of your mean steak dinners?"

Dymphna felt her hackles rise. She felt she was being treated as a put-upon wife and yet she wasn't even marriage material, it seemed. "Thanks, but no thanks. Jeez, Mark, the last thing I want to do tonight is stay in and cook. I'm having a lousy day here and if that's all you're offering, I will call one of my girlfriends and go out with them. Surely we don't need another couple with us to enjoy ourselves?"

A small silence emerged. "Course not, I hope you're not going to go off on one of your 'Where are we going with this?' lectures, Dimples, 'cos I'm kind of busy myself. Tell you what, we'll go to Zorba's on our own, just you and me for a nice romantic meal, on Sunday."

"Sunday?" Dymphna echoed. It was only Thursday today.

"Yeah, well, Todd and Joe are having a boy's night tomorrow night and Saturday I'll be cactus, so I thought Sunday would be good."

Dymphna tried to stay calm. Really she felt like slamming the phone down and dancing all over it, but she reckoned her boss would take exception to that kind of behaviour.

"And tonight?" she said waspishly.

"Well, we could still get a video, but I'll bring over a takeaway, if it'll get you in a good mood."

"Make it Indian and you have yourself a deal," she murmured, making a mental note that tonight she would wear big knickers and kick him out by midnight. She wasn't going to make it easy for him. Or was she?

She had become as comfortable as a pair of old slippers and just as downtrodden. Mark was definitely taking her too much for granted and this was the fifth Friday and Saturday in a row that he was going to be amongst the missing. It just wasn't good enough.

She dialled Grace's number. She needed some of that great sense Grace spouted in bucketloads. She knew Grace would advise her to dump Mark, but she still needed the "you're too good for him" lecture.

Grace's number rang out, so Dymphna rang Kate's house and hoped Grace would be there and not traipsing around the Blanchardstown Centre for Christmas presents.

Grace answered, sounding very chirpy.

"Whatever you're on, bottle it and I'll be over for half a dozen cases," Dymphna quipped.

Grace laughed. "Oh, it's just this house – it's just so perfect this time of year. It looks like those Christmassy ones on those glossy American movies, lots of fairy lights and warm fires. It just makes me so cheerful and about to break out into Christmas carol tunes any minute!"

"Lucky you – I'm up to me arse in wads of paperwork and old Scrooge is alive and well and inhabiting my boss's office. Can you talk for a minute, or are you too busy knitting argyle jumpers and making mince pies?"

"I'm decorating Kate's hugely expensive but tasteful Christmas tree with Orla, who is determined to eat all the decorations. Hang on and I'll put her into her cot for a nap. Ring me back in five minutes. I'll get a coffee and you can tell me all about your nasty boyfriend."

Dymphna laughed as she put the phone down. How had Grace known it was going to be about Mark? Had she been an absolute whinge for ages? She hoped not. She felt bad unloading all of her baggage on her best friend. But who else could she talk to about Mark, except her good friend and confidante?

She called back after a few minutes and tried to be more upbeat.

"Cut the crap, Dimples, it's me you're talking to, and you and I both know that you're miserable, so spill the beans," Grace interrupted after a few moments.

"That obvious, eh?"

"Afraid so," came the deadpan reply.

"All right, here goes. I think Mark is going off me, Grace, or else he's cheating on me. He seems to go missing most of the weekend. He takes me so much for granted and we only seem to go out when we're meeting up with his boozing pals and their insufferable girlfriends. It just doesn't seem to be going anywhere."

Grace asked her if she knew where his ex-wife lived in Limerick.

"I don't, but I could find out from Maria on Reception at the Ballsbridge office.

If he hadn't left the company altogether I could keep tabs on him better. Maria was my eyes and ears over there but, now he's working out at Dun Laoghaire, I don't know what he's up to. Why do you want the address?"

"Well, we could find out once and for all what Mark is up to if we take a trip down to Limerick. I'm prepared for a girly night away from Paul and the kids if your need to find out the truth is great. We could have a night in a nice hotel, a few beauty treatments and a bit of detective work on the side. What do you say?"

Dymphna paused. Was she sure she wanted to know the truth about Mark? Could she handle the reality that he might be two-timing her? But she knew she couldn't bend Grace's ear for the next six months about her lousy relationship if she didn't take Grace up on the offer. Anyway Mark would be history by the New Year if he was being a love rat and at least Dymphna could move on and become Bridget Jones properly, a real spinster with a lousy love life.

"I'd love to," she replied, sounding cheerier than she felt.

A sinking feeling told her she was about to find out the truth about Mark, and although that truth would set her free, it wouldn't make her happy.

That night Mark duly arrived laden with a huge chicken korma, naan bread and a video. Dymphna felt so guilty as he dished up the food and chatted away. His wife's address lay nestled in her handbag just a few feet away, as did the address for the Marriott Hotel, just outside Limerick. She and Grace were driving down to Limerick the following afternoon. Grace reminded Dymphna that if Mark was lying to her all along then surely she could lie for just one night. Still, Dymphna found the subterfuge difficult. She couldn't believe it, but she actually felt sorry for Mark tonight. What if she was just so wrong about all her suspicions? She ate in silence and half watched the video, which was full of gory murders and car chases. Mark, of course, seemed oblivious to her quiet mood as he chomped away on his Indian takeaway and revelled in the blood-spattered bodies that littered the screen.

By eleven o'clock Dymphna pleaded an oncoming migraine and shunted Mark unceremoniously from her apartment before she spilled all the beans and confessed everything. As she shut the door firmly behind his confused face, Dymphna wondered if he would ever be standing earnestly in that hallway again. It depended on the outcome of tomorrow's foray into the west.

She went straight to bed afterwards and found she couldn't sleep, guilt and worry mingling with too much rich food. Tomorrow's truth couldn't come quick enough, whatever it meant.

Grace tossed and turned also. An uneasy truce had been declared between herself and Paul over finding Jordan's father. They had endured an icy ten days at the beginning of hostilities in which neither spoke much, before a huge row ensued. Grace had tried to tell Paul that finding Samir wasn't about him, but about Jordan. At which Paul had demanded to know why he hadn't been enough of a father for Jordan. Grace replied wearily that Jordan was reminded of his parentage every time he looked into a mirror and saw that brown face. Finally, that seemed to pacify Paul, and no more had been said. But Grace dreaded the time that would come when she and Jordan would find Samir and the next step would be taken. Paul seemed hurt that Jordan still favoured the absent disinterested mythical father figure over the real-life loving one that existed in front of him every day. Grace hadn't yet told Paul that she and Jordan had already looked on the net on an absent friends website for news of Samir, so far without luck. But sooner or later something would turn up. Grace felt torn between the love she had for her husband and the love she had for her son. Perhaps Paul felt that Grace harboured a few leftover feelings for her first love, and when she saw him again, he would be somehow discarded. Grace tried to reassure Paul that this would never happen, but still somehow he burned with a kind of juvenile jealousy that frustrated Grace.

She was glad to have the distraction of the debacle that was Dimple's love life and this proposed information-gathering trip to Limerick, to take her mind off her own domestic troubles. She had told Paul about Dymphna's mistrust of Mark and that they were going down to Limerick and would be staying overnight. Paul, who was normally more than pleased at a night alone with Jordan and little Orla, seemed put upon and peeved at the news. Grace bit her lip and quashed the urge to roar at her husband that surely it was his responsibility to look after his children in her absence, but she held her opinions to herself. She didn't want him to make any smart comment regarding Jordan that would plunge them back into another row about the whole father/stepfather debacle again.

Still, she fretted about it endlessly, because she knew things would inevitably get worse before they got better.

The following day, Dymphna collected Grace and they headed for Limerick.

Dymphna felt strangely nervous. She hoped in some way that Mark would be exonerated and she could go back to falling in love with him again. She knew Grace wanted the best for her and Grace didn't believe that was Mark, so she tried to keep the conversation away from the inevitable topic of her errant boyfriend as long as possible, at least until they got past Kildare.

So she asked Grace how was Paul doing with Jordan and if they had found any information in Samir yet.

"Not much," replied Grace, while fruitlessly trying to decipher the map. "All the airlines are very circumspect about giving any information, however innocuous, about their staff, and Gulf Air were the worst of all. They're probably suffering crank calls."

"He doesn't work for Gulf Air, hasn't for years," Dymphna blurted out, before realising she'd even spoken.

Grace stared at her dimly, unsure Dymphna had actually said those words. "How do you know?"

Dymphna glanced at her friend's shocked face. Oh shit, she thought wildly, be careful here, this might be a shorter trip than you imagined! "Well, Sammy phoned me, after you had left, years ago, Grace. You had just met Paul and you had fallen in love with him. Sammy telephoned one day to see how you were."

"And you didn't think to tell me?" Grace wasn't sure how she felt about this. Angry or betrayed, or just glad her friend hadn't confused her at a time when she might have forgiven Samir simply to have Jordan's father back in his life.

Dymphna sighed heavily. "I tried, Grace, I really did. Remember I asked you that time, a few months after you moved in with Paul, what would you do if

Samir came back into your life and you said 'I'd throw him back out'. Well, it was then."

"Tell me everything," Grace said evenly, trying not to lose her cool.

"You had met Paul, moved in with him and seemed very happy. Then one day out of the blue, Sammy calls me up on the telephone. I asked him why he had waited so long and he said he had changed jobs and now worked for British Airways and felt it would be easier to be open about things.

I asked him if he was still married, and he admitted he was. I told you were happy with someone else and had moved on. It was after that, I asked you. It was really hard, Grace, but you seemed so settled and happy for the first time since he made you pregnant and then swiftly fecked off. It was me who had to pick up the pieces and hold your hand through that pregnancy, and I just felt you needed to stay happy. When I asked you how you felt about him and you told me you still hated him, I decided to leave well enough alone. I just couldn't see him hurt you all over again."

Grace's anger suddenly dissipated. She knew Dymphna's intentions to be honourable; she might have done the same thing if she were in Dymphna's shoes.

"It's OK," she replied, touching Dymphna's arm. "I know you were just looking out for me, but you could have told me later. And you knew that recently I needed to know that information in order to find him."

"I was afraid," said Dymphna, close to tears. "As time went on, I felt more and more sure that you'd never forgive me for not telling you. I hoped I'd never need to. Now, Jordan wants to find Samir, and I decided to tell you. You should try British Airways – he just might be still working there."

"I will, just as soon as I get back. We need to sort out your love life first before I go and wreck my own."

Somehow being closer to finding Samir was an uncomfortable thought for Grace. She knew that soon enough she might be taking Jordan to meet his father, and it was something she would have to deal with, hopefully keeping her marriage intact. She put the idea out of her mind and decided to focus on Dymphna for the moment. Her own crisis would dawn in its own good time.

They arrived in Limerick by four o'clock and settled into their hotel room after downing some tasty seafood chowder and sandwiches at the bar. The hotel was luxurious and quiet, and Grace sank into the fluffy towelling robe and slippers that were provided, and raided the minibar while Dymphna called out the varied selection of pamper treatments that the hotel spa specialised in. Grace felt decadent and girly, lounging in a hotel room and actually spending more than ten minutes on herself, and was quite delighted to be away from the madness of being a mother. Dymphna was trying to forget the real reason they were there – basically to break her heart – so they both kept their feelings to themselves while quaffing Baileys and chocolates and poring over the spa menus.

After they had enjoyed a blissful afternoon of Indian head massage and water flotation therapy they got dressed for dinner and afterwards they were going to head for Mark's wife's address and find out the truth. If Mark were cheating he would doubtless be there.

"How are you feeling?" Grace ventured, over her honey-glazed monkfish.

Dymphna pushed her Thai chicken curry around the plate listlessly. "Dunno, I suppose I feel nervous. Either way it can't be good. Either Mark is cheating on me or else he's just plain gone off me. I'm not sure which I prefer."

"At least you will know the truth. If he's not cheating then you can at least talk it over and sort out the problems, but if he is cheating – well, at least you will find out before too much harm has been done."

Dymphna grimaced. "Enough harm has been done already. I just feel emotionally drained by the whole thing – I wish I had never come here . . ." Her eyes filled with tears and she swallowed hard.

Grace put her hand over her friend's. She hadn't realised Dymphna's feelings ran so deep. Dimples did a good impression of a hardnosed businesswoman who cared less about anyone, but inside she was pure marshmallow. Even so, Grace hadn't spotted that she had fallen so hard for the errant Mark.

"Look, I am here with you, every step of the way. If we find out bad news we'll go out on the town and find you a real man, right here in Limerick, and you'll forget the little toe-rag by the third vodka, OK?"

Dymphna smiled through her tears. "You are totally right. We'll go straight there as soon as dinner is over, and get this finished with, once and for all."

An hour later, Dymphna's car sped towards Shannon where Mark's wife lived. It was a pitch-dark night and fine misty rain fell softly. Dymphna was dressed entirely in black, like someone prepared to perform a bank heist instead of looking casually into someone's front garden. Grace had stifled a giggle as Dymphna donned a black beanie.

"What?" Dymphna barked, irritated.

Grace let her laughter have full rein. "Do you not think you're going a bit overboard with the disguise?"

"No, I don't want to be spotted by her or worse still, Mark, if he's there. I might have to go closer to get proof."

"You could be inside the bedroom with that get-up and they still wouldn't see you," Grace guffawed.

Dymphna finally saw the funny side. "Black is my best colour, anyway," she smiled.

At least her nervousness seemed to be abating.

But as they neared Rathsallagh Estate her butterflies returned in abundance. The numbers on the houses were either too small to decipher or else they didn't exist, so they spent several minutes cruising up and down the tree-lined avenue before figuring out Number 28, which was where Mrs Carla McCabe apparently lived.

So far so good, thought Dymphna at first – there was no sign of Mark's smart Mazda. Then it occurred to her he might have taken the train down instead.

Grace pulled up. She was the designated driver in case of a quick getaway. If Dymphna was to see something she dreaded, she had decided she wanted to be the one to see it with her own two eyes.

They sat in silence for a minute.

"Right," Dymphna said eventually after taking a deep breath. "I suppose this is it. I'd better go and do this."

"Yeah, get it over with," Grace replied. "I'd wish you good luck, but I'm not sure that's appropriate for this kind of thing. Just be careful, OK? And don't go mad and knock on the door if you see himself in his boxer shorts. That'll ruin all your plans for your leisurely revenge agenda back in Dublin."

"Agreed," murmured Dymphna, as she pulled the beanie low over her eyes and got out of the car.

Her heart was beating loudly as she first walked past the property, trying to spot any sign of life. The house had several lights on and a small Micra sat in the driveway but all the curtains were pulled tightly. She thought she could hear a television on, but unless she walked right up to the door and risked being rumbled, she wouldn't be able to see anything.

She walked back to the car, the warmth enveloping her after the cold night air as she climbed back in.

"Well?" Grace asked impatiently, all ears for some juicy gossip about Mark's domestic bliss.

"I can't see a bloody thing!" Dymphna fumed.

"What about the back garden? You might see something if you can get access through the rear."

"I can't tramp through a dozen gardens to get to his one, I'd get myself arrested," Dymphna replied, all irritation.

"Not if their garden isn't overlooked," said Grace,

warming to the challenge of discovering Mark with his pants down, "and at the back of this avenue lies a soccer pitch!"

"Brilliant!" declared Dymphna triumphantly. "Drive around the corner and I'll try that way."

"I think I might have to come with you," ventured Grace, reluctant as she was to get herself wet and frozen on this awful night. "If it's a high wall I'll have to give you a boost."

"You're really a bit too good at this, Grace Kelly. All those nights of climbing over walls into the hockey pitch with Johnny Coleman in your teens, I'll bet."

"I resent that remark," quipped Grace as she drove off.

They both tramped through the wet grass until they got to the rear of Number 28, and found the wall was over six feet high. Grace began to regret the trip for the first time since they left County Meath. Dymphna wasn't the most athletic of women and her heavy black boots were hurting Grace's hands, but after several tries and numerous expletives, Dymphna managed to get up on top of the wall. She then disappeared over it and Grace heard muffled curses from the other side as her friend landed heavily.

"Are you all right?" Grace whispered to the cold concrete wall.

"Shit!" Dymphna cried. "I think I've broken the heel on my boot."

Grace smiled, Dimples was ever the fashionista. "Can you see anything?"

"Oh shite!"

Then silence.

A few minutes and several frozen toes later, Dymphna peered over the wall.

"Are you OK?" Grace asked. It seemed like forever since Dymphna had disappeared.

"No," came the small hurt reply.

Suddenly Dymphna dropped down beside Grace.

"What is it?" Grace prodded, but Dymphna seemed unable to speak.

"Go and see for yourself," she whispered at last and motioned for Grace to climb up. She cupped her hands and gave Grace a boost up. Grace grabbed the top of the tall wall and she pulled herself up until she was astride the top.

Bright lights shone from the patio doors and kitchen of the house, lighting up the long garden, which was strewn with numerous children's toys. Slides, trucks and toy cars jostled for position with the patio furniture, but more riveting than that evidence was the sight of Mark cuddling his wife affectionately at the kitchen sink, while a little toddler who had to be at least eighteen months old played happily in the conservatory. Mark's pretty wife then wandered into the conservatory to the little boy, and Grace gasped to see that she was also heavily pregnant. It was such a cosy domestic scene that seemed all the more shocking for the tenderness that obviously existed between Mark and his wife. It would appear that they were very much together and judging by the cosy scene, Grace doubted if they were ever apart.

She felt a great deal of anger on behalf of her friend, and if it hadn't been a pregnant woman that she had spied in that house, she would have marched up to the front door and shattered Mark's comfortable domestic situation.

She got down gingerly.

"Come on, Dimples, what you need is a stiff brandy and a hot bath." She touched her friend's shoulder.

Dymphna was crying quietly. "What I need is a bloody shotgun! The rotten bastard!"

"You will get your revenge, and it will be sweet, but not tonight. That girl in there is the worst poor fool in this whole mess. Can you imagine Mark being the father of your children?"

Dymphna didn't reply that, yes, indeed she had imagined that one day Mark would be the father of her much-desired children – she felt too much a gullible idiot. "Brandy it is then," she said instead and they wearily trudged back to the car, mission accomplished and one heart decidedly broken.

Dymphna had seldom felt so low.

Back at the hotel Grace ran a hot bath for a wet and miserable Dymphna and towel-dried her own hair. She then poured them both a brandy from the minibar and opened as many packets of chocolates and nibbles as she could find, thinking hang the expense. She prepared a mental ego-boosting talk for her best friend, who appeared crushed to have her worst fears not only confirmed, but exceeded.

It was far beyond them to go to the nearest nightclub

and get sloshed and Grace knew her friend would need a lot of support.

Dymphna emerged from the bath eventually, looking tired and pale. She had obviously been crying some more.

"Just in time, Dimples, I've already consumed enough calories to last me until January. Now, get that brandy down you and we'll scoff as much choccy as we can stomach."

Dymphna sat down dejectedly and started to comb her hair. "I can't believe I was such an idiot! How could I have taken in by him? I feel so ashamed, Grace! I had plans for Mark and me. How could he be such a liar, to sleep in my bed and then go home and play happy families with his wife and child, and with another child on the way? It simply defies belief!"

"Dymphna, don't be so hard on yourself. How were you to know? You had him checked out by that receptionist. He was obviously a very good liar as he had everyone else in work fooled too. Just think, Dymphna, you had a very lucky escape. If you hadn't found out now, it could be six months later and you could be thinking about getting engaged or you could have got pregnant – then where would you be? A whole lot worse off, that's where. You can do so much better than Mark McCabe and you will. Just get that twerp out of your life and out of your head, and in a few months' time you will forget it ever happened."

Dymphna frowned. "Do you seriously believe that?"

Grace fell on her own sword. "No, I don't. You will

never forget this happened, but I do feel that in a few months' time, when you have put some distance between you and this disaster, then you will wonder why you ever expended so much energy worrying about such a waster as him."

Dymphna swigged on her brandy and snapped a piece of chocolate in two, wishing it were Mark's bloody neck. "Revenge will be sweet, as they say. I've just had a great idea. I am going to make that boy sweat before he gets his comeuppance, just you wait and see."

Grace clinked her glass with Dymphna's.

"Spare me no gory details," she replied with a grin and was relieved to find a genuine smile grace her friend's face.

And so they sat on their beds, clearing out the minibar and plotting Dymphna's revenge. And Dymphna thought that she was lucky indeed to have a good girlfriend to lean on in times of need like these. Somehow it eased the deep ache of pain and shame that she felt in her chest for loving another liar and a cheat. But when would she ever learn?

Chapter 18

Kate placed the last freshly wrapped Christmas gift underneath the Christmas tree.

She stood back and admired her handiwork. Well, hers and Grace's. Kate had been too busy to decorate the tree, so Grace had done it with Chloe, Jade and baby Orla.

Kate remembered the frisson of jealousy that ran through her when she had arrived home to the splendid tree and the excited children. Someone else had done what she had enjoyed every year with the children since they were born. But she herself had asked Grace to decorate the tree, knowing she was running out of time and there would never be enough of it to do everything she would normally do. It just seemed a high price to pay sometimes. Her mind drifted on to Des. If she felt jealous that she was missing out on time with her kids, then no wonder Des was a bit jealous that she had less time for him.

She glanced at her watch. He was later than usual, even considering his ever more rare appearances these days. He seemed to be saying that if Kate had a busy lifestyle, well, his was even busier and he had even less time to spare.

When he was home he was pleasant but rather like a polite but uninvolved lodger, appearing at breakfast and sometimes dinner, but sequestered in his study for the remainder of whatever time he spent at home. And he often arrived home long after the children had gone to bed.

Their sex life, which had become a bit intermittent over the past year, was virtually non-existent these days. Des had made a smart comment two months ago about how her bum was increasing in girth, seeing as she was spending much of her time sitting on it in college instead of being at the gym staying taut and slim like she used to. The comment, though jovially said, had stung Kate and she burned for days afterwards, and when Des had touched her in bed a few days later she had brushed him off coldly, remembering with pain his earlier remark and feeling undesirable. She couldn't just forget about it because Des was feeling randy. Des knew Kate's Achilles' heel was her former fat self and he knew a thoughtless cruel comment like his barb was enough to make Kate doubt herself. She was bright enough to know that Des's jealousy of her lurked at the heart of the comment but somehow that made it all worse. If you loved someone, why would you want to deliberately sabotage or undermine them?

Kate was flourishing at college. She felt for the first time in her life that she was doing something that she loved and enjoyed and it was something that made her feel worthwhile. Yet her sketches lay in the wardrobe unseen by a disinterested Des who refused to be encouraged to look at them. Kate had hoped his icy opposition to her career would melt but it simply hadn't and Kate fretted that he would become even more difficult next year, when her workload would increase.

Grace had been an absolute godsend; she was not only an invaluable employee but also a good friend. Kate enjoyed hearing about Grace's sister Olivia, who had walked away from her fiancé, and the hapless Dymphna who seemed to be so unlucky in love. Kate absently wondered how Grace and Dymphna were faring down in Limerick on their voyage of discovery.

It was after ten o'clock by Kate's watch. No sign of Des. She switched off the living-room lights and let the magic of the Christmas tree sparkle. Underneath the hundreds of glittering white fairy lights lay all the carefully gift-wrapped presents. It was the perfect scene, but it all looked a little forlorn this year for some reason.

No heart in it, Kate thought suddenly, and felt very tired and emotional. She hoped this apathy between herself and Des would dissipate over the Christmas holidays and they could begin the New Year afresh, but somehow she doubted it.

Just then the phone rang. Kate lifted the receiver, expecting Des with a trite excuse at the ready as to why and how he would be late again for the third time this week.

"Kathleen?" her mother's raspy voice came down the line.

Kate felt immediate panic. Her mother never telephoned her just for a chat; it had to be an emergency of some kind. "Yes, Mum, are you all right?"

Her mother appeared to be sobbing. "Kathleen, come quickly, it's your father. He collapsed a few hours ago and has been taken to the Mater Hospital. The doctors have said it's a massive stroke and he's very bad. I've called all the others and they're on their way. He mightn't last the night. You'd better get here as soon as possible."

Kate sat down and tried to think. Her mind felt as if a fog had descended. "OK, Mum, I'll get there as soon as I can. Des isn't home yet but I'll try to get a baby-sitter. Just sit tight till I get there."

She replaced the receiver and automatically dialled Des's mobile again. It was switched off. She then phoned Barbara Tormey to see if Melody would baby-sit.

"She's not here," Barbara sniffed in vexed tones, "and baby-sitting is the last thing on that young madam's mind at the minute. She's found herself a new boyfriend, one with a car no less. Me and her poor father hardly ever see her at all lately – we're at our wits' end."

"I'm sorry," Kate interrupted impatiently. Barbara Tormey was off on a tangent and Kate simply hadn't got the time to listen. Her father could be dying. "This is an emergency, Barbara, and I just have to get to the hospital. It's my father . . ." her voice faltered. "He has

209

collapsed and I can't get Des on the mobile. Is there any chance you could mind the children for an hour or so?"

Barbara Tormey was suddenly solicitous. "Of course, Kate, I can help you out, you poor dear. That's awful news. Just get yourself ready and I'll cycle up. I'll be there in ten minutes."

At last Kate could exhale.

She cursed Des. Where the hell was he when she needed him? He'd have some answering to do when he finally got home.

But right now she needed to get into Dublin to see her dad. Even though he had never been much of a father to her, she suddenly wasn't ready to lose him. She thought of all the long years of alcohol abuse that her father had inflicted on himself and his family, and she felt sad that the one abiding memory of him she had was of him being drunk in the corner. The years of him being out of work and yet never at home during the day because he was always in the pub, eventually being increasingly joined by her mother who first matched then exceeded his thirst for drink. He wasn't very lovable yet deep down she still loved him, in a hopeless resigned sort of way, rather like the unrequited love of a suitor who knew deep down he was wasting his affections. Christy loved alcohol and everything else was a dim second.

All these thoughts raced through Kate's mind as she kissed her sleeping children and waited for Barbara Tormey to arrive. She had given up on reaching Des. She hoped he'd feel entirely shitty when he eventually arrived back and found out what had transpired, but right now she was too worried to be very angry. That would come later.

Des was at that very moment in a luxury suite at the Westin, where Melody was giving him his Christmas present, herself gift-wrapped in black La Perla underwear that Des had purchased for her earlier at the Westbury Shopping Centre.

Melody was incredibly sexy and so adoring that she made Des feel like a teenager again. In her youthful eyes he was an invincible successful gladiator, who needed to be feted and soothed at the end of a difficult day – not harangued or ignored by his increasingly absent and ambitious wife. No, Melody indeed soothed him with her solicitous words and her perfect ripe body. She reminded him of how eager to please Kate had been all those years ago, when he had transformed her from that plain little fat girl to a classy slim woman he was proud to have on his arm. Des felt little guilt that he had been cheating on Kate for the past three months with a girl young enough to be his daughter. He felt Kate had brought it all on herself. Des had made it plain that he regarded her choosing to go off on him and have a totally separate life in her career as a callous betrayal.

Melody seemed to totally understand him and she focused herself entirely on his needs. That sexy little body of hers was a bonus of course and he couldn't help but notice the jealous looks he got from other middle-aged businessmen as they spied Melody on his arm while shopping in Grafton Street today.

Melody giggled as she sipped on the champagne and carefully unwrapped the red bow that tied her sexy bodice together. Des laughed and dived onto the massive bed towards his prey. He knew it was getting late but he wasn't in any rush to get home to his cold and frigid wife any time soon.

Kate got to ICU at the Mater in record time, her jeep skimming over the narrow country roads in the inky December blackness. Somehow, thankfully, she got there safely.

Her two brothers were waiting in the triage area, each one looking poorer and more dishevelled than the next. Both Christy Junior and Jimmy had a teenage boy each with them, both of whom had shaved heads and the tracksuit uniform of the underprivileged. Kate spotted a tattoo on one of their necks as she asked Jimmy how their father was. Kate felt all at once guilty and irritated. She knew it wasn't the time or the place but she somehow couldn't help but be shocked each time she saw her siblings and how little they had moved on from their awful background. Didn't they notice how dreary and self-defeating their parents' lives had been? Surely they should have at least tried to escape their fate.

Jimmy told her that it didn't look too good but so far their father was holding his own and the next twenty-four hours would be crucial. Kate saw that he looked a bit old and forlorn and he tried vainly to smooth his unkempt hair while he eyed her expensive jewellery and her real suede full-length coat. Jimmy was two years younger than Kate and had five children by two different mothers. Calvin was the spotty teenager who accompanied his father tonight. Kate wouldn't have recognised him if she had seen him on the street. All she might do would be to pull her bag more tightly to herself, he looked so threatening. She felt horrible for not seeing Jimmy more often, as she loved him dearly, but Jimmy had never worked and saw Kate as being some sort of portable Banklink whenever she did visit.

Also she never knew where to find him. He seemed to live with one or the other of his "girlfriends" intermittently. Her other brother Christy Junior did work as a baker but he still lived close to their parents' house, seemed to spend an inordinate time in the pub with his parents and believed Kate had sold out. Her baby sister Joanne was living in New York. She had escaped much like Kate had and seldom came home to visit.

"Did anyone phone Joanne?" Kate asked Jimmy.

Calvin was busy playing a game on his mobile, while Christy's son Joe was kicking the nearby coke machine.

"Yeah, Mam did," Jimmy replied, "but she's gone off skiing to Colorado or somewhere with her boyfriend and she can't be located. Ye'd think she'd leave a contact telephone number at least."

"She wasn't to know . . ." Kate began and then realised it sounded like a lecture to Jimmy. She had to be very careful what she said to her two brothers who took offence at the least comment. Kate knew they felt she had forgotten her humble beginnings and had swiftly moved on as fast as she could, and she knew that they were right, but they didn't know how essential it was for her to move on away from them. She had to, in order to survive and not let her own children suffer the same childhood she had.

"Might have known you'd take her side," Christy muttered as he walked off to give Joe a clip round the ear for his assault on the coke machine.

Kate swallowed her reply and looked around for a nurse to find out some more valid information on her father.

"Only one person is allowed in at a time," Jimmy explained quietly. "He's not up to visiting. Mam is in there with him now."

Just then a nurse appeared at the nurses' station.

Kate told her she was Christy Cassidy's daughter Kate and asked if there was any news on her father's condition.

The nurse eyed Kate's garb and Kate noted the surprised look that often flickered across people's faces when they discovered she was a part of this family.

"There's been no change, but I'll see if I can get a doctor to talk to you. Your mother is with him now but I'm sure she's due a break soon, so I'll see if I can get you in to visit him then."

So Kate sat in the waiting area with her two brothers and her nephews, feeling like an uncomfortable distant cousin, making small talk and wanting to be anywhere else.

She dearly wished Des were here, angry and all as

she was at him. Eventually her mother emerged in the hallway, looking incredibly small and old. Kate felt her heart fill with love and pity. Her mother seemed bereft; her eyes were red and her hands shook.

"Jimmy, please get Mum a cup of tea, would you? Mum, sit down," Kate dictated.

Josie Cassidy meekly obeyed and sat down slowly. Her gnarled hand reached out and found Kate's.

"He's in a really bad way, Kathleen," her mother said, almost in a whisper. Tears filled her eyes. "He can't talk or move any of his left side and he's on a respirator. The doctor said if he makes it through the next twenty-four hours he might have a chance, but he looks terrible – they don't think he is able to fight it, his body is so weak."

Kate swallowed hard, the realisation hitting her that one of her parents might be about to die.

Jimmy came back with a cup of tea and her mother's hand shook so much she spilled half its contents before she got any to her lips. Jimmy gave Kate a look that said Josie's trembling hands were as much due to alcohol withdrawal as shock.

"Oh, I could do with something stronger," her mother said, right on cue.

Kate ignored the comment. Instead she approached her brothers. "Do either of you want to see Dad again now or will I go in?"

"You go," Christy Junior said. "We'll look after Mam, you go on in. Just don't be too shocked by all the wires and machines. It's a bit scary at first."

Kate smiled at Christy's kind words. "Thanks," she replied and walked with trepidation towards her father's room down the long hallway.

She almost didn't recognise him. Christy Cassidy seemed to have aged ten years overnight and now his thin and undernourished body seemed sunken into the large bed. Tubes and drips were attached to him everywhere, and a large respirator wheezed noisily. But most shockingly were her father's eyes. In them Kate saw real terror. She breathed in deeply so she wouldn't come to tears, then she sat down gently and took his hand in hers.

"It's all right, Dad," she murmured over and over until at last he closed his eyes and seemed to rest. Kate instantly forgave her father for all the bad years of her childhood and neglect and she held his hand gently while repeatedly telling him everything was OK.

After ten minutes she saw he was sleeping and quietly got up and went back outside.

Sadness, intermingled with relief that she was finally at peace with her father, made her suddenly feel exhausted. The registrar was speaking to her mother who appeared confused and Kate knew that she was barely even hearing any of the information he gave her.

She went and stood by her mother and heard the registrar tell her that there was little or no chance of any improvement, and indeed if her father did survive, which was unlikely, he would be severely disabled and unable to speak.

Her mother seemed to wilt under this news and Kate

and Christy Junior led her to a chair where she crumbled into tears. Kate felt a rising panic as she realised that if indeed her father did die, the very thing Kate always fretted over might come to pass. Her mother could hardly survive alone, and who would look after her? She pushed the panic from her mind and tried to focus.

She tried Des's mobile again and this time thankfully the phone was answered.

"Hiya!" Des breezed. It sounded like he was in the car. He sounded happy, exhilarated and totally unlike a wayward husband apologising for being hours late home.

"Where the hell are you?" she tried to hiss quietly.

"Sorry," he laughed, sounding anything but. "Bit of Christmas cheer with clients, I'm afraid, took a lot longer than I thought."

"You could have telephoned!" Kate was close to tears. She was so angry. She was terrified her father was dying and her husband couldn't be even bothered to ring in.

It could have been one of the children in intensive care. "I am in the hospital because my father is seriously ill. Now please get home as quickly as possible to the children. I might be here all night."

She clicked the phone off before Des could reply. Let him stew for a little. She didn't want her brothers to see her having a domestic with her snobbish husband that they already despised. It would only please them and have them commenting on how they knew he had never been any good for her. Her mother hated Des too.

In fact all of her family had never accepted him. That was partly what made him so attractive.

She went to get another cup of tea for herself and her mother. It was going to be a long night.

Melody saw Des scowl and up the speed considerably on the Lexus. She ruffled her fingers slowly through his shiny black hair. "What's the matter, honey?"

Des pulled her hand away abruptly. "Kate's father has taken ill suddenly and she's had to go to the hospital. I've got to get home immediately. I'll drop you off first."

Melody realised that the earlier fun-filled Des had disappeared and Des the husband and devoted family man had replaced him. She infinitely preferred Des her lover to this cold steely Des. Somehow or other, bloody Kate and those damned brats always interfered and took precedence over her. She couldn't seem to win. Oh, he was all right when he was in her bed, bonking her senseless, then he was completely hers, putty in her hands, or legs as it were. But outside of that, she didn't have enough sway over him. But that could be fixed easily. Des always used condoms but Melody was sure she could arrange a pinprick or two. She was determined that now she had Des in her clutches she wasn't ever going to let him go. A baby would see to that. He would always be a part of her life if she had his child.

A plan began to form in her beautiful head, one she would have to keep to herself. Not even Suzie could know she was this calculating. This plan was one that would change her life forever

Chapter 19

Grace got a call from Kate the following morning, telling her that her father had died at seven a.m. in the Mater Hospital from a second massive stroke and that Des was at home looking after the children. Grace wouldn't be needed today after all, but could Kate call on her later, if she needed a baby-sitter or some help with the children?

"Of course, Kate," Grace had replied reassuringly. "Anything you need, just call. I mean that, even if it's just to talk. I'm really sorry about your father, Kate."

Grace's words had brought Kate to tears. Grace felt deeply for her friend, as she knew Kate had a chequered history with her parents. She had told Grace all about their alcoholism and how guilty she felt about her ambivalent feelings. Somehow it seemed to make Kate's loss all the worse, all the guilt that was attached to it.

It made Grace think about her own father and

mother and how dysfunctional her own family was, more now than ever.

Olivia had not returned to Dublin after Moira's bombshell about her father and she had not been in contact with either of her parents since that awful day in Clifden. She had spoken to Grace over the phone and seemed blissfully happy with her new life with her hunky dairy farmer, but yet Grace felt she was living in a fantasy world. She couldn't stay like that forever. Sooner or later she would have to face reality and talk to her mother and find out about her real father. It wasn't really fair to her dad either. He was the innocent party too in all of this and so far he had been left in the dark entirely as to Olivia's reasons for practically disowning the family for the past three months. Christmas was only a few days away now and so far there was no news of Olivia coming home even for a couple of days. Grace would be left to suffer Depression Drive all alone – or even worse having her awful parents to her place for the day, which was a fate worse than death. She shivered involuntarily as she envisaged the terrible scene of herself up to her armpits in stuffing and Brussels sprouts with her mother complaining all the while that she couldn't make gravy for toffee and there was no taste off the turkey – while her father meanwhile got quietly sloshed with Paul and left her to the mercy of her mother's complaints.

It didn't bear thinking about. There was also the matter of Dymphna. She was in a deep depression after the disastrous trip to Limerick that uncovered Mark as the lowest louse that ever crawled God's green Ireland.

And now poor Kate. God, when had life got so complicated? It seemed to Grace that everyone in her life at the moment was in a state of flux: Olivia, her mother, Dymphna and now Kate. Kate with the perfect life, the perfect house, the hunky husband and figure to die for. Kate, whom Grace had envied so much for the past four months – even Kate it seemed had her own heartache. Not to mention Grace's own dilemma. How to please her husband and son at the same time over Jordan's deadbeat father? One thing was for sure, when Christmas was over, if they all ever made it intact to January, there were going to be a lot of secrets uncovered and skeletons unearthed. She was going to London, as she had finally located Samir.

Now she just had to build up the courage to tell Paul.

It had been so easy. As soon as Grace had got back from Limerick she had called British Airways in London and asked to speak to Samir Sala. The receptionist had replied in clipped British tones that Mr Sala was not on duty this week and they were not permitted to release personal phone numbers of staff, but did Madam wish to leave a message? Grace panicked and put the phone down, but at least she knew where Jordan's father was. The difficult part was yet to come.

Dymphna telephoned Mark on his mobile.

"Hiya, babes," she murmured silky in her sexiest tones.

"You sound good," Mark replied, pleased.

221

"I look even better," Dymphna continued, rolling her eyes heavenward – this acting bit was tough. "I'm wearing your favourite outfit."

"Your black dress?"

Mark was drooling, she could tell. "No, silly, nothing. I'm wearing nothing, absolutely nothing at all. I was just wondering if you would like to have dinner here in the flat with me tonight, just you and me, some nice wine and a steak – how does that sound?"

"That's sounds just terrific, Dimps. What time will I come over?"

Dymphna grimaced. "How about eight?"

"No problem. I'll bring the wine, honey. Dying to see you in that outfit!"

"I'll bet you are," Dymphna replied, while curling the phone wire into a nice garrotte knot. "I'll bet you are."

The plan was in place. Tonight Mark was going to get it, and it wouldn't be what he expected.

That evening Dymphna got ready for her special date with Mark. She showered and dressed in her clingy and very sexy black dress that Mark loved, sprayed herself liberally with *Angel* and clambered into her highest killer heels. After she had slicked on her glossy red lipstick and chilled the wine, she carefully set the table, perched her high-domed silver platter in the middle of the table and lit the candles. The scene was set.

Shortly after eight, Mark arrived looking smart and sexy in an Armani shirt. Dymphna's heart gave a little lurch when she caught a whiff of his *Joop* aftershave and he gave her his most winning smile. Then she quickly remembered the winning smile he gave his wife a few days ago and her heart grew hard again. He was going to regret ever cheating on Dymphna, but not for the moment. She was going to make him suffer first.

"You look amazing," he grinned, as his eyes ran over her body, every sexy curve of which was accentuated, thanks to the black dress.

"Told you," she smiled in return, offering her cheek for a kiss and relieving him of the wine he proffered.

"Can't smell anything cooking, Dimps. What are we having?"

"It's a surprise. I changed my mind about the steak. Don't worry – all shall be revealed later. Would you like a glass of wine?"

Mark seemed perplexed but nodded yes and flopped down onto the sofa and flicked on the television. Dymphna was filled with rage but had to swallow her anger. The bloody cheek of him! Lounging about like she was some fifties wife serving him, while he relaxed and watched the box.

She took the remote and flicked off the television. "I haven't seen you in days, honey. You can watch TV later. Now come to the dining-table – your starter is ready."

She led him by the hand to the table where he was suitably impressed by the silverware and the huge platter.

"Looks wonderful – you have made a special effort. I am impressed."

He sat down expectantly and Dymphna quickly refilled his wine glass.

Dymphna placed the large platter in front of Mark, then sat down. She motioned him to lift the lid.

"Please. Go ahead," she purred as Mark quizzically eyed her while slowly lifting the lid.

He stared, gobsmacked.

"Aren't you thrilled?" Dymphna gushed, while flashing her brightest smile.

Mark lifted up a tiny pair of baby's bootees. He had turned a ghostly shade of white.

"Do y-you mean you're telling me you're . . . you're –"

"Yes! I'm pregnant. Isn't it the most amazing news? We're going to be parents! Now you can move in and we can start making plans to be a real family. I am so happy about this Mark, and I knew you'd feel the same way. It's a miracle, that's what it is, and I know you'll be a terrific father!"

Mark tried a wan smile.

Dymphna felt like laughing into his weak little face. She knew he'd be too much of a weasel to be honest about how he really felt. There wasn't a genuine bone in his body, and Dymphna was going to show him what it was like to be lied to and fooled.

But not right now. He hadn't suffered sufficiently.

"Are you sure? I mean, I thought you were on the Pill?" He looked sheepish for even asking the question.

Dymphna smiled again. "I was, but remember those dodgy kebabs Sue served us at the awful barbecue a couple of months ago and we both got sick stomachs? Well, it must have been then, so you can blame your mate Dave's girlfriend, or thank her, really. It was due to her terrible cooking that my pill didn't work."

She watched his face: it was a classic. Mark's

precious Dave and Sue would get short shrift for that one.

He nodded mutely, looking panic-stricken.

Dymphna took his hand and smiled her sweetest smile. "You are happy, aren't you, honey? Because I'd be devastated if you weren't." She saw real fear in his cheating blue eyes.

"Yes," he lied, badly. "Of course I am."

"Good, now call up the Chinese and order us both a feast."

A look of irritation replaced the fear. "I thought you were cooking us both a steak?"

"Can't, I'm afraid. The very smell of meat cooking is making me queasy. It must be morning sickness or all-day sickness or something. I just can't cook, but I can still eat Chinese food. My sister was just the same. Order me some king prawns, will you, Mark – and the duck, yes, I'd love some crispy duck with fried rice. I'm eating for two now!"

Mark flicked open his mobile phone and began dialling dejectedly.

Round one to me, I think, Dymphna sniggered inwardly. This was going to be good. This was going to be very good.

Revenge is a dish best eaten cold.

Kate decided to have the wake for her father at The Beeches. If Des was incredulous he never mentioned it. He was still feeling guilty for being missing the one time that she really needed him.

She sounded out the idea to her mother, gently

explaining that there was little space at the family home and they could fit lots more people in at Kate's large house and Kate would do all the catering.

Her mother nodded agreement absently. She was in another world and Kate felt none of it seemed to have sunk in yet.

She got a call from Christy Junior less than an hour after she had returned home.

"We'll be having no wake in your house, Kathleen. Da loved O'Toole's and that's where we'll be havin' the wake. You can pay for the soup and sandwiches if you feel you must, but there's no way all Da's mates will trudge up to County Meath just so you can show off yer mansion."

Kate was aghast. "I'm sorry, Christy, that was never my intention. I only offered so Mum didn't have to worry about anything and as I have the biggest place –"

"Yeah, yeah," Christy Junior replied belligerently, "we all know you've got the biggest place, the secret mansion in the countryside that we've never even been to. How many times was that man, your father, ever in your house?"

Kate felt tears emerge. Why was her brother attacking her like this? She had known they were resentful but had never realised there was so much bitterness towards her position. "Christy, what do you mean? What is this really about?"

"You tell me," Christy Junior snapped. "You're the one with the problem with O'Toole's and the fact Mam and Da and the rest of us like a few jars. You might forget where you came from, but I don't, and your father was happy living in Kilbarrack and goin' to O'Toole's every day, so you can like it or lump it, that's where the piss-up will be. You don't have to come if it's beneath you."

With that he slammed the phone down.

Kate burst into tears. It was bad enough trying to accept the fact that her father was truly gone and she would never get to tell him how she felt, now she had to endure the obvious disgust of her family for trying to better herself. She had never realised they felt so rejected by her. She felt like calling Des and pouring her heart out to him but she knew he would never understand. She felt so alone and bereft of any support that she sobbed as if her heart would break.

The phone rang again shortly afterwards and Kate almost didn't answer it because she feared it would be her other brother to further berate her, but she picked it up eventually and was relieved to find it was Grace calling to see how she was.

She cried her heart out to Grace despite her best intentions to remain stoic, and within ten minutes Grace was at her door to offer a friendly shoulder to cry on. And Kate gladly availed of it.

Grace was awash with advice and ego-boosting talk after her weekend in the trenches with Dymphna. "Your brother had no right to upset you so much, Kate. He probably feels a bit jealous that you have all this." She looked around at the living-room that wouldn't have been out of place in *House and Garden*. "If I'm really honest I'd have to admit a bit of green eye myself over your life."

"My life?" Kate echoed. She never even envisaged anyone would covet her lifestyle.

Grace looked a bit guilty and a little crestfallen. "Yes, Kate. I have always wanted a life like yours: your glamorous looks, your thin thighs, a luxurious home and plenty of money. You seem to have it all. I have a lovely husband and two lovely kids, but the rest of it seems to elude me. Surely it's not that surprising that people envy you?"

Kate looked shocked. It seemed to have never occurred to her. "I've never thought of myself as being anything special. In fact I'm always trying to fit in and be good enough. Did you know I was a fat child and an even fatter teenager? Not one man ever gave me a second glance until Des took me on and gave me a gym membership as a gift. He was the only man to ever give me a second look and it's thanks to him that I have all of this. None of it was my doing. I just travelled on Des's coat-tails. That's why I am trying to get a career going for myself now. I need to feel I am useful, that I can do something on my own, and ironically it seems to be tearing me and Des apart."

It was Grace's turn to be shocked. She could never imagine Kate even remotely overweight, never mind fat. As for all this talking herself down, making Des out to be a saint! Grace was most surprised that Kate seemed to have low self-esteem and seemed unaware that the mighty Des was a total control freak.

"Kate, you are a beautiful-looking woman. Des simply spotted that and acted on it, he is the lucky one to have you, and didn't you work for him, helping him set up his computer company before the children came along? And what about your worth as a wife and mother? Des can relax and concentrate on his work because he has you here keeping his whole life running smoothly."

Kate sighed heavily. "That's the problem. He says I am never here any more, that I am only interested in my bloody self lately and my 'idiotic dream' of being an interior designer. Things haven't been the same since I took up the course. I sometimes feel like giving it up. It would certainly make my life a lot simpler with Des."

Grace felt her heart fall. Was she soon going to be out of a job, going to be reduced to running back to Pervy Conroy in a low-cut top and begging for her job back? It was a hideous thought. "Kate, I can't begin to know what it is like in your marriage, but surely the past few days has taught you how short life is, and this is something you really want to do. Des will eventually get used to you being more independent, and if he doesn't, well, do you really want him to be telling you what to do for the next thirty years?"

Kate gave a slow smile. "No, of course you are totally right. I just got so used to being at home and putting Des first all the time I never realised I had created a dependent monster. I've never had a close friend before to talk things out with. I relied so much on Des's opinion that I had quite forgotten I had one of my own. I do regard you as a good friend, Grace. And I admire your honesty. I have never told anyone about my parents or my fat past. I felt so ashamed that I've spent the past ten years trying to get away from it. That's probably why I haven't had my family out here very often – it's all such a reminder of how ugly and unhappy I was. You know, they still call me Kathleen and it feels like they are talking about someone else. I haven't been her in years and I never want to be again."

Grace spotted tears in Kate's eyes. She didn't know what to say so she just put her arm around her friend. "I'm happy to be your friend, Kate. Don't ever feel guilty about wanting to better yourself. It sounds like they are the ones with a chip on their shoulders because you have succeeded where they haven't. Go to the bloody wake in the pub and wear your finest clothes. It's not about them anyway. It's about saying goodbye to your father."

Kate sat up straight and began to feel a lot better. She wasn't going to be the inferior person she always had been. That was what this course was all about. Kate needed to be someone who counted to herself and not just Kathleen, the fat daughter who raised her siblings, or Kate the slim glamorous accessory of a wife who hung on every word of the great man and had no mind of her own. She realised for the first time that she had swapped one trap for another. That would have to change. And if Des didn't like the new independent self-assured Kate, then he would have to lump it.

Chapter 20

Grace was meeting Darren for a nice Christmas lunch at the Harbourmaster Bar. She had kept in touch with her skinny mate and had received a mysterious telephone call from him begging her to meet for lunch as he had some juicy scandal to impart. So Grace used a valuable day off to do some Christmas shopping and meet Darren and find out the much-promised salacious information. She missed all the office backstabbing and the hustle and bustle of city life but not enough to endure the three-hour traffic jams it would cost her to return to it. Darren was already waiting with a glass of cool Bailey's for her when she arrived laden with parcels and sore feet. He looked good for Darren, still wafer-thin and much freckled, but in an infectiously happy mood. He gathered Grace up in the nearest thing he could muster to a bear-hug and kissed her check.

"You look really good, Princess – the old country life suits you. I think you've lost weight too."

"Love ya forever, Daz!" Grace replied, thrilled, as she sat down gratefully, falling on her drink like a woman possessed.

It really was great to see him.

"Now spill the beans," she demanded, as she settled in with her bowl of hot soup and sandwich. "I'm dying to hear what's so important."

"I couldn't talk in the office because this is all so top secret, but Pervy Conroy has been suspended without pay and is being investigated for stealing from the company!"

"What!" screeched Grace, in total shock. Amazement just didn't cover it.

"I kid you not," Darren replied, savouring the moment. "The word is, the fraud squad was called in after thousands of pounds worth of foreign currency went missing. It would never have been missed except for the new software package that they installed for the euro."

Grace just couldn't believe what she was hearing. She had always felt Pervy would get his comeuppance one day for his sleazy-eyed ways with his staff, but his pilfering money would never have occurred to her. "All those times he was furious with us for no reason, he must have known his luck was running out, that he was going to be discovered. What an idiot!"

Darren grinned triumphantly. "Who are you telling? He was always so holier than thou, making us feel like imbeciles when all along he was cheating Interfex out of thousands."

"At least I won't have to worry about ever having to work for him again," Grace remarked. "Seeing as there might be a good chance I have to come crawling back looking for my old job."

"I'd love to have ya back, Princess. It's like working in a morgue at the moment, but what's the problem? Is slaving for little Miss Perfect not working out for you?"

"Kate is fine," Grace frowned. "But I feel she's getting cold feet with the study thing. Her husband is acting like a real bastard and she's afraid that he will sabotage the marriage if she continues. It doesn't give me a warm and fuzzy feeling for the New Year. I could be out of a job and searching for another childcare facility for Orla."

"Cheer up," said Darren as he motioned over a waiter for another round of drinks.

"It'll all turn out for the best. Now how is the delectable Dymphna? Still playing hard to get to my obvious charms, or is she still chasing married toads around?"

Grace launched into the sorry tale of the trip to Limerick and Dymphna's subsequent plotted revenge.

"I knew I remembered that name!" said Darren. "Mark McCabe. Yes, that idiot is married to my second cousin! What a total waster. He's got another sprog on the way too."

"I know," replied Grace, suddenly worrying that if Darren knew too much he might spill the beans to Mark's wife and spoil Dimples' plan. "But Dymphna has it all worked out, so you mustn't say anything, Daz, because he is another creep who has to get his just desserts. Don't spoil it for her."

"I won't," assured Darren darkly. "That Carla he is married to is such a cow in anyway – they're perfectly matched, much like me and Dymphna, I suppose."

Poor lamb, Grace thought, he lives a deluded life. Dymphna would joyfully join a nunnery rather than date poor old Darren, but she wasn't about to spoil his dream at Christmas time. So she just gave her skinny friend a hug and hoped someday some woman would spot that he was a lovely person and well worth a second look. She just knew it wouldn't be Dymphna. That was for sure.

Olivia looked at the Christmas card again. It was signed "*Love, Mam and Dad*" whatever that meant. Sean Casey, the man she had always called Dad, wasn't her father but one Seamus Costigan *was*, whoever the hell he was when he was up and dressed.

It had been an absolute shock, like a bad nightmare that wouldn't go away. Everyone seemed to think she should just get over it and somehow put it all behind her and forget that her whole childhood was a complete lie. But how could she? No wonder she had always felt slightly out of kilter, like it all didn't add up. The way her mother had treated her, all those years of trying to please her – it had all been just a guilt trip on her mother's part. And all that fuss with Grace, Moira being so hard on her younger sister – well, that was probably just a cover-up to conceal her stronger feelings for the daughter that belonged to her husband, and not the one who was spawned of a feckless ne'er do well who had abandoned his girlfriend and their unborn child as fast as his legs could carry him.

Olivia had spent countless moments since that fateful day scanning the mirror to see any resemblance she might have to this mysterious biological father. Even though she was thirty-six years old she somehow felt like an abandoned child.

Now Grace was putting pressure on her to go play happy families over Christmas.

She was apparently supposed to sit across from her bloody mother and choke on her turkey while trying not to blurt out to her ex-father that he had been lied to for over thirty years. She just couldn't face the man she had called Dad for all her life and not weep and wail and tell him the awful truth. How could she do that to him? And yet, on the other hand, how could she tell him? It was a great source of sadness that he would be hurt as deeply as she had been by any revelation.

She just couldn't face the family, not yet. Her head still hadn't got around the whole idea of being a product of some sordid little affair that resulted in the huge lie that had become her life. No, she would not travel for Christmas to Grace's no matter what pressure was applied. Moira Casey would have to come clean to Sean before any bread could be broken between them, though she had no idea how her mother was going to do that without ruining her marriage. Olivia could gleefully wring her mother's neck for all the lying and pretending.

Olivia's mind drifted on to James. Wonderful James, she smiled – she just couldn't help but smile when she thought about him. James had been an absolute rock. He was such a strong and gentle man. He was there when Olivia had burst into the pub later on that awful evening that Moira had unleashed her bombshell.

He had held her hand and offered an old-fashioned cotton hankie when she wept and wailed about her misfortune. He didn't offer any advice or meaningless platitudes and she had loved him for that. He had just listened quietly and half carried her back to the guest-house when she was so drunk that she could hardly stand. It was then that Olivia kissed him, wildly and passionately, and as tears sped down her cheeks and splashed onto his, he kissed her back, then gently prised her off him and told her he'd see her the following day, that he didn't want her to do anything she might regret.

Then the following day when she hurt from a king-sized hangover and severe embarrassment in equal measures, he brushed aside her mumbling apologies and took her for a long drive out onto the coast road where the salt air improved her mood and frazzled mind.

"Did you like it?" Olivia had asked suddenly, realising that she must still have a bit of alcohol in her to summon up such courage.

"What?" James slowly smiled, flashing those gorgeous white teeth.

"When I kissed you, did you like it?"

"Yep!" he replied glancing at her, his eyes mischievous.

"One more question," Olivia continued, matching his smile. "Any butterflies?"

"Hundreds," came the reply.

And that was all Olivia needed to know.

That night James McCarthy took Olivia to his large bed and she knew right then that he was the man that she would marry. It was like coming home.

That had been weeks ago, and if it hadn't been for the awful debacle of discovering her parentage Olivia would have been on cloud nine. She still retained a terrible guilt when it came to Connell. She had been so awful to break his heart like that, he hadn't deserved it, but she knew she had done him a favour in the long run. She just didn't handle the whole thing very well. He deserved better and eventually Olivia realised she would have to see Connell and explain herself, but not yet.

No one knew about her and James yet – that was, no one in her former life. Everyone in Clifden just smiled at them both indulgently as they watched the romance unfold. James was a local and had managed to get to his mid-thirties without getting hitched.

One day he had quipped that half of the older women thought for years that he was gay and had mothered him incessantly.

And why didn't you get hitched? screamed Olivia inwardly, the question biting into her tongue, but she dare not ask it. It would be death to a budding relationship.

"I had a serious girlfriend for four years," James said suddenly, as if reading her mind. "Her name was Jane, but she couldn't hack the life up here long term. It had seemed like a great idea to escape the big city and go country, but the reality fell a bit short . . . she eventually went back to Dublin, and then onto London. I just couldn't leave here – you know I'm welded to this place, Olivia."

Olivia felt he was trying to tell her something deeper. "I know, James. I see what you love about this place, there's such a calmness and serenity. I can see myself living here permanently, too."

"You can?" James asked surprised.

"I can," Olivia had smiled.

"Well, that's as much as I can hope for, for now," he had replied, and they had been inseparable ever since.

Now Olivia sat looking out at the moody purple mountains and wondered how she was going to get out of going home for Christmas without making Grace angry or her father suspicious. She didn't give a damn what her mother felt. She could go to hell as far as Olivia was concerned.

Kate buried her father on a crisp sunny December day that seemed oddly out of synch for such an occasion. Des stayed closely by her and they both looked so out of place among the small group of shabbily dressed mourners, none of whom seemed to possess a black garment among them. Even her mother was clad in pale grey and the large group of nieces and nephews were in bright tracksuits and trainers. Des was dressed entirely in black as was Kate and, even though she had worn her plainest outfit, she still looked incredibly overdressed compared to everyone else.

There weren't many people there. It made Kate sad to see this was what her father amounted to, a few stragglers from the local pub and a few relatives. He hadn't worked in over twenty years, so there was no one from a job or any work colleagues. After a short service where the priest never alluded to her father's desperate alcoholism and the congregation pretended to believe the accolades, Christy Cassidy was finally laid to rest at Balgriffen cemetery.

Afterwards, as previously insisted on by her brother, the entourage ended up in the awful O'Toole's pub, where soon a wake ensued with a loud singsong and copious amounts of alcohol. Kate endured it for as long as she could, but as each minute passed and she saw her brothers and her mother consume so much, she felt she had to leave. She knew they would accuse her of being snooty and looking down on them but she just could not be there any more in that shabby pub with the faded brown curtains and the balding velour chairs, in the pall of cigarette smoke, and deify her father as a great man and loving husband and father when they all patently knew it wasn't true. Or perhaps it was – maybe Kate had a skewed view of their childhood. She kissed her mother and arranged a visit before fleeing to the car where she wept silently on the way home. Des tried his best to be supportive but Kate felt totally exhausted and just retreated into herself. At least it was over, now she had to try and move on. She doubted if her mother was capable of being saved at this point, so Kate was going to have to try and save herself.

Chapter 21

Christmas day dawned in the Kelly household. Grace smiled as she watched Orla's large brown eyes crease up with happiness and awe at the Christmas tree and all her new toys. Jordan was excited by his new mobile phone and even Paul seemed a lot cheerier than of late and kissed her warmly when he had opened his gift from her.

Grace tried to be upbeat but the idea of having to endure her mother and father alone (well, not alone exactly but without Olivia to back her up and defend her from the turkey-basting policewoman that was her mother) caused her dread. What made matters worse was that Moira had insisted that they all have dinner at Depression Drive, a fate worse than death and twice as painful, and despite Grace's feeling of foreboding a pleading preliminary phone call from her desperate father had precluded Grace from any excuses. Her father reckoned that Moira was a couple of Valium away from a nervous breakdown because of some silly little row with Olivia so Grace and the family "simply had" to come and spend Christmas day with them. So there it was.

Grace would have dearly loved to be travelling up to Donegal to be with Paul's happy crew and the effervescent Nell who would make every one welcome and relaxed. Relaxed just didn't enter into it when you were dealing with Moira Casey. But, with all the problems going on with Olivia, Grace would have to live up to her name for once and just grin and bear it.

Just then the phone rang. It was Dymphna.

"Merry Crimbo!" she exclaimed, sounding full of life.

"Same to you," smiled Grace. "What's your plan for today? Are things going according to plan with the bould Mark?"

"Right on target," Dymphna giggled. "It's just as well my sister is pregnant with all the baby-grows and teddy bears he's bought me. But he hasn't cracked yet. I reckon it won't come to a head for another while, but I'm enjoying all the irritated looks and painful silences when I convey doctor's orders that we abstain from sex for another few weeks and the possibility of it being twins."

Grace laughed guiltily. "Oh Dymphna! Don't you think that's enough suffering? Put the poor eejit out of his misery and send him back to his wife – how long more are you going to keep this up? After three months you'll run out of time and will be expected to be showing."

"He hasn't suffered enough!" Dymphna replied fiercely. "By the time I get through with Mark McCabe, he'll *never look* at another woman again. He needs to know what it's like to be lied to and cheated on, how humiliating it is to be treated like a fool, and so far I don't think he's feeling totally trapped yet. Wait until I tell him I'm considering quitting my job and moving in with him – now that will really see him running shit-scared back to the lovely Carla in Limerick." She gave a vicious laugh.

Grace had to admire her tenacity.

"And today," Dymphna continued, "today I suffer my three sisters and their insufferable brats, and the kids are even worse! I wish I had anywhere else to go. Mark has gone home to be with his 'parents' or so the fiction goes, but I have him on tenterhooks that he's got to be back by New Year's to face the relatives. How about you?"

"Can't get out of Depression Drive, I'm afraid. So it's Moira and the dreaded dry-turkey drama for us Kellys."

"Why don't you escape from there early and tell your oul' wan that I'm coming over for the evening with my boyfriend and I'll do the same – that way we can both escape the endurance test that's the tea?"

Grace giggled. "That's a great idea, Dimples. And I'm sure Paul will think so too! We'll get out of there by five and see you at six. You can stay over if you like."

"It's a deal," replied Dymphna triumphantly. "At least I can have a few jars in peace. Every time a beer passes my lips bloody Mark gives me a lecture on alcohol. Being fake pregnant is hard work, I can tell you! See ye later. Remember to stay calm today despite all the things that'll drive ye insane, and we'll have a bit of *craic* tonight."

"I promise," replied Grace, hoping she could keep it.

Kate was having a very different kind of Christmas morning over at The Beeches.

She was feeling frazzled as she cooked up a huge fry while her mother sat listlessly chain-smoking in the conservatory, looking totally out of place in her shabby nylon dressing-gown. Des was sulking somewhere upstairs. He was such a selfish person, Kate thought, as she flicked over the sausages. He only ever seemed to have concerns about his own needs and wants. He nearly had a pink fit when Kate informed him her mother was coming to stay for a few days over Christmas.

"How long is she staying?" he had hissed when her mother had fallen over after copious sweet sherries before six o'clock on Christmas Eve and had to be put to bed.

"She has just lost her husband!" Kate had hissed back defiantly.

Kate railed at Des's callousness. She knew her mother was a liability and scared the girls with her drunken lurching about and her raspy voice, but she knew Josie needed her at the moment. Des seemed to resent Kate's relationship with her family, however tenuous. It seemed she was supposed to recover from the death of her father in a matter of days, yet when Des's father passed away suddenly a few years ago, Kate had supported and carried Des through six months of the deepest depression that she had ever witnessed. It was a shame Des couldn't do the same for Kate – it hardened her heart against him a little.

So she cooked a fry-up almost to spite him, for she knew he would be counting the calories she consumed and it would irk him to see her stuff down all that fatty food, but he could suffer it for today. She just hoped he would have some Christmas cheer and not be truculent in front of her mother, because she knew any sniff of discord between them would be multiplied by her mother, then embroidered and talked about to her cronies in O'Toole's to prove that all was not well up at the mansion and she just knew it would never last.

Kate's cheeks burned with stress and the heat of the stove and she silently prayed that she could get through the next few days and fall apart later.

Des meanwhile, was lying on his bed reading a sexy text message from Melody.

It had been an inspired idea, mentioning to Kate that he intended to go for a long run after the heavy Christmas dinner. He was jogging all right, all the way to Hog's Lane and an assignation with the delectable Melody. He would need several hits of her sexy little body if he was going to get through the next few awful days with Kate's deranged and alcohol-sodden mother. He just couldn't wait until she took her filthy cigarettes and grotty carcass back to her little hovel in Dublin. He hated to be in the company of any of Kate's relatives because it reminded him of where she had come from and slivers of doubt about her crossed his mind still, even after twelve years together. While they were out of the picture she could be his perfect wife, but after a few days with her crone of a mother, he did have to wonder. That's why Melody made such a refreshing change. To her Des was omnipotent instead of impotent, which is what he was increasingly feeling in his marriage. This affair with Melody made him feel so alive again. He was getting quite fond of living on the edge. His phone beeped and another text arrived that was so raunchy it made him blush to his roots. He couldn't wait for this afternoon – he hadn't had sex outdoors for years and was really looking forward to shagging Melody senseless among the haystacks in Corcoran's barn.

Paul meanwhile, was watching Orla playing happily with her dolls and Grace smiling as she showed Jordan how to use his new mobile phone. His heart ached when he looked around the room. Everything he ever wanted was right here and although things seemed to be perfect on the surface, he couldn't help wondering if next Christmas they would all be here, still together and happy. He could never tell Grace about that sinking jealous feeling that came over him whenever he so much as thought about Jordan (who was *his* son in his heart) and Grace seeing that useless bloody flier again. Paul just felt deep down Grace would fall for him all over again and Jordan would encourage her all the way and before he knew where he was, their lovely little family would be broken up. He had always wondered if Grace harboured a secret passion for the Arab. She never discussed him, but somehow Paul always felt there was unfinished business there and he worried about what that was. Soon he would find out. But he would never let Grace know what his fears were. It might make her feel even less for him.

So he smiled and would do his best to enjoy this time with his little family before outside influences might destroy it forever. If Grace only knew how much his heart ached with love for her and Jordan she would never take this family reunion stuff any further. But he wanted her to decide for herself, without any more pressure.

He dreaded the next few months. He just didn't feel he was good enough to keep her. He lifted little Orla onto his lap and cuddled her tightly. Suddenly Grace looked over and smiled at him. He almost said something then but Orla tugged at his hair and suddenly the moment was lost. He would never get up the courage again to tell Grace how he felt. Now he would just have to wait and see what the new year would bring.

Mark McCabe was staring at his bedroom ceiling feeling panicky. In the distance he could hear his wife

Carla singing Christmas carols to little Sean in his room. What an idiot he was! He had everything – a wife who loved him, a wonderful son and another baby on the way. But had he been happy with that? No, he had to get smug and greedy and now he was in deep trouble. Trouble that could, no, *would* definitely cost him his marriage. How was he going to explain to Carla that he had a girlfriend and another child on the way? And how was he going to support two families on what he made? Oh, he *liked* Dymphna well enough – it had been fun at first, he was the envy of his mates, all that attention and excitement – but now he felt well and truly trapped and at last understood what karma meant and that stupid saying that all your chickens would come home to roost.

And he hadn't the faintest clue how he was going to extricate himself from this mess. It was an absolute fucking disaster that was for sure.

Chapter 22

Christmas hadn't been so bad after all. Grace had endured a heavy lunch with her parents, heavy both in food and mood, as her mother who was suffering from missing Olivia and feeling the weight of her secret bear down, was obviously depressed. She tried to be cheery in front of the children but Grace knew the red face and martyred look well.

At least she escaped early and got to spend the evening with Paul and Dymphna, where they had lots of fun and Irish coffees. Dymphna had both Paul and Grace in knots of laughter with tales of her own debacle of a dinner with her parents. Grace remarked it was amazing that they had ever survived their childhoods with the amount of dysfunction that seemed to linger around their part of Raheny.

Grace wondered how Olivia was getting on up in Clifden. It was New Year's Eve tomorrow and she would have liked to have at least seen her for one night. She'd give her a ring later and see how she was. She knew Olivia wasn't quite ready to confront her mother but she couldn't hide away in the wilds of the west forever. She had to come back sometime, and face it all, even if it was only to collect her things and at least see her mother and father – well, the only father she had ever known.

Her thoughts drifted on to Dymphna. She was going to see Mark McCabe tonight and make him suffer a meeting with her parents.

"If that doesn't put him off cheating forever, nothing will!" she had quipped. After that she would finally admit her deception and pack him off to his poor unsuspecting wife with a blistering lecture and the vow that if she so much as sniffed a rumour that he was playing around again she'd be on the train to Limerick to spill the beans. Grace would love to be a fly on the wall for that confrontation but she guessed she would have to do with Dymphna's blow-by-blow account later.

Dymphna was getting ready for her date with Mark. She couldn't wait to see the look on his face when he was forced to sit through two hours of her mother's frosty looks, her father's boring stories about things being better back in the seventies or even the bloody fifties when he'd got an orange for Christmas and was happy with it. She'd make him endure salty elderly ham sandwiches and watch him squirm as her father interrogated him about his prospects. She had to endure her awful parents all the time so surely he could suffer them for a few hours. She'd have to warn him on pain of death not to mention under any circumstances her pregnancy, because that would require too much explaining later on to her mother.

She loved her parents really, she thought, as she put the finishing touches to her make-up. They were sweet, really, if from another planet most of the time. But right now, she hoped Mark would hate them on sight – it would make his suffering all the more enjoyable. Part of her felt she would like to drag on his misery for a few more months, but she knew that poor cow Carla was due in a few weeks and she didn't want the poor girl to go into premature labour if the errant Mark decided to come clean. So tonight he would get his marching orders.

She felt in some way also a little bit sad, because even though Mark was a shit and had cheated on her so badly and she hated his guts, she didn't exactly relish the thought of being alone every night all over again. She never admitted it to anyone, even Grace, but the idea of the loneliness that would follow his departure was too depressing to contemplate. Back to dinners for one and all that silence. It would be almost unbearable. But she would get used to it, she supposed.

When Mark arrived, Dymphna almost lost her nerve. He looked haunted, as if he hadn't slept in days. Large dark circles dominated his eyes and he seemed jittery. But then Dymphna thought of all the deception and the fact that he had probably spent Christmas in the loving bosom of his poor unsuspecting wife and she became adamant again.

"Are you nervous?" she asked him while they were in the car.

"A bit . . ." he replied quietly.

"Don't worry, they'll love you just as much as I do, sweetie." She smiled widely, "Soon you'll be just like part of the family."

She could see him wilt after that comment, and they drove the rest of the way to Raheny in silence.

The evening lived up to Dymphna's high hopes in its awfulness.

Her father, for some reason, took an instant dislike to Mark and interrogated him in a way that would have made the Gestapo proud. Her mother on the other hand, was fawning and fussed about incessantly and practically stuffed Mark senseless with Christmas leftovers. Mark sat uncomfortably, sandwiched between both her parents and the marmalade cat, which seemed to fall instantly in love and made her bed on his lap. The best part was when her father gave Mark a lecture on the men of today who seemed to prefer just ruining girls' reputations instead of marrying them.

Mark was a nice shade of pale green by the time the night groaned to its predictable end (her mother proffering Christmas cake and pudding for his mother, and her father hinting none too subtly that he hoped Mark was going to just kiss Dymphna chastely at her door) and Dymphna had to bite her lip to prevent herself from laughing wildly into his face.

"Well, that went better than expected," Dymphna breezed, as they pulled away.

"You reckon?" Mark replied waspishly. Obviously the pressure was getting to him.

"Well, you'd better get bloody used to them!" Dymphna spat. "They are going to be your baby's grandparents, after all."

Mark groaned audibly. "I just can't do this, Dimples. I can't lie any more. I've something to tell you, something serious."

"What? That you're still married to the lovely Carla and you've been stringing me along all this time – or that you can't be a father to *our* baby?"

She stopped the car at the traffic-lights and stole a look at him. He was opening his mouth and shutting it like a demented fish. That mighty gob was shocked into silence for once.

"Well, nothing to say, Mark? I always thought you had an answer for everything."

She looked over again. Oh shit, he was actually crying!

"I'm such an idiot, I never meant any of this to happen . . ."

"I don't suppose you did," Dymphna replied icily. "You just thought I could be your little piece on the side, your midweek bit of sex, as it were, nothing too serious, just a bit of fun for you and all your mates to gloat over, then you swan down to Limerick for the weekend playing happy families. Tell me this much, Mark, were Dave and Sue in on it too? Were they also laughing at poor stupid Dymphna?"

Mark nodded.

They had known all along. No wonder that smart bitch Sue was so smug when she met Dymphna – she must have felt so superior. Mark deserved everything Dymphna had done to him and more.

"I am so sorry, I can't go on with this. I can't move in with you or be your partner, Dimples, I just can't."

"Yes, you'll be rather busy, won't you? What with being up to your arse in nappies with your wife's new baby!"

Mark looked as if he had been slapped. "You know everything?"

Dymphna smiled slowly. "Yes, I do. I've been to your house in Limerick, I even saw you with her. I could have boiled a bunny in your kitchen, if I had wanted to, and I could have told Carla, the poor silly cow, but I didn't want her to go into early labour. You're a bloody twit, Mark McCabe, for not appreciating what you have and for almost losing it. As it is you've lost me anyway – you lost me weeks ago. It's over and I never ever want to see you again."

Mark looked relieved and aghast in equal amounts. She could see the wheels turning in his duplicitous little mind. He was half overjoyed but worried about the phantom baby. "But, what about the baby? Can I see it when it's born?"

"There is no baby, Mark. I just thought *you* might like to see what it's like to be fooled and deceived, for a change. So, you're off the hook."

Mark's face contorted into an angry scowl. "You fucking bitch!"

"Careful," Dymphna smiled sweetly. Venomously. "You don't want to get me upset, Mark. I might decide to go down to Limerick for a few days after all. I'm sure Carla would be very interested in what I had to say. Just thank your lucky stars that you got off as lightly as you did. Now piss off out of my life, you creep! Get out right now, I never want to see you again."

Mark looked her incredulously. "What, here?"

Dymphna looked out at the steady rain that was now turning into a deluge. "Yes, right here. A nice long walk home – it's about five miles – somehow concentrates the mind, I always think."

He got out of the car and pulled up his collar ineffectually against the elements.

Dypmnha gave a parting shot. "And one more thing, sweetie. If I ever hear of you even sniffing around this side of the Liffey again, I'll be down to the Shannon to tell Carla before you can say Irish Coffee. Just remember that, you creep!"

She slammed the car door shut and sped off, hooting her horn triumphantly.

That horrible chapter of her life was over and she hoped that the New Year would bring a better bit of luck for her.

She turned on her tape of Gloria Gaynor and played 'I Will Survive' at top volume all the way home.

Survive and thrive she would, she would make sure of it.

Chapter 23

Kate was having lunch with Des's mother Lucinda at the Shelbourne Hotel. They had stomped all over Grafton Street for the sales and were now exhausted.

Lucinda Green had been a top model in London in the sixties when she had met George Heathcoat, Des's father, who had been a successful older businessman.

George had fallen for Lucinda's elegant beauty. She had resembled Audrey Hepburn and even now she still had a timeless elegance and beauty that belied her sixty-eight years. Kate was still spellbound by her now as she sat poised and immaculate and as slim as ever, completely comfortable in the luxurious surroundings of the grand old hotel.

"Darling you're a little pale, have you had a beastly time of it, losing your father so close to Christmas?"

Kate nodded. She didn't trust herself to talk about Christy yet, it was still too raw, but she did want to discuss Des with his mother. Perhaps she could give an insight into why Des was acting so distant and cold. Even the death of her father hadn't really warmed him to her and she felt suddenly adrift.

"Can I ask you something, Lucinda, about Des?"

Lucinda smiled and tossed her elegant grey bob as she cut her scone and buttered it thinly. "Of course, Kate, anything."

Kate related the tale of Des's change in attitude over the past few months.

Lucinda's face appeared to darken as she told her the sorry story of all the late nights when Des appeared distant and icy, and the lack of interest in her or the children.

"He does sound incredibly spoilt, my dear, but then he always has been. He is incredibly like his father. Did Des ever tell you about George?"

Kate looked at Lucinda blankly.

"What?" Lucinda was amazed. "I can't believe after all these years he has never told you! Oh, Des. He always did lionise his father. Well, I will tell you. The truth of the matter is that when George died, I was about to leave him. If he hadn't dropped dead of a heart attack we'd have been divorced. He actually had the heart attack in a hotel with his mistress and she took him to hospital. I had to meet them there."

Kate was aghast. "Oh Lucinda, I had no idea. How awful for you! Did Des know?"

Lucinda smiled grimly. "Yes, he found out years ago. He would have been about fifteen. He blamed me.

He said if I hadn't been so busy and given his father more attention he might never have strayed. The poor kid, I'd been a stay-at-home mum for years, and it never made a blind bit of difference to George. He had been cheating ever since I had the children and no longer could devote myself entirely to his wants and needs. He had several mistresses during our marriage. I had known for years, but I wanted to wait until Des and Lucy grew up before I left him. But when he met Linda, his last mistress, he fell in love with her and I felt like a bit of used tissue, simply cast aside. By then I had enough. I had already filed for a divorce when he died. Des looked on it like it was another form of betrayal. Somehow it never occurred to him that I had been betrayed for years. Des is very black and white, as I'm sure you are aware, Kate. He only sees his own side of things."

Kate laughed hollowly. "Yes, I'm beginning to see that."

Lucinda grabbed Kate's wrist. "Just be careful," she warned in a strained voice. "The apple doesn't fall too far from the tree. Make sure that Des doesn't do to you what George did to me."

Kate felt a sudden chill cross her. "Lucinda, my husband is not the same as yours. Des loves me!" She sounded a bit hysterical, even to herself.

Lucinda regarded her carefully. "Yes, of course he does. Don't mind me, Kate. I'm just an embittered old widow. I'm sure Des is just fine. Don't let me worry you."

Kate smiled wanly. She felt something was amiss in her marriage but she didn't really want to entertain any of the awful ideas that Lucinda had put into her head. She had enough to cope with at the moment – beginning to suspect her husband just wasn't an option.

But all the way home she felt uneasy. Was she just burying her head deep into the sand and not wanting to see what was happening to her marriage? Was Des really like George? Her mind raced all the way home, where Grace was looking after the girls. She hoped Grace was in the mood for a talk because she felt so muddled she needed to chat to her friend and see if she was just being histrionic or if she needed to confront Des and see what the real problem was.

Either way she wasn't looking forward to that confrontation when and if it happened.

What she really wanted was Grace to tell her she was being silly and not to listen to her mother-in-law, but she knew Grace was legendary for her straight talking and she would tell Kate exactly how she saw it.

Grace was finger-painting with the girls in the conservatory when Kate got home. They all seemed so happy and cosy she was reluctant to break up the scene. She would talk to Grace another time, but for the moment she would watch Des a bit more closely and try and keep track of his whereabouts. She had been far too trusting and naive in the past, and that would have to change.

Chapter 24

3 months later . . .

Kate was on her way home from college. It had been an interesting and stimulating lecture, where they had studied the architecture of the Georgian era. Rather than go through a boring dry lecture, their tutor had taken them around a Georgian house in Fitzwilliam Square so that could see it properly for themselves and make comments. Kate was really enjoying the course and Tom Carter the tutor, was extremely enthusiastic about interior design and his enthusiasm was infectious. The fact that he was handsome helped also and every woman in the class thought he was gorgeous.

She blared her favourite Coldplay CD all the way home, the watery spring sunshine giving a glimpse of the summer to come. She was pondering what she'd cook the girls for dinner. She always felt like spoiling them when she had spent a bit of time away at college, so she generally cooked a treat for them that evening.

As she pulled the jeep into the gravel driveway, she spotted Barbara Tormey's battered little Volkswagen outside the house. That was a bit odd, she thought. She hoped fleetingly that nothing had happened to Grace or one of the children and Barbara called upon to baby-sit.

She hurried inside. She heard Grace's melodic voice wafting from the kitchen and by its tone she seemed calm enough.

Barbara and Melody Tormey and Grace, having coffee on the large chintz sofa in the lounge area. Beyond them, in the conservatory, were Kate's girls having their own little tea party with little Orla.

Grace jumped up and announced too cheerily, "Kate, you're home. We have visitors. Would you like me to get you a coffee?"

Kate nodded blankly and followed Grace into the kitchen area. Grace hissed quietly, "They have been here for over an hour and I can't get anything out of them. They just kept saying that they wanted to see you and just wouldn't go away, despite me trying to get them to come back later."

Kate felt somewhat nonplussed. "It's OK – you get off home and I'll sort it out," she said nonchalantly, her heart sinking with every possible scenario that flew through her mind.

Grace gathered up her possessions and went to fetch Orla.

Kate hurried back to where Barbara and Melody

Tormey sat silently, with stone faces. "I'll just see Grace out," Kate said brightly.

They barely nodded a response.

Kate and Grace carrying a protesting Orla walked quickly to the door.

"I'm sorry about this, Kate. I'm sure you're exhausted and don't need visitors at this hour, but they wouldn't go." Grace put her into her little car seat.

"It's fine, Grace. It's not your fault. Did they say anything at all?"

"Well, not really. They had words between them and Barbara seems very cross with Melody but other than that they were like a pair of cranky oul' nuns."

Kate grimaced. "Right, I'd better go face the music."

She slowly went back inside, her heart beating wildly. Whatever it was, it apparently wasn't going to be pretty.

Barbara was perched stiffly on the couch, staring blankly out the window, while Melody was sitting on the floor in the conservatory playing with the girls. Kate looked at her and thought briefly how childlike she still was in lots of ways.

"Now, Barbara," she breezed, sitting down on the sofa beside her, "what can I do for you?"

"Melody, get over here!" Barbara barked at her daughter.

Melody sulkily got up and slouched over. She sat on another chair a few feet away and chewed industriously on her bubble gum while staring obliquely at her fingernails.

"Kate, we are here because I have reason to believe

that my Melody is pregnant and she insists that your husband Des is the father!"

Kate's blood ran cold.

She felt at once that she was outside herself watching some kind of weird play. Yet at the same time it all felt too real and somehow right, as if she had been waiting for this to happen – which of course she hadn't been.

Finally she found a word. *"What?"*

She looked askance at Melody, looking for some sign of regret or shame or even sadness, but all she saw in Melody's small smirk was defiance.

"He doesn't *love* you any more," scowled Melody, her tone matching her defiant look.

Kate had to muster all her dignity not to fly at this teenage slip of a girl and slap her smug face good and hard.

"Melody Tormey!" Barbara roared, her already red cheeks reddening even further.

"Don't you think you have done enough damage already, young lady? Now be quiet and only speak when you are spoken to!"

Melody stared angrily out of the window and rolled her eyes heavenwards.

"I am sorry, Kate," Barbara continued in a more conciliatory tone. "None of this is your fault, but I believe that your husband has a lot to answer for. Melody is after all young enough to be his daughter and Des should know better. It's an absolute disgrace so it is. She tells me that she's in love with him and he loves her. She seems to think this is rather more than what it appears to be to me, a sordid little fling with an older married man who corrupted an innocent teenager. Melody says it's been going on for months . . ."

"Months?" Kate echoed dimly. This just could not be true.

"Yes, months," Barbara confirmed querulously. "But I want to hear it from him, Des bloody Heathcoat. So, after she told me I confiscated her mobile phone so she couldn't warn him off. That is why I am here and I'm staying until he gets home, so he can explain it. Just be thankful it's me and not Mr Tormey. When *he* finds out, he's liable to take your husband's block off."

Kate heard herself saying, "Are you sure it's Des's?" She looked at Melody.

Melody's triumphant look told her all she needed to know. "I just knew you'd ask that. You are so predictable Kate! Yes, as a matter of fact, I am *perfectly* sure. We've done it hundreds of times, everywhere. Do you want to know actual times and dates? I told my mam and I'm telling you: Des loves me and he wants to be with me and now that I'm havin' his baby, he's definitely going to leave you, Kate. You don't treat him right in any way, otherwise why would he come to me?"

Kate felt tears of shame prick her eyes. How could this teenager say these hard hurtful things to her unless her husband had made her feel important enough to do so. She wanted to scream and rant and rave and throw them both out this minute but she glanced over at her little children, oblivious to all that was unfolding, and felt that for their sakes she must remain calm.

She stood up. "I am going to call Grace and ask her to take the girls over to her place and then I am going to call my husband and get him home. I, too, am anxious to hear him explain himself." She walked purposefully from the room into the hallway, although her legs felt like jelly and her hands were shaking so hard she could barely lift the phone.

As soon as she heard Grace's voice she began to cry. "Grace, can you come and take the girls?" she managed to say. "I'll – I'll explain when you come."

"I'll be right over," Grace said immediately.

Then Kate composed herself before she dialled Des's mobile.

"Hi, Kate!" he breezed. "I'm just at Kentstown Cross, I'll be there in ten minutes."

She couldn't even reply so she just put down the phone. She steeled herself before going back into the room.

"Please don't discuss this any further until the girls have left," she warned Barbara and Melody sharply. She told the girls to get their coats and she fussed about with them in the hall until Grace arrived. Tears were sliding down her face and she wiped them away immediately but Chloe noticed and kept asking her what was wrong.

"I've just had some bad news, that's all, darling. Now Grace is going to take you over to her place for tea while I chat to Melody and her mum. You'll both be good girls, won't you?"

"Yeah!" they both chorused, delighted at the idea of having tea with Orla.

Grace arrived and Kate burst into fresh tears when

she saw her. Grace quickly got the girls into the car and then went back into the hallway to see to Kate.

"Are you OK, Kate? What is it?"

Kate flew into her arms. "Oh Grace, it's just too awful for words. That little bitch in there has just told me she's having an affair with Des and she's pregnant by him. I am so devastated! I just can't let the girls see me like this. He is on his way home now and they seem dead set on a showdown. Can you take the kids for a while?"

Grace's heart went out to her friend. As if she hadn't been through enough lately.

"Of course I can. I can take them overnight if you want. Just give me a call later on. If I don't hear from you by about nine, I'll put them to bed. Try not to worry, Kate – perhaps it's not as bad as it seems."

Grace felt a bit of a hypocrite for saying that. Of course it was as bad as it seemed – it was so much worse than that, but what else could she say? I knew your husband was a complete shit almost as soon as I met him and this was bound to happen?

She gave Kate a big hug and drove off with Kate's chattering children and a heavy heart. Whatever was about to transpire back at The Beeches, nothing would ever be the same again.

Ten minutes later Des Heathcoat strolled into his kitchen looking debonair in a pinstripe shirt and a new Louis Copeland suit, wondering a bit uneasily why Barbara Tormey's VW was parked outside, and stopped dead in his tracks. What greeted him was the spectacle of three furious women sitting like broken statues scattered around the room.

As soon as Kate saw his shocked reaction she knew all of it to be true. He just seemed to wilt and he dropped his briefcase onto the floor, then leaned on the kitchen counter and looked at Kate beseechingly.

"Kate . . ." he said. Nothing more seemed to be able to come out.

Melody got up and walked to him. She took his hand and held it to her face. It was a poignant scene, Kate thought, if it hadn't been someone else's husband. Her husband.

"I've told her, Des, I've told her you don't love her any more. And I've got some news to tell you. I wanted to tell you this in private but my mother discovered it today and all hell has broken loose. I know we hadn't planned it yet but I'm having your baby Des, *our* baby."

Des took his hand away from her face slowly – tenderly, it seemed to Kate – and he then looked at Kate and Barbara Tormey who had jumped to her feet and tried to pull her daughter away from him, as if somehow by physically separating them she could undo the damage. But the damage had already been done.

"Is it true?" Kate asked softly.

She was asking Des if what Melody had said was true. She knew by his reaction that the affair had happened and Melody was probably carrying his child, but she needed to know if Des no longer loved her as Melody had so brazenly bragged.

"Yes," Des replied quite casually, as if Kate had just asked him if he wanted steak for dinner.

"*All* of it?" Kate now asked, an edge of hysteria creeping into her voice. "Including the part about you not loving me any more?"

Des looked at the Italian tiles on the floor. "You've changed, Kate. Melody loves me and wants me, she's given me what you obviously can't or rather won't lately – so yes, I love you but I'm not *in* love with you any more."

Kate felt as if someone had just stabbed her in the heart, the deep physical pain that gripped her in the chest stopped her breath. It was some kind of sick nightmare. She felt her head swim and thought for a moment she was going to faint, but that feeling faded as she saw Barbara Tormey pick up Des's briefcase and started hitting him about the head with it. Kate felt like joining in and tearing both Des and Melody limb from limb, but now Melody seemed to be pulling her mother off Des who had shielded himself somewhat pathetically with his arms.

"You bastard!" Barbara Tormey roared. "She's my little girl, not even out of her teens, and you've bloody ruined her life. You're old enough to be her father! You're perverted! You disgust me!"

Melody succeeded in grabbing the briefcase from Barbara. "Mam, would you just calm down? We love each other. It's not Des's fault. We want to be together and we will – you're not going to stop me!"

Kate somehow gathered herself together and stood

up. She walked over to Des and Melody and took a deep breath.

"Well," she said icily, staring Des down, "if you want to be together, I suppose now is as good a time as any. No time like the present. You can start right now. Go and pack, Des. As far as I'm concerned you are welcome to one another."

Des seemed to flinch for a moment.

Kate hoped deep inside her soul that he would say that this wasn't what he wanted and all he really wanted was her. Then she could have some hope, some dignity. But he didn't. He was lost to her and fighting to keep him would only cause her more pain.

"I see what you mean, Des," Melody quipped gleefully. "She *is* a cold bitch."

That was it.

Kate slapped Melody hard on the face and then turned to Des. "I don't expect you to be here when I get back."

Before he could answer she walked away. Out of the room, out of the house of her dreams and out of her dream but obviously fake marriage.

Her heart was broken, and she had never felt so scared in her entire life.

Chapter 25

The next few days passed in a blur. Grace looked after Kate and the girls because Kate was barely capable of getting out of bed. Only the first few seconds after she woke felt normal, until she remembered what had transpired and then the dark mist of depression would swiftly fall and she would weep until there were no more tears.

"After this you'll get angry," Grace assured her, "and when the anger comes you will start to hate him but you will feel a bit better."

All Kate felt at the moment was crushed. She kept reliving that awful evening like a terrible video, with Melody smirking and totally confident that Des would choose her and being right! That was the worst part – she had lost a husband of ten years to a teenager, barely out of school. It had shattered her self-esteem. She didn't tell Grace, but she ached for Des. If he had lifted the phone and begged forgiveness she would have had him back immediately. They could try counselling, they would have worked it out – but there had been nothing. There hadn't been even one phone call to see how the girls were and that had shocked Kate to the core – how easily and comfortably Des had moved on. She had been cast off like an old boot. And what about the children, didn't he even miss them?

She would have to call Lucinda and tell her about Des but not yet. She couldn't bear to admit it to anyone. No one knew yet except Grace. Grace and bloody Barbara Tormey, which meant half of the village probably knew all about it by now. Kate felt so ashamed.

Eventually Grace forced her to get up. "Come on, now, the girls need you. They will be asking questions about their daddy sooner or later but it'll be sooner if they guess that you're upset. What you need is a nice long bath and then I'll take you for a long drive out to Howth along the coast road. You can get a bit of wind in your hair and I promise you, you will feel better."

Kate had thought Grace was crazy but she went along with it and had a long soak and an even longer cry before she dressed up warmly in her velvet tracksuit and long sheepskin coat then clambered into the jeep. Grace sped them along the coast road towards Howth. The three of them had ice cream at Maud's on little Orla's insistence and then walked along the coast wall. Grace simply listened as Kate railed and ranted about Des and what a pig he had been and suddenly Kate felt a little bit better, as if she was still alive, which is what she hadn't felt since Des had left and she was thankful to Grace for being there and being such a good friend.

"You need to meet Dymphna – she has a degree in hating men at the moment. Why don't I arrange a girl's night out for us soon. You'd love Dimples and you really need cheering up."

Kate gave a grim smile. "Right, I suppose I do. Anyhow, if I'm not up to socialising I would still love to meet her. She sounds totally amazing and from what you've told me I just know I'd like her."

"You should also see a solicitor soon. You may need one to sort out the finances."

"Do you think so?" Kate looked alarmed.

Grace faltered. Kate had no idea how awful this might yet get. "Well, perhaps you won't need one if Des plays fair, but it wouldn't do any harm to get some advice on your options. Des is the sole earner after all and you have no other means of support."

Kate looked stricken. She had been so completely devastated about Des's betrayal, she had totally forgotten that Des provided everything for her and their children. Even her course and Grace's wages depended on Des. If he decided to be difficult everything could change and things could get infinitely worse. She could even lose her beloved home. Kate had been Des's backbone and the primary carer of their children but she hadn't earned any money in years and she could never earn enough to cover the household expenses and Grace's wages. It would all be different, very different. Bloody Melody could end up living in The Beeches. Suddenly her prospects looked a lot worse than just a broken heart.

She hoped Des would call soon and at least she could find out what his plans were.

She decided that she would call Lucinda as soon as she got home and tell her what happened. At least Lucinda would have a direct line to Des and Kate knew she would be on her side. She would make sure Des knew he had to be decent after all his terrible behaviour.

Kate suddenly felt worse than she had when Des admitted his affair with Melody and she hadn't believed she could ever feel worse than that. But now she felt as insecure as she had when she had been that fat unloved little girl – she felt like Kathleen again. Somehow she had to get past this and make herself financially independent and secure. She owed it to herself and she owed it to her little girls. She wasn't going to crumble, for their sake and for herself. Somehow she would have to get past this. Now she was alone and suddenly she had to face the fact she would have to become independent and responsible and it terrified her.

Grace got home late that evening to find Paul peeling the spuds and Jordan quietly doing his homework.

"Am I in the right house?" Grace quipped as she put little Orla down. She was tired and worried about her job but it cheered her up no end to see the lads trying to pitch in and help.

"I figured you could do with a wee hand, love," Paul

smiled. "You've a fair bit on your plate so you have. Me and Jordan are going to cook dinner, so you put your feet up. It'll be another twenty minutes or so. How is Kate?"

Grace sighed heavily. "Oh, she's bearing up, but she doesn't have the first clue about what this all could mean. She was totally stunned when I mentioned solicitors and the fact that things won't be the same as before, especially in the area of money. I don't think the reality of the situation has sunk in yet."

It was Paul's turn to sigh. "It's not good, is it? We could do without the worry of it."

"Who are ye telling?" Grace replied. "I never expected this. I know you had doubts about me doing this job, but it was going so well. I just can't imagine having to go back to that madhouse that's the city – and where am I going to find a new crèche for Orla so soon?"

Paul came over to Grace and gave her a hug. "Look, it's not that bad yet. Sure, you might get a local job if Kate's situation gets worse. Let's not get carried away too soon – we'll cross all those bridges when we get there. We should just be glad we're not in their particular boat – money didn't seem to do them much good."

He was right, Grace thought. She and Paul might have their problems but at least deep down they had an abiding love to get them through. That was worth all of Des Heathcoat's money and more. For the first time in ages Grace felt lucky and incredibly satisfied. Whatever problems she and Paul had to overcome with Jordan's natural father and their re-uniting, she felt sure that in the end they would all be fine and more importantly still together.

She regarded him seriously. "I do love you, y'know, Paul Kelly," she said kissing his nose.

"I know. Me too. Now get in there and put your feet up while you have the chance, I'll call you when dinner is ready."

Grace did as she was bid, flopped onto the couch and flicked through the channels to find some evening news. Just then the phone trilled.

"Grace, it's me," barked her father.

It never rained but it poured.

"Yes, Dad what is it?"

It had to be something awful – he never ever phoned with good news. "It's your mother, she was in hospital today with chest pains. Honestly, I thought she was at death's door, I can tell you. Doctor Davis thought she was having a mild heart attack so we spent all the day in the Mater with her hooked up to machines and what have ye . . ."

"Why didn't you ring me?" asked Grace, alarmed. "Is she OK? Where is she now?"

"She's fine. She's at home now under bed-rest orders, and I *did* call – I've been ringing your house all day, no answer – you'd better get one of them mobiles, we can never get you in a crisis."

Grace rolled her eyes upwards. She never got away without a lecture no matter what had transpired. "And what did the doctors say?"

"They said it was a classic panic attack. They said your mother must be under severe stress and she must rest more. It's all this business with Olivia – she just hasn't been herself in ages."

"I know," replied Grace, anxious not to give too much away to her poor unsuspecting father.

"Look, Dad, I'll give Olivia a ring to see if I can get her to come back and sort things out with Mam. This isn't doing anyone any good."

"Couldn't agree more. You get Olivia to come back. I don't want my Moira upset any longer."

With that he hung up before Grace could even say, "I can't promise anything."

Grace dejectedly dialled the number of O'Sullivan's guest-house where Olivia had become an employee since she had moved on from being a guest.

"Jesus!" muttered Grace in irritation. "I'm like the fecking United Nations here – I think me next job should be a diplomat."

She fervently hoped Olivia was in a forgiving mood, because the Northern Ireland peace agreement was like a walk in the park compared to the bull-shitting it would take to get Olivia and her mother together.

Olivia was about to go home when she received the call from Grace.

She felt suddenly sorry for Grace being in the middle of all this and also a bit guilty for not seeing anyone in the family over Christmas, but she just hadn't felt ready.

It had been such a shock that awful day she found out her whole world was a lie, and she just couldn't face her mother over the turkey and play happy families. Still, she couldn't imagine how she would feel if something happened to her mother and she hadn't sorted it all out.

"OK Grace, I'll come to Dublin and see her. I can't promise it'll solve anything. I suppose it has to get sorted out sooner or later. So Dad is still in the dark – I thought she might spring it on him over the Christmas pudding? She usually chooses the worst moments."

"I don't think there is a good moment for that kind of news, do you? Anyway, how do you feel about it all now?"

"How do you think? I am still angry and shocked. I find myself staring in the mirror and wondering if I look like him and where he is . . . he could be dead for all I know. Moira didn't exactly give me a biography!"

Grace could hear the tension in Olivia's voice – she was nowhere near any type of reconciliation yet. Grace wondered if the proposed visit to Dublin to see their mother was a good idea after all. She decided to change the subject. "And how is the handsome James?"

Olivia brightened up immediately. "He's fantastic, Grace. I'd love you to meet him properly, but he seldom leaves the farm. You must come up for a few days with Paul and the kids – we'd love to have you stay."

Grace agreed readily and then laughed.

"What?" Olivia said obliquely.

"I'm just thinking of how far we have come. You've

277

never extended an invitation to me and the family before."

Olivia laughed now. "God! I don't suppose I did. Sorry, Grace, I must have been a right cow."

"No, not at all, but I have to say I do like this new improved Olivia. That James has had a good affect on you – you're all loved up."

"You have no idea," Olivia laughed a dirty laugh as they said goodbye.

Let's hope she brings that good mood with her, Grace thought as she went to the kitchen to give Paul the latest. It was at times like these that she wished fervently she had stayed in London. She'd need all her wits about her for the Olivia/Moira Peace Accord that was for sure.

Chapter 26

Olivia arrived at Grace's townhouse early the next day. Grace couldn't believe the transformation in her sister. Olivia had shed most of the weight she had gained in the previous year, but that wasn't all. Olivia had changed beyond all expectations. She had grown her hair long again and instead of the severe bob it lay loose and blonder in long layers. She was wearing a simple pair of faded denims and a loose linen shirt and she looked years younger. But most of all she looked happier and it was a relief for Grace to see her sister looking so well and relaxed.

"You look amazing!" Grace blurted out in surprise.

"I know," Olivia laughed and hugged her sister. "They say a woman is only truly beautiful when she is loved and I don't know about that, but I seem to have recovered from my little detour from reality. I am happier, Grace. Since I broke up with Connell I haven't had one binge and James just gives me goose-bumps. I love my new job because it gives me lots of time to sketch and paint. The colours and light in Connemara are fantastic for painting. And James thinks I have some talent. Everything is going so great. In fact, I'd be the happiest girl in Ireland if it wasn't for the reason I'm here."

"I know, ye poor thing. Come in and we'll have a coffee and plan our tactics." Grace said.

She didn't want Olivia and her mother to have a full-on row that would send Moira back to hospital with heart palpitations, but yet she knew all the issues would have to be addressed if progress was to be made. Yet the one person she truly worried about was her father – how would this all affect him. It was a big lie to hold for so long and she wondered if he could forgive his wife. The thought of her parents heading for the divorce courts in their sixties was appalling. So it all needed careful handling. Olivia would have to keep her temper for a start.

"Tell you what, forget the coffee. Maybe we need some camomile tea to calm ourselves before the onslaught on Depression Drive," quipped Grace.

Olivia laughed but Grace could tell she was a bit nervous. "Yeah, maybe we could give George Mitchell a call to negotiate."

"We could do, but the oul wan would only flirt uproariously with him. You should have seen the shenanigans in front of Connell when we went to see you in Connemara. She was like some fawning fifties schoolgirl – so Bill Clinton is out too, he's far too attractive. I think that Ian Paisley is about the only one who she doesn't fancy. Anyway, are you really up to this, Olivia? Do you think you can see her and talk to her without losing your cool?"

Olivia's face darkened. "I honestly don't know. I don't want to upset her or cause her any health problems – she is an old woman after all – but I am still very angry with her. She's lied for so long. And she is still lying to Dad."

"That's who I'm worried about," replied Grace worriedly. "Poor old Dad has been married for almost forty years to someone he doesn't even know. We need to tread carefully here, Olivia, for Dad's sake."

"Agreed," said Olivia solemnly. "I won't bite her head off so, not this time anyway."

So they set off for Raheny and a showdown with the wanton Moira.

Their father answered the door and uncharacteristically gave them both a large hug.

"She's up in the bed still," he whispered. "I've just given her the mother and father of a breakfast, which she seems to be enjoying. Come into the kitchen for a minute and we'll give her a chance to finish. And how are you, Olivia? You certainly look a lot happier, the country air must be doing you good."

"More like the countryman doing her good and proper!" Grace whispered, out of her father's earshot, and Olivia gave her a puck.

"Now, Olivia. I know you and your mother haven't exactly seen eye to eye lately but I hope you can sort it out. Now when you go up to see her you'll have to keep calm and not get all riled up. You know she's uptight and gets upset easily. Do you think you can manage that?"

Olivia bit her lip. She couldn't bear the idea that this poor man wasn't her father and was being kept in the dark, but yet she still couldn't summon up the courage to tell him. "OK," she said quietly instead. Her mother would have to break his heart because she couldn't.

Her father smiled and touched her hand.

"Jesus, I've died and been reborn into *The Waltons*," Grace quipped and they all laughed, tension broken.

"Right, up ye go," Sean said to Olivia. "I'm going to make Grace a nice cup of tea now – you can have yours later." And he gently pushed Olivia towards the hallway.

She finally left and they heard her tread upstairs on the creaky stairway.

"Sit down Grace," her father said amiably. He busied himself making the tea.

"How is Mam, *really*?" Grace asked.

"Oh, she's worrying herself to death, that's what's really the matter. I can't help her. She's bottling up all her worries over Olivia."

Grace didn't reply. She was afraid she'd blurt out the truth.

Her father placed a steaming mug of tea and some hot buttered toast in front of her, and sat down.

"It's OK, Grace," he said quietly. "I know Olivia is not my biological daughter. It doesn't matter a damn to me, I'm that girl's father no matter what the blood test says. I have always known."

Grace was aghast. She couldn't believe what her father had just said. "How long have you known?" she managed in a small voice.

"Since day one. I knew as soon as Moira chose me over Seamus Costigan. I knew there had to be a reason. She had been so besotted with him. As besotted with him as I was with her. I just loved your mother and I was happy and proud to have her on my arm. I never questioned it but as soon as he hightailed it out of Mayo, I knew it. Then shortly after he left, Moira announced that she was pregnant, and it wasn't too difficult to put it all together. Oh, she liked me well enough, I knew that, but she didn't love me then, not like she had loved him." His eyes misted over and he seemed to be very far away.

Grace had never heard him talk like that before. She never knew he had loved her mother so much. It was heart-warming and heartbreaking at the same time.

"Why have you never said anything to her, over the years?"

Her father smiled ruefully. "Because she has never forgiven herself. I see it in her every day. I loved every hair on her head and still do. I just couldn't cause her any more pain. I felt she'd tell me eventually in her own time, when she was ready. So I just wanted to forget all about it. I love you and Olivia equally. I never wanted there to be any differences between you."

Grace smiled ruefully. Her father hadn't a clue that

there had been differences made, quite a lot of them in fact, over the years. Perhaps they were both so anxious to make sure Olivia felt loved that they hadn't realised they had compensated to such an extent that Grace had felt unloved.

But now wasn't the time to discuss it. There was enough to focus on for the moment. There would be time for all her own issues later – right now she needed to get her parents to communicate with each other more. Her mother would be a lot happier if she was aware of the fact that her big secret no longer existed.

"Can you tell her for me?" her father interrupted her reverie.

"Me?" Grace echoed.

"Yes, I feel it would be easier if you told her that I know the truth. She could get herself together and we need never discuss it. It's a thing of the past, long gone as far as I'm concerned."

Grace felt like saying that it was all this secrecy that led to all the problems in the first place. But whatever strange set-up her parents had, it seemed to work for them.

"She thinks you linger in the shed all day to stay away from her," Grace revealed.

Her father smiled. "I *do*. She's not the easiest of women to live with. But part of it has been that she's been miserable with herself and she just takes it out on me. That's why I spend a lot of time escaping to the shed. But after this who knows? We might even take a second honeymoon!"

Grace laughed. "One step at a time there, Romeo! Let's just see how Olivia gets on first. I haven't heard her being hurled down the stairs yet, so it all seems to be going better than expected. I'll go up and see if they're both still alive."

Her father took a sip of tea and chomped on his toast. "I think it's safer down here, if it's all the same to you, Grace. I'll stay here in the relative safety of the kitchen – you know where to find me."

"Coward!" Grace said as she walked towards the door. "If I'm not back in ten minutes, you can send in a posse."

She went upstairs to face the music. She hoped that somehow Olivia and her mother had reached some kind of acceptance of each other's standpoint, but she knew her mother was never big on apologies or even empathising with anyone else. So she didn't hazard a guess to what she might find.

She walked upstairs slowly past the lurid red telephone seat and the Infant of Prague, on to the landing with the picture of the Sacred Heart. It had stared out at her for years, petrifying her as a child whenever she had to go to the toilet at night. It was funny how you instantly reverted to feeling like a child when you were at your parents' and surrounded by the things of your childhood, Grace thought, as she spotted the eighties shag-pile carpet that still adorned her faded bedroom.

She knocked lightly on her parents' bedroom door.

"Come in," her mother's voice answered, sounding high and squeaky.

Grace opened the door. Her mother was sitting up in bed, her face bright pink and her eyes red-rimmed from crying. She looked kind of old and even a little bit frail, Grace noted.

Her mother was always so bossy and strident, Grace never had considered her to be in any way fragile, but that was exactly how she looked right now, in her yellow nylon nightdress and padded bed jacket. The bedroom was a riot of flower-patterns, apricot curtains and frilly bedspread competing for attention with the brown and apricot carpet. Her mother's taste was appalling but now Grace found it oddly reassuring and comforting.

Olivia was sitting on the bed, hankie in hand. She had obviously been crying too.

"Are you both OK?" Grace ventured.

"Yes, we are. We've had 'frank discussions' as they say on the telly when they've had a major dust-up, but we've sorted quite a lot out. Olivia can fill you in later – I'm just too exhausted to go over it all again. How is Sean?"

Grace took her mother's chubby red hand in hers. "He knows, Mam. He has always known, he says."

Her mother froze and she heard Olivia's gasp

"And you know something? He says it doesn't make a blind bit of difference to him. He loves you very much and he feels Olivia is every bit his daughter. He just wants you two to get on so he can get back to his shed and some peace and quiet."

Tears rolled down her mother's face in quiet succession. "I am so . . . ashamed . . . what I have done to that man . . . I don't deserve him."

"What's done is done, Mam. You always say that yourself. Dad loves you and says there is nothing to forgive, so you just need to get well and get on with your life with Dad. He's already talking second honeymoons!"

Grace looked over at Olivia. She worried that making it seem all sorted with her mother and father might leave Olivia feeling as if her justified anger wasn't important.

Olivia seemed to pick up on Grace's discomfort. "It's OK, Grace. Mum and I have come to a kind of . . . an understanding, so to speak. I feel a lot better about everything. As Mum said I'll fill you in later. So if you don't mind I'll go downstairs and speak to Dad and have that cup of tea. I really need it now." She gave a little laugh and got up to leave. "I'll talk to you soon, Mum," she said quietly and touched her mother's arm. And with that she disappeared from the room.

Moira grabbed Grace's hand. "Is it really OK or were you just saying that for Olivia's sake?" she hissed.

"No, Mam, it's really OK. Dad has always known from day one but he didn't want to upset you any more than you already were. He loves you more than you know, more than I have ever seen. You're one lucky woman. Just make sure you make the most of it. And go easy on him, will ye? He might not stay in that bloody shed so much if you were a bit nicer to him."

Her mother clucked. "Ah, get away out of that, would ye!" but she was as pleased as punch.

Grace and Olivia made good their escape within

another half an hour. Grace couldn't wait to get Olivia on her own and find out what her mother had said to defuse Olivia's anger about all those years of lies that she had endured.

"Well, spill!" she said urgently, as soon as they had reached the corner. She risked a glance at Olivia who seemed to be lost in her own thoughts.

"You won't believe it if I tell you . . ." Olivia said at last.

"Try me," Grace replied. "Very little surprises me these days." She briefly thought of Kate's life falling apart, planes crashing into tall buildings and Dymphna admitting she had talked to Samir after their break-up. She was no stranger to shocks recently.

"Well, she knows where my father is, what he does and she even furnished me with his business card!"

"What?" Grace screeched. She stopped the car in amazement. "Run that by me again!"

"She told me that she had kept tabs on him over the years – that was enough of a shock for a start. Then when we had the blow-up in Clifden she went to see him – to tell him she had a daughter by him. Imagine, after all those years, how shocked he must have been. She led us to believe he dumped her when she found out she was pregnant but he never even knew!"

"What! I am amazed at that woman! And I can't believe she has had a pining for him all these years – poor Dad!" Grace was annoyed. Her father had poured out his love for his wife and there was Moira having secret yearnings for her ex-boyfriend and having even more secret assignations with him. She wondered if she had ever known her mother at all.

"It's not quite like that," Olivia replied. "She only went to see him for me, to try and put things right, so I could contact him if I wanted to. She told me all about him and about him not wanting to settle down in those early days, even though she loved him – she knew when she found herself pregnant that he would probably not stand by her and marry her. And as you know in the sixties, especially in Mayo, she'd have been sent away to some kind of home for unmarried mothers to have me and she'd have to give me up for adoption and she couldn't bear that. Dad was a good friend who she knew loved her and she knew would be a good husband and father, so she chose him. She did it to keep me and to prevent shame. But she grew to love Dad and she never regretted her decision. The reason she was able to keep tabs on Seamus over the years is because he has an Art Gallery in Dublin and is quite well known. I've even heard of him myself." She took out the business card and gave it to Grace.

It read: *Shay Costigan: Costigan Galleries Mount Merrion*.

"Well . . ." said Grace, unsure of what to say to her sister – this was uncharted territory. "What are you going to do next?"

Olivia looked at her seriously. "I haven't the foggiest, but I feel it might involve copious amounts of vodka."

"Right so," replied Grace. "I'll get on the phone to Dimples and Kate. This calls for a secret women's meeting. It's about time you met up with my friends. We could all do with a girl's night in. You can stay another few days, can't you? Before your lusty loins drag you back up to Clifden."

"Yes, why not," agreed Olivia. "I do want a bit of fun. Anyway I might stay until I can gather up enough courage to meet my, quote, 'biological father'."

"You do sound a bit like a Jerry Springer guest," Grace allowed. "Don't worry – we'll get you pissed tonight and we'll hatch a plot, OK? Anyway, Kate's life is like a TV chat show – 'My husband ran off with the teenage baby-sitter' – so things could be worse. And as for Dymphna's current status – well, that's another great headline: 'My cheatin' boyfriend has a wife already'. So you're only in the ha'penny place, Olivia!"

Olivia laughed long and hard. She couldn't wait to meet Kate and see Dymphna again. At least she wasn't the only one to have conflicts in her life.

Grace called Kate on her mobile. "Hiya, Kate! Listen, we need an emergency rescue mission for my sister, Olivia. So are you free for copious drinks and a severely disgustingly fattening takeaway later?"

"You bet!" enthused a lonely Kate.

She had been having a difficult day. Des had finally taken the girls on an overnighter to his new apartment in the village with Melody and she was feeling rather fragile. She was more than happy to have a diversion.

"Would you like to come to my place, Grace – I'd love to have you all over here. Are you going to ask Dymphna too? I'm absolutely dying to meet her."

"I am," Grace replied smiling. "And I'm sure she'll come. How about eight – is that OK?"

"Can't wait," said Kate. "And don't bring any booze. We've got to go through Des's massive collection of rare wines in the cellar. We can't see them going to waste, now can we?"

"Agreed!" laughed Grace.

She hung up.

"She's in fighting form," she told Olivia. "I think we called at the right time. Perhaps Kate's needs may be even greater than yours. Better call for reinforcements – we need Dymphna's cool head and jaundiced eye to complete the posse." She dialled Dimples' number. "This should be a great night – four mad women together – hang on a sec – Hi Dimples, it's me. Yeah, how would you like a marathon bitching session, several bottles of expensive wine and a delicious hip-enhancing takeaway? Thought you would – OK, be at my place by half seven tonight."

She hung up. "We're sorted," she told Olivia.

And Olivia believed, with her sister in charge, they would be.

Chapter 27

Dymphna arrived at Grace's townhouse by seven looking impossibly glamorous and chic. Grace took one look at the slender legs lithely clad in sheer black tights, her hips encased in a black leather miniskirt. She was wearing a classy black mohair jumper. Dymphna couldn't be casual if she was going down to the shops for a bottle of milk at midnight, Grace thought, as she cast aside her envious thoughts. She looked terrific and always did. Grace had long since come to accept it.

"I'm a bit nervous meeting the Wicked Sister from the West!" Dymphna whispered in the hallway.

Grace laughed. "She has changed, Dymphna – she's a lot more chilled out, you'll see!"

Dymphna was surprised to find Olivia was different. She was dressed in a simple pair of Levis and a white T-shirt and she was not as slender as she had been or as stiff in manner. She was smiling and apparently happy to see Dymphna, which was a first.

Dymphna had never had a warm fuzzy feeling whenever she encountered Olivia in the past. She had always been made feel inferior in some way – at least that's how she recalled it.

"I've called a taxi," Grace half whispered as Paul was putting a fractious Orla to bed. Orla seemed to have a sixth sense whenever Grace crossed the door without her and went into immediate tantrum mode. "I intend to get well and truly blotto. It's been quite a day – I'll fill you in later."

Just then the taxi beeped and they all piled in and headed for The Beeches.

As the electric gates opened and revealed the well lit-up mini-mansion Olivia and Dymphna realised that, unusually for her, Grace hadn't exaggerated at all in her glowing references for Kate's house. The Beeches was a stunning home. Olivia and Dymphna were enthralled. The large door opened as the taxi pulled up on the gravel drive and Kate came out to greet them.

"Welcome, everybody," she smiled shyly. "Hope you all brought healthy kidneys for the ruination of."

Kate was so down to earth that both Olivia and Dynphna took to her immediately. Grace had filled them in on all Kate's problems with the cheating rat Des and Dymphna for one couldn't believe that anyone could treat this stunning girl in such a cruel and callous manner. Dympha had thought herself unlucky in love until she heard Kate's story – imagine being cast aside after ten years of marriage for a spotty teenaged baby-sitter!

She watched a slender Kate gracefully pour the wine in the meticulous well-appointed kitchen and wondered if her chunky knit cardigan was Lainey Keogh and if her wristwatch was really Gucci. Kate *was* beautiful, Dymphna thought, noting the vivid blue eyes, the clear skin and shiny blonde hair. Grace had been right – it would be easy to envy Kate except for the fact that she had the worst problems of them all.

Kate proffered the drinks. "I've got menus from the local Indian so we can order whenever we feel like it. In the meantime I've got some horrendously expensive wine of Des's for us to enjoy – he'd have a seizure if he knew. But who cares?" She laughed a bit too hard and Grace exchanged knowing glances with Olivia.

They all sat down in the conservatory sipping the fine wine and Grace regaled them all with Olivia's news of her father and their visit to their parents.

"Oh you poor thing," sighed Kate forgetting her own problems and gladly focusing on someone else's. "How do you feel about it all, now?"

Olivia frowned. "I dunno. I feel a bit numb if I'm to be honest. I just feel like flitting back up to Connemara to my handsome farmer and forgetting the whole thing, but I suppose that's the coward's way out. I should really face my father and get it over with. I need a few days to sort out my brain. It feels totally frazzled at the moment."

She smiled weakly. Grace felt really sorry for her sister. It was a lot to come to terms with, all this time believing your life to be one thing and finding out it was something completely different after all. She briefly thought of Jordan and how confused and isolated he must feel sometimes wondering about his natural father and naturally feeling jealous of Orla. She inwardly decided she was going to procrastinate no longer but was going to make definite arrangements about him meeting his father.

"You should see the handsome farmer," Grace announced hurriedly, anxious to keep the mood upbeat – this place was in danger of turning into a Wailing Wall if everyone became down over their respective traumas. She was determined that Kate and Olivia in particular would have a great time. "He'd give old Brad Pitt a run for his money. Glenroe's Miley was never like this – you should see him, girls – no wonder she's running back to Connemara! I would too if I had that waitin' in an Aran jumper for me!"

Everybody laughed at that one. That's better, thought Grace. The mission was to rescue Olivia from depression and that was what they would do.

After that the night became a raucous success.

Dymphna related her tales of Mark the Snake and how she stalked him in Limerick and then got her revenge by pretending to be pregnant by him.

"The look on his face when I told him the truth before dumping him on the coast road for a nice five-mile walk back to civilisation, was priceless. He won't be climbing into anyone else's knickers quite so arrogantly in the future."

"I need some of your backbone to wreak revenge on *my* evil husband," Kate said admiringly, "and we'll talk about that later. But all this man-bashing has made me ravenous – I think we should order the curry first and plot revenge after."

"Yeah," quipped Dymphna. "Revenge is best discussed on a nice full stomach."

"What are we like?" laughed Grace. "We'll have to rename this house The Bitches instead of The Beeches if we get any worse."

Kate laughed uproariously at that comment. She had visions of a new plaque on the granite wall outside when Des came to visit.

She and Grace went to order the Indian.

"Thanks, Grace, for tonight," said Kate. "It was just what I needed – I don't have many friends and I'm so happy you've introduced me to yours. Things don't seem nearly so bad when you can share it all with other women who understand."

Grace stood silently while Kate gave the order over the phone. She felt Kate wanted to talk about Des, yet she didn't want to upset her by raising the subject herself.

"And how did things go, with Des having the girls overnight?" she ventured.

Kate grimaced. "Oh Grace, I hated to hand them over, but what could I do? Melody was driving the Lexus, and it was just the way she seemed so cocky with her sly smirks – like she had been Des's proper wife all along – I felt like tearing her hair out then and there! But I had to be civil for the girls' sakes and Des, well, he looked a bit downcast and embarrassed which of course he should be, the shit! He's only bought an apartment in that posh new development just outside the village."

"Peyton Park?" Grace was incredulous. The cheapest three-bedroom apartment in the new and expensive development cost over four hundred thousand pounds.

A pained look crossed Kate's face. This had to be hurting her deeply.

"Can you believe it? I'm sure we're the talk of Kilmadden. Barbara Tormey is not going to keep quiet about her teenaged pregnant daughter snagging the likes of Des Heathcoat and landing herself a posh apartment in Peyton Park. Meanwhile I just have to sit back and take it. If I cause too many problems with Des at the moment or tell him I don't want Melody to see the girls, I could lose everything, I wish I wasn't so dependent on him, you know? And now she's got her own baby on the way . . . well, it's only a matter of time before she replaces my family with hers. Her little plan has worked a treat and there isn't a damn thing I can do about it."

"Oh Kate, you must feel very angry," Grace replied sadly.

"I haven't even reached anger yet – I'm still at the numb-with-shock stage, but I'm going to need your help, Grace. I have to figure out a way to make myself financially independent in the next twelve months. I don't want to have to leave this house or go back to my mother's if Des decides he's not going to continue to fund my lifestyle. I mean it's only going to be a matter of time before Melody gets in his ear over it – you should see the looks she gives me. I know she envied me all along and now she detests me. It won't suit her eventually to be in an apartment, no matter how nice, while wife number one is in the big house on the hill."

Grace regarded Kate seriously. She looked desolate, so Grace decided the gloves were off as far as Des Heathcoat was concerned. "I think you are underestimating Des here, Kate. I found him to be very controlling where you were concerned and he only played away when you decided you needed a life of your own. He just couldn't handle it – he was scared you would become strong and you have. He's going to be just as controlling where Melody is concerned. You should pity her – she's going to be so under his thumb. Just think of this time as your chance for freedom. You can be whatever you want to be without answering to anyone. For the first time in your life, you can be yourself – just try to think about that for a while."

Kate smiled slowly as if it had only just dawned on her that there was another side to this. "You know something, you are absolutely right! While I sit here fretting over him he still controls my life. I have to get my control back and I'm going to start right now. Thanks, Grace! I think this calls for some champagne. Let's delve into Des's secret stash of mega-expensive champers. It's time we celebrated freedom."

And so they did.

They fell out of Kate's house firm friends after 3 a.m.
They had sorted out all their problems and indeed the
problems of the world and had decided that they would
help each other in any way possible in the following year.
Dymphna made a promise to meet Kate for lunch in
town when she was in college midweek. Olivia invited
Kate and the girls to Clifden for a much-needed break
and indeed they were all invited for a girly weekend in
the summer. Dymphna promised to go scout Olivia's
father's gallery and report back to Olivia, and Olivia
promised to draw up a business plan for Kate for the
following year when Kate had finished her design
course. Grace vowed to support them all and make sure
all the inebriated promises were kept.

All four realised that it would be friendship that
would get them through.

When they got back to Grace's house Paul was still
awake. He had suffered a bad night with Orla who
appeared to be getting a back tooth and made some
strong coffee and made put-you-up beds for the guests.

Over coffee, Dymphna stated that for all her various
love affairs she never enjoyed the warmth and fun with
a man that she did whenever she spent time with her
girlfriends and they all agreed.

"Still, have our uses though!" Paul quipped as he
led a drunken Grace haphazardly towards their bedroom.

"Damn right!" agreed Grace. "Do you know how
lucky I am to have you?"

Paul laughed. "I do, but do you?"

"We all do," Olivia remarked dryly. "Gracie's going

to rent you out to the rest of us – she's decided you're one in a million."

"Stop! Me head's swellin'!" Paul replied, pleased. It almost made up for a tormented evening with a cross toddler.

It looked like his wife loved him after all.

And Grace did feel lucky, luckier than most. She had a man that she loved who loved her. And that it seemed was very difficult to find.

Chapter 28

3 months later . . .

Dymphna sat on her bed in her towelled robe and looked at herself in the wardrobe mirror. She thought she looked rather small and insignificant and more than a bit worried, which was exactly right.

She looked skywards. "What else? What else are you going to bloody throw at me – is it not enough that I have no one to love me and a job that I hate? And now this?"

She felt the lump again. It was definitely there: a small hard pea-sized bump on her left breast that she had first discovered in the shower ten long minutes ago.

She felt her blood run cold. She would have to visit the quack. There was no way she could ignore this one. Pap smears were one thing you could put off till the last dreaded moment, but this was something different.

God. What if it was really something serious? The thought of losing her tiny but much-loved breast! Then that horrible treatment afterwards. She tried to imagine having to undergo chemo and all her hair falling out. And that might be the best-case scenario . . . She just couldn't bear the idea of it all and without warning large salt tears fell rapidly down her cheeks.

She lifted her mobile phone and went to dial Grace's number but dialled her local GP's number instead. There was no point in worrying Grace until the doctor said that there was something to worry about. But Dymphna felt deep down that there *was* something to worry about here. Now suddenly everything else in the room seemed extra bright and sharply defined and she vowed, if this scare was just that, that she would live her life differently. She'd no longer drift along aimlessly and let life just happen to her. She would go out and grab it with both hands and seize happiness.

"I promise!" she said to the ceiling or what was beyond it as she heard her doctor's receptionist answer the phone.

She made an appointment for later on that evening.

It was going to be a very long day indeed.

Up in Kilmadden, Grace also held a telephone in her hand. She had shakily dialled the number of British Airways in London twice and quickly put the phone down before anyone answered.

She felt nervous because she knew if she went through with this simple phone call that everything else would be changed utterly forever. There was no going back. She knew it would upset Paul and gladden Jordan and she wasn't sure where it would take them all, but thinking of Olivia and her sadness over her father's identity, Grace knew she owed it to Jordan to complete the jigsaw that was his parentage. She worried how Sammy would take it – would he even want to know his son after all these years? And of course Paul would be more than unhappy about it all, but it had to be done. With stronger resolve she pressed the redial button. This time she was going through with it. She was going to call Samir and arrange a meeting between him and his son.

The clipped British tones on the other end announced British Airways.

Grace told the telephonist that she had a message for Samir Sala, then she gave her telephone number and asked that he contact Grace Casey, stressing that there was nothing wrong in case he got alarmed.

After she put the phone down she realised she had really let the cat amongst the pigeons but there it was, it couldn't be changed now. If and when Sammy rang back she'd tell Paul and face the consequences.

Kate was shopping in the village with Jade and Chloe. They had bought a present for a party that Chloe was going to later on that day and were buying some cold meat in the deli when Kate suddenly spotted Des and Melody across the street. Kate was first taken aback at seeing them walking along as a couple, then she was stunned by Melody's appearance. Apart from the fact that she was now very obviously pregnant – she would be about six months along by now – it was still a shock to see it, somehow. Even more shocking was the transformation in Melody's appearance. She had lost a considerable amount of weight – in fact, she looked gaunt. She was painfully thin and she looked eerily like a younger clone of Kate. Her long caramel hair had been chopped into a bob and was now a lot blonder and she was wearing clothes that were classically cut, but way too old for her. Des was holding her hand and strolling along looking smug and contented, but Melody looked utterly miserable.

Kate suddenly started to laugh and surprised herself. She had been feeling particularly down the last few days, since hearing the news that Melody was expecting a boy and observing that Des was over the moon about it. But now she felt like a great weight had been lifted from her.

That was me, she thought to herself incredulously. She had never imagined that she had been that controlled or ruled by Des, but there it was as large as life walking alongside him down the street. It was *her* – a few months ago, a million years ago.

Kate watched them disappear from view as they entered the little Italian restaurant on the corner. True to form, Kate thought – that was Des's favourite restaurant. She wondered idly if Melody had any say in the matter.

As Kate collected her Parma ham she asked the assistant for six gooey éclairs that she had spotted on the counter. It was like a little act of defiance and of freedom. She was celebrating not having to put up with Des's smart remarks every time a cake passed her lips or comments on how many gym workouts she had missed that week.

Once again, she realised that her new life had strange and wonderful possibilities. Rather than focusing on the things about her husband and marriage that she missed, she was facing the delicious fact that she was now an independent woman who answered to no one. And that felt good. Today, for the first time in months, she didn't hate Melody or envy her, in actual fact she pitied her. She gathered the illicit cakes and her daughters and headed for home with a much lighter heart. For the first time in nearly three months Kate was feeling something approaching hope. Perhaps there was a light at the end of the tunnel after all. She had turned a corner. Instead of feeling her usual depressed fragile self, she felt strong, she felt free.

The phone rang, making Grace jump. Her heart thumped as she ran to answer it.

She didn't want Paul or, worse still, Jordan to answer the phone first and end up speaking to Samir. She suddenly realised that she hadn't thought this through at all. They were due home soon and she could hardly stand by the phone twenty-four seven. Anyway she'd have to cross that bridge later, she decided, as she answered the phone and heard Kate's voice.

"Hi," Kate breezed. "I'm in the car and have some sinful cakes and a bit of gossip. Do you fancy a coffee?"

Grace smiled. She could do with a diversion. "Sure do, but can you make it my place? I'll explain later."

Ten minutes later they were both scoffing cakes and swapping stories as they sat in Grace's tiny cramped kitchen.

"Honestly, Grace," Kate said, mid mouthfuls of gooey éclair, keeping one eye trained on Jade who was trying to force-feed Orla some cake with mixed results.

"I've been seeing Melody all along as some sort of vicious little viper casting an evil spell over Des. She was so smug and bitchy in the beginning, like the cat that got the cream, but today I *actually* felt sorry for her. I was glad it was her and not me with Des today going into that restaurant being all meek and mild and acquiescent. I finally realised what you tried to tell me – he is such a control freak. She now looks like a mini-me: blonder, thinner and even dressed in my style. It was spooky. I felt strangely released somehow, like as if I can finally be myself."

Grace smiled equably. Watching Kate eat a cake with such abandon was a change, for starters. "Good for you. Was it a while since you've seen her?"

Kate nodded. "I couldn't stand her rolling up to the house like she owned it, so I told Des he was to collect and take the girls alone until we both told them about Melody's condition. It was such a shock for them – they're already missing their father, but to find out he's having another child makes them feel even more insecure. Poor things! I think that's the main reason Des is playing so fair at the moment. He realises that the girls have suffered enough and at least he has enough guilt not to make them suffer any more. So your job is safe for the moment, Grace – he told me as much the other day when delivering the girls home."

Grave blushed. She felt guilty that she and Paul endlessly pored over Kate's love life. They couldn't help speculating on Des's motives as the break-up affected their family too, Grace being at risk of losing her job.

"That's great, em . . . thanks," she managed, relief evident in her voice.

"Yeah," Kate continued in a half whisper, glancing over at the girls who were now trying to comb a reluctant Orla's hair, "he's been in an expansive mood lately. They just found out Melody is expecting a boy. All Des's Christmases must have come at once. You know he always said it didn't matter to him before, that we had two girls, I mean. He even forbade me to consider another pregnancy – that's why I took this bloody course on. And he's like a fecking kid in a sweetshop now he is having a son. It really makes me mad – for the past few days I've been feeling cheated on all over again."

"Yes," Grace gently reminded her. "And if you had got pregnant and had another baby, how much more awful would it have been for you if he had left you then, for her? You just have to keep focusing on yourself and your new life. You know what they say – living well is the best revenge."

"You're right," Kate agreed, brightening up. "Now, I'll brew us another coffee while you tell me more about your phone call."

"Well, if you hear me suddenly changing the subject when Jordan and Paul get back don't let on. Anyway, that's all there is to it – I called British Airways and left a message for Sammy to call me. I don't still know for sure if I've done the right thing but I was driving meself nuts worrying and fretting over it. So, it's done now, there's no going back." She flashed a nervous smile.

"Are you worried about Paul?" Kate enquired.

Grace frowned. "Yeah, I just don't know how he is going to react. He is so dead set against it. It's almost like he's jealous of Jordan's father though he has no reason to be. I have never given him any reason to distrust me, but somehow it's like he thinks as soon as I clap eyes on Sammy again, I'm going to fall at his feet and we're going to ride off into the sunset with Jordan in tow. It's so ludicrous but to Paul it seems entirely plausible."

Kate eyed her quizzically. "And do you have any feelings left over for Sammy, like . . . er . . . unfinished business?'

Grace looked flummoxed. "Yes. No! Oh, I don't know. I suppose a part of me still wonders about him. I see him in Jordan every day. I felt so bloody angry with Sammy for the longest time, because he was such a complete shit and I was hopelessly in love with him, but that's long since over. I suppose I'm curious more than anything else. Like you would be about your first boyfriend, but that's about all."

Kate put a fresh coffee before her. "Say it like you mean it – at least when you say it to Paul."

Grace groaned and put her head into her hands. "What am I like? Am I coming across like an overgrown schoolgirl with a crush on a pop star?"

"A little," Kate replied gently. "But we can knock that out of you by the time you get your story straight for Paul's ears. You can't sound at all girly, or even remotely curious about the pilot or else he'll smell a rat –"

Just then they heard the front door slam. The lads were back from football. So that was the end of it for now. But Grace felt more worried than ever about what she had just unleashed.

Chapter 29

Dymphna sat in the surgery looking absently at the yellowing map of the human body on the wall while Dr Cleary examined the offending lump on her right breast.

Normally Dymphna would be chatting incessantly to Dr Cleary, who loved nothing better than a good gossip, but today she was too worried to even speak. Her throat was dry with the stress of it all, and she hadn't been able to do a stroke of work all day, what with her whole life flashing before her every ten minutes.

"Well?" she urged impatiently, looking up to read Sandra Cleary's face, which seemed a bit concerned. Dymphna spotted the dark grey eyes narrowing as the doctor felt around the area.

"It's probably just a benign cyst, but I am concerned enough to have it checked out. We'll send you for an ultrasound, and perhaps a needle biopsy just to be sure."

She heard Dymphna's muttered "Shit!" and touched her arm, her motherly face full of concern. "Now, Dymphna, it's far too premature to panic. Breast cancer is extremely rare in anyone your age, so let's not get carried away, OK? I'll get you an appointment for Thursday, so you won't have long to wait, as you seem a bit nervous."

A bit? Dymphna thought incredulously, her mind racing. How was she supposed to cope for another two days and even then perhaps she'd have to wait for lab results.

This was just so unfair. She had so wanted Dr Cleary to laugh and say she was a bit of a hypochondriac and of course there was nothing to worry about, but now she had to have further investigations, and who knows what they might find?

"Are you OK?" Dr Cleary was asking her.

"Fine," Dympha flashed a wan smile. "I'm fine. As you say, it's probably nothing to worry about."

She got dressed, took the referral and paid the doctor and then drifted to her car in a daze.

The day was bright and sunny and Dymphna felt the warm sun seep into her bones. She had never been so terrified in her entire life. She sat in the car and cried in huge racking sobs for a full five minutes until, exhausted, she lifted her mobile and dialled her friend's number. It was time she told Grace.

The phone rang and Grace raced to get it. Paul hardly ever bothered to answer it first but Grace wasn't taking any chances.

"Grace?" The voice was unmistakeable.

Grace's heart leapt in her chest. "Sammy?"

He gave a little laugh, that boyish laugh that used to melt her heart. In an instant thirteen years were wiped away and she was twenty again – red-faced, stupid and up the duff.

"Yes, it's me. I was so surprised to hear from you after all this time? Everything is OK with you and the baby – I mean, our son?"

Grace sighed. This was so awkward. "Yes, everything is OK, Samir. Just fine in fact. Our son is a wonderful boy and he's very dear to me and to Paul, who is his stepdad. It's just that Jordan wants to see you, to meet you and know who you are. He is at that age now . . ." Her voice trailed away – surely Sammy would get the picture. She didn't want to appear too desperate or too eager, in case he wasn't amenable.

"I understand," Sammy said evenly. "I too have thought of him every day all of these years, and of course you too, but I feel if he is happy then it is not for me to interfere."

Grace felt like saying 'Well, you've changed your tune – when I told you about him we couldn't see you for dust!' or 'It's shag all thanks to you that we're happy!' but she realised that wouldn't help Jordan much, so she demurred.

"Yes, he is very happy," she replied a mite sharply. "But he still wishes to see you. How do you feel about that?"

Sammy laughed again happily. "Grace, I would love

it. I am based now in London and I have lived here for many years. Would you like me to come to visit you or would you prefer to meet me here? I am on long-haul flights mainly, so I am in London only every second weekend."

"I'll, I mean *we'll* come and see you – we can get cheap flights now with Ryanair," she replied hurriedly, imagining him calling to the door and getting a black eye for his trouble from Paul.

"OK – I'll give you my mobile number, then you can sort out the details and call me. Or I can call you again if you prefer?"

"No, I'll call you. You see, Samir," she said awkwardly, "I'll need to talk to my husband about the trip . . . so, for the moment, please don't call unless it's an emergency – and then only on weekdays before six – he's never home before seven."

"I understand, Grace."

After he had hung up, Grace felt so weird – she wasn't sure how she felt, really. Angry, excited, misty-eyed, cynical, curious, scared. Mostly scared, she decided, because she still had to sell the idea to Paul.

The phone rang again while it was still in her hand, making her jump. At the other end was a sobbing Dymphna asking who the hell was Grace talking to for so long and could she visit right away, that she had some awful news but she wanted to tell her face to face.

Alarmed, Grace agreed immediately. What a weird day this was turning out to be! She hadn't got a chance to adjust from one emotion to the next without something else happening and demanding her attention. She absently looked at her watch. It was only one o'clock. Was the sky going to fall down by two? It looked like she would have to put Paul on the back burner for the moment as it looked as if old Dimples needs were greater for the moment. She hoped Dymphna hadn't been seeing that bloody Mark McCabe again even though she had swore blind that she wouldn't – she seemed so heartbroken over the phone, it just had to be man trouble. What other kind was there?

"It's a stiff vodka I need after the morning I've had," she said out loud to Orla who was the only one listening. Maybe Paul might look after Orla while Grace took Dimples off to the local for some vodka and sympathy. On the other hand, maybe not. She needed him to be in the best of form when she landed him with the news that she and Jordan were off to London so see the wayward pilot. She'd send Paul off to the pub instead. A few pints of the black stuff, a sexy negligee and she could sell him anything.

Chapter 30

Dymphna was due at Beaumont hospital by nine o'clock, fasting for her ultrasound and needle biopsy. It was only day surgery but Grace insisted on coming with her. Dymphna was glad her friend was there, but there was something so isolating about being ill, you travelled in your own terrified little cocoon where nothing or no one could actually touch you. She found herself going through the motions and cracking feeble jokes, but deep inside she felt like screaming and running a mile down the long corridor out of this place to the nearest pub. But the pubs weren't open and, besides, Grace had her bag and the nurse had already led her to her bed with its crisp linen sheets so she was stuck.

"I'd love a rest for the day, any chance of a swap?" Grace quipped as she eyed the bed in mock envy.

"I wish!" Dymphna retorted in a strange wispy voice while biting her lip. She was determined not to cry.

Grace squeezed her friend's arm. "You are going to be fine, Dimples, I promise you. By the end of today or whenever they get those results back, you'll be in the clear and we'll have a laugh about this."

Just then the nurse came back with the awful paper gown that had no back in it and an envelope for all Dymphna's jewellery. She checked Dymphna's chart, put a plastic identity band on her wrist and took her pulse.

"Still alive, so," Dymphna said, to no one in particular

The nurse glanced briefly at Grace and informed her that she had another ten minutes before she had to leave. "She'll be released by about four o'clock if you want to come and collect her," she informed her crisply.

Grace looked at a stricken Dymphna.

"You'd better go, Mummy," Dymphna tried a joke.

"Right so," Grace smiled, pushed Dymphna's bag into the locker and wondered if she should give her best friend a kiss and a hug or would it seem too melodramatic. Dymphna could be as prickly as a hedgehog when it came to physical contact with people other than gorgeous hunks.

"Grace?" Dymphna held out her hand.

Grace took it in hers.

"Thanks, you've been so great."

"Ge'way, ye big eejit! I only came in case I saw a dishy doc. Now, no asking for a boob job while you're on the operating table, Dimples – you know the only bloody advantage I have on you is my magnificent bosoms, OK?"

Dymphna grinned. "OK, see ye at four o'clock.

Bring me anything chocolately and totally fattening, all right? I'll be famished by then."

"It's a deal." And with that Grace was gone.

This had to be faced alone. Dymphna retreated into her mind full of worries as she got into the awful backless number and waited.

Grace drove out of the carpark in a mist of tears. She had never seen her friend so unhinged. She prayed fervently all the way back to Kilmadden that this was just a scare and not the real thing. Grace just couldn't bear her dear friend having to endure cancer. It was so scary. She had never seen Dimples so terrified, which in turn frightened Grace. This was going to be a very long day indeed.

Dymphna was staring at the ceiling contemplating her future when the nurse came in with two orderlies and a trolley to take her down to day surgical. She hopped onto the trolley trying in vain to preserve her dignity and they whisked her along the corridor to the x-ray room.

The nurse informed her gently that the ultrasound was first. It would take a detailed composite of her breast tissue and then after that, depending on the results, the needle biopsy was next.

A handsome doctor type in a white coat emerged from the x-ray machine and took Dymphna's chart. He studied her notes and issued a wry smile that went all the way up to his pale blue eyes.

"Well, I never! If it isn't Dymphna Coffey as I live and breathe!"

Dymphna snapped out of her fear for a minute and found time to smile. "Sorry?"

He shook his long blonde hair and grinned boyishly. He was gorgeous, she thought. Maybe I'm not that sick after all.

"I'm Derek. Derek Mooney. From St Kevin's in Raheny. I had a king-size crush on you in fifth year and you couldn't stand the sight of me."

Dymphna searched the handsome face for some sign that she knew him in a previous life, but she couldn't believe that she'd ever have knocked back a dish like this.

The nurse glared at Derek and he became businesslike again.

"Anyway, Ms Coffey. Today I'm going to examine your breast with this device and the doctor will be along to discuss the results in a while. Now please open the gown – this gel will feel a little cold."

Dymphna was too perplexed by this blast from the past to focus on the worrying reality of her breast lump. "Aren't you a doctor?" She gazed at the vision that was Derek.

"No," he smiled, checking behind him to see where the cranky nurse had gone. "I'm a radiographer. I'll come and see you later on, Dymphna, and I'll try and get you to remember me. I mustn't have made any impression at all, which has me mortally embarrassed -- but anyway, Nurse Nasty is on her way back so we'll have to talk later."

Minutes later Dymphna was undergoing one of the

scariest moments of her life so far having this sonogram, and yet here she was thinking about the blonde bloke who was scanning her boob and wondering how and why she had ever passed him up. It was a bizarre moment but soon it passed and now she saw that the handsome radiographer was carrying her future in the form of the x-ray charts to the wall where he looked at them carefully in the fluorescent-lit screen. She watched as he conferred with the doctor who had come in and she tried to pick up nuances from their expressions that might tell her anything, but they seemed to be cheerful enough.

After what seemed like an age, the doctor came over and introduced himself as someone unpronounceable and informed Dymphna that there was indeed a mass there and they were going ahead with the biopsy. Moments later with tears sparking her eyes, she was whisked into theatre and after a local anaesthetic they took a little piece of her breast away. The sample was going to be sent for assessment to the laboratory and the results would be known within a few days.

As she was led back to her room, she prayed that the lump would prove to be benign.

Now all she had to do was wait. But it was the impossible waiting for the axe to fall that was the absolute worst.

"I'll bring you some tea and toast now," the nurse said kindly and returned minutes later with hot buttered toast and strong sweet tea. Dymphna surprised herself by scoffing the lot and strangely she did feel better afterwards. She found herself drifting off to sleep amid all the noise and bustle of the busy hospital. She hadn't slept a wink the night before so she was exhausted.

When she awoke sometime later she was surprised to find that Derek was sitting quietly by her bedside studying her chart.

"Hi, sleepyhead," he said cheerfully. "How are you feeling?"

Dymphna tried to sit up. "A little bit sore, actually."

Derek pressed her bell. "You're due for some painkillers right now as a matter of fact. I've summoned the nurse. They're very busy today – would you like some water?"

Dymphna nodded and Derek poured her a large tumbler, which she sipped self-consciously. She was thinking she should have bought those new silk pyjamas in Marks and Spencer's that she had seen yesterday. She was sure she looked like a train wreck. Suddenly her appearance seemed to matter a great deal.

"So, you don't remember me at all?" Derek was saying.

"Can't say I do, no," Dymphna replied in a tone that tried to convey 'If I had noticed you I'd have grabbed you'.

"Well, Miss Coffey – it is still Miss because I checked your chart – I was the geeky bloke with the glasses and spots that was on the debating team. Your mate Grace had a few dates with Johhny Miller who was in my year. You must remember the famous debate about the Dublin Bay oil refinery that we had with your year. We trounced you." He smiled at the memory.

A blurry image fleetingly graced Dymphna's mind, one of a blonde brainbox type in an argyle jumper and thick glasses. "Ah, I think I remember you now! Were you the captain, and did you wear an awful argyle jumper?"

"Guilty as charged!" laughed Derek, wincing. "And if I remember correctly, a horrible fat silk tie and black drainpipe jeans. I thought I was the cheese."

"And you weren't even the cow on the box!" Dymphna grinned, remembering the old insults they traded in the eighties.

Derek's eyes crinkled in amusement. "You caused me many a sleepless night. I saw you at all the discos in the Grove, but I could never gather up enough courage to approach you."

"I wasn't that bad, was I?" Dymphna tried to remember her appearance and demeanour back then. She and Grace would flounce into the disco every week, heads held high, pretending to smoke in a sophisticated world-weary way, and ignoring all the boys, hoping by their open disdain they'd be noticed all the more. With mixed results. She laughed at the memory and admitted, "Perhaps I was."

The nurse arrived with some welcome pain relief and Derek and Dymphna chatted some more about people whom they had in common at school and what had happened to them since.

"So is your boyfriend coming to pick you up then?" Derek enquired innocently enough.

"Don't possess such an item," Dyphmna replied, a

glint in her eye. "A very dear friend is taking me home. A female friend as it happens."

Derek grinned back. "So you won't mind if I ask you out for coffee sometime, so I can put the awful rejection of 1985 behind me?"

"Perhaps," Dymphna said coyly. "We'll see."

The doctor who had performed the procedure arrived presently and re-assured Dymphna that although the results of the biopsy would not be available for another five days, the lump didn't appear too 'nasty' as he put it and they were 'optimistic' that everything would be OK.

Grace came at four o'clock to see a much brighter Dymphna all packed and ready to go home.

En route to Dymphna's coast-road apartment, she recounted her meeting with the handsome Derek.

"You are truly fucking amazing, Dymphna Coffey! You go into hospital a fragile shell of your former self, worried to bits about cancer and you emerge a few hours later totally reborn and armed with a date – with a dishy radiographer to boot!"

Dymphna looked out at Dollymount Strand. It always had a calming affect on her whenever she felt stressed or worried in the past and today was no exception. "I'm not out of the woods yet, Grace. They only said it *looked* promising. Or less nasty than expected, to quote the doctor directly."

"And did you ask Derek for his professional opinion?" Grace enquired.

Dymphna started to giggle. "What am I like? I was too busy flirting . . . I forgot all about it."

"Sound's serious," replied Grace.

Dymphna eyed Grace but there was no underlying cynical grin. "He is different to anyone I have ever met before, Grace. It's like I have known him all my life, and I suppose I have in a weird way, him being practically the boy next door and all that stuff – but there was no me trying to make a good impression by my smart comments or cynical lines. Maybe it was the fact I was wearing pyjamas, and old comfortable ones at the time, but I felt so at home with him. I would love to see him again."

"But minus the white coat just to see if those feelings are real?" Grace finished.

"Yeah, how did you know?" Dymphna was amazed.

"Saw it last week in *Casualty*!" Grace quipped, before ducking a puck from her friend. "Well, I *did*! I can't help if your life is one long melodrama. Anyway, look on the bright side. Your mother will be delighted for a start – someone from Raheny that she can look down on. After the high dramas of all your foreign London blokes, then the married Mark, it'll be a relief for her to meet someone normal!"

"Jesus, you have me gallivanting up the aisle already and we haven't even had a first date yet! No pressure there, then."

They both laughed at that and the overhanging cloud over Dymphna's health seemed to lift a bit, at least for the rest of the afternoon.

Chapter 31

Kate was busy studying a modern architecture book for her exams in the college library when suddenly she felt a tap on her shoulder.

She swung her blonde hair around to see Tom Carter, her tutor, standing over her.

"Sorry to interrupt, Kate, but you look totally perplexed. Is there something I can help you with?" He was smiling at her with those dark sooty eyes, flashing those perfect teeth.

Kate could feel a blush redden her cheeks. "Oh sorry, no, I was miles away. It had nothing to do with the course, I'm afraid – I was just wondering what I'm going to cook my daughters for tea tonight." She suddenly felt stupid for saying that, like as if her brain was filled with no more than domestic chores, when she should have been pondering modern architecture or something to actually do with interior design.

Tom grinned. "You know, I was thinking exactly the same thing. What exciting meal for one could I plunder my freezer for, or will it be another Chinese for a change?"

Kate smiled back. So he lived alone. She had been wondering about Tom Carter a lot lately, in fact so had most of the class. He was handsome in a dishevelled Heathcliff bohemian sort of way. He sloped about the college clad in various teacher-style cord jackets and jeans, his dark eyes and mood intent most of the time. Lots of the students fancied him but he seemed to keep himself very private and didn't generally socialise. Everyone wondered if he had another half.

Leila, a student in Kate's class, said that he had recently been divorced but no one knew for sure. He had always seemed professionally polite but aloof when Kate came into contact with him before. But she had been in the midst of such a deep depression that even Brad Pitt could have escaped her notice.

She wondered if she had just transferred some residual feelings she had for Des to Tom. After all, she felt incredibly lonely still, mostly at night, alone in her large bed – the bed she had shared with Des for all those years. She literally craved the feeling of his body next to hers. Now she had accepted that she would never have that again and she missed the close physicality of her husband. Even though she hated his guts for what he had done to her, to them, she still missed him. So Tom was a nice bit of eye-candy to focus on instead. Des was getting on with his life and building a new family, so she should get on with hers.

"So is it egg and chips or beef bourguignon?" Tom was saying.

"Sorry? Oh yes, I don't quite know. I'll be probably too tired to cook by the time I get home. I live in County Meath – it's quite a drive."

"And would your husband not cook you the odd meal?" Tom enquired, his eyes cheeky.

Kate laughed hollowly. "Des wouldn't know his Aga from his ass. No, I can never recall my husband ever cooking for me. Besides, his feet are under someone else's table these days, so it's not really relevant."

Tom appeared suddenly crestfallen. "Oh, I'm so sorry. I didn't mean to pry. I've been that soldier as they say and it's not very pleasant: hence the cooking for one and all that. It's funny – it's the little things you miss.'

Kate winced. Tom had a faraway look in his dark eyes. This was getting seriously maudlin and they were beginning to attract some funny looks. "Yes, well, I'd better be going. I've got to get back to Kilmadden and cook the poor little neglected children something." She gave a nervous laugh, shut the book she hadn't been studying and then rose quickly, grabbing her bag.

Tom followed in her wake. "I'm sorry, Kate. I didn't mean to upset you."

"You didn't upset me," Kate forced a small smile. "I really do have to get on the road soon."

Tom regarded her with his dark sooty eyes. "Kate," he said softly, touching her arm. She stopped in her tracks. "I only came over to tell you that I'm leaving the college to take up another position at the end of term and ask you in my idiotic way if it was possible for you and me to maybe have dinner sometime. But as I am hopelessly out of practice in all this dating lark, I messed up magnificently. Sorry, I'm really rusty at this!"

Kate smiled genuinely this time. She was flattered anyone gave her a second look. Des had done a good job in crushing any self-confidence out of her. "You didn't stuff up – and I am also out of practice with even talking coherently to someone of the opposite sex that's over the age of ten. And yes, maybe we could have dinner sometime but I would prefer lunch to start off with, if that's OK. Baby-steps are best for the moment. By the way, how did you know – that I was single again, I mean?"

Tom smiled and dropped his gaze to the ground. "Apart from the same tortured look that I had worn myself for the first six months, you twiddled your wedding ring constantly in class for about three weeks and then stopped wearing it altogether."

Kate was amazed at how observant he was. She looked down at her bare fingers where her huge diamond solitaire and matching wedding ring had once nestled. Now the white tidemark had even faded long since like her marriage. Ten years didn't seem to count for much, it would appear. "Really?"

He had the decency to look sheepish. "Well, partly – your friend Leila told me you had recently separated, but I had to be sure, hence the husband question. I could never imagine anyone being stupid enough to leave someone like you."

Kate tried to decide whether or not to be annoyed

over this. "Leila seems to have spilled the entire can of beans."

"Sorry, I told you I was crap at all of this." He started to move away. "Sorry, Kate."

"I'm free for lunch Friday, if you like," she said suddenly, triumphantly.

She felt as if she had jumped off a cliff. But it was time to move on.

"Oh, I like!" Tom said, the sooty eyes all sexy. "I like quite a lot."

And there it was.

Olivia at that very moment was standing outside Costigan Art Gallery in Mount Merrion trying to get up some courage to go in. She peered in the window and tried to spy her father – well, her biological father. The word father didn't really fit someone she had never met and it seemed insulting to the man she had always called Dad.

Dymphna had come by, as promised a couple of months ago, and had carried out a reconnaissance mission, but after some inquiries had discovered that Seamus Costigan was away in Australia for six weeks. So now thanks to James's persistence and nagging encouragement Olivia found herself about to meet the man who was her father.

She felt as if she was going for an important interview or something, but the queasy feeling that engulfed her stomach meant it was so much more. What if she hated him on sight or he hated her? She went through various scenarios in her head, of what she would say and what he would look like, but nothing could really prepare you for this.

"You can't move on until you sort this out," James had said. "It's not as deep for Grace or Moira as it is for you. It is essentially between you and him. You have to make your peace with this."

So she was here, terrified and feeling like a fourteen-year-old on a first date.

If James hadn't insisted she just wouldn't be here, but he insisted on facing up to things which was probably why she loved him so and why she had come so far and was happier than she could ever remember. She felt her stomach and patted her little secret, then calmly walked up the tall granite steps and went inside.

Inside the quiet luxury of the gallery Olivia spotted a large man in an expensive suit hovering about the paintings and wearing a frown.

"Em, Mr Costigan?" Olivia ventured.

He was bald and red-faced and more than a little bit unfriendly-looking.

"No," the man barked, even though he wore a fake smile. "Charles O'Leary – I'm Shay's partner." Then he called out loudly through a doorway that led into the back of the showroom. "Shay?"

Olivia could hear her heart pound even louder.

Charles O'Leary smiled lasciviously at her. "There's a pretty lady out here to see you."

Moments later Shay Costigan emerged, into Olivia's life.

He was tall and fair like her and he had the same eyes. It was weird to look at him – it was almost like looking at herself sometime in the future.

He smiled, the pale blue eyes crinkled. He had been handsome – he still was, even though he must be now over sixty.

"Yes?"

"I'm Olivia," she said simply in the end, all the rehearsed lines thrown out the window.

He didn't even look remotely surprised. "Yes, you are, aren't you? Hello, I've been expecting you."

She looked at him quizzically.

He tried to explain. "Oh, I wanted to come and see you straight after your mother came and told me of your existence. But then I realised that it had to be your decision, your choice. And here you are." He seemed to be genuinely excited.

She stood there, taking him in. The tallness of him and the nuance of his smile that mimicked her own were very familiar, yet he was a stranger. It was the oddest experience.

"Let's go somewhere nice for a coffee so we can talk properly," he said, taking charge, ushering her out of the gallery and leading her away to a chic little coffee house a few doors down.

Over cappuccino they seemed to be both suddenly shy and chatted awkwardly about the plethora of coffee houses in Dublin lately and how cosmopolitan it had all become.

"I never knew about you, you know," Shay Costigan

said suddenly. "Until, that is, your mother arrived a few months ago to tell me. It was quite a shock. I wondered why she never told me before, but I suppose I wasn't much of a boyfriend to her in those days. I hated Mayo – always wanted to leave and head for the big smoke and make my fortune. She probably guessed that I wasn't good husband material and in those days I wasn't. And so I did leave, and soon after I heard through the grapevine that Moira had married Sean. So I moved on and ended up here – but I couldn't help wondering, since I had that visit recently, if it all could have happened a lot differently."

Olivia nodded. She had never thought of how all this had affected him. He must have felt as unhinged as she did. All those years he missed out on too. Then all the anger and fear just drifted out of her and suddenly she felt very tired but oddly satisfied.

"My father is a wonderful man, you know," Olivia said. She needed to say that, in defence of her real father, Sean. "He gave me all the love in the world, but I'm sorry you were denied the chance."

Shay went to put his hand over hers and then stopped short. "Well, it can't be helped. Perhaps we can be friends now though, that would be nice. I can't pretend to make up for thirty-six years, it wouldn't be possible, but you and I can become good friends."

Yes, Olivia decided inwardly, her heart lifting and soaring as never before. That would be perfect.

"Well, I have a little gift for you, in a way. A gift only a daughter can give her father . . ."

Shay Costigan looked surprised and touched. He waited.

"I want you to be the first to know that you are going to be a grandfather. I am expecting my first child. I just found out today, in fact."

Shay was openly amazed. "I am honoured to be the first to know! Haven't you even told the father yet?"

Olivia shook her head. And then explained all about James and the aborted wedding to Connell and the fact that this pregnancy was neither planned or expected and that it was early days in the relationship, but that despite all of that she was ecstatic.

"Well, go home and tell him," her father advised. "He sounds like he is a person with great integrity who loves you to bits, so he is going to want your child just as much."

After Olivia learnt a bit more about her father's past life (two marriages, one divorce and one step-son), she left the coffee house a very different person to the one who went in. She made her way to the train station where an unsuspecting James would be patiently waiting for her four hours later at the other end. Despite what Shay had said about James, she felt equal mixes of excitement and terror at the prospect of telling him their news. James had never mentioned the "C" word, commitment, never mind the "M" word. His parents were still so old-fashioned that she had to pretend she wasn't even living there when they visited from the big farm a few miles away. She wondered how this news would go down. But deep inside she felt at peace because this baby, though a surprise, was very much wanted by Olivia, whatever lay ahead.

She suddenly realised she wasn't all that different from her mother after all, unmarried and pregnant and unsure of her future. The irony wasn't lost on her and she started to giggle in the train carriage to herself. She thought Grace would get a great laugh out of this. Olivia had always held the high moral ground and had openly criticised her sister for getting knocked up so easily.

But James would be the next to know, and everyone else including Grace would have to wait – they'd all know soon enough.

Chapter 32

The day had dawned for Dymphna's biopsy results.

Grace had been a fantastic support over that time and had rarely left Dymphna alone, even though Dymphna assured her that she was perfectly fine. But she hadn't been. She had been surviving on autopilot and denial in the daytime and with copious vodkas at night in order to find some sleep. It had also been a tense five days in which Dymphna had avoided Derek's many and frequent phone calls. She just couldn't think about starting something while this question mark still remained over her health. She also knew that if Derek did know something about her results she wouldn't be able to help herself – she would persecute him for information. So she managed to avoid him until today, after which she would definitely contact him. The text messages were piling up too.

She sat with Grace in the packed waiting-room in the oncology outpatients. Funny how the cancer department was termed oncology – they were probably trying not to scare the first timers. Dymphna looked about and wondered what trials and tribulations each patient had endured. At least some of them here today would receive bad news, even though most looked surprisingly cheerful.

"Are you OK?" Grace asked for the ninth time.

"I'm fine," Dymphna lied, her throat constricting so much she could barely speak.

Why the hell did they ask two hundred people to attend at nine o'clock in the morning anyway, when it was painfully obvious that they wouldn't be all seen until well after four? The suspense was almost too much to bear.

"Have you heard from that guy Derek at all?" Grace enquired, at a loss to think of anything else to say.

"He's like a bloody stalker!" Dymphna muttered darkly. "I've had about seven phone calls and forty-three texts so far. Honestly, I'm rapidly going off the bloke already. He must be some sort of weirdo, the way he's been calling me."

Grace laughed out loud at this and received some dour looks from the other out-patients in the exceptionally quiet room. "Dimples you are a scream! You moan and bitch about guys not being attentive or ever phoning when they say they will and yet when they do you don't return their calls. Didn't you think that maybe there was a chance he was ringing to tell you that he knew your results and that you were in the clear?"

Dymphna looked contrite. "Oh you don't think so,

do you? Maybe he was trying to re-assure me that there was nothing to worry about. I'm such an idiot – I should have called him back."

She took out her mobile phone and began to go over her texts. Just then the nurse emerged from the inner sanctum and called her name loudly. She almost jumped out of her skin. She leapt up as if she had been scalded and Grace ran after her. She grabbed Dymphna's arm and squeezed it tightly.

"I'm coming in with you," she whispered.

Dymphna smiled and nodded mutely.

Inside the consultation room sat the nurse and an elderly doctor. He pored over her file for what seemed like an age and then airily introduced himself in a posh accent as Professor Carthy.

"Miss Coffey," he said, looking at her over his pince-nez and under his bushy eyebrows, "we removed a lump that you found in your right breast and sent it for assessment and culture in the laboratory . . ."

Dymphna held her breath and tried to focus on the words.

"And the results . . ." he continued while scanning her chart.

Hurry up! Hurry up! She felt like screaming…

". . . were normal. I am happy to say the lump was benign. So Ms Coffey, you are in the clear. I'll just have a look at the biopsy site to see if it is healing well."

Dymphna couldn't believe it. The words fell over her. It took a moment to sink in and then she thanked the professor so profusely that she embarrassed herself and him. Grace just sat there with tears misting up in her eyes – it had been a sobering experience.

Within minutes they were both out of there and Dymphna had got her life back.

Grace and Dymphna went out for lunch to celebrate and telephoned Kate, who was looking after Orla, with the good news.

"Come here as soon as you can," Kate said excitedly. "I want to celebrate myself. I've got some news and I need to share it."

"Will do," Grace said happily. Everything was turning out OK. Kate sounded happier than she had in ages and Dymphna was like a woman reborn.

They had a lovely lunch in Malahide and then made their way to Kate's house in Kilmadden where, champagne bottle and glasses at the ready, she imparted the news of her first proposed date in over twelve years.

"Fair play to you," Dymphna replied archly. "It's about time you had some fun after watching Des lord it about the village with Miss Malicious Melody."

"Don't mince your words there, Dimples, tell us how you really feel." Grace quipped, watching Kate's crestfallen look.

"It's OK, she's right, Grace. I do have to move on and Tom *is* totally gorgeous. It's just a bit weird that's all, sort of like the end of an era. Therefore, I think this calls for champagne."

Kate popped the champagne cork and poured and they all sipped the frothy bubbles in unison.

"We'll have to give you pointers on how to dress and trap a man, seeing as how you are so out of practice," Dymphna said, tongue-in-cheek. "I can give you a few tips . . . or you can borrow my collection of *Sex in the City* videos. I think you're probably more like Charlotte – you need to learn a few things from Samantha."

"I prefer Carrie meself," Grace mused, the champagne bubbles getting to her.

"What *are* you pair like?" Kate laughed. "It's only lunch, you know! I don't want to scare the poor bloke off! It's early days yet, and he's been through a separation himself, at least that is what I gathered from what he has said, so he'll understand how I feel. It just feels weird that's all, even contemplating a romantic life with someone else – it was just never part of my plan."

Grace watched Kate as she spoke, the faraway look in her clear blue eyes intimating a great deal of hurt still very evident.

"No," she said sadly, touching Kate's arm, "I don't suppose you did."

To think she had envied Kate's life so much and now look at her: alone and abandoned by her husband and so unsure of her future. Despite her perfect looks and her obvious devotion to Des, it still didn't matter – Des had walked away from his beautiful wife, perfect home and lovely children. There was nothing to envy.

Grace felt ashamed of every time she jealously coveted this fabulous house or Kate's slim thighs and suddenly became painfully aware of all the things she possessed. She promised herself she would treat Paul to a romantic dinner tomorrow night because he had been so understanding and helpful the past few days and because she had been so preoccupied over Dymphna that she had hardly been present.

She glanced at her watch. It was well after five and Jordan would have been home from secondary school for almost an hour. She hated to be late on the evenings Jordan was home early from school. It made her feel like a bad mother. Teenagers needed you even more than babies, it seemed.

"Sorry to break up the party, but I really have to get going. Poor old Paul has been totally neglected lately and here I am again quaffing champagne and not a spud on the boil. I'd better go."

Kate looked a bit dejected. "You'll stay, won't you, Dymphna? You have to help me finish off this champagne. You don't need to be anywhere tonight, do you? We can have a girly night in and you can stay over . . ." Her voice trailed off.

Dymphna noticed the edge of desperation in Kate's tone. She was obviously lonely.

Dymphna smiled. "I'd love to, Kate. Of course I'll stay. Better than facing an empty flat." She glanced knowingly at Grace who nodded her assent back.

Grace rose and gathered a fractious Orla who was never too keen on leaving Jade and Chloe after a full afternoon of play.

She headed home through a deluge of rain and the ever-increasing traffic-jam that recently clogged the small narrow village at rush hour. Dublin had seemed to up sticks and run to the countryside. She arrived back to find all the lights on and Paul's van parked in the tiny driveway outside.

She was bursting to tell him Dymphna's good news.

She ran inside, clutching Orla and the usual myriad of baby necessities, and found Paul sitting like a statue in the tiny front room, staring at a large closed suitcase that loomed large in front of him.

Grace stared at the suitcase and then at Paul. "What's going on?" she said in a voice that sounded terrified, which is exactly how she felt.

Paul continued to stare straight ahead at the suitcase. He wouldn't even look at her.

"I think that's my line, don't you? I should be asking you the same thing. What is going on, Grace?"

Grace's mind raced. It could be only one thing. Oh no! It couldn't be, could it?

"What do you mean, Paul? You're scaring me, what is the matter?"

She eyed the suitcase; it seemed to be getting larger by the minute.

"I had an interesting phone call a while ago. It was your old flame Samir asking about your arrival times in London – you and Jordan. He sounded so excited, couldn't wait to see you both. Of course I pretended to know all about it, unlike the eejit I really am, being the last to know. I would just like you to tell me when I was going to find out about your little plan. Or would I ever have known until after you were gone, if I hadn't happened to come home early today? I was planning to make you a nice meal as a surprise. Instead, I got the surprise, didn't I?"

Grace's heart fell to her boots. She had fully intended to tell Paul about the trip almost since the day she had phoned Samir, but it had never seemed like the right moment and then with all the problems over Dymphna's scare it had receded into the back of her mind. She had never expected this.

"I can explain," she said in a rising panic.

"I'll bet you can!" Paul roared, his voice dripping with disgust. "Just when was I going to find out about this little moonlight flit? Were you going to pin a note to Orla's bib to say that you and Jordan were off? How *could* you, Grace? How could you deceive me like that and plan in secret to meet that – that *idiot* who walked out on you all those years ago and never looked back. I have never felt such a fool or so cheated on in my entire life!"

Grace couldn't even tell him that it wasn't how it seemed. It did look bad but it wasn't the way he was portraying it – he made it sound so sordid.

Grace went over to him and stood inches away, trying to connect with him, to make him look her in the eyes, but the dreamy chocolate eyes were cold, icy even.

She tried anyway. "Do you trust me Paul? Have I ever done anything in all these years for you to doubt me? Surely you don't believe there is anything between Samir and me? I am doing this for Jordan, and only because he insists on knowing his father – why don't you believe that?"

Paul stood up abruptly. Grace noticed that there were tears in his eyes.

"How the hell would I know? I don't even know you any more!" He took the suitcase up and marched past her, stopping briefly to kiss Orla. "I'll be in touch to see the kids – well, my kid anyway, seeing as I'm obviously superfluous to requirements for your precious son."

He slammed the door loudly behind him and with that he was gone.

Grace felt like she had been slapped. She felt shocked but also very angry. Paul could at least have heard her out! To walk out just like that after all these years! She couldn't quite believe it! They had never even had a row that left them anywhere close to one of them packing their bags, so she knew this was very serious. She stood in the front room for what seemed like an age before she heard the door slam and Jordan calling out for her while gabbling on that he was sorry he was late, that he had football practice. With tears streaming down her face, Grace told a shocked Jordan to fetch Orla and himself some biscuits from the kitchen while she telephoned Paul's mobile. She would have to sort this out. As expected, Paul's mobile was switched off so she did the only other thing she could think about through the fog of shock – she called her friend

"Dimples, it's me, come quickly. It's urgent. Paul has just walked out."

There it was: the words she never dreamt she'd ever utter. But it was all too real. Paul had left her.

Chapter 33

Within minutes, Dymphna, Kate and Kate's girls arrived en masse to Grace's aid.

They found her cooking dinner in the midst of tears while Jordan eyed her silently and quietly from the corner.

Kate took over the cooking while Dymphna led Grace away into the front room for an explanation.

"What the hell has happened?" Dymphna was incredulous. In all her wildest imagination she never could have dreamt that what seemed like the happiest couple she knew were splitting up. Dymphna had envied Grace's happy marriage for years.

"It's all my fault!" Grace wailed. "I arranged to go to London with Jordan to meet up with Samir. I hadn't yet told Paul, with all the hassle of the past two weeks and it never seemed the right moment and I had warned

Samir to only call me if he absolutely needed to and then before six o'clock on weekdays because Paul is never home before seven, but today Paul was home early. And Samir called and Paul answered, put two and two together and made two billion. He thinks there is something going on and he's left. Packed a suitcase and just walked out! I can't believe it!"

"Oh you silly, silly cow, Gracie! You should have discussed it with Paul first – you know he has a blind spot when it comes to Samir. But don't worry, I'm here and so is Kate. It's about time someone else took care of you for a change. Kate's cooking the tea, and I'll stay for as long as you want. I'll call Paul on his mobile in the morning and try to get him to see some sense. When he calms down, surely he'll realise you'd never do anything to jeopardise you and him, won't he?"

"I don't honestly know, Dimples. I have never ever seen him so angry or devastated. He looked at me with real hate. I don't know if he'll ever come back. He has never even spent a night away after a row – we never have those sorts of fights. You should have seen the look on his face . . ." She dissolved into fresh tears.

"Come on now, Grace. You don't want the kids to see you so upset, do you? This will all blow over tomorrow and you'll be wondering why you ever got so worked up. Now dry your eyes, we'll get the kids sorted out and the three of us will have a nice cup of tea and talk it over, OK?"

Grace nodded gratefully. Dymphna smiled widely but inside her heart was sinking. She didn't believe for one minute Paul Kelly would get over this betrayal – a betrayal at least in his eyes – any time soon.

After Kate cooked all the children something to eat and put on a video for them, the three women sat in Grace's cramped little kitchen with a bottle of wine and tried to make sense of what had just occurred. Grace's marriage to Paul had been the one stalwart rock in their lives. They had all envied the relationship and pinned their hopes on finding a similar one. It was unthinkable that it was now as insecure and wobbly as everyone else's. Kate felt awful for Grace. She had just about crawled out of the abyss of misery and now she had to watch her friend go through something similar. She found it difficult to mouth platitudes when she felt deep down that they just didn't help, in fact she had felt like slapping everyone who mouthed one to her over the past six months.

Looking at Grace's distraught face brought back all the feelings of utter despair that she had felt that first night she had discovered Des's affair. It was as if the ground had been suddenly removed from under her feet. Her world had never been the same.

Dymphna chatted on to Grace, trying to find a loophole in the rationale behind Paul's quick departure and some way to try and mend fences. She was pouring Grace another glass of Chardonnay when Jordan came in.

"Mum, I'm really sorry that this has happened. I feel it's all my fault. If I hadn't talked so much about my father and pushed you into finding him, none of this would have happened. I didn't want to see him if it means you and Paul are splitting up because of it."

Grace regarded her son whose grown-up speech was the most he had ever spoken to her in the one conversation in the past year. His dark brown eyes were serious and she could see the beginnings of an adult face emerge.

She never loved him as much as she did right now.

"It's not your fault, Jordan. You have a right to know your natural father. Paul is just angry with me because I didn't tell him about it, and he is right about that. But don't worry, we'll sort it out. You will still go to London and see Samir like I promised." She'd have hugged him but it just wasn't cool for Jordan to be seen receiving affection in front of anyone else so she just winked at him and he departed with his sloped jaunty walk, the ragged denims straggling along the floor.

"Did you mean it? Are you still going to go to London?" Dymphna enquired in a surprised tone.

"You'd better believe it," Grace replied bitterly. "If Paul wants to believe that I have ulterior motives then that's his problem. I know I was wrong not to tell him but I had intended to. If he wants to believe after all these years that I'm a two-timing bitch then he can get stuffed. This is about Jordan and what he needs and if Paul can't be a grown-up about it, then I want nothing more to do with him."

Dymphna watched a silent tear slide down Grace's cheek but there was a steely resolve in the tone and in the words that meant she was serious. It would break her heart but she wouldn't bend when her mind was made up. This might prove to be more difficult than she had first anticipated. Both Grace and Paul could represent Ireland in the Olympics for sullen obstinacy, so it might take more than a few phone calls to sort out, that was for sure. She would give Olivia a ring – Grace needed all her friends right now and her sister too. Dymphna would call her in the morning.

Chapter 34

Grace woke up to find her head was muzzy and her mouth dry. For a few seconds she wondered why she felt so awful, then the previous night came back to her in awful glorious technicolour. She was suffering from a hangover and a broken heart and not necessarily in that order. She felt like weeping and wailing into her pillow but it wouldn't help feed and dress a demanding toddler and equally needy teenager. So she dragged herself out of bed and pretended that her whole world hadn't fallen apart. Wasn't it bloody weird that women couldn't even enjoy a nervous breakdown without getting up and making breakfast and looking after everyone else first?

The phone trilled. Grace's heart gave a little jump. No one would ring this early – it must be Paul. She took the stairs in twos and dived for the receiver like an Olympic medallist.

"Grace!" Olivia's singsong voice these days was refreshing but today it wasn't what Grace wanted to hear.

"I've got some news! I'm just bursting to tell you! I was thinking about coming down to see you for a few days and I need to visit Mad Moira and Dad too so – can I stay?"

"Yep," Grace replied deadpan. "Plenty of spare room – in fact we've got room in my bed as it happens. Paul has vacated the premises."

"Oh Grace!" replied Olivia in a shocked voice. "I'm so sorry. Look, I'll be there in a few hours. James is lending me his jeep."

"Well, drive carefully," said Grace. "We don't need you breaking your neck to get here – Dimples got rid of all the razors so you're OK on that score. Take your time. I'll be at The Beeches all day."

She put the phone down without even wondering momentarily what news her older sister wanted to impart. Her mind was filled with thoughts of Paul and where the bloody hell he might be.

The phone rang twice more in quick succession but both times it was someone other than Paul. Firstly it was Dimples offering to take the day off work and then it was Kate wondering if Grace was up to going to work. It was just that she had a lunch date with Tom, she admitted in a guilty voice, and she needed to tell him if she was able to go or not.

Grace assured both of them that she was totally in control and that Olivia was coming to stay and no she didn't need to be baby-sat and yes she was going to work and would be there in time to help Kate pick out a suitably sexy outfit. Grace asked Kate if she wouldn't mind Olivia coming over to The Beeches, considering the circumstances. Kate said she'd be delighted if they'd all stay for dinner, Jordan and all.

Grace almost tried Paul's mobile before she regained her steely composure and she got both children ready in record time and wore her best linen pants suit to convince the world and more importantly herself that she was absolutely fine. She took her mobile out of her handbag and put it in her pocket just in case Paul was trying to contact her. Just in case.

Kate was over at The Beeches trying on half her wardrobe. She was desperate not to give Tom the wrong impression, yet she wanted to look sexy and desirable and confident – all the things she rarely felt.

She wondered what Des would say if he could see her now, going on a date. He'd find out soon enough. Jade and Chloe had heard her talk to Tom on the phone and no doubt they'd chatter on all the information over at Des's apartment either to Melody or him. She didn't care. He'd moved on, even started a new family – she wasn't going to remain nun-like forever. She felt a mixture of paralysing fear and girlish excitement fight for supremacy in her head. Then there was Grace. Kate felt so awful to be going on a lunch date today of all days when Grace's marriage seemed in real trouble.

She flung another three outfits on the bed and

instantly hated them all – this was going to be more difficult than she thought.

Within an hour Grace had helped Kate select a black Donna Karen dress, simple yet sexy, that showed off Kate's slender figure but yet was demure enough to suit the day-time lunch date.

"Perfect," Grace admired, while sitting on the bed wondering if she'd ever fit into Donna Karen's clothes, never mind afford them.

Kate was contrite. "I really appreciate this, you know. I feel horrible having you help me out when it's my turn to be there for you."

"Nonsense," Grace replied emphatically. "This *is* helping. I'd rather be here and keeping busy than at home miserable. Paul will come to his senses, he'll calm down and we'll talk it over, you'll see." She almost but not quite convinced herself.

Her mobile phone still remained stubbornly silent.

She waved Kate off on her day and then brought Kate's children to school. Everything was as normal except for the crushing pain deep in Grace's chest.

Kate arrived early for her lunch date with Tom. She knew she should be cool and fashionably late and sweep into the restaurant in wafts of Angel perfume but she was far too nervous. So she got there ten minutes early and freshened up with shaky hands in the ladies'. Giannini's was an unpretentious little Italian restaurant off Temple Bar, but it had a homely air and excellent food. It wasn't upmarket enough for Des's taste, but

Kate had had several nice lunches there in the past with his mother Lucinda and felt quite at home there. So she had suggested it to Tom in the hope that she would feel more relaxed being somewhere familiar, but so far that hadn't worked. She felt almost nauseous, she was so apprehensive.

She looked at her watch and decided she would give him ten minutes' grace when suddenly he was there in front of her, looking taller and more handsome than she remembered. Her heart gave a little lurch as he bent over and kissed her cheek. He smelled of Aramis and sandalwood and looked a lot different than he usually did in college. He was wearing a smart navy jacket, dark navy jeans and a crisp white linen shirt. Not a teachery corduroy in sight.

"Hope you're not as nervous as me," he laughed. "I had half a mind to have a stiff whiskey to steady my nerves, but I thought you might think me a dipso, so I had three bars of chocolate instead!"

Kate laughed in surprise. A man who turned to sweets in times of stress could only be someone a woman could relate to. "You're the first man I ever met who ever admitted being hooked on chocolate. I'm a Cadbury's woman myself – it calms me down every time."

This time they both laughed.

"I've had a long love-hate relationship with the stuff," Tom confessed. "I was a bit of a tubby child. My parents owned a sweetshop and were very busy, so I comforted myself with all the confectionery I could get down. That little fat boy is still lurking in there unfortunately."

Kate stared openly at him.

Tom blushed profusely. "Sorry, I'm rambling now – I do that when I'm nervous. I told you I was a bit rusty at dating. My line in small talk is non-existent."

Kate wasn't sure how to reply. Should she admit to being a former fatty herself and open up her inner torment to a man she hardly knew or should she just fire back some witty repartee? Tom was being honest and it endeared him to her. Des would never admit to any insecurity or fault. It was just strange to hear a man admit to some frailty.

"It's fine, Tom. I've been there myself, to be quite honest. But I don't like to admit it. I feel everyone then watches what I consume after I tell them – or look for telltale signs of bulimia or even worse cellulite!"

"Let's not order a pizza between us then, just in case we're surreptitiously watching each other's consumption!" joked Tom and Kate laughed out loud, and from then on all her own nervousness fell away.

Tom was a kindred spirit. Over a long and leisurely lunch, in which they discovered each other's likes and dislikes, they touched on their respective break-ups.

"Des liked the baby-sitter so much he moved in with her," said Kate, derisively.

"My wife ran off with my cousin," replied Tom, deadpan. "My cousin Linda to be exact."

"You win," grinned Kate.

Tom wolfed down the last of his tiramisu. "That was two years ago and I'm only now feeling somewhat back to normal. That's why I've been such an old grouch most of the semester – so sorry if the lectures were a bit tedious. But now I'm finally moving on. I'm putting the past behind me. I need a fresh start, hence the new job."

Kate found herself a bit perturbed. She suddenly didn't like the idea of Tom just coming into her life to then leave just as quickly. "Oh yeah?" she said nonchalantly. "And where's your new post?"

"I'm setting up my own design team with a friend actually. It's something I have always dreamt of doing but yet never had the nerve. Jill and I sold the house after we broke up and made a bundle. So I'm investing a chunk with an old college buddy and we're going to give it our best shot. It's a bit scary, but we figured it's now or never. I've nothing to lose but my reputation and my life savings and probably the shirt off my back!"

Kate smiled at the self-deprecation. He was so different to Des. "You'll be a huge success, Tom. You're a fantastic design teacher so I'm sure your talent will be recognised. You'll be an enormous loss to the college – never mind your large female following!"

Tom blushed profusely.

"You're embarrassed," Kate said.

"I was hoping you thought these red cheeks were from the Chianti. Have I? A large female following me, that is?"

Kate nodded. She didn't want him to get bigheaded but she had already said it. "You know what I meant."

"I'd settle for one female admirer, you know."

"Stop fishing for compliments!" Kate retorted.

"I meant you, Kate! Just say that you'll consider another date with me and you'll save me from another week of overdosing on Munchie bars."

Kate gave a slow smile. "Purely in the interest of your waistline, all right, you're on. But I'll cook for us next time. Something healthy – that fettuccine was delicious but I'm stuffed."

"What a relief!" Tom exclaimed. "I thought I'd either bored or scared you to death."

"Quite the opposite," remarked Kate, thinking she hadn't had so much fun in absolutely ages. "It's been really fun."

And so it had.

Des stared out of the office window over the rooftops of Dublin city. Somewhere out there, down below, his wife was having lunch with another man. Des had discovered the juicy facts from Chloe, who, while trying to elicit another CD from him, told him she'd relate her mother's secret if he would buy it for her.

Des didn't know why but he felt a jealous rage deep within. He couldn't bear the thought of Kate being pawed by another man or worse still, some bozo spending time in his home, quaffing his wine and playing daddy to his kids.

It unhinged him to feel this bad – after all he had left Kate for Melody and he was happy, wasn't he? Well, as happy as he could be, he supposed. Things hadn't been as heady recently as those first days with Melody were. Since she became heavily pregnant sex had become sparse and Melody had become increasingly moody, but that wasn't it really.

It didn't explain why he felt so enraged that Kate was finally moving on and finding a life without him. He had liked the idea of her pining away, studiously raising his girls alone. He even entertained the idea sometimes of getting her back.

Well, one thing was for sure, if she was going to get serious about this guy and he was going to be a surrogate daddy to Des's girls, he'd be doing it elsewhere. There was no way in hell that Des would let Kate live on at The Beeches with another man while he lived in a glorified flat with his new son. Kate would regret this new liaison. It would cost her a lot more than she imagined.

Chapter 35

Olivia swung James's Land Rover into the long sweeping gravel drive of The Beeches. She would never get tired of looking at this beautiful house. No wonder Grace loved working here. Although there was a price to pay for everything, it seemed, and Kate was paying it.

The large oak door opened and Grace stood there with Orla on her hip, looking a bit crestfallen.

"Hi!" Olivia enthused. She was bursting to tell Grace her brilliant news. But she guessed it could wait. "Are you OK? Any word from Paul yet?"

Grace frowned and led Olivia to the gleaming kitchen where she'd prepared them both some lunch. "Nope, I suppose he's staying with his brother Kevin. I called his mother this morning and she knows nothing yet, so I think maybe he's not sure what to do next. He rings Nell if he breaks a fingernail and she always cossets him back to normal, so I'm not sure if that's a good or a bad sign. Do you want some bread with the salad?"

Olivia grinned. Grace was funny – her world had tipped on its axis and she still remembered her hostess manners.

"Grace, Paul will eventually get over this, he is just being the jealous caveman. Just give him some time. He loves you and that will never change."

Grace nibbled on some salad listlessly, for once her legendary appetite deserting her.

"I hope so. Anyway, enough of my depressing tales of domestic blitz – what has you scurrying down here to Dublin in James's fancy jeep, no less?"

"Well, in a nutshell, I am joining the club. I am in the club as they say, up the duff, preggers or whatever the term is, the fact is – I am with child."

Grace was amazed. Olivia's eyes were shining with pure happiness.

"Olivia, you brazen hussy!" she exclaimed.

"Pot calling the kettle black-arse!" Olivia retorted, laughing.

"I was paraphrasing Mrs Maxwell as a matter of fact. I had to put up with that comment for long enough. I can't quite believe it – you're actually pregnant! You realise Moira is going to do her nut, of course?"

"She is the blackest pot of all." Olivia grinned – nothing was going to dampen her upbeat mood.

"And James? How is he taking the news?"

Olivia took Orla onto her lap and began stroking her black curly hair. Hormones were kicking in already, Grace mused.

"James is both delighted and shell-shocked all at

once. His mam and dad make Moira look as wild as Pamela Anderson. They are so old-fashioned they don't even know we live in sin at his farmhouse. I have to scurry away like a scarlet woman as soon as they hare up the drive. He wants to make an honest woman of me as soon as possible. Luckily I am so mad about him I'd run up the aisle this minute."

"Olivia, you have changed so much from the wedding-shy woman who fled her forthcoming marriage and fiancé and ended up in Clifden! A scant six months later and now look at you! About to be a mother and a farmer's wife all in one go! If you weren't so happy I'd be worried you were on the rebound."

Olivia was suddenly serious. "Grace, I have never been so sure of anything in my life. Since I have got my life in order and met my real father, I finally know who I am, and what I want. That's why it's so important to Jordan that you do this for him, meet Sammy I mean. Even if it's a disaster, at least Jordan can go forward in life and he'll know who he really is. It's very important, Grace. Don't change your mind because Paul disapproves. It's much too vital an issue for that."

Grace looked pensive. "I know." She just wished that she could fulfil her promise to Jordan and hang onto her marriage at the same time.

Olivia watched Grace bite her lip nervously and decided it was time to change the subject. "And where is Kate today?"

"Believe it or not, she's on her first date with a new man. She looked like a movie star going off, even though she was shaking like a leaf. I really hope this man at least gives her back some of her confidence. That Des has a lot to answer for. He swans about the village like Lord Muck with his pregnant teenager in tow, while Kate has to endure the sniggers of the neighbours. Her ego has taken quite a battering and I'm amazed she's even gone through with the date. I'm dying for her to get back so she can tell us all the gossip. She wants us all to stay for dinner, if that's OK. I think she's trying to take my mind off Paul. To think that a few months ago I was doing the same for her, smug in my own happy little world. I never realised how precarious it all was until right now."

"Yes," Olivia replied dreamily, recalling her near-miss with Connell and the dream home and settling for a companionship marriage. "Did I tell you that Connell has found a new woman for himself?"

"No!" gasped Grace suddenly intrigued. "Spill, immediately!"

"OK. Remember I was in Dublin to see Shay Costigan? Well, I called in to see Connell at his practice to apologise to him over everything. I just felt I had to put it right. I didn't expect a great welcome, to be honest, but I felt he needed a better explanation. Anyway, he was on top form. Ushered me in with full attention and I realised why a few minutes later when Nuala, his legal assistant, burst in with a sheaf full of swatches for the new house. Turns out that he has been squiring Nuala since our break-up and they are already planning a wedding – plus she also has a couple of kids from her first marriage. So he has totally moved on and there was I thinking he'd be heartbroken forever."

"Men!" Grace muttered darkly. "They always manage to surprise you, don't they?"

"Yes," Olivia replied gracefully. "I think they do."

"Anyway, when are you off to see Mad Moira and impart your great news?"

Olivia rolled her eyes heavenward. "God, can you not let a poor woman enjoy her lunch before you pose the stomach-churning questions? I'm going to see them tomorrow and as a matter of fact you are coming with me."

Grace was aghast. "You got to be kidding! Where were you when I had to fess up and face the music?"

"Grace, you fessed up at the airport fronting a huge bump and without any warning if you remember. We had no advance notice. I really want you to be there, help me catch her when she faints, so say yes, please, pretty please, I'll owe you one."

"All right," Grace replied grudgingly. "But please, no mention about Paul and me and our current troubles – d'you hear? She'll have a grin the size of Dollymount if she finds out. She's not too keen on 'the man from the mountain' as she calls him."

"Right so, agreed," replied Olivia, exasperated with the convolutions of her family.

"I for one am not looking forward to it."

Chapter 36

Melody was having a freshly percolated coffee with her mother in her new penthouse apartment at Peyton Park, which lay at the top of Kilmadden village and gave panoramic views of the Meath countryside. It was a glamorous apartment that was all steel appliances, marble surfaces and large floor-length windows. They were having their coffee in the lounge, which had a small patio that overlooked the local churchyard and onwards towards The Beeches and the rolling green hills.

Barbara sat somewhat uncomfortably on the low leather sofa, while Melody sat some distance away on the chaise lounge flicking through some magazines. Melody always sat uncomfortably in Barbara Tormey's company. Blood might be thicker than water but it didn't always flow quite as easily and their difficult relationship made Melody feel like a naughty toddler most of the time. Lately though, her mother vacillated between fawning admiration for Melody's audacity in snaring a successful businessman and outright indignation for being an unrepentant hussy parading her bump with pride around Kilmadden like a medal, confusing Melody more than ever.

"You'd better mark my words, Melody Tormey, and make sure that Des is going to divorce that Kate and marry you. You don't want to be left high and dry with a baby to look after. These uppity-type fellas have a habit of getting fed up when the sleepless nights and cranky babies arrive. You've got to make sure he doesn't hightail it back to his wife. Then where will you be? I'm certainly not in a position to take you and a baby on, not with all I've got on my plate as it is –"

"You won't have to take me on," Melody spat emphatically. "Des isn't going anywhere, he'll never go back to Kate. Not now I'm giving him a son, something he has always wished for. Anyway, from what I hear, Kate is sporting a new man, so it looks like she's moving on too. Either way you won't be seeing me back in my scruffy little bedroom ever again, Mum, no thanks. I'm never going backwards – just you wait and see. I want *her* house. I'm not staying here forever. The Beeches is Des's place and as soon as I have his son, I'm going to put pressure on him to get his house back. She's not going to sit pretty up there in any case, when Des sees another bloke up there, where Des rightly belongs – and I am going to make sure of that."

Barbara Tormey watched her daughter's honey-brown eyes harden and become flinty.

She was a cool one, that was for sure. Barbara didn't know if she was proud or ashamed of her calculating daughter, but she was in awe of her – she was finally coming to believe that, whatever happened, Melody wasn't going to be the loser in this.

But still she was worried. Melody seemed to be rail-thin and she was forever studying magazines and books about style and entertaining. It seemed like she was becoming a clone of Des's wife Kate and she never seemed at ease or contented despite her new luxurious surroundings. She still was exercising strenuously despite being well over six months pregnant. Barbara Tormey might not be the best mother in the world, she was aware of that, but it didn't mean she didn't worry about her headstrong eldest daughter who had altered so much.

"Are you happy, Melody?" she asked suddenly out loud. It was a question that was out of character for her to pose normally – happiness was never high on the agenda in the Tormey household – but right now she had to know.

Melody looked up from her book about fine wines and considered the question for a brief moment. "Yeah, I suppose I am – whatever happiness means."

Barbara suddenly felt a fleeting moment of panic and then sorrow for Melody. She knew by the reply that Melody wasn't in love with Des Heathcoat and she had let herself in for quite a bit more than she had bargained for. She just hoped Des would be good to her and that Melody would find happiness and love for her baby when it arrived.

At least the father wasn't some pimply farmhand with no money or sense.

"Even if I'm not totally happy," Melody added with a small smile, "at least I can be miserable in total comfort."

Unaware that across the village Melody was coveting her home, Kate was enjoying a pleasant morning with her girls before Des arrived to take them to ballet lessons. She tried not to smile as she recalled Tom's gentle kiss or the scent of his aftershave as he brushed her lips with his. "Don't get carried away," she said aloud, berating herself for being smitten with the first man who paid her any attention. "It was only one date, after all." But still she felt strangely lighter and happier than she had been in ages. It wasn't just because gentle honest Tom had been such a revelation after the studied control of Des, it was the fact that someone found Kate attractive again. It made her feel more hopeful that life could be good again. She was also more hopeful about her mother's circumstances than she had been in years. Josie had invited her daughter down to the house in Kilbarrack for lunch a few weeks ago and Kate had been astounded by the transformation that had taken place. Instead of her mother languishing around, missing her father in a sea of vodka, Josie had instead cleaned up her act and had got Christy Junior to move in with her. Christy had painted the entire house and had new wooden flooring laid and suddenly everything seemed so much more cheerful and promising. Josie seemed to have a new purpose to her life and Kate hoped it would last.

"I'm really proud of you, Mum," she told Josie in the new spruced-up kitchen.

Josie smiled happily. "It's thanks to Christy Junior, really. But I'm quite proud of it. I don't drink as much since your father died. Half the time I just wanted to be with him, you see, and he was in the pub, so that's where I went to join him. I loved your father so much and I miss him a lot, but having Christy here is great. I feel like there is something to live for again and the grandkids come around a lot too, so the house has got a bit of life back, things are going well and I feel better than I have done in years."

Kate gave her mother a warm hug. She never envisaged a happy ending for her mother given the past few years, but she seemed to be realising that there was more to life than yet another bottle of whiskey.

It made Kate feel hopeful about her own situation – if Josie Cassidy had made a new life for herself after a lifetime, than so could Kate.

Des arrived late that afternoon in a black humour, and barely acknowledged Kate with a brief and terse hello before speeding off with the girls in a cloud of gravel.

Kate's earlier brightness dimmed as she worried and fretted over Des's dark mood. It brought back many memories of when she had displeased him and the coldness of his wrath that always gave her a deep pain in her stomach. Now her nerves clenched at the memory of it and she suddenly realised that was how she had felt a lot of the time for years. She had been so miserable the past few months that she hadn't realised that tense feeling in the pit of her stomach had gone.

Immediately anger replaced the feeling of dread. How dare he make me feel like that, she raged inwardly. He was obviously put out because he got wind that Kate had been seeing someone else. Well, he could get stuffed! Kate thought hotly. How could Des have the audacity to treat her with such disdain, when he had walked out of the marriage after having an affair?

She stormed about the house in a bad temper – at that moment if she could have got her hands on Des she would have throttled him gleefully. Des would not call the shots on her life any more, she decided. She would give him that power over her no longer. They would have to be civil as parents over their girls well-being; but Kate decided that she had been graceful enough considering the circumstances of their break-up and there was no way she would allow Des to call the shots where her love life was concerned. Des would be getting a few home truths when he got back with the girls, that was for certain.

Grace and Olivia arrived over at Depression Drive to break Olivia's news to their parents. They both giggled nervously like giddy schoolgirls as they rapped on the large brass knocker and awaited their fate. It was funny, Grace thought, as her father opened the door, they never had enjoyed this closeness when they were giggly schoolgirls. Still, they had it now and it was wonderful to have a sister that she genuinely liked at long last.

"Your mother is in the kitchen," their father said flatly, rolling his eyes heavenwards. "Cleaning out the cooker."

Some things never changed and there was Moira knee-deep in oven cleaner, fully knowing that her daughters were due to arrive. "I'll be finished in ten minutes, just wait in the parlour."

"No, I'll just wait here," Olivia said in a firm voice. "After all, we pregnant women need a nice firm chair."

Moira leapt up like lightning from her earlier urgent task. "Was I hearing things or did you just say that you were . . . *pregnant*?" She studied Olivia's face for a moment and then switched to glaring at Grace.

"Don't look at me, it's not my fault." Grace murmured, while ushering the children out to the garden where her father had escaped and closing the door after them.

"Yes, I am, Mother," Olivia announced calmly, proudly.

Moira sat down heavily, putting her rubber-gloved hands to her stricken face. "I can't believe it. Olivia. How *could* you?"

"It wasn't planned, Mother, but James and I are very happy about it and we want you to be happy for us too."

Olivia looked serene, and that seemed to silence her mother for a moment.

Grace was feeling increasingly irate when she recalled the endless lectures and talks of scarlet women that she had to endure all those years ago. Was her mother going to play favourites yet again with Olivia?

"You are bringing shame on this house, Olivia Casey," Moira began in a slow deliberate voice.

Spoke too soon, Grace thought, be careful what you wish for. She felt suddenly contrite.

"We've just about got over the fact that you dumped your great job and perfect fiancé to run off with some farmer and now this!" Moira was in full predictable flow. "I just don't know what to call it, I really don't."

Olivia issued her mother a bright smile. "Well, I *do*, Mother. I'd call it a hat trick."

Moira looked at Olivia as if she had finally gone mad, then looked at Grace for some backup.

Suddenly Grace realised what Olivia meant and she began to giggle despite herself.

"Yes, Moira, a hat trick. You, Grace and me, we've all done it now, so I really feel part of the family. Let's call it a family tradition, shall we? The Casey girls always get knocked up and then get married later. I am going to get married, by the way."

Her mother looked quizzically at Olivia and then suddenly a smile crept across her face. She began to laugh, a large belly-aching laugh that both pleased and surprised her daughters. "I suppose it is a family tradition!" She laughed and wiped her eyes with her Marigolds. "Lord above but you girls don't half give me heart failure sometimes!"

"That's because we're just chips off the old block, Mam," Grace quipped, glad that at least her mother saw the funny side and the worst was over.

Her mother blushed crimson and suddenly looked a bit tearful. "It's all my fault, of course. I haven't been a very good mother to you both. I was hard on you, Grace, and I lied for so long to you, Olivia, but I want you both to know that I did my best, the best I knew how to anyway, if that makes any sense."

"Of course you did, Mam," Olivia replied softly. "We love you and you *are* a good mother."

"Lovely clean ovens too!" Grace added and they all laughed again.

And that was as good as it was going to get with their mother. At least she hadn't taken out the rosary beads and challenged Olivia to go immediately to confession.

Grace made tea, while they all chatted about Olivia's forthcoming nuptials.

"By the way, Grace," Moira said, suddenly back on form. "You'd better keep an eye on that fella of yours. I met him up at Artane Castle shopping centre yesterday coming out of Penney's with a glamorous blonde. Oh, he tried to pass her off as a customer but I know a guilty look when I see one."

Grace blanched visibly. Olivia saw her open panic and stepped in. "That's rubbish, Mam! Why, you and I both know that Paul would never cheat Grace or his family. If Paul said she was a customer then that's what she was. Now, speaking of Paul, you probably should get the kids home and get the poor guy's dinner organised, Grace. And I want to head back to Clifden before it gets too late."

Olivia got them all out of the house as quickly as possible as she gleaned from Grace's black looks that tears and anger were welling up inside her.

Once inside the jeep Grace broke into silent tears but tried to hide her upset from Jordan, so she looked out the window unseeingly at Raheny flying past, trying to make some sense of what she had just heard.

"We'll go to MacDonald's for lunch, kids," Olivia announced cheerily as she put her hand on Grace's arm and gave it a squeeze. They drove to Artane Castle and got the children their favourite meals and talked as Jordan played with Orla in the kiddies' play area.

"I'm sure it's not like Mam said, Grace. It was probably totally innocent. You have to talk to Paul before you jump to any conclusions."

Grace looked miserably at her chips. Normally she'd have wolfed them down but she just felt sick with worry. "I don't know, Olivia. He scarpered pretty quickly from my life, as I seem to remember – maybe the issue of me seeing Samir again was just a cover. Maybe this other woman was just waiting in the wings and he caused a row in order to leave. How do I know? His mobile phone is switched off and he hasn't exactly been burning down the phone lines with his passionate pleas to re-unite. Hell, he hasn't even called to see how the children are. Probably having too much fun with Blondie Knickers to remember his own little girl!"

Olivia started on Grace's unwanted chips. "Now you're being totally paranoid, Gracie. Just talk to the guy. You can sort it out. Phone him this evening, OK? Otherwise you'll drive yourself nuts over nothing. Please promise me."

"OK, I will."

But Grace wondered what kind of reason could explain her husband being at their local shops with a mystery blonde. One way or another she was going to find out.

Chapter 37

Dymphna was rushing through Grafton Street on her lunch hour in a desperate attempt to purchase some black court shoes for an important conference she was attending soon and not having much luck. She looked at the time. It was almost a quarter to two and she still hadn't managed to find the elusive shoes or even a sandwich. Her stomach rumbled noisily and she decided that her hunger would have to be fed before she could look at another shoe shop. She ducked out of the rain and into the Stephen's Green shopping centre and raced to O'Brien's in a tizzy, then bumped straight into dishy Derek, her radiographer friend from the hospital.

Dymphna was stunned into an uncharacteristic silence while her brain tried to picture her rag-tail damp hair and fading lipstick. Somehow she had imagined meeting Derek again in more glamorous circumstances.

"Well, if it isn't the disappearing damsel, no longer

in distress!" said Derek in a mocking tone. He wasn't joking.

Embarrassment flooded Dymphna, making her turn a nice shade of dark pink. "Derek, hi! I'm sorry I haven't returned your calls, I . . . em . . . meant to, it was just . . ."

Derek's pale blue eyes blazed with ill-disguised annoyance. "It's fine," he said in a flat voice, while looking at Dymphna coolly. "I suppose the memory of my awful argyle jumper was just too much for you to bear. Sorry I bothered you with all those calls. I might have guessed you hadn't changed much after all. I won't be bothering you again. I got the message. See ya."

He sidestepped her swiftly and moved off into the crowd of customers milling around the Stephen's Green Centre.

Dymphna was rooted to the spot with pure embarrassment for a few seconds. Then almost without thinking she ran after him. She spotted his tall blond frame in the distance, striding purposefully toward the large exit doors.

"Derek! Stop!" she called loudly to him and he turned around. "What do you *mean* I haven't changed? Of course I have. Just because I haven't had the time to return your call doesn't mean I didn't want to see you again, you *idiot*!"

Derek looked unconvinced. "Is that your version of an apology?"

"No! This is all coming out wrong. Look, Derek, let me buy you a cup of coffee and explain, please."

His brow unfurrowed for the first time since she'd

met him today. "OK," he allowed, "but make it a mug of cappuccino and I want a double chocolate-chip cookie as well, plus you only have ten minutes to convince me."

Dymphna smiled. She was glad he wasn't a pushover. "You drive a hard bargain, but OK." Suddenly it seemed very important that she not let this one go.

Over their frothy coffees Dymphna tried to explain. "I'm sorry I never returned your calls or texts. I was so distracted with worry over my results that I just couldn't focus on anything else. Then when I found out the results, I was so embarrassed by my fobbing you off that I couldn't find the courage to phone you. I had let it go too far and I knew you'd be annoyed and you are, so I just hoped I'd bump into you sooner or later and we'd sort it out." She gave him her most winning smile.

With relief she saw Derek's face soften.

"Pretty unlikely, don't you think? It's lucky that you even met me here. I seldom come into town."

"Not luck," Dymphna replied silkily. "It's fate. I was meant to have a lousy time looking for shoes and you were destined to be having lunch in the very same place I was. Why are you in town, then?"

Derek blushed. "I'm on a late shift today. So I decided to come in to Grafton Street and see what all the fuss and bustle was about." He grinned then. "Plus, a certain patient of mine told me that O'Brien's did the absolute best sandwiches and she spent most of her lunchtimes there."

"So we're friends again?" Dymphna asked.

"Yes, I suppose we are," said Derek, draining the last of his cappuccino.

"Right so," Dymphna replied impishly. "You can help me on my desperate mission to snare a pair of shoes before escorting me back to the IFSC – if you've got the time, that is."

Derek looked at his watch. "Well, I've got to be back at Beaumont by three for my shift. I'm on three to eleven this week. The shifts can be murderous. The X-ray department isn't a nine-to-five sort of place. But I will escort you down Grafton Street, if you'd like."

Dymphna wasn't sure whether Derek was still keen on her or not, judging by that last remark. She now wanted him to want her. He was so attractive and sexy she regretted her earlier reticence – she really must have been high on painkillers and sick with worry to pass him up the first time.

"No problem," she replied lightly and rose swiftly to leave.

This time Derek had to hurry after her.

"God, you are hard work," he said, exasperated, after several silent minutes of following Dymphna as she strode down Grafton Street.

"What?" Dymphna retorted in irritation, swinging around to face him. She was late back to work minus the much-needed shoes and she'd just made a fool of herself with the first man that she had found attractive since the awful Mark had been dumped from her life.

"Yes, *you*. You are so bloody irritating! I chased you for over a week and you totally avoided me, then today you sort of apologise and before I know it you're annoyed with me all over again over something else I said. What do I have to do to make you realise I haven't been able to stop thinking about you? I came into town today to try and see you. But to be honest, I don't know why I bothered."

He stood facing her, both hands on hips. He looked so handsome she just wanted to throw herself into his arms and kiss the face off of him.

"Me too," she said instead. "I have been thinking about you non-stop and I thought that you were just trying to give me the brush-off back there as some sort of payback for me being such an idiot."

"I don't play games, Dymphna. If I want to tell you something I'll tell you out straight, OK? Now – will you agree to meet me for dinner on Sunday night? It's my first night off this week."

"Yes, I would love to, Derek." She felt unbelievably relieved.

He then took her into his arms and kissed her right then and there. She almost melted with the softness of his kiss and all around her Grafton Street fell silent and everything was still. Then he let go and she came back to reality again.

"I've waited years to do that," he said, a grin flickering around his mouth.

"Yes, well, let's hope it won't be so long before the next one. I quite enjoyed that," Dymphna replied brazenly.

"Plenty more where that came from," quipped Derek. "Now I really have to go or I'll be late. I'll call you, right?"

"Yes," replied Dymphna, staring after him, not quite believing all that had just occurred. "You do that."

And there it was – no shoes but a new boyfriend. You just never knew what you could achieve in Grafton Street on your lunch hour.

Kate was in a black mood by the time Des arrived back laughing and cheery with their two daughters. She watched him in disgust as the Lexus came to a crunchy stop on the gravel driveway. He got out of the car with his usual languid grace and ambled to the doorway without a care in the world. This above all angered Kate greatly. She had fretted and stewed about all afternoon after he had stormed in earlier. Now she was supposed to be all sweetness and light because he was finally in a good mood. Kate rushed to the door – she didn't want him strolling in like the Lord of the Manor.

"Girls, please go into the den, I need to speak to Dad for a moment." She tried her best to sound light but the words somehow slipped out petulant and harsh.

"Don't want to," Chloe said defensively, eyeing Des and waiting for Kate to be overruled.

"Go on, pet, it's OK," Des said sweetly, which infuriated Kate even more. Let's humour crazy Mummy while she has a rant, the tone said.

Kate began to recite the words that had stormed through her mind earlier. "Des, I would prefer if you wouldn't come up here to see the girls and take whatever ill feelings you have out on me. If you can't at least be as civil as I am, then we'll have to meet on neutral ground where you'll have to behave in a better fashion."

Des's full red lips curled into a now-familiar sneer. "Oh, please, do me a favour with the sanctimonious saint routine. I know what you've been up to."

Kate was incredulous. Who had left whom? Was he completely out of his tiny mind?

She regarded him carefully. No, he was serious and aggrieved. He actually was pissed off that she had taken her life back and was moving on. In fact he seemed, well, *jealous*. She couldn't quite believe it but there it was, right in front of her.

Six foot two of pent-up jealousy.

Suddenly she felt rather calm and in control. "Des, perhaps the tiny fact has escaped you, that you in fact left me for the teenaged baby-sitter as I remember, and as and from then my private life was no longer your business. You gladly gave up that right."

Des clenched and unclenched his fists.

She felt he might actually hit her if it wasn't for his legendary control.

"It is my business if he's spending time in *my* house while I'm still paying for it. And if he is seeing my kids, pretending to be their new Daddy then I have a right to vet him. In fact, I don't like the idea of them spending time with some stranger."

Kate smiled sweetly. "You are within your rights to do that, I suppose. Of course I didn't need to – the children were very much aware of Melody beforehand, weren't they? No, they haven't met Tom yet, nor will they in the near future. I think they've had enough upset in the lives for the moment."

Des ran his hands though his black hair manically. "Kate, all this pretence doesn't work, you know. Why don't you come to your senses? You know you want to patch things up. This new guy, it's got the desired result. You win, so let's talk it over."

He moved a bit closer to her.

She was almost gleeful with satisfaction. He was trying to crawl back into her life, away from his teenaged pregnant love, just as soon as his control over her had waned. She was just supposed to say all is forgiven and accept him back, just like that.

She hadn't guessed until now that she would never have Des back under any circumstances. She never wanted to feel that nervous knot in the pit of her stomach ever again, or the edgy jittery feeling when Des walked through the door, wondering what mood he'd be in or if he'd be pleased with her strenuous efforts at a cordon bleu meal – all the pandering to his every whim and being controlled for the past twelve years.

It was over – she knew it deep in her heart. She didn't want him back.

"Des, what you and I had, it has gone and it can never be regained. I don't want to be your wife any more. You have to take ownership of at least half of that. I want a divorce."

Des recoiled as if he had been slapped. Then he recovered a second later. "Fine. That's totally *fine*. Just don't think for one minute that you're going to stay

A Life Like Yours

here at The Beeches, because you're not. I'll speak to the
estate agent in the morning and put the house up for
sale. I'll send you back to where you came from. You
won't manage without me, you never could!" He strode
to the door.

Kate's heart was steel to his taunts – they simply
didn't work any more. "Des, you can have this house. I
don't need it. It was your dream, your fake little world
that I was a prisoner in. This house has been more like
a jail to me. And I have no intention of falling apart. My
daughters and I will be fine. So do your worst, Des,
because as they say, frankly, I don't give a damn."

With that she slammed the door in his face. She had
never felt so exhilarated in her life. Ten minutes later
she was pouring a glass of wine with shaky hands and
crying silently at the death of her marriage but she still
was defiant. Defiant and free.

Chapter 38

Grace had finally plucked up the courage to phone Paul's mobile that evening. Her heart was pounding as she tried to gauge his reaction to her. Would he blithely inform her that she had been replaced by glamorous blonde shopper woman, or would he slam down the phone? Who knew . . .

"Hi," he said calmly, coolly, as if she was ringing him to ask what he wanted cooked for his tea.

This stoked up Grace's ire immediately but she gritted her teeth and ploughed on regardless. "Hi, yourself. I was wondering when you wanted to come and see Orla – she misses you." She knew she was using the ultimate weapon in the arsenal – guilt – but she was desperate to break the ice somehow.

"Yeah, I was about to ring myself. I miss both of the kids. How about I have them for the weekend?"

Grace was aghast. Here was Paul calmly talking

about having the children for the weekend like they were an old divorced couple discussing access visits! They had only been apart for less than a week and she didn't even know where he was staying or what his long-term plan was. Paul's tone was all so benign and carefree. She had expected at least a little terseness to indicate he missed her and their marriage.

"Well, first of all, where are you staying? And who is the blonde you've been squiring about, for that matter?" She couldn't help herself – the dam broke and the thin veneer of casual friendliness had evaporated.

"I knew it!" Paul retorted triumphantly. "I knew your crazy mother would put two and two together and come up with six million. The blonde I was with was my brother Kevin's fiancée, Jill. I happen to be sleeping on their couch for the past few days and I was in the shopping centre with her to buy a duvet for me. I get freezing at night sleeping in their ice-cold house. So there! I'm not having a ball and it ain't no picnic being away from you and the kids."

Grace's heart did a little back-flip. At least he was as miserable as she was. "Well, why don't you come home then? We can talk it over and come to an agreement of some sort."

There was an overlong silence at the other end. "OK," he said finally. "After I have the kids for the weekend, we'll sit down and have a wee chat."

Grace's heart did another different kind of back-flip. This break-up business couldn't be good for your health, she decided – her heart was doing a tango in her chest.

She knew Paul was going to be unhappy with her next sentence.

"It'll only be Orla, I'm afraid. This is the weekend that Jordan and I go over to London to see Sammy."

She held her breath as she glimpsed herself in the hall mirror. She looked red and blotchy and entirely like someone who was under great stress, which is exactly what she was. If Paul could see her now he wouldn't exactly be overwhelmed with passion – with her greasy hair and blotchy skin and her oldest track pants, she looked like an unmade bad.

She calmly waited for the explosion.

"What?" Paul exploded, rewarding her. "You mean to tell me, you only called me to be a baby-sitter for wee Orla while you swan off to London with Jordan?"

It was now Grace's turn to shout down the phone. "Now hold one minute! Do you mean to tell me you regard looking after your own daughter as baby-sitting? You are at least as responsible for your child as I am and, as a matter of fact, why don't you just grow up, Paul Kelly. You're acting like a bloody child over this entire situation. I can and will go wherever I please if it involves making my son's life better, whether you like it or not. So you can bloody get over it! And as for Orla, in fact, I won't disturb your single man's weekend. I'll make other arrangements for our daughter and you can go fuck yourself!"

She slammed down the phone and burst into tears. After a minute she calmed down and looked at her tear-stained face in the mirror.

"Well, that went well then," she said to her

reflection, then picked up the phone and dialled Nell Kelly's number. It was time to call in the heavy artillery.

Paul sat at the other end of the phone in Raheny in a stunned silence. How did a perfectly civilised phone call end up such a disaster? He was further than ever from getting back with Grace and his family and he was totally miserable. Yet Grace couldn't seem to see why he felt betrayed that she was jetting off to see the person who had broken her heart so badly all those years ago. Paul had felt so belittled – he was consumed with insecurity and the feeling that somehow he knew this time would arrive sooner or later. He had never felt good enough for Grace and now it was all coming true that he wasn't. She hated that tiny little townhouse and being almost poor most of the time. He wasn't a good husband or, at least, not good enough. An airline pilot could make Grace and Jordan very comfortable.

He had thought if he had made the grand gesture and packed his bags that Grace might come to her senses, but it had backfired badly and now they were in a real mess, a mess that they might never recover from. He lifted the phone and tried to call his mother but her line was engaged. Nell was obviously talking her head off to one of his legion of aunties. He really needed his mother's advice right now before this mess got even worse. He'd try her later – right now a man needed a pint to drown his sorrows and that was exactly what Paul was going to do.

The following day Nell arrived from Donegal at noon,

festooned with freshly baked bread, apple-pies and copious knitted jumpers for the children.

Grace heated up the apple-pies and they tucked into them, with gallons of strong tea for Nell.

Nell was larger than life and very strong matriarch who ruled over her large brood with buckets of sense and a strong hand. Grace knew if anyone could get through to Paul, Nell could, and she had been so happy when Nell had immediately agreed to come and stay for the weekend and look after Orla, after she had heard the long sorry tale.

"Don't worry your head about that wee man at all, Grace. You and Jordan head away to London and forget all about it. I'll have that man back with his feet under the table by the time you get back, just you see. But he does have a point, you know. I know you didn't mean it but he feels a bit left out and I have to say that I agree with him."

Grace was alarmed. "Why, what did he say?"

"Well, Paul called me late last night and poured his heart out to me. He just feels he's not good enough for you and that you want more. He felt angry that you never consulted him about the plan to visit Jordan's real Dad. I have to say I agree with him there. He also told me that you've been a bit low since you've been working up in that big house and that now you're very unhappy here."

Grace was shocked and chastened. She had never considered that Paul was feeling that insecure or that he felt responsible for her happiness. She felt so sad that she had made him feel that way and she longed to make it up to him. She was such a stupid cow and it took Nell's sensible words to make her see sense. But would Paul ever forgive her?

"I'm not unhappy here. I love Kilmadden. This townhouse is a bit cramped and of course I envied Kate's huge house at first – but I'm far happier here than poor Kate ever was in her house, or at least I *was* happier. Oh Nell, I miss him so much . . . Paul made me happy . . ." Her voice trailed away.

"And you'll be happy again," Nell insisted kindly. "I've told Paul I'm coming down for the weekend, so I'll give him a call when you're gone. Don't worry, pet, it'll all be fine by Monday, just you wait and see."

Grace regarded her mother-in-law gravely. With that strong jaw and those dark brown eyes that she had bestowed on her son, Grace knew that Nell had a steely determination that could turn the strongest opinion and Grace fully believed if anyone could turn this disaster around, it would be Nell.

"I believe you just might," Grace said and she smiled for the first time that day.

"You know I will," Nell affirmed. "Now off with ye to get ready."

An hour later, Grace and Jordan were packed and ready to go. Jordan was so excited. This was all such a great adventure for him. He didn't have that nervous feeling of dread that Grace had. So many things could go wrong. She fretted that Samir would be dismissive of Jordan and talk about his other children too much and hurt Jordan's feelings. She wanted so much to protect her son and she had no way of knowing how his father would be. She just hoped and prayed it would all turn out perfectly. She had gone through a lot to make this happen and she hoped that it would be worth it.

They said their goodbyes to Nell and Orla and set off for the airport.

On the flight Jordan was chatty and animated. Grace hasn't seen him so happy in absolutely ages and it made it all worthwhile just to see the shine in his eyes and the growing confidence he displayed. Whatever happened, he knew she loved him enough to risk everything and it seemed to bring them closer together. After all, it had just been the two of them in the beginning before Paul happened and later Orla arrived. Grace tried not to think about the awful early days after Samir had left her, how abandoned and idiotic she had felt and how insulted that he hadn't loved their son enough to stay around. She wondered if Jordan still felt those feelings of abandonment – he must do if she still did. She reminded herself that she wasn't here to settle old scores but to engineer a fledgling relationship with his father. It wasn't about her and she was going to be grace itself – for once living up to her name.

They arrived and got a cab to Belgravia, where they had booked a family room in a bed and breakfast. London looked incredibly different after only a couple of years and Grace found herself excited to be back and for the first time she actually felt hopeful about the whole exercise. They had a mobile phone number for Samir and they were to call him to tell him they had arrived and to make a rendezvous.

"Do you want to call him, Jordan?" Grace ventured as they flopped down onto their beds with their cases.

"No, Mum!" Jordan was horrified. "You do it. I'm too nervous."

Grace felt like saying she was nervous too, but she just dialled the number while Jordan fiddled about with the television channels. Samir seemed to be excited that they had arrived and they arranged to meet at a Pizzahut restaurant in Oxford street, as it was Jordan's favourite place and Grace wanted somewhere busy and bustling in case there were long embarrassed silences, or Grace got the urge to smother Samir in bolognese sauce if she got angry with him. She really hoped she wouldn't.

"This is it, Jordy. You're finally getting to meet your father – let's go."

It was after four by the time they got to the restaurant. The afternoon lull meant that the place wasn't packed and Grace spotted Sammy immediately. She was shocked by his appearance. Gone was the thick black curly hair that he had – all was left were some thin wisps at the side, cut short. He was a lot thinner and seemed to be slightly stooped and not as tall as she had remembered. Of course it had been thirteen years since she had seen him and he would now be about forty-four. He wasn't wearing his pilot's uniform, which had always made him more handsome. He seemed a bit world-weary somehow, dressed plainly in an oilskin jacket and jeans. Only his smile lit up his face, making him look more like his son.

"Grace, Jordan, hello." Samir held out his hand to Jordan and shook it warmly.

Jordan seemed bashful and looked down at his sneakers. Samir had a small model of a Boeing jet in his hand and gave it to his son. Grace knew that Jordan was too big for such a gift and had he received it when he was five or six years old he would have loved it, but they had lost a lot of time and nothing could get that back.

They chatted about the flight and where they were staying, while Jordan silently eyed the man he had wondered about all his life and fiddled with the toy plane.

When the meal arrived, Jordan began to open up and asked Samir about his job and his other children. Grace held her breath, hoping that Sammy would be diplomatic and explain it carefully. She was pleased to hear Sammy tell Jordan that in fact Grace had never known that Samir was married, and as a Muslim Samir would have been in great trouble with his family and his employer and would have lost his job if they had known about Grace and Jordan.

"I was a coward," he admitted, "and I owe your mother a great apology for running away from her and you. I don't deserve a second chance, but I am very honoured to have one."

Sammy then told them that his wife had died many

years before and he had raised their three teenage children. They were now all grown up, two were in college, and one, the eldest girl, was getting married. Jordan seemed indifferent to the fact that his half siblings had enjoyed the full attention of their father – he just seemed politely interested. Grace was amazed at his resilience. She resisted the urge to tell Sammy how happy she was that she had met Paul and what a good father and partner he was – in fact she suddenly realised that all the anger she had stored over the years had strangely left her. She also realised that Sammy was not a bad person but just a weak man and he had had it tough too over the years. She wasn't going to waste another minute feeling any bitterness towards him – she had her son from that relationship and that was all that mattered now.

After almost two hours they left the restaurant and Sammy accompanied them both back to their guest-house in a cab with a promise to call early next morning to take them out for the day. Grace was exhausted by the time they got back but was dying to probe Jordan for his take on the big day.

They flopped onto their beds tiredly, both stuffed from too much pizza and all-you-can-eat dessert and exhausted after an eventful day.

"Well, what did you think, Jordy?"

Jordan sat up and leaned on his elbow. "He's nice . . ." he said slowly. "A bit like a sort of an uncle I'd never met. I don't feel like he's my dad or anything. I thought I'd feel like he was but I don't. I don't feel I love him or anything, not like I love Paul anyhow."

Grace's heart had never felt as glad or as sad as it did at that moment. Glad, for that was the one thing she had always wished that Jordan would feel for the man who was to all intents and purposes his father; and sad, because this one thing she had wished for only came about by the destruction of her relationship. She couldn't even ring Paul to tell him what he had waited all those years to hear. She choked back a rising urge to burst out crying.

"I'm really glad I met him though," Jordan was saying. "Now I can say I have a proper dad and more brothers and sisters and I feel I belong properly to a big family now. He even looks a bit like me, doesn't he?"

Grace smiled. "Yes, he does, and you both have the same long beautiful hands."

Jordan looked at her from under those long black eyelashes. "Did you love him?"

Grace had waited for that question. "Yes, I did. I was very hurt when he left me. I never thought I could trust anyone else ever again"

Jordan frowned. "Until you met Paul. Oh Mum, I hope I haven't ruined things for you with him. I kinda miss him, you know."

Grace's heart lurched. Her beautiful brown son seemed older than his years all of a sudden. "You haven't ruined anything," she insisted, "but I'll ruin your carefully managed coolness, if I tell Paul what you've said about him tonight."

"Don't you dare!" Jordan laughed. "Ah no, I don't care. I think I resented him a bit because he wasn't my real father and I thought you just loved him more than you loved my dad, but now I know that's not what happened and he's not so bad. I just hope we can get him back."

"So do I," said Grace ruefully, throwing a prayer to heaven that Nell could work her magic. "So do I."

Chapter 39

The aeroplane landed jerkily on the runway and lurched itself forward, before screeching to an eventual halt. Grace looked down on the twinkling lights of Dublin and slowly exhaled. She'd never admit it to Jordan, but she was glad that was all over. They'd spent a hectic two days with Samir, traipsing all over London playing at being tourists, and now she was totally exhausted and anxious to get home to Orla and her normal life – well, whatever passed for normal these days. If she had been totally honest with herself, she would admit that she was anxious to get back and discover if Nell had managed to talk to Paul and if she would get her husband back. Her stomach churned with the thought of another night without him. She couldn't wait to get off the plane and get home to find out.

"It was really great, Mam, thanks a lot. I had such a good time. Sammy is a lot of fun, isn't he?"

"Yes," Grace smiled. "He is."

And he had been. He'd worn himself out trying to please Jordan and he even endeared himself to Grace with his genuine effort. They left him with a promise that he would come to Dublin next and perhaps in time Jordan could meet his half siblings. Grace was happy that Jordan seemed contented and hugely relieved at the way things had turned out. She had secretly feared that Jordan, once he had met his father, would want to go to London to live with him.

Jordan proudly clasped the teddy that he had bought for Orla in Oxford Street and after they had alighted from the plane they quickly went to the baggage carousel and fetched their bags.

Grace always felt a bit guilty walking through the green channel, like the customs officers were going to pounce any minute and find a hidden stash of drugs. Today was no exception, even though all she had was a solitary bottle of whiskey – a thank you for Nell's efforts, which she fervently hoped weren't wasted. She soon discovered they weren't. Waiting to greet them both was Paul, standing right in front of the arrivals door with a huge bunch of flowers.

Grace's heart leapt and she ran into his arms, not caring who saw her, and Jordan stood beside them, pronouncing them both an ancient embarrassment and muttering things like 'Would they ever get a room!'

"I'm sorry," Paul whispered in her ear. "I've been a total fool."

"No, Paul, it's me who owes you an apology," she

replied quietly. "I'm sorry that I've been so selfish and didn't discuss Jordan and his father with you, but I promise you it'll never happen again. We'll discuss everything to do with both of our children – but that's not for here and now – we'll talk later. Just take us home please – I've missed you and Orla so much and I've got so much to tell you."

They kissed again.

"Right son," Paul beamed at Jordan. "Granny's orders are that I've got to take you home for one of her oven dinners and she is looking after yourself and Orla for a few hours, while I take this lady out to dinner and start making things up to her."

"Please tell me that it's stuffed steak," Jordan said, his eyes lighting up at the idea of his favourite meal cooked to perfection by his grandmother.

"The very same," Paul replied, grinning. "Now, let's get you back to your wee sister. She missed you both, so she did."

"We missed you too, Dad," Jordan said, giving Grace a secret wink.

Grace caught the look of amazement that flickered over Paul's face.

"Right, son. Well, let's get you into the car and you can tell me all about your trip."

"He's never done that before," he said, beaming, as Jordan raced on ahead with the luggage trolley. "Not purposely, anyway."

Grace looped her arm around her husband and gave him a tight hug. "You see? I told you that it was important for him to see Samir so he could find out who he really was. The mystery of his real dad was always going to be more tempting than the reality. You didn't consider that he might actually discover that you are the best dad he is ever going to have."

Paul was contrite. "I know I've been really stubborn over this, but I was so scared of losing you. I just lost me cool."

"You had a right to be angry, because I left you out of the decision and I'm sorry for that, but I only did for Jordan what I thought was for the best, and I didn't realise how much I was hurting you in the process. I was devastated when you left me. We're a pair of eejits all right – we very nearly lost a whole lot more than we bargained for."

"Who are ye telling?" Paul said, putting his arm around her shoulder. "Me mother has left me under no illusions as to the error of me ways. I suppose you got a similar lecture?"

Grace smiled. "Indeed I did."

She wasn't sure what Nell had told Paul, but she was dying to find out. Nell was some woman and Grace was going to get as many tips as possible from her mother-in-law for the future. She was just glad for the moment that the worst was over and she had her wonderful husband back and she would never let him go again.

Her thoughts turned to Kate and she wondered how her friend was. Her own marriage troubles had focused her mind greatly and she felt worse than ever about

Kate and all she had gone through. She resolved that she would call her later on tonight and see how things were. But first she was going to have a romantic dinner with her husband and enjoy every minute of it.

Kate at that very moment was staring out of the window at the large For Sale sign that had been posted in the garden some time that day. She had arrived back from seeing her mother with the girls when she discovered it. It had been a total surprise. She knew Des would try something like this, but to actually see it happen gave her a shiver up her spine. The Beeches was up for sale and Kate knew her past life was finally over. It still came as a shock. She felt bereaved all over again. It was one thing to endure Des strolling around the village hand in hand with his pregnant lover, but this was a really stinging humiliation. The thoughts of the malicious Melody being ensconced at The Beeches like the Lady of the Manor filled Kate with dread. But she had to get stronger. She just had to survive and thrive for herself and her girls.

She finally knew what it was like to wish someone dead, because right now she wished Des was dead and although she felt thoroughly ashamed of herself, she spent about ten minutes imagining all kinds of horrible ends for her estranged husband.

She decided to call up Des's mother and see if Lucinda had been informed of the latest development. Lucinda had been a stalwart supporter of Kate, even though she adored her son, and she said she always would be. Kate needed some support right now, so she poured a nice glass of Chianti and dialled Lucinda's number. She wondered when Grace would be home, so she could break the news. The fact The Beeches was now up for sale meant things would change for all of them.

Dymphna was in the throes of cooking her first ever meal for Derek.

She desperately wanted everything to go perfectly. The wine was chilling nicely and the chilli prawns seemed to be just right. She was worried about tackling the stir-fry beef noodle dish, while trying to look glamorous and also conjure up witty conversation at the same time. She should have just secretly ordered a Chinese from the posh restaurant in Clontarf and passed it off as her own.

It was just after eight by the time Derek arrived. She ran and sprayed herself liberally with Dune and then opened the door to find Derek standing there looking incredibly handsome in a white linen shirt and jeans – apart from, that was, his thick black glasses that bespoke instant nerd and reminded Dymphna of the brainy swot that she could never previously remember.

Derek took in her obvious surprise. "Sorry – nerd alert! I have an infection in my right eye and I can't wear my contact lenses for a few days."

Dymphna resisted the urge to immediately rip them from his face, they were that awful, but she knew that Derek felt she had been superficial in the past and she was anxious that he would see that she had changed after all. But had she? If Derek were still that nerdy guy, however wonderful, would she have given him a second glance?

She banished those thoughts from her mind and tried to focus on the dinner and her otherwise handsome date.

She sloshed the wok around and the beef sizzled impressively, while Derek opened the wine and poured them both a glass while chattering on about his day. Soon the dinner was ready and Dymphna managed to serve it up like she was a domestic goddess, which of course she wasn't. Derek *oohed* and *aahed* over the meal, which he said was delicious and all the time Dymphna, despite herself, kept staring at the offending nerd glasses and memorising all the people she could recall with such awful frames. Ronnie Corbett, Frank Carson, Roy Orbison . . . she had got to the Proclaimers when she just burst out laughing.

"What?" Derek enquired, bemused.

"Those *glasses!* I'm sorry Derek, but you look like a demented refugee from the fifties! I'm looking at you, but I just see Ronnie Corbett – *please*, could you take them off? They're just too horrible!" She dissolved into laughter again, but at the same time she felt like a bitch for saying it.

"Hah! I *knew* it. I knew you hadn't changed a bit, Coffey – you are still that stuck-up snobby person you always were. I tricked you!"

He pulled out a trendy pair of rimless glasses and replaced the awful black frames.

"I searched for hours for these things. I haven't worn

them since college, when I couldn't get a date for love nor money. Someone then told me that it was face furniture like this that seriously turned off the girls, and still does, it would seem."

He smiled then.

Dymphna breathed a sigh of relief. She didn't think he was going to dump her after all. "Am I a total cow?" she asked in her most plaintive little-girl voice

"Yup, it's just as well I am falling in love with you and am prepared to overlook your obvious failings. But I doubt if you would do the same for me?" He looked at her quizzically, a hint of a smile playing on his lips.

Dymphna blushed. Had he actually said that he was falling in love with her? She knew that her next reply meant everything. "Derek, I have got out library books on the subject of Chinese cookery, made six attempts at this meal during the week and spent forty quid on a fresh haircut. I haven't eaten a thing in three days, because I haven't been able to get you off my mind and I'd be devastated if I couldn't see you again – but those glasses, they would definitely still have to go, sorry."

Derek regarded her seriously. Then he laughed. "I do like a woman who sticks to her guns. So, are you saying that you feel the same way too?"

Dymphna nodded, not trusting herself to speak.

"Yes!" Derek exclaimed. Then, "Sorry, was I too happy?"

Dymphna grinned. "No, just right. You did warn me you wouldn't play hard to get and anyway I've had enough of game playing."

"Right so," Derek replied, jiggling his eyebrows up and down suggestively. "What's for dessert?"

Dymphna recalled Grace's entreaties in the past for Dymphna to play at least a little bit hard to get.

"Bailey's Cheesecake," Dymphna replied innocently.

Derek gave her a slow-burning smile that reached his eyes. "Wonderful," he said.

And it was.

Chapter 40

Grace leaned over and stretched out languidly like a cat. She was feeling all loved up from her night of romance with Paul. They had enjoyed a wonderful meal at *Ban Thai* the previous evening, with a few glasses of wine and some passionate making up later. They toasted Nell more than once for making them both see sense.

Things seemed to be back to normal, even better than normal, Grace thought, because Paul and Jordan now seemed to have turned an important corner and had a new appreciation for each other.

Nell was due to head back to Donegal later on in the day and Grace was looking forward to a lazy day off, scouring the shops with shopaholic Nell and a long leisurely lunch, before Nell boarded the three o'clock bus northwards.

Just then the phone rang. Grace groaned. Paul had

taken Jordan to school and she had put Orla back for another sleep. Who the hell could it be, disturbing her peace and quiet?

She stumbled downstairs to the phone, smelling en route the bacon that Nell was cooking up for breakfast. Suddenly she was famished and even more irked by the intrusive phone call.

"Yes?" she barked, a mite more aggressively then she had intended.

"Oh Grace, I'm sorry, is this a bad time, I didn't get you out of bed, did I? I feel awful."

It was Kate – only Kate was ever this apologetic and sensitive to people's nuances.

She sounded mouse-like and timid, a tone Grace hadn't recalled since the early days of their meeting.

Grace felt terrible. "Kate, I'm the one who should be saying sorry. It's fine, really. I just had a few too many wines last night. How can I help you? Do you need me to work today?"

"No, not really . . ." The voice was wavering.

"I could just do with a chat, that's all. Des has put the house up for sale."

"The absolute shit!" Grace blurted out before she could stop herself. "Sorry," she then backtracked.

Kate gave a mirthless laugh. "No, be my guest. You are perfectly right – he is an absolute shit. In fact that's the kindest description I could come up with."

"Right," Grace said assertively. "Nell is cooking up a storm – so do you want to come over for breakfast? She is a rock of sense and had just sorted us two idiots out –"

"I'll be over in ten minutes," was the reply.

Grace hoped Nell could offer some words of comfort for Kate and to Grace herself, who was feeling the rising panic of a redundancy coming along.

Fifteen minutes later, Kate, Nell and Grace were ensconced in Grace's kitchen tucking into grilled bacon and tomato, perfectly poached eggs and freshly home-baked muffins.

Nell got straight into her no-nonsense advice mode. "I think you've had a lucky escape, Kate, from what you've told me Des is a self-important man who regards you as another piece of his property. He was always going to do this to you, just as soon as you showed signs of moving on with your life. You have to decide whether you want him back and, if you're not sure about that, you need to take some time to consider it. And I would think very carefully. Controlling men seldom change and the same goes for men who have affairs. Do you want that kind of life for you and the girls?"

Grace almost choked on her breakfast – talk about laying your cards on the table!

Nell pulled no punches.

Kate was stunned into silence and just nodded sagely.

"You seem to be doing quite well, taking your diploma course, meeting other people. Don't let the idea of losing the house, beautiful and all though it sounds, decide your marriage for you, because it's still a form of control. It's all just bricks and mortar at the end of the day, and it'll be there after you're gone. It's really a question of trust – could you ever trust Des again?" She took a sip of tea and continued. "And what about this Melody person? She's hardly going to go away with a wee'un on the way, is she? There'll always be reminders and contact between her and Des because of their child." Nell shut up for a minute and sipped her tea serenely, while Kate and Grace digested all the cold hard truths.

Grace watched and waited. She half expected Kate to burst into tears and flee from the room.

"You're absolutely right, Nell," Kate finally said, after what seemed like an age.

Grace exhaled with relief.

"I don't want to lose my home, but I can't let Des call all the shots either. It's just that for years I have never had to cope on my own. Des has always been the strong one."

"Steel is never stronger than when it's been tested in the flames, Kate. You are already strong – you just have to realise it."

Kate nodded. There were tears in her eyes. Grace was amazed that they hadn't appeared sooner, but Nell was only voicing what everyone else felt deep down: Des was a cheating bastard who regarded women as trophies. It still wasn't easy to hear it.

So she decided to come to the rescue.

"Nell, it's hard for Kate. She is used to a comfortable lifestyle with Des, a lovely home, plenty of money and her two girls having everything. It's come as a bit of a shock to see a For Sale sign on The Beeches and have to think about leaving there. Also, what about Kate's studies? She won't be able to afford to continue with her college course. Des won't pay for me to help her out any longer. It'll be a whole new life for her. It's not going to be easy."

Nell looked pensive. "No, it won't. But whatever Kate achieves now, it'll be her that achieves it. Those girls are going to be proud of who she is. And at least she'll be able to look at herself in the mirror. She can't be going back to her husband just because he controls the purse-strings. That would make her a purchase, just like everything else he possesses."

Kate put down her cup of tea.

Grace was unsure of what she would do next.

"You know, Nell, that's it! I wasn't sure of it until right now when you said it. My mind has been in such turmoil. I can't go back, because I would never forgive myself. He thinks he can just buy everything, well, Des Heathcoat has just exceeded his purchasing power, because I will never be a possession of his ever again."

Kate's eyes blazed and Grace knew immediately that she meant every word, vehemently. She looked at Nell in amazement. "Whatever you've got, Nell, I wish we could bottle it."

"Ten kids and grinding poverty focuses the mind, I can tell ye," Nell replied dryly.

"But at least I had the love of a good man. That carried me through. There were many in my family that weren't as lucky, but I've seen a lot in my day and eventually you get to know people. I know by you, Kate, you've already been tested in the past and you rose to it, I'll bet. You can do it again."

"I'm sorry for you too, Grace," Kate said sadly. "I think you may have to start looking for another job."

Grace smiled ruefully and tried to reassure her friend. "Don't worry, Kate," she said. "Interfex are just dying to take me back and sure Pervy Comb-over is in handcuffs and can do no more poor accounts clerks any harm. I still have you. We would never have met if I hadn't gone to work for you at the mansion."

They both laughed.

To think I had envied her for so long, Grace thought. Silly stupid envy about the life she imagined Kate had.

And there it was.

Kate left about midday with a lighter heart and a new determination to be her own person, and shortly after Grace drove her mother-in-law to Dublin for the Donegal bus. Tears misted her eyes as she said goodbye to this formidable woman, to whom in many ways she was closer than to her own mother.

"I'll miss you, Nell," she said tearfully. "And Paul and I can never thank you enough for sorting the pair of us out."

"Ach, sure it was nothing! That big lad of mine just needs a good talking to every now and then. You're a good girl and he needed to realise it. A short lecture from his mother always brings him back to reality. Next time you can all come up to Bundoran to visit me and you can bring Kate with you – she's going to need a lot of support if she's to get away from that man for good. You look after her now!"

Grace smiled. She had known there would be some orders. "Don't worry, I will."

With that, she was gone in a fluster of sensible tweed and a cloud of 4711. Grace wondered if she would ever have that easy relationship she enjoyed with Nell with her own mother. One thing was for sure, she wouldn't be holding her breath.

Life with Moira was interesting but never easy.

Kate was shopping later on that day in the village and was coming out of the small local supermarket laden with supplies, when she literally bumped straight into Melody, who happened to be walking in. Kate had dreaded this moment for ages – she had been lucky enough so far only to glimpse Melody from a distance. But Kate was unsure of what she would actually do when she saw her. Would she remain ice cool or would she go to scratch Melody's eyes out like she really wanted to?

It was Melody who spoke first.

"Kate," she breezed, shaking out her toffee mane of hair. "Des tells me that The Beeches is up for sale."

As if you didn't know already, you poisonous bitch, Kate said inwardly but outside she was icy cool. "Yes, that's correct – though I fail to see what business it is of yours."

Melody issued a fresh sneer. "It's becoming more of my business by the minute, as a matter of fact. Look at this." She lifted her left hand to reveal a large rock straining to stay onto her third finger. "Des and I are engaged. It happened only last night, as a matter of fact. He asked me to marry him and of course I said yes." She looked triumphant.

Kate tried to hide her shock. Every time she thought Des couldn't shock her any more he went ahead and did it. The bastard.

She smiled sweetly. "I see, Melody, but you'll have a bit of a wait, *as another matter of fact* – considering he hasn't issued divorce proceedings yet."

Melody flinched slightly. "How do you know?" she demanded.

"Well," said Kate, flicking her own blonde mane back, "considering he was only asking me to take him back into my bed a few short days ago, I doubt if he has had the time. I told him to get stuffed of course – hence your new gift, I suppose. Anyway, I wouldn't advise you to be in too much of a hurry to step into my shoes, Melody dear – after all, you know what they say . . . when a man takes his mistress as his wife, it creates a new vacancy."

Leaving Melody open-mouthed and staring after her, Kate sauntered off, feeling ten feet high. She was finally going to fight back and show that she had some backbone. Kate would make little malicious Melody regret the day she ever set her greedy eyes on her husband.

She had a feeling that large rock would make quite a dent in Des's head when it hit it later on tonight. She would love to be a fly on the wall for that little argument.

"One nil to Kate, I think," she smiled as she got into

her jeep. She gave a moment of silent thanks to Grace's mother-in-law, who had spoken so strongly to her. Thanks, Nell, I like being strong. I like it a lot.

As she drove away she saw Melody still rooted to the spot. She hadn't moved a muscle. She even looked a little bit dazed.

Kate's grin lasted until she got home.

Chapter 41

It was a beautiful day for a wedding. The sky was a flawless blue and the clear fresh air of the west of Ireland assailed Grace's nostrils. The air was fresh in Meath but here it was different, suffused with peat and the scent of the nearby ocean. Grace felt exhilarated. Her big sister was getting married.

Somehow, the wedding had been hastily arranged in a matter of weeks. There was the small matter of finding a venue, a church and of course most importantly, a dress. Olivia had arrived in Meath and in four scant hours they had managed to find a beautiful gown in the Design Centre that would conceal an emerging bump from James's so far unsuspecting parents.

James knew the local parish priest and a few quid donated to the poor box managed to find them a place for their marriage. They couldn't get the large hotel in Clifden for the reception, so settled for a small country manor outside Letterfrack, which had a lot more charm and some enchanting views.

It had all worked out perfectly and now Grace sat with Olivia getting her prepared for her big day. They had managed to get Moira ensconced with the flower arranger so they could have some valuable but more importantly peaceful time together to get ready.

"I just can't believe this is really happening and I'm actually getting married to James. I am so lucky, Grace." Olivia's eyes were shining.

"He's the lucky one," Grace replied, while fingering Olivia's beautiful dress, which was a pale silver floor-length gown with a beaded bodice. It was simple yet stunning and Olivia was just going to carry a tied bouquet of cream lilies and wear a single flower in her hair. "What's happening with James's parents?" Grace enquired mildly.

Olivia grimaced. "I feel Sheila suspects that I'm pregnant though she hasn't said anything. The haste with which the wedding was planned threw the cat among the pigeons – but so far so good. Poor James is so nervous that she's going to twig and carry out a huge scene in the chapel about me being soiled goods and us both being in a state of sin and not fit to darken the church's door! Just as well I'm not wearing the traditional white."

Grace rolled her eyes in disbelief. "God, don't let Moira and Sheila get together then, it would be a nightmare. Can you imagine? They'd be trying to outdo each other in their superior knowledge of all the Saints in Heaven! Moira already thinks you're wasting yourself on some old farmer and Sheila doesn't believe her little boy of forty should take up with a wild Dublin woman, never mind marry her. It's going to make for an interesting day, trying to avoid them both and also getting them to stay away from each other."

Olivia laughed. "*Oh, very* funny! It will be interesting though. Shay Costigan is coming and I can't wait to see Dymphna's new love. I reckon her and Derek will be next up the aisle. Is Kate bringing Tom?"

"I don't know yet, she seemed very evasive. I'm not sure she's quite ready for the dating game just yet – not like you, just stepped out of one engagement and into another, albeit a much more delectable one."

Olivia shivered. "God! Don't remind me. I had a lucky escape there. Imagine I could be miserably married to Connell and have never felt those butterflies I craved so much."

Grace looked at her older sister, who seemed to be suddenly miles away. "And do you? Still feel the butterflies, I mean?"

"Hundreds and thousands," Olivia said breathlessly.

"Then you made the right decision. Right, let's get you ready for your groom, so. Enjoy today, Olivia. It will be very special and just remember to enjoy every minute."

Olivia smiled. "Don't worry, I will. And thanks, Grace, it means a lot for you to be here with me being my bridesmaid."

Grace winced slightly. She recalled her own wedding and how distant she had been to her older sister, so distant in fact she insisted that Olivia wasn't even part of the wedding party. She had asked Dymphna and one of Paul's sisters instead, yet Olivia bore her no malice.

"I'm sorry that I never had you as my bridesmaid . . ." she offered guiltily.

Olivia brushed away the apology. "Don't be so silly. We weren't even friends then, but I'm so glad we are now. So are you going to help me into my dress or what?"

An hour later the congregation were outside the quaint old church awaiting Olivia's arrival.

Grace spotted Shay Costigan arrive and Moira's eyebrows rise in alarm, but Olivia had organised it all perfectly. Sean was going to give his daughter away and was made aware that Shay was just going to be a guest.

Shay went inside unobtrusively and Moira visibly relaxed. Then James arrived looking splendid in a smart navy suit, his wild long hair trimmed and tied back into a discreet ponytail. Grace thought he looked more handsome than ever. He was definitely a brother-in-law she felt she could be close to, rather than the uptight stuffy Connell. James had made Olivia lose all her stuffiness too, for which Grace was eternally grateful.

Then suddenly the flower-adorned pony and trap arrived, carrying Olivia and her father. She looked amazing and Sean looked as proud as punch.

Moments later, Olivia was gliding up the aisle to her husband and her future and Grace followed in her wake spotting Dymphna and Derek holding hands in the pews. Dymphna was looking cool and classy in a cream trouser suit. Kate was seated nearer the back in classic Lainey Keogh, looking elegant and beautiful as usual. Grace noticed that Tom was absent. She hadn't time to wonder what had transpired, but she would talk to Kate later. Right now she had to witness her only sister get married.

Sean gave his daughter proudly to James while the congregation looked on. Grace threw a look at Moira who was wiping her damp eyes furiously while James's mother Sheila looked stern and irritated, with pursed lips and a barely concealed frown. James's father Dan looked benign enough, although he seemed quite elderly and it was obvious that Sheila McCarthy ruled the roost. Grace didn't envy Olivia's task in converting Sheila to their son's union, never mind the soon-to-be disclosed news about their baby. Still, once the baby arrived things should become easier. At least Olivia and James weren't teenagers. At forty, Sheila should be delighted that he was at last becoming a father and husband, but somehow Grace doubted that would be the case.

However if anyone could convert her, Olivia could.

Olivia and James exchanged the personally written vows an hour later and there was hardly a dry eye in the house, all except his mother of course, whose steely gaze hardly altered throughout. The congregation burst into spontaneous applause when Mr and Mrs James McCarthy were announced and finally Olivia's dream was realised. She had married the man of her dreams.

Afterwards, they all clambered onto the ancient bus to take them to Clew Country House for the reception.

Grace managed to get sitting next to Kate in order to see how things were. Kate had been incredibly quiet and reserved so far and Grace hoped it wasn't the wedding ceremony that had been too full of memories for her to cope with.

"They got such a beautiful day for it, didn't they?" Kate said wistfully, as she looked out the window onto the bright sunny day that lit up the countryside into vivid greens and gold, the sky dotted with white fluffy cotton balls.

Grace watched her. She was twisting a handkerchief tightly around her fingers.

Kate, who normally seemed serene and totally in control, appeared a little on edge.

"Are you OK, Kate?" Grace enquired. She knew that Kate probably wouldn't want to discuss it, especially today, but she was concerned. Kate's newly acquired bravado had suddenly seemed to desert her.

"Just a bit sorry for myself, that's all. I suppose the wedding brought back a lot of memories, things I'd thought I had forgotten. There's still a part of me that loves Des even though I know it's over. I know it's over deep inside and it has made me a bit maudlin, you know? We did have some good times, in the beginning."

Grace didn't know how to answer that. She couldn't know what Kate was going through. All she could do was try to be a good friend. "And Tom? You didn't ask him to come with you?"

Kate seemed thoughtful. "No, I didn't. I just don't know if I'm using Tom as a sort of crutch to get over

Des and make myself feel good just because someone else wants me. Tom's had a rough time getting over his marriage break-up and he's too nice for me to just use him, so I've being keeping my distance."

"Oh Kate," Grace said wryly. "Even now, you're always thinking of someone else's feelings before your own. Maybe Tom is big enough to take that risk for himself, just give him a chance – you need to do what's best for Kate for a while."

Kate smiled. "I probably shouldn't have come today. I'm like an old poisonous divorcee, sad and bitter. I don't want to feel this way or ruin Olivia's happy day but I so wanted to see her and James get married. I need to believe that I can be as happy as they are sometime in the future."

"And you will," Grace insisted. "You will, Kate, you will."

Kate bit her lip and stifled a tear. "I hope you're right, Grace, I really hope you are right."

Grace hoped so too.

The wedding was a huge success and even Kate managed to have a good time after Grace enlisted the help of every single male friend of James, who in turn kept her entertained and whirled on the dance floor all evening. The happy newlyweds were showered in hugs and kisses as they left eventually for their honeymoon, which was a week in sun-drenched Sardinia, a wedding surprise from James to his bride.

Grace noticed that Moira and Sheila were having words over at the bar towards the end of the night and she saw several frosty looks exchanged and then Moira stormed off in a huff.

"Looks like she's met her match there!" Paul chuckled as he too looked on at the standoff.

Grace considered going over to sort it out or mediate, but then she decided Sheila looked a nasty piece of work and Moira's sharp tongue might be just what was required.

Dymphna and Derek were entwined on the dance floor, Dymphna still clutching the bride's bouquet which she had performed an Olympic dive for. Grace smiled at them both. If ever there were a match made in heaven, it was Derek and Dymphna – even the names had a ring to them.

Grace looked over at Paul and felt a rush of love for him. She was so glad they were back together and happy. She felt so lucky to have him. It was only Kate that Grace was worried for. She still had a long way to go before she would get through this – she still hadn't even got through the divorce or Melody's baby yet.

And as Grace was led by the hand by her merry husband upstairs to their quaint bedroom at the manor, she saw Kate go into her room alone.

"I'll be just a minute love," Grace said, whipping out her mobile phone. "I'm just going to make a quick phone call."

The following morning, after they all had a huge country breakfast, Grace looked out onto the long green lawn that overlooked the gravel drive and saw Tom Carter's battered MG sports car roll up.

Grace smiled magnanimously as she eyed Kate pick at her breakfast half-heartedly.

This new arrival would either make her friend very pleased or extremely cross that Grace had invited him down for the rest of the weekend. Tom had been delighted and surprised when Grace phoned. He told her that originally Kate had invited him and then later retracted it.

"She told me that people would think we were an item," Tom explained. "I replied, I thought we *were*. And it was then she told me not to get my hopes up. She just wasn't ready for anything heavy. The point is, Grace, I'm not sure if I am ready either – but I do feel we should give it a try and see how things go before we write the whole thing off."

"Couldn't agree with you more," Grace replied, deciding she liked him more already and promptly asked him down to Clifden. It was only after she put the phone down that she worried what she had done might really annoy her friend.

Ten minutes later, as they emerged from the dining-room, Tom was at the check-in desk and Kate spotted him.

"I just happened to be in the neighbourhood and I thought you might like some company – I hope you don't mind," Tom said sheepishly, issuing a bright and hopeful smile.

Kate gave him a huge hug and returned the smile. "I'd be *delighted*, Tom," she said warmly and then flashed Grace a look that said, 'Thanks so much, but I'll still kill you later'.

420

Grace breathed a sigh of relief and knew it had been the right thing to do. Kate had been so low last evening and Grace knew that fear of what might or might not happen with Tom was preventing her from enjoying his company. And Grace just couldn't let Kate deny herself some happiness because she was worried she might hurt someone other than herself.

The rest of the weekend was full of fun, with lots of delicious food, plenty of sightseeing and, for Grace, the satisfaction of seeing both her dear friends happy, which was a first for all three at the same time. Grace just hoped that this happiness would last.

Chapter 42

6 months later . . .

Kate was moving house. The Beeches had been sold and that part of her life was really over. It was difficult to leave this large and wonderful house that had held such promise for her. The house that had defined her status in Kilmadden when she had arrived all those years ago, that anxious self-conscious young bride who never felt she would be good enough for the rarified country air and upmarket neighbourhood. Now she was leaving it all behind and moving back to a smaller house, not far from Grace's townhouse at The Gables. It was thanks to Lucinda, Des's mother, that Kate had got a fairer deal from Des, with a veiled threat that she would leave her own considerable money entirely to Kate and the girls if Des didn't play fair.

The Beeches had been sold and the money divided

equally, so that both Des and Kate were able to purchase outright two detached houses at opposite ends of the town, so that Des could still be close to his daughters and Melody close her family. Kate would have preferred not to have the constant threat of bumping into Melody and her offspring in the local supermarket, but she had to swallow her pride for the sake of harmony for her daughters.

Tom arrived early to help. He had been Kate's rock over the past few months. He asked for nothing and sometimes that was what he got. But he had stuck it out and become a close friend and, even though Kate knew he wished for more, Tom would never dream of pushing it for fear of losing her. Grace had got Kate to see that she didn't have to survive alone, but that she would survive and succeed with the help and love of friends.

As they packed the myriad of boxes for the removal men, Kate tried to be upbeat and philosophical. Des had taken the girls for the day so she didn't have to pretend for them, but she somehow felt she had to be cheerful for Grace and Tom. No one must see that it was breaking her heart to leave this house, the home where her girls had been babies and had lived all their lives.

But it was time to move on.

"I'll make a pot of tea," she announced too brightly, as she saw Grace's battered Starlet pull up.

As she disappeared indoors, Tom greeted Grace.

"How is she bearing up?" Grace enquired. She knew this would be a difficult day.

"She's shining brighter than Liberty Hall," Tom

quipped wryly. "But you and I know this has to be tearing her apart. Still, my guess is after today, she will actually start to feel better. We've just got to be there for her."

"Spoken like a true new man," Grace smiled devilishly. "You watch way too much Oprah."

"The perils of starting your own business, I'm afraid – too much daytime television, waiting for the phone to ring." Tom replied, grinning as they went inside.

The house looked even more enormous emptied of all the luxurious furnishings that mostly were too large and ornate for the new house and were to be sold. Grace recalled the first time she had ever set foot inside The Beeches and how she had envied Kate so much to the point of jealousy that evening just over a year and a half ago.

Now, it seemed, everything had come full circle. No longer would Grace be working for Kate. She had called Darren at Interfex, who had passed her CV along and she had been offered her old job back. But after thinking long and hard about the awful traffic jams and abandoning little Orla again to the clutches of *Cute and Cuddly*, Grace changed her mind. So, she had managed to get a part-time job with an engineering company in Kilmadden and Kate's mother-in-law, Lucinda, had offered to look after Orla as well as Kate's girls – she had informed Kate that she would look after the girls until Kate finished her course and got her career off of the ground.

Grace would miss Chloe and Jade and working in this beautiful house too, but at least she had gained a dear friend in Kate and circumstances would not change that.

"Tea break already, oh goody!" Grace said cheerily as she found Kate making the tea in the kitchen.

"I'm tired even before I begin," Kate replied with a weak smile. "I hate moving, it's apparently almost as stressful as a divorce."

"Well, that's OK then. Tom, check her pulse, it seems she's about to collapse with a heart attack."

Kate laughed despite herself. "I knew I asked you over here for something, and it certainly wasn't for your packing skills."

Grace frowned. "I presume you are referring to my packing of Dymphna's and Derek's engagement present. It wasn't my fault the box was as flimsy as paper. Anyway, they had way enough Waterford crystal!"

They both launched into giggles and Tom guessed this was some girly joke that he wasn't a party to.

"The best bit was when you suggested that we stick it all back together!" Kate guffawed, her earlier dark mood forgotten. Grace had that affect on Kate, Tom noticed. She seemed lighter and more fun when Grace was around. Tom was so hopelessly in love with Kate, though he would never admit it to her – he feared she'd run a mile. But as he watched her giggle and laugh like a schoolgirl with her friend, he had to resist the urge to carry her outside and propose to her on the spot.

"Any chocolate-chip cookies?" was all he said instead.

"Already packed," Kate said and launched into more giggles. Maybe this would be easier than she thought.

After the truck was loaded, they all headed for Kate's new house at the other end of Kilamadden village. The house was a nice roomy semi-detached with big Georgian windows and a large garden, but it still seemed tiny in comparison to her previous pile.

Grace thought the house was lovely, with its spacious rooms and huge kitchen. She could have gleefully imagined the Kelly brood living here, but she realised that for Kate it was a bit of a comedown.

The removal van reversed into the cobble-locked driveway and they began to unload the numerous boxes – it was going to be a mammoth task.

Across the village at Beaufort Downs, Melody looked around her bare living-room with its dozens of unopened boxes. In the midst of the debris, was endless baby paraphernalia. Melody felt rather aggrieved that Des had point-blank refused to take even a few days off work to help her move in. She was supposed to cope with the unpacking and look after a new baby at the same time. Connor was a lovely child, but he seemed to cry and fuss such a lot, there were days when Melody felt as if she might go out of her mind with just a cross baby for company. Of course her mother had refused to be of much help. After all, she had said, she did have her own large brood to look after and muttered a lot of nonsense about Melody making her bed and having to lie on it – whatever the hell that all meant.

Somehow, Melody had got all she had hoped and wished for. More or less. She never would be mistress of The Beeches, Des's witch of a mother had seen to that. But she still had Des, a lovely house that was the envy of all her relatives and now a baby, but deep inside she felt a bit hollow. It was probably just that Suzie was doing so well, off at college, living in a flat in town and hanging out with the trendy university crowd. She told Melody hair-raising tales of nights in Temple Bar and all the gorgeous guys she had slept with, none of whom stuck around – but that never bothered Suzie. Melody felt deep down that she had missed out a bit.

Connor grizzled away in his pram and Melody stared out of the window onto the grey drizzly day. The words that Kate had said to her that day in the village had come to haunt her. When a man takes a mistress for a wife it creates a new vacancy.

She had already seen Des's eyes wander when they were out in town and a glamorous blonde walked past and he had been most insistent that she return to the gym six weeks after Connor was born to get rid of her "baby blubber" as he termed it.

Melody was consumed with the idea that Des would stray. After all, as Kate had so rightly said, if he cheated on her with Melody, what was to stop him doing it again?

She certainly saw less and less of him lately. Oh, he seemed enamoured enough with Connor when he was home – it was just that that didn't occur too often.

Still, that was her life now and Melody supposed she would get used to it.

An hour later, Kate and Grace had managed to open most of the kitchen utensils and Tom had unloaded the beds into their respective rooms with the movers and at last things were beginning to take shape.

Shortly after, Dymphna's car pulled up and she and Derek alighted with a couple of bottles of champagne under each arm.

"Leftovers from the engagement party," Dymphna announced happily. "We figured it was time to celebrate Kate's new life and give a hand at the same time. Who says you can't move and have some fun as well?"

Derek kissed her cheek. "See why I'm marrying this girl," he beamed. "She definitely has her priorities right. You open the champers, Dimples, and I'll go and give Tom a hand with the sofa. But keep me a glass." He disappeared down the hall.

"This is wonderful," Kate smiled as she searched for the glasses that she knew were just in the next box or two.

"Not at all," Dymphna replied, looking glossier and more polished than ever if that was possible. She was wearing a simple white T-shirt and a pair of dark denims but still looked as if she was bound for the boardroom. "I wouldn't have missed it for the world. We're still a man down, though – it's a pity Olivia isn't here."

Grace rolled her eyes. "I doubt she'd be much help, seeing as she is so huge with baby that she hasn't seen her feet in months. We should give her a call on the mobile – then she can be at least here in spirit." Grace pulled out her mobile and called her sister.

"I'm like the side of a house!" Olivia exclaimed when Grace asked her how she was.

"We are all helping Kate move," said Grace, "and we're knee-deep in boxes and could do with some of your organisational skills. Dymphna has arrived with champagne and we just had to call you and include you in the celebrations, at least by proxy."

Olivia laughed. "Well, if I was there I wouldn't be much use. Tell Kate not to let any of you have any champers until all the boxes are empty."

"I will not!" Grace retorted. "So, how are you really?"

"Fat and blissful," Olivia replied. "We had Moira up visiting last weekend. Honestly, she and Sheila are having a competition to see who is the best granny already and the baby hasn't been born yet! There are so many Infants of Prague and holy pictures in the nursery that now it looks like a convent. If ever there were a pair of oul wans who should never have to be in the same room it's that pair, but sometimes it's funny – Moira is well able for Sheila in a way I would wish to be but can't, seeing as I love her son so much. And that's quite enough about me. Can you put me on to Kate for a minute?"

Grace passed the phone over and Kate slowly walked out of the room, listening no doubt to one of Olivia's legendary pep talks. Olivia would have Kate feeling invincible in about two minutes.

"We've got to keep her spirits up," Dymphna said quietly, looking around the kitchen.

"This is nowhere near as nice as The Beeches."

"Well, don't ever say that, for starters, Dimples." Grace frowned. Dymphna was never great on tact. "It's all new, but she will come to love it here. She's free of

Des the control freak and that is the main thing." She stole a look out the window at Tom who was busying himself carrying armchairs with Derek through the patio doors into the dining-room.

"Tom is so totally in love with Kate but he still hasn't had the nerve to tell her, poor bloke."

"Why not?" Dymphna was agog. Tom was a catch in any woman's language, even one who had recently become engaged to a divine man. Kate would be mad to pass him up! Those sooty eyes and handsome dark features! Dymphna thought he was a dish.

Grace shrugged. "Stuffed if I know. I think maybe she's just scared. Scared of letting someone in to hurt her again. It's a damn shame though – he could make her very happy."

Dymphna smiled. "Ah, you're an old softy, Grace Kelly, aren't you? You want us all happily married and settled like yourself."

Grace grimaced. "Only if Kate wants it. Trouble is, I think she does, she just doesn't know it yet."

Kate came back. "Don't know what?" she enquired.

"Oh, just where to put those dishes, that's all," Grace replied hurriedly.

"What did Olivia have to say for herself?" Dymphna enquired quickly.

"Oh, just telling me that this was the start of my new life. And a new beginning was always scary but also very exciting and she reminded me of when she fled to Connemara and she was just so miserable and mixed-up that she never could believe what has turned out to be her happiest and most exciting year. She's even managed to sell a couple of her paintings, and there she is expecting a baby with a man she truly loves. It made me feel a whole lot better about things."

Good old Olivia, Grace thought, she'd managed to do it again. She'd turned Kate around in minutes. Kate now seemed a lot more upbeat. Now Grace just had to get Kate to see what was under her very nose. A handsome dedicated admirer that would do absolutely anything for her. Fear wouldn't stop Kate from really being happy. Not if Grace could help it..

Chapter 43

It had been an interesting day.

They all worked like slaves and unpacked until their collective backs could bend no more. In the end the champagne was all that kept them going and they all became a little merry. As there was no food in the house, Kate decided to order in an Indian takeaway.

Grace called Paul and sweetly asked if he could come and collect her, as she was too inebriated to drive. Paul laughed and said he'd order himself and the kids a takeaway and to stay put and enjoy herself for the moment – he'd collect Grace after dinner.

"He is so nice," Kate said, her words slightly slurred. "If that had been Des on the phone, he would be so irritated and furious that I hadn't dinner ready for him and I was out enjoying myself, that I would be given the silent treatment for days. I have always envied your easy relationship with Paul."

Grace smiled slowly. "Well, he's not perfect, he has his moments. Look at his attitude to Sammy that time, he was so stubborn about it all . . ."

"And how is that now, with him and Jordan and Sammy?" Tom was asking.

"Well, it's a bit like the Good Friday agreement, they will never be bosom buddies but they work together for the sake of Jordan – and Jordan is very happy."

She turned to Kate. "Kate, Des was unusual, not every man is like him. Here you are now, ordering curry and quaffing champagne with a bunch of friends in your new house – and you can do this any time you want, this is your time now."

Kate smiled and looked around the table at Grace, Dymphna and Derek – and at Tom. Dear reliable Tom, who was a kind and gentle man.

She thought of Lucinda and how much of a dear friend she had been. As the mother of Des she could have dropped Kate and supported her son unquestionably. Yet she had stood by Kate and now even had taken the girls on in order to help Kate graduate. Things were looking better, better than they had been in a long time.

"You know what, Grace? You are absolutely right. I can do what I want. I had been so long thinking about Des and what I lost, I wasn't thinking about what I've gained."

"I think this calls for another bottle of champagne," Derek yelled out loud and they all laughed.

"I'll get one," Dymphna replied rising to her feet. "We have a secret stash in the car."

Tom grinned, his dark eyes glittering in the candlelight. "I hope you ordered lots and lots of food," he said to Kate.

Kate felt a faint stirring – it could have been a fluttery feeling in the pit of her stomach, or maybe just too many bubbles in the champagne.

"Bucket-loads," she smiled.

Des couldn't help himself. He just felt he had to drive up to The Beeches and have one last lingering look. He pulled up in his Lexus, shining the headlights onto the property. The house looked dark and rather forlorn. Already Kate's warm lived-in homely look, that had made the house a home, had drained away.

He felt inexplicably saddened by that. The family life he had so carefully built up and the perfect lifestyle with the perfect family had all been destroyed. Oh, he knew that he had stuffed up monumentally with Kate over that silly fling with Melody. If only she had given him another chance, it could have all blown over. But Kate was so stubborn. She would rather lose all this than back down. Well, she was the loser. Des would move on. He had enough money tucked away so that he could buy another Beeches if he so wished, but he couldn't do that at the moment, not while his mother was interfering. Lucinda hated men and thought they were all like his father and maybe Des was – he was certainly as successful. He then thought of Melody. She had become more and more like a wife lately – always looking for more attention – and she had even lost her youthful sexy disposition since the arrival of their son. He loved baby Connor totally, but already he was becoming bored. Still, Sabrina, his new personal assistant was certainly easy on the eye. The way she sashayed about in that black leather skirt, now *she* would be a classy prospect. Yes, Des would move on from Kate. He just hadn't reckoned it would take as long as this. Or that he would feel so inexplicably sad, but there it was.

Grace woke up with a pounding headache and Orla bouncing on her bed feverishly, making Grace's head feel even worse. She shouldn't have had that last glass of champers – correction: those last three glasses.

Paul breezed in with the brightness of a person who hadn't touched a drop of alcohol for weeks and rescued her. He placed a strong cup of tea on her bedstand and scooped Orla up.

"Let's give your mum a wee rest there, Missy," he said and they slipped quietly from the room.

"I love you, Paul Kelly," Grace called after him and she did, realising how incredibly lucky she was. She might not have everything that she wanted, but she did have everything she needed: a loving husband and two beautiful children, a few really good friends and her family. And that was fine by her.

Over at the new house, Kate and her guests were enjoying a big greasy fry, which Tom had cooked up, saying that it would either kill them or cure them, but that it always worked for him.

They all fell on their food after momentary protests and Kate ate it all like the rest of them, abandoning her usual fruit and muesli, with obvious relief. She had already gained half a stone since Des had left her – there was no one to badger her into going to the gym religiously Everyone said she looked a lot better and Grace remarked that she was still pencil slim and to relax, but somehow Kate felt if she did relax that fat Kathleen could come back and she wasn't ready for that. But for now she brushed those negative thoughts aside and just enjoyed having some adult company at the breakfast table for a change.

Dymphna was regaling them all with the story of her ill-fated trip down to Limerick to catch the two-timing Mark.

"What a fecking eejit I was," Dymphna was saying "traipsing all over the countryside, dressed in black fatigues, looking for this two-timing idiot who was still with his wife! Talk about a cringe factor of ten!"

Kate was amazed. Dymphna obviously had such a good relationship with Derek she could be entirely open with him without arousing jealousy or irritation She stole a glance at Derek to confirm this.

There was something about the way Derek was looking at Dymphna – a look of pure adoration and love – that it almost made Kate wince and she found herself feeling a stab of jealousy, so she looked away and glanced at Tom. And then the most wonderful thing happened. Kate caught Tom giving her exactly the same look of love that Derek had just given Dymphna. In that instant it all became clear to Kate. Just a second ago she had being envious of Dymphna and yet she had the exact same thing right under her nose. A man who it seemed adored her. It was now up to her what she wanted her life to become.

She lightly touched Tom's hand and saw the sooty eyes light up with hope.

After Dymphna had finished her funny story and they all laughed, Kate spoke.

"Have you two lovebirds got any plans for later?" she asked, a smile playing on her lips.

"Just survival of this hangover," Dymphna replied, chomping on another piece of toast. "This is a really good breakfast by the way, Tom. You'll be kept."

Kate grinned. "Just what I was thinking."

Tom glanced at her quizzically.

Kate continued. "The reason I asked you, Dimples, is that I wondered if you and Derek would like to hang around for the day and hopefully baby-sit the girls this evening, because . . . I want to take this wonderful man out to dinner."

Tom squeezed her hand tighter. "Are you sure?" he said quietly so only she could hear.

Kate was suddenly serious. "Totally."

Derek grinned and poured them all another cup of tea.

"I think this calls for a celebration but I doubt if any of us could cope with the bubbly stuff at this hour of the day. I'd just like to say if this sounds like what I think it does, then both Dimples and myself couldn't be happier for you both."

"Me too," Kate responded.

And she realised now that happiness was very much up to her and she decided she wasn't going to live in fear because of her past. She was going to grasp at happiness wherever she found it.

Everyone had envied a life like hers, except it had never been the life that it had seemed. Her new life however was a life which she was going to take pleasure in and it began right now.

Tom leaned over and kissed her gently. Butterflies billowed forward in her stomach – those damned butterflies Olivia placed so much store on.

"*Weheeeew!*" hollered Dymphna loudly, while grabbing her mobile phone. "I have *got* to call Grace, she just has to know about this."

Kate laughed – to have all this and friends like these too, she thought.

My life is not so bad after all.

THE END

Published by Poolbeg.com

Happily
Ever After

It's the 1970s in Dublin, and Ali O'Neill and Trisha Costello – best friends since forever – want nothing more to dance the night away at the Grove disco. But soon both girls are falling in love for the first time, changing their lives dramatically.

As they approach their twenties, family tragedy and class snobbery threaten to overwhelm Ali, while Trisha struggles to break the mould and have fun. Desperate to escape, the best friends book their tickets and set off on an Australian adventure. But Trisha doesn't expect to have to return home suddenly, and Ali finds herself stranded thousands of miles from home with a pressing problem.

But is there a chance the girls will live happily ever after?

Sometimes you have to go halfway round the world before you realise that the best things are on your doorstep.

ANNETT HOLLIDAY

ISBN 1-84223-118-9

C.C.